PUBLIC LIBRARY
W9-AJP-932

Run Afoul

Also by Joan Druett

IN THE WIKI COFFIN SERIES

Shark Island
A Watery Grave

OTHER FICTION

Abigail
A Promise of Gold
Murder at the Brian Boru

NONFICTION

In the Wake of Madness
Rough Medicine
She Captains
Hen Frigates
The Sailing Circle (with Mary Anne Wallace)
Captain's Daughter, Coasterman's Wife
"She Was a Sister Sailor" (editor)
Petticoat Whalers
Fulbright in New Zealand
Exotic Intruders

Joan Druett

Run Afoul

ST. MARTIN'S MINOTAUR NEW YORK

This is a work of fiction. All of the characters, organizations, and events portrayed in this novel are either products of the auhor's imagination or are used fictitiously.

www.minotaurbooks.com

Library of Congress Cataloging-in-Publication Data

Druett, Joan.
Run afoul / Joan Druett.—1st ed.
p. cm.
ISBN-13: 978-0-312-35336-0
ISBN-10: 0-312-35336-7
1. Coffin, Wiki (Fictitious character)—Fiction. 2. United States Exploring Expedition (1838–1842)—Fiction. 3. Linguists—Fiction. 4. Fathers and sons—Fiction. 5. Americans—Foreign countries—Fiction. 6. Brazil—Fiction. 7. Scientific expeditions—Fiction. I. Title.

PR9639.3.D68R86 2006
823'.914—dc22

2006045282

First Edition: October 2006

10 9 8 7 6 5 4 3 2 1

For Helen and Jill,
with appreciation for the poisoning

Run Afoul

One

South Atlantic Ocean, November 1838

As he slumped exhaustedly in the cutter that pulled from the brig *Swallow* to the expedition flagship *Vincennes*, Wiki Coffin wondered if he smelled as bad as Lieutenant Forsythe. Over the past five days, while the cutter and its battered, miserable crew had been struggling to rejoin the expedition fleet, the steward of the *Swallow* had painstakingly mended and cleaned Forsythe's uniform, and so the lieutenant's appearance was smart enough, considering his bulky frame. Forsythe's lumpy, battered face was reddened and scraped where he had shaved off a week's worth of hard stubble, too. To spoil the effect, though, he stank like a skunk.

Wiki was wearing his best broadcloth, which was even cleaner than Forsythe's uniform, because he wore it so seldom. Despite the urgency of Captain Wilkes's summons, he had taken the time to wash in a bucket of fresh water, and had lashed up his long black hair. Still, though, he couldn't help wondering if the effluvium of the past five days clung to his skin—a qualm that became full-blown as the boat clicked against the starboard side of the *Vincennes*.

The oarsman in the bow stopped the cutter by holding on to a dangling rope. Then all six men of the crew silently contemplated Wiki and Lieutenant Forsythe, while Wiki watched them back with great respect. These seamen had also endured five horrible days of bucketing about in the thirty-foot cutter while they struggled to rejoin the expedition fleet. They had regained the brig *Swallow* just four hours before, but now they were as shipshape and smart as if they had never been away. Even the cutter was clean.

Their expressions were noncommittal, but, to Wiki's surprise, as Lieutenant Forsythe clambered to his feet, the men stood, too, and saluted their commander. It was a remarkable compliment, and an eloquent sign of their respect for his seamanship. Forsythe was universally disliked for his unpredictability, brutality, and foul tongue, but it was a tacit recognition that few other officers could have brought the thirty-foot craft to a mid-Atlantic rendezvous with the fleet. Characteristically, Forsythe didn't even bother to return the salute, instead casting his crew a suspicious and aggressive look before turning to grab one of the rungs of the side-ladder.

Wiki reluctantly followed. When they clambered over the gangway at the top of the tall side of the ship, the squad of marines on duty stamped loudly to attention, while the two side-boys, one at each side of the ladder, saluted, and the boatswain piped on his call. A comradely wink from one of the marines was an unwelcome reminder that every jack tar in the U.S. Exploring Expedition knew that both he and Forsythe were in deep disgrace. Wiki lifted a brow in wry acknowledgment, but Forsythe stayed blank-faced as he headed past the mainmast to the great deckhouse where Captain Wilkes and the shipboard scientifics lived and worked. The two men at the ship's wheel, which was stationed just in front of the house, glanced sideways with sympathetic looks, too, and the corporal of marines who was standing sentry in the alcove stamped and saluted with unusual fervor.

Obviously, there was no need to state their business, but Forsythe barked that they were here in reply to the captain's summons. The corporal saluted again, turned smartly, and led the way into the lofty, white-painted corridor beyond the open door. To the left-hand side of the long passage, a credenza topped with wooden spindles half hid a saloon furnished with a table large enough to seat twenty, with revolving chairs screwed to the floor all around. This dining room was empty, and the varnished doors at both ends were closed, as were those to the four staterooms on the far side of the corridor. The soldier kept on going, heading for a set of double doors at the end of the passage, while Forsythe and Wiki followed.

Their steps echoed hollowly, then stopped. With a double stamp as he brought his feet together, the marine knocked deafeningly. At the preoccupied sound of a distant grunt, he opened the doors with a flourish, and stood aside to let Wiki and Forsythe pass through. Then the doors slammed shut again, and Wiki heard the retreating thunder of boots as the corporal marched back to his post.

The room smelled of preserving alcohol and ink. Long rays of bright late afternoon sun streamed in a great skylight, and the glazed windows in the stern let in water reflections, which moved hypnotically over racks of glass jars where enigmatic creatures floated, and the shelves where many books and charts were securely stacked. Rows of chronometers in padded boxes solemnly ticked, not quite in unison. This was the place where the shipboard scientifics worked alongside the ship's officers who had been assigned to surveying duties. Right now, however, only the commander in chief of the expedition was in residence.

Captain Wilkes, though standing, was bent over a chart that had been spread out on one of the tables, filling in figures along the line that marked the last track of survey. For some moments, he ignored their arrival. Wiki stood beside Lieutenant Forsythe, his feet braced apart to counter the slow roll of the ship, and warily contemplated the tall, lean, ascetic figure. The last time he had been summoned here, he'd been given the brief of hunting pirates on Shark Island. It was hard to believe that it had been only four weeks ago. Just as before, every small movement betrayed Wilkes's inner tension. There were patches of red high on the cheekbones of his narrow face, and he occasionally lifted a hand to rub his forehead, as if it hurt.

Wiki already knew that the commandant of the exploring fleet was under great pressure—that he had been under stress for years, for Charles Wilkes had been intimately involved with the expedition since the very beginning. As a decade had dragged by in an endless chaos of political and scientific lobbying and public controversy, he, unlike many others, had remained loyal to the project. After he had been appointed to the position of fleet commodore, following the resignation of his fiery rival, Captain Thomas ap Catesby Jones, powers in the navy had received the news with open outrage, but the humiliating acrimony had been the least of Wilkes's problems. Ships had proved unsuitable, and he'd been forced to replace them at incredibly short notice, and then have the replacements provisioned in a navy yard where the outfitters and victuallers had been unwaveringly hostile. The papers had dubbed the enterprise "the Deplorable Expedition," and it had become the butt of cartoonists and music hall comedians, but Charles Wilkes had stubbornly clung to his vision of an American scientific triumph. Despite his notoriously volatile temper, Wiki still found him admirable.

At last he looked up, right into Wiki's face. "So I finally see you!"

"Aye, sir," Wiki warily admitted.

"Well, what do you have to say for yourself? I *distinctly* recollect giving you instructions to report back without a moment's delay—and yet I had to send Lieutenant Smith with the *Flying Fish* to remind you of your obligations. Almost *four whole weeks* have elapsed since I saw you last!"

"I'm sorry, sir."

"Being sorry is not sufficient! Lieutenant Forsythe—what is your excuse for keeping me in the dark, sir? I want to know what the *hell* you were thinking!"

Before Forsythe could open his mouth, Wiki forestalled him, saying firmly, "The delay was entirely my fault, sir."

Captain Wilkes's large eyes opened wide with affront; for the first time Wiki realized how bloodshot they were. He echoed, "*Your* fault?"

"Aye, sir. When we found an American ship in distress at the island, I thought the priority was to render assistance. After all, she was a fellow national—"

"Now, wait a bloody minute," Forsythe interrupted. The glance he cast at Wiki was inimical. "Who was in charge of the goddamned mission—you or me?"

"Exactly!" Captain Wilkes exclaimed. "You're supposed to be a linguister, damn it—a *civilian*! Your job was to *investigate*, not to decide priorities! Just who the bloody *hell* do you think you are?" He crashed his fist down on the desktop and shouted, "It's high time you carried out the *proper* duties you've neglected to perform!"

"Duties?" Wiki felt puzzled, because he thought he had worked extremely hard, both off and on the brig *Swallow*. "What duties?"

"You were shipped to work as the expedition's linguister, Mr. Coffin—to translate for us, and coordinate with the other scientifics! Not only have you done no translating at all, but you've failed to answer questions about Pacific languages that Lieutenant Smith has posed—and he has now filed a formal complaint about your lack of cooperation."

My God, thought Wiki—he wouldn't have believed that even the petty-minded Lawrence J. Smith would do this to him. The overbearing little prig had asked him no questions about Pacific languages at all! And even if Smith *was* the commodore's particular crony, Captain Wilkes should have had the intelligence to realize that the pompous little prawn was far too proud of what he considered his vast and superior knowledge to ever listen to the ideas and opinions of anyone else, let alone deign to ask advice.

He said hotly, "If Lieutenant Smith ever *did* ask questions, I would have answered them to the best of my ability—but he's never given me the chance!"

"That is not what he tells me, Mr. Coffin! And you do yourself no service by accusing him of telling lies!" The patches of red on Captain Wilkes's cheekbones stood out; he was obviously building himself up into a right royal rage. "What the hell did you think you joined the expedition for?" he demanded. "To loaf away your time on board the brig *Swallow*, at the expense of the U.S. Navy? To stand by while Lieutenant Smith carries out all the language-related research, and then grab the honor and glory after the expedition returns?"

Wiki's mouth fell open. *"What?"*

"If I'd had my way," said Captain Wilkes, obviously harping on an old grievance, "the scientific corps would have been entirely manned by naval officers! There would not have been a single goddamned rascal of a civilian on board to usurp all the credit when we get back home!"

Insulted to the point of indiscretion, Wiki protested, "I have no intention of claiming any credit at all—I don't want it, I'd never ask for it, and I resent the slur on my character, sir!"

"But there's more, Mr. Coffin! Even though you're expected to assist the other scientifics, you have not bestirred yourself to make their acquaintance! You're not even aware of their specialities! Have you made any attempt to share your knowledge of the Pacific—or educate the members of the crew about the places where they are going? No, you have not!"

"I have answered all the questions I've been asked," Wiki exclaimed.

"How dare you interrupt! You have not played your part at all! Did you bother to make any measurements at Shark Island—did you collect any plants? No, you did not! You have done *nothing* to earn your place with the expedition."

"Captain Wilkes, that's unfair and unwarranted!" Wiki was angrier than ever. He was a translator, not a teacher or a surveyor or a botanist, and no one had given him any kind of hint that he was supposed to *measure* the ground he covered.

"Unfair? Unwarranted?" Captain Wilkes savagely echoed. "I don't *think* so, and you will find that I have *ways* of making you fulfill your obligations." Again, his fist hit the top of the desk, and he roared, "You are reassigned to the *Vincennes*!"

Wiki opened his mouth, but then shut it again as alarm took over from affront and fury. He had joined the expedition only because his old friend George Rochester, the captain of the brig *Swallow*, had repeatedly asked him to do so. If George hadn't found him the civilian job of linguister with the fleet, right now he'd be on board some workaday whaleship, heading off to the Bay of Islands, New Zealand, for yet another visit with his *whanau*—his folks. The only reason he'd agreed to employ his vast knowledge of the Pacific and its languages in the service of the exploring expedition was that the prospect of sailing around the world with his old friend on his dashing little brig had been so appealing. The horrible notion that he might be assigned to a different ship had never even crossed his mind.

Battling a sense of panic, he said quickly, "Give me a moment to write my resignation, and you'll see the last of me in Rio."

"How *dare* you argue with me!" Wilkes exploded. "Don't force me to remind you of the terms of agreement you signed! Get it into your head that you are reassigned, Mr. Coffin—to the *Vincennes*!—where you will live and work in this afterhouse, and satisfy the questions posed to you by the other scientifics! Try to understand that you have absolutely no choice in the matter!" And with that he barked that they were both dismissed, and the exceedingly unpleasant interview was over.

As they escaped from the afterhouse, Wiki could hear Captain Wilkes marching up the corridor behind them, his steps still ominously angry. Everyone on the quarterdeck jumped nervously to attention. Wiki and Forsythe stepped smartly aside to let him by, and watched him make his way to the waist deck, where Lieutenant Smith was supervising a couple of men who were untangling strands of seaweed from dredge nets. Then Forsythe headed off to a nearby companionway, and Wiki was left alone, standing about in the alcove without a notion of what he was supposed to do next.

Above his head, massive masts lifted to the late afternoon sky, interconnected with an intricate web of rigging. The lower sails of the *Vincennes* were brailed up, just the great main topsail being set to keep the ship still, and so Wiki could see all the way along the decks to the galley forward, where the food for the people who lived in the afterhouse was cooked. The smokestack plumed, and steam issued from the open doorway. Supper would be served soon, he thought, but he was far too tired to feel hungry.

Instead, Wiki was overwhelmed with something that felt perilously close to panic. Between the galley and the doorway of the afterhouse the vast expanse of planks was teeming with what seemed like a hundred men, and he couldn't even guess what most of them were doing. Groups of seamen were gathered about the foremast and mainmast, hectored by boatswains' mates with their shrilling calls, while others were hammering away amidships, where the ship's launch and two cutters were stored inside each other, the largest at the bottom, and the smallest—which also served as a pigpen—at the top. If he had been told to climb to the main topgallant crosstrees and then lay out along the yard, he would have had no trouble at all, but finding his way around this daunting seven-hundred-ton flagship—more than seven times the size of the *Swallow!*—seemed utterly beyond his powers, let alone making an adjustment to the unwritten laws of life on an overcrowded sloop of war.

A concerned Yankee voice said in his ear, "Be you quite fine, sir?"

It was the corporal who was on sentry duty. Wiki summoned a reassuring smile, though every muscle hurt and every bone ached from the aftereffects of the passage in the cutter. He had not slept for more than an hour at a time in the five days since leaving Shark

Island, and it was an effort to focus his grit-filled eyes. Then he jumped a foot, as the marine glanced at the ship's clock hanging in the alcove above the door to the afterhouse, looked up at the officer who was pacing the roof, and bellowed right by Wiki's ear, "Time, sir!"

The officer lifted his trumpet, shouted, "Strike the bell!" and a boy rushed out of nowhere and energetically hammered at the ship's bell by the wheel. He rang the bell eight times—it was four o'clock, the end of the afternoon watch and the beginning of the first dog-watch; time for the men going off duty to get their supper and the second issue of grog for the day; a time of relaxation, when songs were sung, and many yarns were told.

If Wiki had been on board the *Swallow,* he would have been relaxed in a warm spot on the deck, exchanging stories in Samoan with Tana and Sua, the two *Kanakas*—Pacific Islanders—of the crew, before heading off to his comfortable berth. Now, he didn't even know where he was supposed to lay his head, except that it was somewhere in the afterhouse. Wearily, he turned and trudged back down the corridor.

Two

To Wiki's surprise, because he had heard no sounds from inside, there was someone seated at the big table in the saloon—or half seated, because he was so hugely fat that he was forced to perch on the forward part of his chair with his belly crammed against the table, as his bulk would not fit between the arms.

When this stranger saw Wiki, he swung the revolving chair around, releasing his great paunch with an audible plop. "You're brown," he observed amiably. "So you must be Wiki Coffin. I believe we are to have the honor of your company in the afterhouse?"

Wiki spun round one of the chairs opposite, and slumped into it. "You overheard Captain Wilkes?"

Blue eyes studied him from above applelike cheeks, and plump lips smiled from the midst of a luxuriant black beard. "I did, indeed—not that it was difficult," he said. "Winston Olliver, M.R.C.S., at your service."

That little formality over, he swung back to the table, using both hands to wedge his paunch in place, and once in place, he picked up a glass of wine, and judiciously sipped a few times. When the wine sank to the halfway level, Mr. Olliver set it down and carefully topped it up from a decanter.

Wiki watched the procedure abstractedly, thinking about those letters *M.R.C.S.* Then he said, "Member of the Royal College of Surgeons?"

"You can call me Dr. Olliver," the other generously said.

"You're a surgeon with the fleet?"

"I'm a naturalist, mostly with the plants."

"One of the scientifics?"

"For my sins."

"Yet, judging by your accent, you are English."

"You are a very perceptive young man."

"I thought only Americans were allowed scientific positions with the fleet?" Wiki himself would never have been given the job of linguister if he had not been half Yankee.

"When visiting friends in Washington, I happened to mention that I'd been helping Charles Darwin classify the specimens he brought to Cambridge from the *Beagle* exploring voyage, and the powers that be in the Navy Department couldn't recruit me fast enough."

"You know Charles Darwin?" Wiki was impressed.

"You've heard of him?"

"Of course," said Wiki, but then was distracted by the sight of the steward coming out of the pantry in the forward part of the dining room, carrying two plates and two mugs. He was a portly, middle-aged man, whose habitual expression of prissy sulkiness became evasive when he encountered Wiki's incredulous stare.

"My *God—you*!" said Wiki. The steward did not bother to answer. Instead, he slammed down the dishes and mugs and went away, leaving Wiki to contemplate his plate, which held a slice of cold, almost raw, salt pork, a weevilly ship's biscuit, and a pile of half-baked beans. The coffee in the mug was boiled to black bitterness, and had a slimy scum on the top.

The surgeon said with lively interest, "You know that man?"

"It's Jack Winter," Wiki said moodily. "He was one of the eight sealers we rescued from Shark Island—their steward."

"If you rescued him from a place with a name like that, he ought to love you. But he don't?"

"He most certainly does not," Wiki agreed, examining his meal with disgust. "And now it looks as if he's trying to poison me off."

"He often threatens to poison off the rats—of which, as I must warn you, we have a biblical plague," the surgeon said. "And as for the food, it is always that awful—it was revolting before he came, and remained horrible after he replaced our old steward. We wouldn't even notice it if he added poison to the terrible mix—practiced on people before he moved on to rats, as it were."

"The food is always this bad?" Wiki was appalled.

"Blame the navy. Each and every one of us has a weekly allowance of meat, bread, flour, and so forth, which the steward draws on Mondays. He stows them in his storeroom and pantry, where the rats sample them at their leisure." The naturalist waved a meaty arm at a door alongside the pantry, presumably indicating the storeroom, and, as if on cue, three fat rats ran out from under the door, scuttled along the skirting, and disappeared under the dresser. "And out of that, three times a day, he prepares a dish, takes it to the foredeck galley to be cooked by the nasty old peg leg, and then dumps the result on the table and calls it a meal. It's not pretty viewing, but it ain't actually his fault. The coffee, however," he added thoughtfully, "is entirely his responsibility."

"Dear God," said Wiki. He was wondering if he would ever eat again.

Then, with utter disbelief, he watched the fat surgeon attack the dreadful meal as if he expected to enjoy it, keeping his fork in his left hand and his knife in his right, and plying them with mincing movements, as neatly as a cat. Between forkfuls, he put down his knife, picked up his glass, and gulped wine—to take the taste out of his mouth, Wiki guessed.

Then, as if struck by a sudden thought, Dr. Olliver looked up, and Wiki found himself the object of his bright scrutiny again. "How odd," he mused aloud, "that there are things you should know that you don't know, while at other times you demonstrate unexpected understanding."

"I beg your pardon?"

"I wouldn't have expected a *Kanaka* to know about Charles Darwin."

"Why not?" Wiki queried. "People in South American ports have been gossiping about Darwin for the past five years, ever since he arrived on the *Beagle* to explore the coasts and hinterlands—he's the stuff of myth and legend."

"Ports?" Dr. Olliver looked animated. "You're a seaman?"

"A whaleman—for my sins," Wiki dryly replied.

"Aha!" said Dr. Olliver, with even more enthusiasm. "You'll find a kindred soul here—Captain Couthouy."

"He's a whaleman?"

"He commanded merchant vessels out of Boston, though I would strongly advise you not to call him 'captain' in Captain Wilkes's hearing." The surgeon stabbed a fat finger in the direction of a door sited next to the big chartroom, evidently indicating Wilkes's cabin.

"Why not?" said Wiki, more puzzled than ever.

"Captain Wilkes gets emotionally upset when shipmasters more experienced than he happen to be in his vicinity."

"So what is Captain Couthouy doing here?"

"He got the mad idea that he wanted to sign up with the Deplorable Expedition, shell-collecting being his passion—he informed President Jackson that he would ship before the mast, if necessary, which entertained Jackson so first rate that he shipped him on the spot as a scientific."

It didn't surprise Wiki that a Boston shipmaster should be an avid collector of shells, exotic seashells in good condition being worth a pretty price in the right market, but Couthouy sounded interestingly eccentric. He said, "Where is he?"

"Somewhere where he can keep clear of Wilkes, just the same as Wilkes is somewhere keeping clear of him."

"They don't like each other?"

"Wilkes don't like civilian scientifics as a species—reckons that they will grab all the credit when the ships get home, relegating his officers to the subcategory of hewers of wood and drawers of water. However, he reserves a special antipathy for Couthouy—on account of the fact that Couthouy has accumulated a lot more sea time than he has. Wilkes wanted to eliminate the civilian corps completely, you know," Dr. Olliver confided. "And he would have done it, too, if he could've located navy officers with the skills to take their places, but there ain't even a common gardener to be found in the U.S. Navy. Not that a man on the breast of the stormy wave has the chance to develop much interest in gardening," he added with a surprisingly womanish giggle.

Wiki had sailed with quite a number of whaling skippers who, to all appearances, were more interested in their boxes of flower plants than in the set of the sails, but he didn't comment, instead inquiring, "So what was *your* reason for agreeing to come along on the Deplorable Expedition? A passion for plants?"

"A passion for curious phenomena, Mr. Coffin! And what could be more curious than an expedition founded on the premise that the world is hollow?"

"What?"

"Goodness gracious, you really don't know much, do you? A few years back, a fellow named Symmes reckoned there were holes at the poles, and that the earth is habitable inside. If you could locate the holes, he said, you could sail into the bowels of the world—down a kind of waterfall, I suppose—and find a fertile paradise. A harmless fellow, quite amiable, they say. My grandfather was rather like that," Dr. Olliver reminisced, contemplating his wineglass as he topped it up yet again. "He reckoned that the sun has a temperate climate—that it stood to reason that the sun is tepid at the surface, because most of its heat is dissipated in our direction. If we could only get to the sun, he said, we'd find it a capital place to live. He and Symmes of the hollow globe would have got along first-rate."

He took a few sips while Wiki watched him unseeingly, lost in a dreamlike vision of sailing to the top of the world, arriving at the North Pole, instructing the crew to brace up a bit, and then plunging into the center of the earth. When Dr. Olliver picked up the decanter again, having reduced his wine to the halfway level, he finally said, "And people *listened* to this nonsense?"

"People traveled for miles to listen to my grandfather's crackpot theories abut the sun—and to John Cleves Symmes, as well. The latter staked his fortune on the premise that inside the earth there is a rich and tax-free land—warmed by volcanic fires, no doubt, though I do wonder how it is illuminated—and lots of people fell for it, including a newspaper editor by the name of Jeremiah N. Reynolds. Like Symmes, Reynolds thought that all that was needed for the United States to become a premier nation was to mount an expedition to locate one of those holes at the poles, only he reckoned that instead of going north, the ships should steer south to where the seals and whales roam."

"Ah," said Wiki, beginning to grasp where this was heading. "So the administration took an interest?"

"And Connecticut sealing interests, too." Dr. Olliver, after taking another little swallow of wine, wobbled his chins in the direction of the pantry, and said, "Those sealers you rescued, were they steering in the direction of the Antarctic?"

"Aye."

"Then that explains why they've been co-opted into the expedition." Dr. Olliver paused, and when Wiki shut his sore eyes and cautiously revolved his shoulders, he remarked, "You don't look too chirpy, young man."

"I've spent the past five days tumbling about the ocean in a thirty-foot cutter. We got here just today."

"Then you must be fearfully constipated. I'll prescribe a draft."

"I'd rather get some sleep," confessed Wiki, rising to his feet.

He was foiled, however, because just as he was about to ask which room might be his, one of the doors on the other side of the corridor opened, revealing a formidable figure. Though he was not large in physique, the newcomer's immense russet-colored beard fairly bristled with all the confidence of a shipmaster who expected his orders to be obeyed, by God, and so it was not hard to guess that this was Captain Couthouy.

The room behind him was equally remarkable, being packed with boxes, chests, books, and scientific gear, stacked tightly above and below a cramped sleeping space, and held in position with a spiderweb of ropes lashed to cleats in the beams and the floor. A tiny table set by the head of the bed had still more paraphernalia stowed underneath, while racks holding specimens of coral and seaweed were bolted to the bulkhead above it. Dead birds swung from strings in the roof—very ripe dead birds. Wiki could smell them. Because of the dampness of the ship, he deduced, they had gone rotten instead of drying.

The newcomer slammed himself into a chair, nodded briefly when introduced to Wiki, and remarked, "So you were one of those who were forced to come away from Shark Island in the cutter? That was a damn long passage, and you were bloody lucky to find us."

"We were very relieved to raise the ships," Wiki admitted.

"Well, it was a close-run thing," Couthouy informed him. "Against my most strenuous advice, Wilkes gave instructions to make all haste for Rio, the *Peacock* being in such dire need of the attentions of a shipyard. We were smartly on our way when he changed his mind, and issued orders to retrace our steps."

"He'd remembered us?"

"He'd realized we'd lost the *Porpoise*."

"*What?*"

"One minute she was there, and the next she was not. We passed a large Dutch ship in the dark, and the theory is that the officer on watch mistook the Dutchman for us, and followed the wrong ship. The *Peacock* was sent on to Rio, but the rest of us are sitting here waiting for the *Porpoise*—and, incidentally, your cutter—to find us again."

"Is Captain Ringgold still in command of the *Porpoise*?"

"That he is."

"Then he's in for a reprimand." Wiki felt sorry about that, because he liked Cadwallader Ringgold, who ran a taut, happy ship, and right now he felt a profound empathy for anyone who was likely to be the butt of Captain Wilkes's overwrought tongue.

Then Couthouy, having poured himself a mugful and taken a cautious sip, exclaimed, "This coffee is disgusting, almost as foul as the food. When is Wilkes going to fire that bastard of a cook who takes good grub and ruins it? By God, he wouldn't have lasted a day on board any of *my* ships!"

"I absolutely agree with you, Mr. Couthouy," said Lieutenant Lawrence J. Smith with a smirk, as he trotted around the corner of the credenza into the saloon. He was flushed, and his tubby figure pushed out the front of his vest even more than Wiki remembered. "And so I have arranged to have him replaced. Good evening, Wiremu," he added, using the Maori version of Wiki's English name, William. It was meant to prove how cultured and knowledgeable he was, but instead Wiki found it highly irritating.

Wiki didn't bother to speak. Not only had Lawrence J. Smith told Captain Wilkes lies, which rankled, but he was the reason Wiki had been reassigned to the *Vincennes*. And as well as that, he had always deeply disliked the pompous little prawn.

Captain Couthouy said hopefully, "Who is the chosen man?"

Smith smiled, and said, "I've requisitioned the cook we rescued from the stricken sealer. Unfortunately, he was inadvertently left behind when the *Flying Fish* sailed, but now that Lieutenant Forsythe has brought him to the fleet—"

Wiki interrupted with horror, "You can't mean Robert Festin!"

"Why not?" Dr. Olliver inquired with an air of interest.

"He doesn't even understand English!"

"Why, where does he come from?"

"We can only guess," said Wiki. "All we could learn from the sealers was that when they shipped him in Rio de Janeiro he'd been suffering so much from the aftereffects of something like a knock on the head that it was a wonder he even remembered his name. Since then, we've learned very little more. He talks a weird mixture of antique French and Abnaki Indian, so the theory is that he hails from some remote village in Labrador that was forgotten when the British threw the Acadians out of the country."

"If so, he's bound to be a fine seaman," Captain Couthouy said. He had the knowledgeable air of a man who had shipped many sailors from the northern maritime regions in the past.

Wiki shook his head with a private grin, remembering how Festin had been obstinately and constantly seasick, to the discomfort of them all, for the whole of the five-day passage in the cutter. Before he could speak, Dr. Olliver demanded, "So how the devil did he get to Rio?"

"We haven't the slightest idea."

"None of this *matters*," Lieutenant Smith said crossly. "What *does* matter is that he's a superb cook."

Dr. Olliver said to Wiki, "Is that right?"

"Aye," Wiki allowed grudgingly.

Smith said reminiscently, "On the brig, I had the pleasure of being regaled with a particularly delicious steamed concoction of pastry and chicken."

"Pastry?" echoed Dr. Olliver. "Chicken? My God!" he exclaimed. "I don't care if he talks Hottentot—let's have this Robert Festin!"

"Robert Festin?" cried Jack Winter, coming back into the saloon. "You don't mean to say that *Festin* is being shifted to our galley?"

"We're assured he's a master chef," said Olliver.

"But he's under suspicion of *murder*!"

Three

Wiki was woken from a dead sleep the next morning by loud halloas from out on the deck. For a long moment he couldn't work out where he was, save that he was in the upper berth of a double bunk, just as he would have been on board the brig *Swallow*. Obviously, this was not the brig, because his berth there had a bookcase full of favorite books, a lamp, and various other little luxuries that he had fixed up himself. However, thankfully, he was not on the jouncing, backbreaking cutter, because this ship was lying relatively still.

Then he remembered the portly surgeon—Olliver—pointing out the door closest to the drafting room, and telling him that it was vacant, because the two draftsmen who had lived here had been banished to the *Porpoise* by Captain Wilkes, on account of the noise they made. "I believe some poor creature of an instrumentmaker from the *Porpoise* is removing here," he'd said. "But in the meantime it's all yours."

Wiki had requisitioned the upper berth, so that he would not have a foot in his face every time his unknown companion got in or out of bed. Now, he dropped lightly to the floor, having regained his natural agility sometime in the night, briskly dressed, and headed out to deck.

When he arrived in the bright sunlight, it was to see the gun brig *Porpoise* bracing up off the stern of the *Vincennes,* white foam streaming off her bows, her men cheering from her yards as they took in sail. Even though she was still hauling aback, a boat was being hastily lowered with the captain and another man in the stern sheets. Wiki had to step aside hastily as a reception committee of marines scurried up to the gangway, to get there before the boat arrived, and deduced that Captain Ringgold was anxious to get the dreaded interview with Captain Wilkes over with as fast as humanly possible.

No sooner had the marines shuffled themselves into a neat squad than to everyone's confusion they found themselves inadvertently saluting a short, squat, swarthy-featured man who sidled off the ladder and over the gangway. A boat from the *Swallow* had arrived alongside, Wiki instantly deduced, because this was none other than Robert Festin, the Acadian cook with the shadowy past.

First, the Acadian's head appeared at the top of the ladder, then his bulky shoulders and torso, and finally his spindly little legs. He was not alone, as two massively muscular brown-skinned seamen arrived close behind—Sua and Tana, Wiki's Samoan shipmates, one with Wiki's sea chest on one brawny shoulder, and the other heaving along a basket of fish.

"Kia ora e hoa ma," Wiki exclaimed, striding around the squad of marines. Being Polynesian, and not *pakeha* or *papalagi,* he and Tana and Sua greeted each other with hugely enthusiastic hugs, instead of hammering each other meaninglessly about the arms and back. When Festin rushed forward and joined the fun by throwing himself into Wiki's arms, it was rather disconcerting, however. Wiki already knew that the cook was the emotional type, but hadn't expected him to be so obviously delighted about shifting onto the *Vincennes.* Then he suddenly realized the reason—that Festin was overjoyed at the prospect

of being on the same ship as Lieutenant Forsythe, whom he adored, though the Virginian would have drowned the Acadian like a cur if he had suspected it.

Now the short, square man looked around, and inquired eagerly about his hero, who was nowhere in sight. Wiki reassured him, and then said to Sua, "Why the fish?"

Sua grinned. "Festin was worried about what kind of rations were available on board this boat, and so we went fishing this morning." Then, after a surreptitious glance about the decks, he said in English, "What's the grub like, anyways?"

"Shocking," said Wiki. He looked in the basket. There were about a dozen fine flying fish—*maroro*—inside, their huge eyes gleaming with the luster of only recently departed life. The two Samoans would have caught them Pacific fashion, he thought, by lowering a boat in the dark before dawn, with a lantern set behind the sail. These fish would have come flying in from the night, slapped against the canvas, and crashed into the bottom of the boat.

They would also be delicious. "Come with me, *e hoa ma,*" said Wiki, with enthusiasm, and headed for the captain's galley on the foredeck.

The cook came out to meet them. He was a battered-looking, one-legged black man, wearing an extremely suspicious expression. An old scar slashed across the top of his forehead, so that he looked like the ill-used relict of some past battle. His eyes slid from Sua to Tana and back to Wiki. Then, completely unintimidated by the three stalwart Polynesians and their strange little companion, he spat in the direction of the rail, and sourly observed, "That's a damn lot of fish."

"It is," Wiki agreed smugly.

"You expect *me* to cook it?"

"I don't," Wiki informed him, and looked around for Lieutenant Smith—who, as usual, was absent when most needed—and wondered why the devil he hadn't told this man that he was being replaced.

He waved an arm at Festin. "This gentleman is the new chef."

"What the *bloody* hell?"

"Lieutenant Smith will give formal notification," Wiki said firmly. Then he turned to Festin, and said, "*E hoa, nadacowaldam*—this is now *your* galley."

Festin eyed the cook, and the cook stared at Wiki, with indentically aggressive expressions. The Acadian said, "*Awani agema?* Who bloody he?"

"Soon he will go away," Wiki said optimistically. "Just fix the fish."

It took some multilingual argument, but finally Festin set to with his knife, while the man he was supposed to be supplanting watched with a supercilious air. Another few minutes, and fins and tails had been lopped off with satisfying celerity, and the Acadian was cutting slits along the backbone and across each side of the fish. When Wiki looked at the old peg leg again, it was to find that he had retired to a patch of sunlight by the scuttlebutt, and was smoking a pipe with a virtuous air, obviously waiting to reclaim his realm. Smith had still not put in an appearance, so Wiki asked Sua and Tana to keep an eye on Festin, just in case a ruckus broke out, took over his sea chest, and headed for the afterhouse.

Lieutenant Smith was not there, either. Instead, as Wiki shoved his chest beneath the double berth of his stateroom, he could hear Captain Wilkes and Captain Ringgold in the big drafting room. Both were laughing, Captain Wilkes seeming very amused by Ringgold's blunder in mistaking the Dutchman for the *Vin*. Quite a contrast to the way his tardy arrival from Shark Island had been received, Wiki thought wryly, then heard footsteps approaching.

He turned hopefully, thinking it might be Lieutenant Smith at last, but instead it was a thin, lugubrious man with prematurely gray hair, a desiccated, skull-like face, and badly stooped shoulders. He was holding a large chamber pot in his left hand, which hung forward from his fingers so that Wiki, fascinated, could see that there was a portrait of Napoleon painted in the bottom.

He had only met the man holding the pot twice before, but recognized him immediately—Astronomer Grimes, who had been a witness in a case of murder early in the voyage. As Wiki remembered vividly, getting testimony out of him had been difficult, as the scientific had been utterly appalled at the very notion of being questioned by a South Seas savage. Now, it seemed not only that Grimes was the man who had come from the *Porpoise* with Captain Ringgold, but that he was to sleep in the lower bunk, which was not a pleasant prospect at all.

Obviously, the astronomer felt the same way. He exclaimed, "*You!*"—and took such a fast backward step that he crashed into Jack Winter, who was carrying a couple of his bags. Then he fell into a furious fit of coughing, which sent tears down his cheeks and stooped his back even more.

Wiki waited, thinking that this boded badly for the nights ahead. Grimes smelled sour, as if he were prone to cold sweats, and his collar was very dirty. When the wet, hacking noises stopped, he said, "Dr. Olliver told me that an instrumentmaker was moving in here. He said nothing about an astronomer."

"I *am* an instrumentmaker. I was only an astronomer's *assistant*," Grimes said. "If you cast back your mind, you would remember that when I joined the fleet I was Dr. Burroughs's instrumentmaker and *assistant*."

Wiki also remembered that Grimes had joined the expedition only because Dr. Burroughs, a very rich man whose hobby was astronomy, had paid handsomely for the privilege. Originally, Captain Wilkes had been determined that no civilian surveyors should be shipped, having given himself the role of expedition astronomer, something for which he was well qualified, as everyone knew that he had learned triangulation methods of survey from Ferdinand Hassler, and geomagnetism from James Renwick, a professor at Columbia College. However, he had been persuaded to make an exception in Grimes's case, as a favor to a friend.

"So why have you been shifted?"

"To carry out duties as Captain Wilkes's instrumentmaker. We'll be conducting a protracted series of pendulum experiments at Rio de Janeiro, which are part of a series intended to establish the precise force of gravity."

Wiki frowned, because this was the first he had heard that they were to stay at Rio for any length of time. Occasionally, though he greatly respected Captain Wilkes's intelligence, he couldn't help but wonder about his state of mind. While it was supposed to be a secret, every man in the whole fleet knew that they were supposed to mount a search for the continent of Antarctica before the southern summer ended in February—and it was now November, and time was running out fast. Was Captain Wilkes determined to arrive in Antarctic seas so late in the season he would endanger the lives of all?

Grimes interrupted his thoughts by saying crossly, "So why are *you* sharing this cabin with me? I had my own room on the *Porpoise,* and I don't wish to live with anyone here, particularly not with a *Kanaka*."

"It's on Captain Wilkes's orders," Wiki said stiffly. "If you have any complaints, then he's the man you should tackle. In fact, I wish you would."

"I certainly will," Grimes flashed right back—and at that unfortunate moment Festin appeared in the doorway, apparently having tracked down Wiki by the sound of his voice.

In his mixture of dialect and the profane English he had learned from Forsythe, he said plaintively, "The officer gave orders for Tana and Sua to go back to the brig, and then that old bastard of a cook threw me out of my galley."

Oh God, thought Wiki, feeling completely at a loss. Then the Acadian complained, "No one has even told me where I will *sleep*."

Wiki did not have a notion where the afterhouse cook slept. When he asked Jack Winter, the plump steward bridled, and snapped, "Not in *my* room, I assure you!"

"*Your* room?" It was the first Wiki had ever heard of a steward having a room of his own. On the brig *Swallow,* Stoker, the steward, bunked with the cook, the boatswain, and the sailmaker.

"I took the liberty of slinging a hammock in the storeroom."

With the rats, meditated Wiki, remembering the fat vermin that had run out of the storeroom the night before. He grimaced. The rats were bad enough, but because of his childhood training, he knew without doubt that laying one's head where food was stored was very wrong.

He said, "Where the devil is Lieutenant Smith?"

Jack Winter looked around, and shrugged. "The officers' wardroom?"

"And where, pray, is that?"

"On the gun deck, aft."

Gun deck. For a moment the word made no sense. Infuriatingly, Wiki was aware that Jack Winter, having the advantage of an extra five days on board the *Vincennes,* was gazing at him loftily, in a most superior fashion. Then he was saved by a memory of being escorted about the three levels of the flagship by the junior midshipmen of the *Vincennes,* several long weeks ago.

The deck where the afterhouse stood, he recollected, was called "the spar deck." Save for the afterhouse and various structures on the foredeck, it was open to the air. Next down came the gun deck, and below that was the berth deck, which was just above the holds. The little *Swallow* had only two levels—the open deck, where the fifteen-man crew worked, and the deck below, which was divided into after cabin, steerage, and forecastle. Suddenly, the adjustment he was forced to make seemed overwhelming again.

Then Festin whined in English, "I want sleep here with you."

"Here?" exclaimed Mr. Grimes. The instrumentmaker's voice was high with utter horror. "In this *room?*"

"On floor," elaborated Robert Festin, grinning coaxingly.

"Impossible!" Grimes shrieked.

"He can't sleep in the same room with Mr. Grimes," said Jack

Winter, his tone shocked. "It ain't bloody *nice*, if you'll excuse my biblical language."

Wiki agreed. If he had been alone, he would have had no problem with Festin curling up in a blanket on the floor—or on the spare bunk, for that matter—but coping with a hysterical instrumentmaker and an obstinate Acadian cook at one and the same time was unthinkable. Accordingly, he took a firm grip of Festin's collar and hauled him down the corridor, while the Acadian squirmed, saying, "Please, Wiki, please."

Hardening his heart, Wiki carried on to the nearest hatchway ladder, keeping a sharp eye out for Lieutenant Smith. As they descended, darkness rose to surround them. The gun deck was very dim, because the skylight had been taken away when the afterhouse had been built, and so it was lit with scuttles only. Farther forward, Wiki could just see the eight twenty-four-pounder carronades which, with the two nine-pounder chasers on the main deck, was all that was left of the sloop's original cannonry. They were lashed along the sides amidships, and their shiny black paint gleamed faintly in the light that peeked in about the edges of the shut gunports.

In the wide space between each pair of guns, chests and lockers were stacked against the side of the ship. A tin number was nailed to the wall above them to tell the number of the mess that gathered to eat their meals here. Wiki wondered how the devil he would manage to find a number for Festin, who was now grumbling constantly in an undertone. There were more metal ciphers fastened above hammock hooks driven into the heavy beams, and he gathered that each seaman had a hammock number, too. The job of getting Festin settled was becoming more daunting by the minute.

Far forward, Wiki could glimpse occupied hammocks hanging like ripe fruit, swaying gently with the slow roll of the ship, the off-duty seaman inside each one snoring away the last half hour of his watch below. Beyond the sleeping shapes, immediately before the foot of the foremast, implike silhouettes labored in front of a fire—cooks working at the ship's galley, where the food for the ship's common company was cooked.

It was tempting to walk the length of the ship, and take Festin there, but instead Wiki turned toward the stern. At last the Acadian's stream of plaintive complaints had silenced. Apart from the creak of the hull, a few footsteps from above, and the squeak of ropes, this part of the ship seemed very quiet—unnaturally so. Then Wiki heard a queer, loud pattering.

Festin whined with superstitious horror. The fine hairs on the nape of Wiki's neck quivered. Then he glimpsed a gray flow of movement, and swung around, narrowly missing cracking his head on a beam. He saw a dozen rats scuttle from one shadowed partition to another in a quick, ragged procession, swore softly to himself, took a firmer grip on the shivering Festin, and carried on.

Here, in the after part of the gun deck, cabins lined both sides of the ship. Through some of the open doors he could see the clutter of officers' gear, and recognized Forsythe's stateroom by the great rack of antlers that hung on the wall, but the Virginian was nowhere to be seen. From the farthest door aft came such a happy commotion that Wiki realized that it led to the lieutenants' wardroom—and was right, because as they hove up to the door, he could hear Lawrence J. Smith's self-satisfied voice as he related some long, boring tale to a long-suffering fellow officer. Thank God, he thought. Even Festin looked relieved.

Indeed, the Acadian's expression, as he looked up at Wiki, was surprisingly cheerful—and yet at the same time full of cunning. "I cook something very tasty and nice for Mr. Grimes, and he say yes, I bet," he announced, going on to confide, "We won't take no notice of that bloody Jack Winter, not when Mr. Grimes say different."

"I'm sure you're right," said Wiki. Without putting any thought to what Festin had said, he knocked firmly on the wardroom door.

Four

When Wiki arrived back in the saloon, it was to find Dr. Olliver ensconced in his usual chair, holding his filled wineglass high as he contemplated its ruby interior.

As soon as he heard Wiki's steps, he turned with alacrity, demanding, "And how is our murderous cook?"

Wiki said patiently, "As Lieutenant Smith has already assured you, he is *not* a murderer."

"Are you quite certain of that?"

"He was under suspicion, but was cleared—we found that someone else had carried out that particular crime. And right now," Wiki added, "he's fine."

As far as he knew, everything in the Acadian's world was indeed fine. Lieutenant Smith, reluctantly pried away from the officers' wardroom, had trotted off to the purser's office with Festin in tow. Now, presumably, Robert Festin had a hammock, a mess, and a number, and had taken over the afterhouse galley, the old black peg leg cook having been sent about his business. There was no reason at all, Wiki thought hopefully, not to look forward to a delicious meal of fish.

The coffee, when it arrived, was not a good augury, being as black and acrid as ever. When the ship suddenly pitched, though, Wiki caught both pot and mug in dexterous hands, simply out of habit. The *Vincennes* was under full sail again, scudding fast for Rio de Janeiro, and the sea was getting brisk. There was another hard pitch, so violent that the two rats came tumbling out from under the credenza, followed by three more. Wiki watched them as they flowed in a small gray tide along the skirting and then disappeared beneath the storeroom door.

"They're breeding like crazy," observed Dr. Olliver, who was watching them, too. "The sailors used to catch them, and skin and dress them, and sell them to the junior midshipmen, who grilled and ate them, which helped to keep the numbers down. Now, however, supply has exceeded demand."

Wiki heard the click of a door and looked up, to see Captain Wilkes coming out of his cabin, which—as Dr. Olliver had indicated the day before—was sited on the starboard quarter, to the side of the drafting room. The purser was with him. They were both wearing uniform, and looked as if they were about to keep an appointment.

Before anyone could speak, another door opened, and Captain Couthouy stepped out of his stateroom, along with a reek of decay and a couple of rats, which disappeared under the credenza. Captain Wilkes swerved around and snapped, "*Mister* Couthouy, did you *not* receive my note?"

Captain Couthouy said distantly, "Note, Captain Wilkes?"

"My note concerning your smell, sir—your *stench*! You're lumbering up the ship with unpleasantness, Mr. Couthouy, and the smell is encouraging vermin—the ship is full of goddamned rats! How many times do I have to tell you *not* to bring your specimens into your room? They should not be inside at all—not here, and not below decks. Keep them out on the spar deck, sir—the spar deck! There are plenty of racks and tubs for the purpose."

"On the open deck?" Couthouy's voice rose in affront.

"What's *wrong* with the open deck, pray?"

"It's too bloody crowded, Captain Wilkes! The scientifics don't have a decent space in which to work, not without the officer of the watch deigns to issue orders to that effect!"

"*Deigns,* Mr. Couthouy? This is the U.S. Navy, sir, not your private goddamned yacht! I would remind you of my instructions," Captain Wilkes said frostily. "The primary object of the expedition is the promotion of commerce and navigation. The Navy Department believes, and quite rightly so, that it is more important to chart the waters than to list their animal and vegetable contents. You will collect no more than one specimen of each variety, and that as small as possible, and you will *not* bring them into your room. If you don't know where to stow them, ask the officer of the watch!"

Then, ignoring Couthouy's furiously red face, Captain Wilkes turned to the purser and said, "It's time we made our appearance in the wardroom, Mr. Waldron. Our hosts will be awaiting."

And with that, the two officers marched off down the corridor. Wiki heard a distant stamp as the marine on sentry duty saluted, just before the ship executed a tremendous lurch to lee. Again, he caught the coffeepot and his mug, but the other mugs went tumbling to the floor with a multiple crash, echoed by many thuds from the deck outside, plus a fair amount of yelling. Dr. Olliver was calmly holding his decanter and wineglass poised in the air, while Couthouy hung on to the corner of the credenza.

Another great pitch, more yelling from outside, and a wash of water came pouring in the open afterhouse door, to gush in a wide stream down the corridor. Couthouy swore, let go his hold, and plunged back into his room, where they could hear him frantically getting dunnage off the wet floor. Jack Winter came out of the pantry as calmly and steadily as if he were walking on land, his expression as smarmy as ever, and unfolded several sets of fiddle boards—sticks which were laid on the tabletop to hold meal things in place.

The *Vincennes* wallowed unhappily. The afterhouse door swung to and slammed shut, and the commotion of taking reefs in the sails became muffled. Another nasty roll, and then at last the feel of the vessel became stiff, indicating to Wiki that the helmsmen had been replaced with more experienced hands. Then, just as he set the coffeepot carefully to one side, he realized that Grimes had joined the company.

The thin man's stoop was more pronounced than ever, so that he had to crane his neck to bring up his head as he surveyed the room, looking like a suspicious tortoise. He came slowly round the credenza, holding on as the ship pitched her head, and silently chose a chair. As he sat down, his harsh breathing was audible. Lieutenant Smith looked at him, but didn't bother to make any introductions. Instead, he sniffed loudly and luxuriously.

Jack Winter had carried the fish to the table. Because of the rough conditions, they were piled helter-skelter into a wooden mess tub, and the top two were speckled with spray, but the aroma was perfectly wonderful. Robert Festin, Wiki deduced with deep pleasure, had regained his culinary abilities at the same time he had settled in the ship. The fish—if the top two, which were all he could see, were any guide to the rest—had stayed straight while being crisply fried, so that the succulent white flesh was evenly cooked.

Wiki had to restrain himself from grabbing. Instead, remembering his manners, he passed the mess tub around. The first to help himself was Grimes, who was evidently hungry, because he took both top fish. Smith and Dr. Olliver took one each, before handing the tub back to Wiki. He could scarcely wait. When he slid his knife along the backbone, his mouth watered. Miraculously, soft bread came, too.

The delectable meat slipped easily off the bones, and Wiki piled it onto a thick slice of bread, and ate greedily with his fingers. No one about the table was talking, producing happy eating noises instead, and so he was able to concentrate. Turning the fish over, he cleaned off the other side.

Just as the mess tub was being handed round again, Couthouy stamped back into the saloon, swung a chair around, and sat down with a bad-tempered thump, judging his timing to the next weather roll of the ship. He readily helped himself to one of the fish, but didn't make any remark about it, exclaiming moodily instead, "What the devil am I doing here, if I'm not permitted to make a collection? Of *course* the aims of the expedition are scientific—to state anything different is nothing less than ignorant bloody-mindedness!"

Lieutenant Smith looked up from starting operations on his second fish. "I should have thought a shipmaster like yourself would agree most heartily with Captain Wilkes's assessment of the primary aim of the expedition—which is to make the Pacific safe for American commerce!"

Couthouy put down his fork, turned in his chair, and stared. "By charting the ocean?" he demanded.

"Not just that, but also by flying the U.S. flag in a thousand lagoons! Our job is to tame rebellious natives and make the Pacific secure for American adventurers like you, sir!"

"Goodness gracious," said Dr. Olliver, lifting his wineglass in a sardonic salute. "So that's why we've been practicing the cannon so assiduously? Is the intention really to terrify innocent natives into abject submission to your flag?"

"Unpleasant, but necessary," Smith declared roundly. "As a Salem shipmaster I know well could tell you, the disasters that have fallen on American adventurers have too often been the outcome of shipmasters putting their trust in savage chiefs. My friend has testified before the East India Marine Society in Salem to the grave dangers faced by American shipmasters, and he has made representations in Washington, too—he knows from personal experience what it's like to see one's crew cut out by bloodthirsty savages!"

"Good God, has he?" said Dr. Olliver, his tone even more colored with irony. "And just who is this passionate gentleman?"

"Captain William Coffin—Wiremu's natural father."

Though Wiki had been half expecting this, he still felt a jolt in his gut. Everyone turned and stared at him, their thoughts—that he was living evidence that Captain Coffin had demonstrated quite a different kind of passion for at least one of the islanders in question—writ plain on their faces.

He watched them back with a deliberately impassive expression. It was a skill he had developed over the years—at moments like this, he remembered one of the proverbs that his *iwi* liked to quote: *I nga ra o te pai, he pai; i nga ra o te kino, he kino*. What is good, is good; what is bad, is bad. Live with it.

For a moment there was an awkward silence, punctuated by a swish and a thump as the *Vincennes* lifted and plunged. Then Couthouy turned to the assistant astronomer, saying with a deliberate change of topic, "Grimes, isn't it? Weren't you living on the *Vincennes* when we sailed from Norfolk?"

Grimes was eating stolidly, while Dr. Olliver, having demolished his second fish, watched him over the rim of his glass. Now the instrumentmaker looked up at Couthouy and nodded.

"*I* don't remember him," the surgeon remarked to no one in particular. "And *I* was on the *Vincennes*, too."

"But you were infamously seasick at the time," said Couthouy, and laughed. Then he looked at Grimes again, saying, "Assistant astronomer—right? And you're an Englishman, ain't you, just like Dr. Olliver here." Again, Grimes nodded silently, and Couthouy turned back to Dr. Olliver and said, "He lived on the gun deck."

"Ah," said Dr. Olliver with satisfaction, and toasted himself with a longer swallow of wine than usual. "That accounts for it. I was in the afterhouse, of course; I've always had the same room."

"After the sudden death of his employer, Astronomer Burroughs,"

Lieutenant Smith elaborated, "Mr. Grimes was moved onto the *Porpoise*."

Again, Wiki found himself the focus of speculative stares. There had been rather a lot of sudden deaths on the expedition, most of them connected with him. Then the conchologist said abruptly, "I know your father, I think."

Considering that Captain Couthouy and Captain Coffin were both Massachusetts shipmasters, Wiki was not amazed. He said politely, "You were in the China trade, too?"

Couthouy shook his head, but did not have a chance to reply, because yet again Lieutenant Smith chipped in. "I know Captain William Coffin very well, indeed—a most remarkable man," he bragged. "His commercial exploits are famous! He left Salem in June 1830 to make the most profitable voyage on record, carrying tobacco for New Zealand, and flour for Sydney, which he sold at the rate of fifteen dollars a barrel—flour which had cost him four! Then he filled his holds with tortoiseshell and sugar, and sold that cargo in New York for no less than twenty thousand dollars. It's for his kind of enterprise that we want to secure the Pacific for Yankee traders!"

Wiki pushed his plate aside. In June 1830, as he remembered very well, his father had sailed away without him—he had abandoned his sixteen-year-old Maori son to the mercies of his legal Yankee wife. While that was an old memory, this was the first time that Wiki had heard that his father had sailed to New Zealand after leaving Salem. Back then, Captain Coffin had told him that he was bound to the Orient.

"Astounding," said Couthouy to Smith, his tone so flat it was rude, and said to Grimes with a deliberate change of topic, "You've been moved back to the *Vin*?"

"Astronomer Grimes has been shifted from the *Porpoise* to assist Captain Wilkes with the apparatus for gravitation measurements at Rio," said Lieutenant Smith, again without giving Grimes a chance to answer.

"So he's working with Wilkes? The poor bastard," said Dr. Olliver, again to no one in particular.

Grimes said stiffly, "Checking and adjusting the equipment is an interesting assignment, and I am not to be pitied at all."

"Nonetheless, you have my liveliest sympathies," returned Dr. Olliver, completely unabashed. He lifted his glass in an ironic salute, and queried, "What was *your* reason for joining the Deplorable Expedition?"

"I must protest that appellation!" Lieutenant Smith exclaimed, but everyone ignored him, instead looking at Grimes, who said in precise and pedantic tones, "Astronomer Burroughs brought me on board in the capacity of his instrumentmaker and assistant."

"And was Astronomer Burroughs a despised Englishman, too?" demanded Dr. Olliver.

Grimes said, more stiffly still, "He was American."

"So how did he find you? Come on, man, tell me," the fat naturalist urged, his wineglass still poised. Wiki was beginning to recognize the look of unbridled curiosity on his face; Dr. Olliver was a man, he mused, who delighted in digging up odd stories, even if he had to be unbelievably ill-mannered to get them.

"Because I was a horticulturalist who enjoyed astronomy," Grimes replied with spirit, and then fell into a fit of coughing.

"Horticulturalist?" Couthouy echoed, looking puzzled. It was as if he had never heard the word before.

"A man who specializes in the science of gardening," Lieutenant Smith informed him.

"But *where*?" said Couthouy to Grimes.

"On an estate near Cambridge," said Grimes, wiping his mouth with the soiled handkerchief.

Captain Couthouy turned to Dr. Olliver. "Weren't you at Cambridge assisting Charles Darwin after he got back from the *Beagle* voyage?" The portly naturalist nodded, and Couthouy said to Grimes, "I can't imagine the connection between gardening and astronomy."

"I was in charge of the glasshouses, you understand—glasshouses that I designed myself. I also constructed heating equipment. Sir Roger—our master, the owner of the estate—was a notable amateur astronomer, and because he noticed I was so handy in the gadget-making way, he paid for me to be taught the science of optical instruments. Then Dr. Burroughs came to Cambridge—he'd paid Mr. Darwin to make some observations on his behalf, and wanted to see the results—and while he was in town he became acquainted with Sir Roger, who was kind enough to show him some of my inventions. Dr. Burroughs was so impressed that he begged Sir Roger to allow me accompany him to America as his assistant."

"That's quite a story," said Couthouy. He sounded admiring.

"Sir Roger—who?" The query came from Dr. Olliver.

"Palgrave," answered Grimes.

Dr. Olliver lifted his glass and emptied it in one mouthful. Then he picked up the stopper that had been rolling back and forth between fiddle boards, and carefully inserted it in the neck of the decanter.

"Never met him," he said without interest.

"He's dead," said Grimes.

"Of natural causes?" inquired Couthouy on a ghoulish note.

Grimes snapped, "Of course," and then added, "His only son sold the estate after he inherited it, so there's no Palgraves there anymore."

There was an odd, awkward little silence, broken, unexpectedly, by the arrival of Robert Festin. The squat little man came around the corner of the credenza with a small covered dish in his hand, and the same sly grin that Wiki had seen before on his face.

He went straight up to Grimes, pushed the plate toward him, and said in English, "For you."

"What?" The assistant astronomer scowled. Then he slowly took the cover off the dish, while they all watched in fascination.

It revealed an individual baked pudding, golden in color and liberally sprinkled with grated brown sugar. It steamed, wafting out a delicious aroma of sweet potato that had been mashed and blended with butter, molasses, and rum. Everyone leaned forward with blatant envy as Grimes plied a fork, puffing damply on each morsel to cool it before inserting it into his mouth. Even when he had finished, he made no comment, but Festin's grin was broader than ever.

"Now," he stated, "you say *aye,* yes?"

Wiki, having suddenly deduced what it was all about, tensed warily. Grimes was slower on the uptake, saying blankly, "What?"

"Me sleep in your room, on floor. You say *yes,* no?"

"Absolutely not!"

"But Wiki said—"

To Wiki's enormous relief, they were interrupted. The afterhouse door slammed open, and Lieutenant Forsythe strode in. His burly form was swathed in a wet oilskin coat, making him look bigger than ever, and he was carrying a speaking trumpet, evidently set to take over the deck when eight bells rang and the watch changed.

He swung around a chair, threw himself into it, reached out, grasped Dr. Olliver's decanter, unstoppered it, and poured wine liberally into a mug, while he used an elbow planted on the table to brace himself against the roll of the ship. Then he gulped deeply, before looking at Lieutenant Smith with an evil grin, and saying, "Found you at last, you treacherous little bugger."

Assistant Astronomer Grimes let out an audible gasp, while Lawrence J. Smith's eyes popped. "So you're back on the *Vincennes,* huh?" the Virginian remarked. "Last time I saw you, you was in charge of what passes for the quarterdeck of the U.S. schooner *Flying Fish,* taking off for the horizon like the devil himself was on your tail, having solemnly promised not to leave me and my men stranded at Shark Island with just the cutter to get us back to the fleet. So what are you doin' here? Your career taken a mighty downturn?"

The pompous lieutenant gobbled, at a loss for a dignified answer, and Forsythe laughed. "Don't bother," he advised. "I'm merely here to deliver a message—that your presence is desired in the wardroom."

The ship's bell rang, and the big southerner drained the mug, heaved himself to his feet, grinned unpleasantly at them all, and left, kicking at a rat as he went.

Wiki got up, too, abandoning Festin to his doomed argument with Grimes. By the time he arrived on the windswept deck, Forsythe had disappeared, but nonetheless he stayed outside. The brisk air was invigorating. Spray, mixed with drizzling rain, flew across the decks, wetting his shirt and trousers, but on impulse he walked forward to the waist, kicked off his boots, jumped onto the bulwarks, and began to climb the mainmast shrouds. The wind tore away the lashing of his long hair, so that it whipped out behind him. Reaching the futtock shrouds that braced the platformlike top of the lower mast, he threw himself bodily outward, swarmed over the top with the roll of the ship, and then carried onward up the ladderlike ratlines to the topgallant crosstrees, where he wedged himself into place, hanging on to a lanyard.

The view was tremendous. The big ship, cracking on with the gale on her starboard quarter, was leaning well over, plunging every now and then, and the wake that curled away from her hull, a hundred fifty feet below, was white with rushing spume. The sky was streaming with broken cloud, full of holes that let through great shafts of rain-streaked moonlight, which gleamed on the spread of canvas below him, and lit up the scudding sails of the other ships of the fleet—the multiple triangles of the two schooners, *Flying Fish* and *Sea Gull;* the double pyramid of the brig *Porpoise,* and the piratical silhouette of the *Swallow,* dashing along at a terrific rate under her steeply raked masts.

The gale was on the rise—it was high time to take in more sail. Wiki heard Forsythe, on the roof of the afterhouse, bellow into his trumpet—"Stand by t'gallant halyards!"—and boatswains' mates shrilling their calls. A sudden gust of rain swept down, and men slipped and slid on the distant deck as they hauled on buntlines and clewlines to slacken the hard bellies of the sails.

Then, "Away aloft!" and hands were crawling up the rigging toward Wiki. Some, braver or more agile, were outpacing the others, and so the first topgallantman arrived well ahead of his shipmates. Wiki moved aside to make room for him, so he could sidle along the jolting yard to take the weather earring, and then, on yet another impulse, went out on the opposite end. Other men arrived on the footrope alongside him, and together they bent over the yard and heaved at the heavy wet canvas.

At last the job was done. The other seamen headed deckward, some casting Wiki curious looks. However, he lingered, watching the *Swallow* take in sail, imagining what it was like on board the smaller and much more lively craft. The decks would be a cacophony of shouted orders and trampling feet, the creaking of blocks and the groan of hauled ropes. Below decks, the little brig would be creaking like a basket, with every particle on the move, the rattling of cutlery punctuated by the smashing of plates.

Yet even in these conditions, he mused, compared to the chaotic state of society in the afterhouse of the flagship *Vincennes,* the atmosphere on board the *Swallow* would be remarkably tranquil.

Five

That night, Wiki woke to hear a grating sound as Grimes's chamber pot was dragged out from under the double berth, followed by a bout of loud, wet coughing as the pot was shoved back with yet another scrape. Worse was to come—at four in the morning, as eight bells rang for the start of the morning watch, Grimes was overtaken with griping pains, and groaned most horribly as he crouched.

The moment he was back in bed, shuddering and whimpering, Wiki swung down from his berth, and retreated into the empty saloon, carrying his clothes. The instant he was dressed he tapped on Dr. Olliver's door. The naturalist opened it almost at once, more whalelike than ever in a billowing nightshirt. After silently listening to Wiki, he nodded and went back inside.

It seemed to take an endless time for the surgeon to put on his clothes and come out again. Then Grimes objected strenuously to a medical examination, vowing that he did not want to be poked and prodded. Marveling that any man could be so obstinate when he was suffering so much, Wiki retreated to the saloon, leaving Dr. Olliver to it. By the time the echoes of the argument faded and the naturalist had set to work on his reluctant patient, coffee arrived on the table.

The ship was still plunging about in lively fashion, but the plump steward minced back and forth with the same steadiness he had displayed the evening before. Undoubtedly, Wiki mused, Jack Winter's remarkable sense of balance was the heritage of years on tiny sealing vessels in tumultuous southern seas. Perhaps, he thought ironically, that was where he had learned to make such horrible coffee, too.

"What's all the early commotion about?" the steward then inquired. "If I may take the extreme liberty of asking?"

"Astronomer Grimes is sick. Something gave him the gripes."

"The fish didn't agree with his innards, huh?" Jack Winter's sideways look was malicious.

Dr. Olliver came into the saloon as Wiki replied impatiently, "I thought you might have more sensible ideas than that."

"When I viewed them fish I didn't like the sight at all—to my mind they threatened something bloody nasty, excuse my biblical language, particularly when I saw their reproachful eyes."

"But we all ate the fish!"

"And maybe we don't all have delicate digestions," Jack Winter said in his smarmy way. "You sure they was fresh?"

Wiki snapped, "*Ehara!* I promise you they were caught yesterday morning! You can argue with Sua and Tana, if you don't believe me!"

As the steward went off with a resentful look, Dr. Olliver said, "I don't trust that fellow an inch—he steals my wine, you know."

Wiki didn't doubt that for an instant. However, remembering the naturalist's little ritual of refilling his wineglass every time it reached the precise halfway level, he said curiously, "Why don't you mark the decanter?"

"Because God alone knows what he would pour into it to bring it up to the mark again. And anyway," Dr. Olliver went on as he swung a chair around and eased his bulk into it, "I brought the Madeira on board in a butt, which is kept in the steward's storeroom, and there's no way I can check how much is taken out of that."

Wiki helped himself to coffee, thinking that he now had a good idea why Jack Winter slung his hammock there. Captain Couthouy came into the room, blinking and complaining about being disturbed in the night, and the surgeon told him, "Grimes is suffering from a bout of diarrhea," adding with relish, "And he reckons he's been poisoned."

"By the fish?"

"Either the fish or the pudding," said Dr. Olliver.

"Then it must be the pudding, because no one else has been sick."

"Whatever, Grimes reckons that odd little cook is out to poison him, and maybe Jack Winter is, too."

"Can't he make up his mind?" queried Couthouy.

"He doesn't need to, because he reckons it's a conspiracy."

Wiki echoed blankly, "Conspiracy? Between Jack Winter and Robert Festin? But why?"

"Oh, you have the honor of being included in the number," Olliver assured him with a smirk. "Not only does he reckon you want him out of that stateroom, but that the cook will stop at nothing to get in there, as well."

"Dear God," said Wiki. He wondered if Grimes were mad.

The surgeon said thoughtfully, "Do you have any idea why Festin made him a dessert all of his own?" He pursed plump lips, and confessed rather plaintively, "I must confess it smelled and looked so enticing I could easily have managed a portion myself—but now I wonder if I was lucky I didn't."

"I didn't realize it until too late, but it was intended as a bribe, his logic being that Grimes would be charmed into letting him sleep on the floor of our room. He gets lonely, you see," Wiki went on, as a lame kind of excuse.

They both stared at him, and then Captain Couthouy barked with laughter. "Well," he said callously, "if the pudding *was* poisoned, he'll have a room all to himself—in the brig—and then a space of his own when he hangs from the yardarm, too."

"Unless the steward sprinkled something on the top two fish—the ones that Grimes ate," said Dr. Olliver.

Couthouy guffawed. "Surely you're not going in for this conspiracy idea, too? Why the devil would the steward want to kill him?"

Dr. Olliver shrugged bulky shoulders. "I agree that Grimes is exhibiting morbid delusions of persecution. The problem is that he's very ill—ill enough to die."

Wiki exclaimed in horror, *"Die?"*

"You've noticed how he stoops? His difficulty in breathing? He suffers from a pronounced lateral curvature of the spine, which is probably congenital, and has led to such a long-standing degeneration of the chest that the left lung has adhered to the wall. On top of his other symptoms, he now has a heightened temperature. If the diarrhea, with its accompanying chills, brings on a pneumonia, then the very worst could happen."

"So what are you going to do about it?" Wiki demanded.

"My first recourse would be venesection, but he utterly refuses to be bled. I have to say he's the most bloody uncooperative patient I've encountered in many a year," Dr. Olliver confessed on a resentful note. "However, I have managed to dose him with carbonate of ammonia. It was the devil's own job to get it into his mouth, and he refused to swallow until I pinched his nostrils shut. Then he had the sauce to call me a goddamned quack because it tasted bitter."

"Will the carbonate of ammonia fix the problem?"

"It should help. It's a cardiac stimulant, but can also be employed as a valuable expectorant. To make sure, however," he said, his tone becoming businesslike as he heaved himself out of his chair and went to his room for a wooden box, "I'll make up some *pilula cinchona composita.*"

Paying not the slightest regard to the fact that the steward wanted to lay breakfast, Dr. Olliver dumped the box on the table. Opening the lid revealed the contents of a medical chest. He then asked Jack Winter for an egg, and by the time it arrived, rattling in a small bowl, he had four bottles lined up in front of him, along with a small stone pestle and mortar.

As Wiki and Captain Couthouy watched with deep interest from the other side of the table, he measured coarse powder out of three of the bottles. Then he picked up the fourth vial, which held a small amount of dried vegetable matter, and shook it, studying it with a frown before emptying it into the mortar.

"What's that?" said Wiki.

"Peruvian bark—and I hope there's more in the ship's medical chest, because this may not be enough."

Having unburdened himself of this ominous news, Dr. Olliver energetically ground up the ingredients of the mortar. That done, he cracked the egg, and separated the white into the bowl. Then, holding the yolk in a half shell, he yelled out to Jack Winter, this time for his decanter and a tumbler. When both arrived, he tipped the unbroken yolk into the tumbler and covered it with wine.

Turning to the mortar again, the surgeon tipped the ground-up powder onto a little marble slab, where he gradually mixed it with egg white until it was stiff. Then he rolled it into a pipe, cut off measured pieces, and rolled them between his fat fingers, in this way manufacturing a row of little balls.

Wiki asked, "What do these pills do?"

"*Pilula cinchona composita* is a compound of Peruvian bark, piperine, *ferri pulvis*, and gentian root," Dr. Olliver pompously informed him.

"I meant, will these pills make him better?"

"*Pilula cinchona composita* is an excellent prophylactic for ague and fever." Leaving the row of pills on the slab to dry, Dr. Olliver picked up the tumbler with the egg yolk and wine, and drank it down in one swallow. Then, with an air of expecting the worst, he mused aloud, after licking his lips, "Unfortunately, the patient's intrinsically feeble constitution doesn't help matters, and his obstinate and contrary nature don't make my job any easier, either."

"But shouldn't he be in the sickbay?" Couthouy inquired. "Dr. Gilchrist—who is the official ship's surgeon, after all!—should deal with the problem."

"Grimes flatly refuses to budge from his stateroom."

Wiki exclaimed, "It's my stateroom, too, you know—and I can't stay in there if he's ill!"

"That's a point," said Couthouy. "Is Grimes's disease contagious?"

Dr. Olliver shrugged. "If he was laid low by something in the food, then of course it isn't catching. But if it's something else, it's possible the air he emanates is noxious."

"Then he and Wiki certainly shouldn't sleep in the same room—*Kanakas* die too easily of white men's diseases."

Though blessed with a naturally robust constitution, Wiki wasn't offended, as he had seen too many Pacific Islanders sicken and die of European illnesses, like measles, that *pakeha* children contracted routinely and recovered from easily. He was worried about something much more dire. In New Zealand, a temporary shelter—a *wharau*—was built for anyone who was gravely ill, because a house where a person had died could never be used again, being *tapu*—forbidden. After the patient expired, the problem of the *tapu* house was solved by burning it to the ground. Obviously, on board ship, this was no solution, but Wiki's problem remained—that living in the same space as a man who might die was spiritually impossible.

Wiki looked at the larboard side of the passage, counted the four doors, pointed at the last one, and said, "Is that a spare stateroom?"

Both naturalists shook their heads. "It's Smith's," Captain Couthouy said, adding with a grin, "You could sling a hammock in the storeroom with Jack Winter."

That idea was almost as impossible as sleeping with a man who might die. Then, to Wiki's deep relief, Dr. Gilchrist arrived.

Unfortunately, however, after a brief inspection of the patient, and listening to what Dr. Olliver had to say, Dr. Gilchrist professed himself perfectly happy with his distinguished colleague's decision to leave Grimes in the stateroom. Not only was the propriety of sending a scientific to the common sickbay doubtful, but the patient demonstrated such a strong disinclination to move that shifting him forcibly could lead to an unfortunate decline. Indeed, that Mr. Grimes was so conveniently close to Dr. Olliver was an advantage.

As for the medication, he declared the choice was impeccable. Unfortunately, there was no Peruvian bark in the medical stores of the *Vincennes,* but hopefully Dr. Olliver's stock would last until they arrived at Rio, as *pilula cinchona composita,* administered four times daily at the rate of two pills before breakfast, four before dinner, three before supper, and two more at bedtime, applied in conjunction with carbonate of ammonia, was an excellent prescription. And, forthwith, the two surgeons took themselves off to discuss a bottle of Madeira in the wardroom, leaving Wiki to contemplate Grimes, who glared balefully back.

"It was something in the food that felled me, and it was naught to do with overindulgence," he hissed. "And I know the reason why I'm being poisoned!"

"You can't possibly believe that!"

"I collapsed when I used the chamber pot, something that's never happened before. I've had the pneumonia, too, and I know the pain that afflicts me ain't due to that—nor the state of my innards, neither! So get out of my stateroom, and don't come back unless you're accompanied by the captain, so I can state the true case to him."

There was no point in arguing further. Without another word, Wiki walked off, heading for the foredeck galley and Robert Festin. It was a strange reversal of fortune, he grimly mused—where Festin had wanted to sleep in his room, now he wished to berth with him.

Six

Though Festin was nowhere near the captain's galley on the foredeck, he was easily located, because his shouts of pain and defiance echoed up from the gun deck immediately below. Springing down the ladder and running through the dimness toward the common galley, Wiki sighted a bunch of seamen silhouetted against the fires, shouting savage imprecations and wielding angry fists.

The man they were attacking was Robert Festin, so hunched down he could scarcely be seen in the center of the group, but defending himself with spirit. As Wiki rushed up, a couple of his attackers came hurtling out of the writhing heap to fall crashing to the planks, while another wave of men descended on the Acadian. Wiki could hear them grunting epithets—"Bloody poisoner! Kill us all with your foreign muck, will you?" Festin's gasps of pain were audible, too, while his short, powerful arms were held up to cover his face.

Wiki put down his head and barged into the middle of the group by sheer momentum and strength, shouldering away one man and fending off another with a palm in his face. Hard blows thumped against him, but in the blur of motion Wiki scarcely felt the impact. He glimpsed snarling faces as sailors turned to fight him off, but kept on going, shoving with his elbows and fists. In the gap that opened up he could see Festin crouched into a fighting stance.

Wiki launched himself full length and tackled Festin about the thighs, bringing him down with a crash. They landed on the planks as one, while vicious boots lashed out. Wiki rolled them both through a thicket of legs toward the galley fires, taking a couple of kicks as he went. Then he shoved the panting Festin away, and lunged to his feet with the hearth at his back, fists up and braced to meet the oncoming rush.

Belatedly, he heard Lieutenant Forsythe's loud yelling, coming fast from the amidships part of the deck. The attackers stopped dead, then made a precipitate dash into the dark shadows on either side. In contrast to the previous racket, the sounds of their retreat were as quiet as the pattering of rats. Forsythe's shouts and rapid steps were very noisy by comparison. By the time he arrived, the last of them had vanished.

The Virginian's face was red with outrage, and his speaking trumpet was gripped so hard in one huge hand that it threatened to be crushed. Evidently, Wiki deduced, the ruckus had happened while he was in charge of the deck.

"What the bloody hell was all that about?" he roared.

"They were trying to murder Festin," Wiki said shortly. He turned to the cook. "Are you all right?"

Festin was not all right. His eyes were crossed, and it was obvious that his ears were ringing loudly, because he kept on hitting the sides of his head with his open palms. Wiki said, concerned, "Do you remember your name?"

Instead of answering, Festin smiled seraphically, giving Wiki cause for even more alarm for his health. Then he realized that the

Acadian was simply enchanted by being rescued not just by his hero, Lieutenant Forsythe, but by Wiki, too, whom he considered his friend. To spoil the effect, however, blood suddenly gushed out of his mouth and down his chin and chest.

Festin spat out a tooth, caught it in his palm, and studied it with an expression of great interest. Lieutenant Forsythe scowled even more deeply, and demanded, "Why the hell did they want to beat the living daylights out of him, apart from being tired of looking at his ugly face?"

"Haven't you heard?" Wiki asked. During his seven years at sea he had often noticed that the common seamen knew shipboard gossip long before the officers, but still it never failed to surprise him. "The men think he poisoned Assistant Astronomer Grimes."

Forsythe laughed in disbelief. *"Poisoned?"*

"Aye. Grimes had an attack of diarrhea in the night, and blames it on Festin, because he reckons that he put poison in either the fish he cooked last night for us all, or the pudding he made just for him."

"Jesus," said Forsythe, and shook his head in disgust. "That was a stupid bloody choice. Why Grimes, and not Lawrence J. Smith?"

"I've not a notion," said Wiki.

"So how did the men hear about it?"

Wiki frowned. Then, remembering the hiss of *foreign muck*, he jumped to the obvious conclusion. "Jack Winter must have told them," he said.

"H'm!" grunted Forsythe, and nodded as if it were exactly the kind of behavior he expected of the steward. Then he looked at Wiki and barked, "I should call the marines, and have you thrown into the brig."

Wiki thought about it, and shrugged.

"You don't care?"

"It solves my accommodation problems."

"What the devil do you mean?"

Wiki paused, studying the big Virginian, wondering if there was a chance he would understand. Forsythe had once hired himself out to a Ngapuhi chief as a mercenary fighter. He had hunted the forest warpaths and voyaged on *waka taua*—canoes of war—and he had lived and fought with Wiki's people, though after Wiki had left the Bay of Islands. So Wiki said, "I berth with Astronomer Grimes, and if he dies I'll have to cope with his *kehua*—his ghost. And the room will be too *tapu* to live in."

"For God's sake!" Forsythe exploded. "Why can't you remember that half of you is a civilized American? Aren't you embarrassed to behave like a bloody ignorant savage?"

Wiki maintained a chilly silence. Then he saw Forsythe's thick lips pursing in and out as he glowered at Festin, who was still contemplating his tooth. Finally, the lieutenant said with an air of decision, "Come with me."

"What? Where?"

Instead of answering, Forsythe cast sharp glances all about the gun deck. Wiki looked, too, but the only life to be seen was a trickle of rats, scuttling from shadow to shadow. The fires glowed redly under the big cauldrons where great lumps of salt meat were simmering, but right now there was no one to tend them. Evidently, he thought, the cooks had been part of the party that had attacked Festin, and had run away with the rest. Then, when he looked back at Forsythe, Wiki glimpsed an odd awkwardness in his expression.

The lieutenant said in a lowered voice, "You can both berth with me until the fuss settles down."

Wiki stared at him, stunned. Involuntarily, he exclaimed, *"What?"*

"Goddamnit!" Forsythe burst out, now openly embarrassed. "Don't ask bloody questions, just come!"

Still looking stealthily from side to side, he led the way aft, almost the whole length of the ship. Wiki followed first, and Festin, still clutching his tooth, trailed behind. No sooner were they inside Forsythe's cabin than the Virginian hastily shut the door.

Wiki looked around. The room was extremely cluttered, and did not smell very wonderful, either, but was more spacious than he had expected. A tier of lockers and drawers, some half open and spilling garments, was set against the side of the ship, its top lipped to hold a narrow mattress and serve as Forsythe's bed. A sidelight above this berth cast grimy reflections of sun and water onto the opposite bulkhead, which was furnished with a sofa. There was a chart desk built between the head of the bunk and the settee, its surface marked with many rings from bottles and tumblers. Forsythe's great rack of antlers was screwed to the wall above the desk, and his rifle hung from one of the horns.

Forsythe was studying the room, too—with new eyes, it seemed, because he started to tidy up in a clumsy fashion, shoving drawers shut with a thump of a boot, and sweeping all the papers and books on the desk into one pile, which promptly fell apart with the next roll of the ship. It was the most bizarre demonstration of southern hospitality that Wiki had ever seen.

"Festin can have the sofa," Forsythe said. "And I'll bullyrag that goddamned excuse for a ship's purser into breaking out a hammock for you."

The cabin was certainly long enough to sling a hammock, about nine feet from the forward partition to the after bulkhead where the rack of antlers hung. Then Wiki forgot it, because the blows he had absorbed abruptly started to sting. He pulled up his left sleeve and gingerly inspected his upper arm, which was swollen even more than usual.

Forsythe said with complete lack of sympathy, "Brown bastards like you don't show bruises much, so no one will notice that you've been fighting, not if you have the brains not to point it out." Then he looked at Festin, who was sitting on the sofa smiling at them both with his tooth in his hand and blood running down his chin, and observed on a much less optimistic note, "But he looks a right bloody mess—which is a goddamned pity, considerin' he has to go back to work in the galley any minute."

"That's true," Wiki agreed, keeping irony out of his voice.

"But someone once told me that if you shove a lost tooth back into the hole, it will grow back into place."

Wiki lifted his brows, thinking that he was learning a great deal in the medical line, this day. There were so many cuts and bruises starting out all over Festin's face that it didn't seem possible that putting back the tooth, even if successful, would be much of an improvement, though.

However, Forsythe looked very animated. "I reckon we should try it," he pronounced, and with no more ado he hunkered down, plucked the tooth out of Festin's hold, spat on it to clean it, and then held the Acadian's mouth wide open with one great hand while he wriggled the tooth back into his jaw with the other.

Then it was done. Forsythe stood back, instructed Festin to open his mouth to expose his handiwork, and then frowned mightily. "It don't look right," he said.

Wiki came over and peered. It certainly did look odd. He said, "You've got it in backward."

"What? You reckon? Goddamnit," said Forsythe, after having another look. "You're right. How about you having a go?"

Wiki shrugged, thinking that he couldn't do any more damage than had been done already. Festin was beginning to whine with pain as the numbness faded, so Wiki plucked out the tooth as gently as he could, washed it in a handy tumbler of water—which immediately turned an unpleasant brown—and put it back in place, with due care given to its orientation.

"That's done it," pronounced Forsythe after another inspection. After grabbing up a tattered pair of drawers from the top of his bunk, he doused a corner with the water from the tumbler, and scoured the blood off Festin's face. "You'll do," he said, standing back for another look. "Off you go to the galley, and don't breathe a word about what happened. In fact, keep your mouth tight shut, or that damn tooth might fall out."

With perfect timing, eight bells sounded from above. Forsythe sprinted up the companionway to hand over the deck, urging Festin along as he went. A remarkably short moment later, he came thundering down again with a hammock over his shoulder. "Now," he said energetically, and set himself into action again. Hammock hooks were screwed into the wall above the desk and into the partition opposite, and when Wiki clambered into the hammock to try it out, he found that he swung quite comfortably with his feet beneath the antlers, though the dead stare from the deer's glass eyes was a bit disconcerting.

To celebrate, Forsythe opened the door and roared for a boy to fetch a pot of coffee. "Wa'al, then," he said, settling down with a mug, "tell me about this poisoning. Was it the fish or the pudding?"

"Neither," said Wiki flatly.

"You reckon the fish were fresh?"

"Tana and Sua caught them just that morning."

"Those black bastards? They put a barbaric curse on them."

Wiki received this in a cold silence which was wasted on Forsythe, because he didn't even notice, demanding instead, "So who carried them over from the galley after they were cooked? Festin? Or that po-faced steward?"

"Jack Winter, of course."

"So he could have done it. Does he have any access to poison?"

"According to Dr. Olliver, he swears all the time that he's going to lay poison for the rats, but the rats are as lively as ever, which probably means he has no poison to lay."

"So who ate the fish?"

"Everyone at the table—Dr. Olliver, Captain Couthouy, Lieutenant Smith, Grimes, and myself."

"And did anyone else get sick?"

"Just Grimes."

"So mebbe it was a *particular* fish."

"Aye, we thought of that, too—or, at least, Dr. Olliver did. The fish were piled in a mess tub, and Grimes ate the topmost two."

"Aha—so that's where we should have a bloody good look at Jack Winter," said Forsythe with an air of triumph. "I betcha that while he was carrying the bucket from the galley, he sprinkled somethin' on top."

"But he doesn't have a motive!"

"He does, if he expected Wilkes to be at the table," the southerner said with an evil grin. "His majesty would naturally take the first helping—and Smith, considerin' himself the next most important, would follow. And I bet what Jack sprinkled was a big spoonful of salts! The way you described it, I reckon it was a dose of salts what sent Grimes to the pot."

"It's a theory," Wiki allowed, concealing his amusement.

"It's more than a bloody theory! And you'd better hope like crazy that I'm right, because if anyone else gets sick, or Grimes gets even sicker, I can't do anythin' more for you and Festin."

Wiki glanced at Forsythe curiously, "Why *are* you doing it?"

"Doin' what?"

"Why are you looking after me and Festin?"

Forsythe looked astounded. "Because you're my men," he stated as if it were obvious. "My crew!"

Wiki blinked. "What crew?"

"Of the bloody *cutter*, of course."

It was then that Wiki learned, to his complete stupefaction, that the horrible five-day passage in the cutter from Shark Island to the fleet had been positively enjoyed by Lieutenant Forsythe—that it had been a challenge he had relished. While for Wiki it had been an uncomfortable ordeal, for the southerner it had not just been a chance to demonstrate his remarkable seamanship and gifted navigation skills, but a triumph of camaraderie, as well.

Festin, Forsythe readily allowed, had been nothing but a confounded encumbrance, while Wiki was one of the best bloody helmsmen he had ever known. However, their various skills and talents made no difference, because now he felt a fierce loyalty to all the men who had shared the experience.

"Well, I never," marveled Wiki.

"As I said, there is only so much I can do for you, though," Forsythe warned. "You and Festin can live in here with me—in the meantime. But you better hope like the devil that Grimes don't drop dead, because if he does all bloody hell is going to break loose, and I'll have to stand by and watch Festin swing, and see you sent back to the States in irons."

Which, in the light of the instrumentmaker's mad accusations, was probably very true, Wiki grimly thought.

Seven

"Did you find another berth?" Dr. Olliver inquired.

"On the gun deck," Wiki replied. He had the comfortable sense of telling nothing but the truth, because Forsythe's cabin was indeed on the gun deck, a few doors forward of the officers' wardroom. However, when he asked about Assistant Astronomer Grimes, the answer was not encouraging.

"His lungs are clogged with pus and full of fluid," Dr. Olliver pronounced, and drank wine as if he needed it. "Listen to his breathing," he said—and Wiki could indeed hear the harsh, stertorous rasping from where he sat at the table.

To make matters even worse, the meal was horrible. The beef was burned and the potatoes almost raw, which was a worrying indication of Robert Festin's state of mind, and maybe even the battered state of his brain. However, a night spent sleeping soundly on Lieutenant Forsythe's sofa improved the Acadian's outlook considerably, with the result that the following day the provender was vastly improved.

Not so the state of Grimes's health, which continued to get worse. At dinnertime on the third day, as Dr. Olliver consumed forkfuls of *pâté à la râpure,* washing down ambrosial mouthfuls of chicken and grated potato with a great deal of gulped wine, he confessed that matters looked very bad, indeed.

"If it wasn't for the nourishing soup that Festin sends up from the galley," he grimly ruminated, "I fear he'd be dead by now."

Wiki frowned, thinking that this boded even more badly for Festin if Grimes did indeed die, and said cautiously, "Does Grimes know that it's Festin who cooks the soup?"

The surgeon laughed. "He still vows he was poisoned by either the fish or that pudding, and I wouldn't get a single drop of the stuff down his throat if he had the slightest notion that Festin was the cook."

Wiki silenced, feeling very worried, indeed. He wanted to suggest that it would be a good idea if someone else prepared the invalid food, but realized it was impossible to do without making it look as if he, too, suspected that Festin laced his cooking with poison.

"I'll consult with Dr. Gilchrist this afternoon, and see if he has any better ideas," Dr. Olliver heavily went on.

"So what did Dr. Gilchrist say?" Wiki asked at supper.

"That we should keep to the same medication," Dr. Olliver said. His expression, as he concentrated on filling his wineglass, was preoccupied.

"Is that a problem?"

"Indeed it is," the naturalist said, frowning as he took his first sip. "I've only seven pills left, and, as you know, I've run out of Peruvian bark. Tomorrow we drop anchor, I hear, and it can't come soon enough for me."

They were certainly close to port. When Wiki went out on deck it was to see land on the horizon, one immense peak with many little hills peeping up from either side of its bulge. In the last of the sunset, the mountain was deep purple, rising from a dark green sea. *Cape Frio,* he thought. It was the first indication of the port of Rio for those vessels approaching from the north, and a familiar sight from previous voyages.

As he headed for the companionway, Wiki heard Forsythe, who was the officer of the deck, relaying Captain Wilkes's orders to take in sail and prepare to lay to for the hours of dark. With the first light of dawn, he mused, the ship would put on all her canvas again, and proceed grandly into port. Provisions and fresh water were low, Captain Wilkes and his officers were anxious to know how the *Peacock* was faring, and the storeship *Relief*, sent on ahead many weeks ago because she sailed so slowly, had not been heard of at all. Getting to port would be a relief for everyone on board.

When Wiki came back to deck at the start of the morning watch, however, it was to find that the wind had died. The glorious morning dawned, and they all waited for the customary sea breeze, but it failed to rise.

The great peak of Cape Frio loomed over them, stealing whatever wind might come from the west. The sea was like shimmering satin, olive in color, with a deep swell that was not enough to break the surface, but made the motion of the ship uneasy. The sailors had spent the last three days preparing the ship to make a fine appearance in port—every glint of brass was burnished to a dazzle, deck planks scrubbed to the color of bone, deck furniture given yet another coat of varnish, bare patches in the rigging carefully touched up with tar—but now the watch did nothing but tend braces and haul up and down the courses for every trifling catspaw of breeze.

To be so close to their destination and yet get nowhere was frustrating for all, but particularly for Dr. Olliver. Wiki watched him pace the decks, massive in form and yet remarkably light on his feet. At noon, when the junior midshipmen lined up along the rail with their sextants to take a sight of the blazing sun, he disappeared to tend to his patient. When Wiki followed, it was to find him crouched at the foot of the credenza with his great rump in the air, swearing as he groped beneath the dresser.

"I'm down to the last three pills," he announced, breathing heavily as he clambered to his feet. "And one of the bloody things rolled underneath."

Wiki cooperatively hunkered down, but couldn't even see the lost pill, let alone retrieve it. A rat darted out from the darkest corner, and he flinched back and scrambled to his feet.

"Maybe the rat ate it," Dr. Olliver said gloomily as he sat down at the table. He filled his glass and drank it all, abandoning his usual ritual. Grimes was worse than ever, quite delirious, he said, and if they didn't get to Rio within hours, he wouldn't be responsible for the consequences.

At four bells in the afternoon watch, a riffle of wind skipped over the tops of the waves. The weather leech of the main topgallant fluttered, and every man leapt to his station. The helm was put hard up, and the ship paid off, but then a flaw in the breeze brought her aback, and she was left hanging in the middle of the maneuver, with the canvas as straight up and down as ever.

After that, the wind clung to the surface of the sea like a lover, undoubtedly affected by the great shadow of Cape Frio. The *Vincennes* wallowed helplessly and the boatswain swore foully at his mates. Cries of, "Ready about!" echoed from the two fore-and-aft schooners, but their efforts were equally useless. Clearly, only very small craft would be able to make way in this weather, and that by using oars as well as sails. Captain Wilkes made the decision to lower one of the ship's boats and send it into port with Dr. Olliver, to procure medicine before it was too late to save his instrumentmaker. Lieutenant Forsythe, who was the obvious choice, having acquitted himself so well on the passage from Shark Island, was assigned the *Vincennes* cutter, and told to choose a crew of good oarsmen.

He immediately asked for Wiki Coffin, but though Wiki was summoned, Forsythe's request was refused. "Not only is Mr. Coffin a scientific and not a seaman," Captain Wilkes said coldly, "but I require his services before going into port."

They were standing in the big drafting room. "May I ask the nature of the services?" Wiki queried cautiously.

The captain's expression became lofty. "I assume you can read and write Portuguese, as well as speak the language?"

Wiki inclined his head, wondering what the devil was coming.

"I want you to write a letter to whoever is the local official in charge of harbor operations in Rio de Janeiro."

"El Capitão do Porto?"

"Exactly." Captain Wilkes's habitual small smile completely disappeared as his lips compressed. "The letter is to explain that we must dispense with the usual salute of cannon—because of the delicacy of the chronometers. Their accuracy is so crucial to the mission that I cannot risk it with unnecessary jolting. I assume *delicacy* would be the right word, once translated?"

Wiki had to pause to keep his astonishment out of his face, because there had been plenty of cannon-firing during the voyage already. Not only had Captain Wilkes ordered all his captains to appoint gun crews and exercise the cannon every flat calm, but he had staged gunnery competitions to boost morale after times of stress, such as murders and storms. Never, to Wiki's knowledge, had any fears been expressed on behalf of the chronometers.

He didn't dare meet Forsythe's jaundiced look, but managed to say, "The word *fragilidade* should fit the bill, sir."

"Excellent. There will be two letters to be written in English, too, each of them bearing the same message. Please attend me in my cabin in an hour." And Captain Wilkes stalked out and down the corridor.

"The bloody hell he's worried about the chronometers," Forsythe muttered a few minutes later. He and Wiki were standing in the waist deck watching a gang sway out the cutter from the main yard.

"So what do you reckon is the reason, then?"

"He just don't want 'em to find out how pitiably few cannon he has at his disposal. When you think of it, all he's got is two long toms.

Can you imagine the poor bastards of gun crews trying to reload and fire without an embarrassing time lag between each pair of shots? The Brazilians will expect him to fire twenty-one guns to their flag as we pass the fort, and then I hear that the British ship of the line *Thunderer* is likely to be lying here—so that's another twenty-one-gun salute, adding up to forty-two. The flagship of the U.S. Brazil squadron will be there, too—and that means twenty-six more, in honor of Old Glory! Firing a total of sixty-eight guns is asking the impossible of the poor sod, and he don't want to knuckle his forehead to a superior officer, anyways."

Wiki knew exactly what Forsythe meant, the matter of rank being one of the greatest of Charles Wilkes's grievances. Though the Navy Department had given him the command of a fleet, they had not thought fit to assign him a rank to fit the position. Both Wilkes and the second-in-command of the expedition, William Hudson of the *Peacock,* were still lieutenants, called "captain" only because they were in charge of ships, and it was an injustice that rankled sorely.

Wiki said, "What flagship?"

"USS *Independence*. The commodore is John Nicholson."

"What's he like?"

"They're all bastards, but he's one of the better ones."

Then Wiki saw that just about the whole of the ship's complement was gathered at the starboard rail, grinning. Dr. Olliver was bobbing slowly down the side of the ship, the progress of his balloon-like form assisted by at least three men. It took rather a lot of persuasion to get him to make the last jump into the boat, and then the craft bobbed up and down madly, with a great deal of splashing, threatening to capsize for quite a few seconds.

"Good luck with your letters," said Forsythe, taking his departure.

"And good luck with your passenger," said Wiki with heartfelt sincerity, because so much was at stake.

"I'll manage. Movable ballast can be bloody useful at times."

And with that, Forsythe scrambled down the side, landing with a thud of boots in the bottom of the boat. Orders were barked, oars were put out and canvas was set, and then the cutter gathered way. Considering the inconstancy of the breeze, she disappeared from sight surprisingly fast.

Ironically, Forsythe had been gone no more than two hours when a southeast topgallant wind abruptly whisked up. Down in the captain's cabin, filling pages with his neat script, Wiki heard the sudden snap of canvas, a shout of, "Ready about!" and the piping of the boatswain's mates. Planks echoed to the thump of many feet as men hurried to their stations.

"Helm's alee!" came the cry. More shrilling of pipes as the jib-sheets and fore-sheet were let go and overhauled, and then, "Mains'l ha-a-a-ul!" Wiki sensed the thump as the main yard brought up against the backstays, and then the stiffening of the ship as the weather mainbrace was hove taut. The ship leaned into the wind and gathered way. By the time the third letter—the one to Commodore Nicholson—had finally been rewritten to Captain Wilkes's satisfaction, and placed with those to El Capitão do Porto and the commander of the British ship, the *Vincennes* was standing up the bay with all sail set, gliding along at a good three knots through a descending afternoon mist.

Another haul, so they could brace up to the north to enter the harbor, coasting along between the two white sentinel-like forts with a dip of the flag. This was the time when the first salute of cannon should have been fired, but instead they glided through with just the hiss of water to mark their passage. Wiki, clambering onto the poop deck, having left the three letters, all signed, blotted, folded, and sealed, lying ready on Captain Wilkes's desk, looked up to see the boys in the mizzen hamper staring ahead in a silence that was so transparently awestruck, that for the first time he fully realized the general youthfulness of the crew.

Then the vista opened—a sight that caught Wiki's own breath every time he entered Rio, because this abrupt grandeur was like nowhere else in the world. Mountains rose above mountains, peak above peak, all dominated by the strange shape of Sugar Loaf, rearing its stark barrenness up against the sky. Wiki heard the officer of the watch, standing close by, shout orders through his trumpet. Men obeyed readily, to bring the flagship even more to the north.

A long way behind, he saw the two expedition schooners change their triangular shapes as they tacked to pass through the entrance of the great harbor, while the *Porpoise* sailed more demurely beyond them. He could just glimpse the *Swallow* flying along under a flamboyant spread of sail, silhouetted by the bold point of Santa Cruz. There was a brigantine, on the same tack, dashing along under an imprudent amount of canvas, too, so that it looked for all the world as if they were racing each other.

Wiki turned and looked ahead again. Now he could see the city, with Praia Grande opposite, shafts of late light pooling on white colonnades and cupolas, and terra-cotta roofs. Distant aqueducts marched in double rows of arches through the riotous tropical growth. Because there were no wharves, ships lay at anchor everywhere, brilliant flags flying, grouped according to nationality, most the lee of one or another of the little islets that dotted the emerald water. One was a huge frigate, with the Stars and Stripes flying brilliantly from her mizzen peak, and the broad blue swallowtail of a commodore's pennant, with its twenty-six gold stars, fluttering from her main—the USS *Independence*. It should have been the moment for another salute of cannon. Instead, seamen clambered about the rigging of the *Vincennes*, harried by the shouts of boatswains' mates, until the yardarms were lined.

Then, just as the first hip-hip-hurrahs were bawled, cheering being the best alternative to the roar of guns, Wiki heard the lookout in the foremast shriek over the din, "Ahoy the deck!"

The seaman was pointing at the water ahead. Wiki shaded his eyes, and the watch officer trumpeted, "What is it?"

"Our boat, sir!" the lookout hollered, and sure enough, it was the ship's cutter, coming fast toward them on the wind. Within seconds she was close enough for Wiki to see Dr. Olliver's massive shape in the stern sheets, and Forsythe at the tiller.

The watch officer called out more orders, and the *Vincennes* was hauled aback, with just her momentum driving her along. Then, just as he heard the cutter click against the side of the ship, Wiki registered that Captain Wilkes had arrived alongside him. When he turned inquiringly, he saw that Wilkes was holding out one of the letters.

With his habitual meaningless smile, Captain Wilkes said, "After we have taken Dr. Olliver on board, you will oblige me by taking the cutter to the *Independence*. Tender this letter to Commodore Nicholson with my compliments, and inform him I look forward to the privilege of a meeting after we are safely anchored and I have attended to my other business."

Dear God, thought Wiki, shocked; was Captain Wilkes really determined to exasperate the commodore of the Brazil squadron beyond bearing? The lack of a salute of cannon was crime enough, without this studied insult. However, there was nothing he could say, so he nodded, took the letter, and headed down the poop ladder to the waist deck.

As he arrived at the gangway Dr. Olliver came up, red in the face and with a hand clapped over the pocket where the precious package was presumably stowed.

"Success?" said Wiki.

"Success," the surgeon confirmed. Thank God, thought Wiki, because the noises he had heard from Grimes's berth while he had been penning the letters had been truly alarming.

Forsythe's reaction, when Wiki arrived in the bottom of the cutter and passed on Captain Wilkes's instructions, was predictably sardonic.

"Wa'al, let's see if we can survive this pretty little mission—and that Robert Festin doesn't get into any more trouble while we're both away from the *Vin*," he drawled.

And with that, he brought the little craft about with a flourish, while the band on the deck of the great U.S. flagship struck up the welcoming strains of "Hail Columbia."

Eight

The harbor of Rio de Janeiro was opening up before Captain George Rochester like a great panorama. The waters were hectic with the local felucca-rigged galleys—*fallua*—battling for room with queer fishing rafts—*jangadas*—which were made of logs strung together, and tacked by shifting their single masts from one notch in a log to another. Big ships of all nations maneuvered through the lowering late afternoon mist.

George stood on the foredeck of the *Swallow* with his hands clasped behind the seat of his trousers and his boots braced apart. His expression was benign as he took in the brilliant scene, but behind it he was wishing that it were Wiki Coffin who held the helm, and that his first officer was something better than an unseasoned seventeen-year-old youth. Despite that, he was determined to make a great show. Green water foamed white as it curled about the cutwater below, and then bubbled as it dashed along the brig's steeply leaning side.

As if in tacit encouragement, the brigantine that accompanied them through the harbor entrance was standing under flamboyant canvas, too, a few fathoms off their starboard beam. Like the *Swallow*, she was heeled far over in the freshening breeze. When she straightened up for the anchorage, Captain Rochester heard Midshipman Keith, who was standing importantly in charge of the quarterdeck, call out orders to do the same. In the distance, he could see two great men-of-war lying at anchor off the city, and hear distant strains of "Hail Columbia" from one of them. The other, he deduced, was HMS *Thunderer*.

Then, just as George was about to request the old boatswain to pass on a message to bring in the topgallants, the totally unexpected happened. A *jangada* piled deep with a load of fish appeared from nowhere. The whole of Rochester's fifteen-man crew was on deck and in the rigging, but not a single hand had seen her coming.

The unwieldy craft staggered athwart their bows, so close that George could clearly see the faces of her crew gawping up at him. He roared, "Hard to starboard the wheel!"

At the same instant, to do him credit, Midshipman Keith screamed the same order, though with an embarrassingly adolescent squeak of panic. Canvas cracked and booms slammed, and for a tense moment Rochester thought the brig wouldn't respond. Then around she came like a game little terrier, and hissed past the raft with yards to spare. For an instant, George was engulfed in evocative smells of charcoal, rice, fish, and cordage. Then, *thank God*, the fishing boat was gone.

Midshipman Keith screamed, "The brigantine!"

George's neck cracked as he jerked round to stare with horror at the brigantine, which, not having followed the abrupt change of course, was now bearing right down upon them. He lifted his trumpet, and bawled, "Brigantine ahoy!"

"I see you, goddamnit!" shouted the reply.

"Keep your luff, sir!"—and to the man at the helm of the *Swallow*, "Hard up the wheel!" Even as he uttered the order, though, he knew it was far too late. He saw the brigantine's mainyard come round and her canvas flutter, but she was right on his starboard quarter.

The crash as she hit was deafening, followed by a series of pounding thumps that were almost as loud. The brig pitched, rolled, and shuddered under the onslaught. George staggered, and the old boatswain fell down. Then it was as if the other craft were determined to utterly destroy his beautiful ship. With horrible scraping noises she carried on forward, breaking up rail as she went. As the two tangled vessels lost momentum their combined wake caught up with them, and again the brigantine slammed hard against the *Swallow*.

The concussion was awful. Again, Rochester stumbled, and several men were thrown to the planks. Looking up in horror as he straightened, he saw the two tall masts of the brigantine, still carrying whole sail, tipping slowly over, casting their slanted shadows over him. *Dear God,* he thought, she was holed! She was sinking! He could hear the rush of water pouring into her, while she became even more intricately tangled with his brig. The terrible commotion of sundering timber was replaced by an ominous creaking.

On both decks, there was a moment of appalled silence, broken by shouts of consternation. On the *Swallow,* seamen grabbed poles to shove the intruder away, terrified that if she sank she would take them down with her. On the other craft sailors were pouring up the hatches with billets of wood in their hands, similarly determined to free themselves of the burden of the other vessel, which they were convinced was taking them down.

George cried, "Belay that!" Like an echo, he heard the other captain roar the identical command. The brigantine wasn't sinking—yet—but she was the one taking in water, not the brig, and it was obvious that she would founder without the *Swallow* to hold her up.

The boatswain had scrambled to his feet, unhurt. "Get a big sheet of old canvas," George snapped. The good fellow nodded in swift understanding, and hurried off to the sail locker, yelling out for assistants as he went. They would have to fother a sail—stiffen it with ropeyarn—

and then maneuver it over the hole in the brigantine's side, to stop the leak as fast as they could. The job required men who were good swimmers and divers—again, George wished that Wiki was on board. As it was, he knew he was lucky to have Sua and Tana.

There was a bump from the waist deck—boots hitting planks. George spun around, to see that the captain of the stranger had executed an athletic leap over the broken gangway rail. Even in the midst of his panic and racing thoughts, George registered that he was a striking figure. Though middle-aged, with an abundance of gray sprinkled in his thick black hair, he was still very handsome, broad-shouldered but otherwise as lean as a whippet.

Otherwise, the overwhelming impression was that he was utterly furious. A small slanting scar on the side of his face caused his left eyelid to droop in lizardlike fashion, half hiding a gray eye that flashed as belligerently as the wide-open right eye, and his clean-shaven jaw was pugnaciously squared.

Though George had certainly never seen him before, he was struck by a strong sense of familiarity. Then he saw the man visibly take hold of his temper, so that when he came to an abrupt stop, he was icily impassive. "Sir," he said with a snap—and the snap clinched the impression.

"My God, old chap," George exclaimed in great astonishment. "You're none other than Captain William Coffin!"

The lizard eye glinted in alert curiosity, but George was interrupted by the arrival of two boats from the *Vincennes*. Obviously, the lookouts on the expedition flagship had seen the emergency develop, and the officer on watch had responded without an instant's delay. Mystifyingly, though, Wiki was not with them. George wondered what was up with his old friend. Surely he hadn't been ordered to stay away? Captain Wilkes hadn't even sent a senior officer, as the fellow in charge of the two boats was a junior midshipman who was scarcely as old as Constant Keith.

"Midshipman Dicken, at your service, sir!" he barked in a voice that squeaked on the last syllable, his chubby face bright red with the importance of his mission. In strictly descending order, he saluted Captain Rochester, then Captain Coffin, and finally Midshipman Keith. Rochester's first officer returned the salute, and after that the two young men shook hands and clapped each other on the shoulder in the manner of two friends getting back together after quite a long time, while Dicken commiserated with Keith, because the accident had made him look so *lubberly*.

"Quite," agreed Captain Coffin dryly.

"The blame, sir, was not ours," said Midshipman Keith stiffly, taking instant umbrage, but Rochester put a swift stop to that, pointing out that there was a great deal of work to be done if both ships were to be saved. In the process of the introductions, George Rochester had found that Captain Coffin's vessel was the brigantine *Osprey*, in the Salem–China trade. How much longer she was going to float, let alone sail to the Orient, was very debatable, though—and if she went down right now, she was going to take the *Swallow* with her.

"My instructions from Captain Wilkes are to carry back a written report of the accident," said Midshipman Dicken in an obstinate kind of voice.

"Report be damned," said George Rochester with vigor. "Get your men on board the brigantine, and see if the pumps are working. And at the same time send over all the members of the *Osprey* crew who are not needed on board; I don't want them to be caught there if she founders."

"Thank you," said Captain Coffin. At that moment George couldn't tell if he was being sarcastic or not—and didn't care, either, there being not a moment to be lost.

Within seconds, in response to hurried orders, a half dozen of the

Osprey's crew were on board the brig, one of them carrying the brigantine's cat. The six hands were astonishingly young, George noted, but didn't waste time on speculation, instead setting them to work threading strands of ropeyarn into the big square of canvas the boatswain had found. They were a good bunch, he meditated as he strode past them some moments later. Even though their belongings, along with their ship's provisions, were all underwater, they were even managing a shaky laugh or two—though maybe that was because Stoker, being the gem of a steward that he was, had produced a huge kettle of hot chocolate.

Meantime, Midshipman Keith was aloft with a gang, untangling the rigging that bound the two ships together, while others tore apart the combined wreckage along the shattered starboard rail. Captain Coffin had jumped back on board his own ship, and could be heard striding around the *Osprey* shouting orders, while the pumps thumped, and water gushed through the scuppers and over the side. Ominously, though, George could hear more water surging in through the hole.

Night fell as they all frantically toiled. When the wreckage that tied the two vessels in their fatal embrace was finally cleared away, the *Osprey* slumped over farther than ever. Obviously, the hole had to be stopped as swiftly as possible, as without the *Swallow* to hold her up, she was doomed. The piece of fothered canvas was lowered on ropes over the rail of the brigantine, the two ships were pried apart, and Tana and Sua dived into the narrow strip of black water between the two hulls, which were bumping back and forth with the tide.

It was appallingly dangerous work. Every sailor held his breath, watching the two black heads bob up and down, each man gripping one of the two lower corners of the fothered sail. Down they dived in the surging water, while the ships sagged perilously close together above them. A fraught moment, and then up they came, gasped for breath, and disappeared again, while the pumps labored and gushed.

The next time their heads bobbed to the surface, they both thrust triumphant fists upward, just before scooting up the side of the *Osprey*. The hands at the top of the canvas hauled manfully, and bowsed the fothered sail tight—and the gush of incoming water quietened. *Thank God,* thought George fervently. Sucked into place by the pressure of the sea, it would slow the leak long enough, hopefully, for them to tow the brigantine to the shipyard.

Rochester sent down the brig's two boats to help the two boats from the *Vincennes,* but even with four boats hauling it was a slow, painfully arduous trip across the harbor. The *Swallow,* sailed by a skeleton crew, slowly followed. It was midnight before they arrived—but, though there were awful signs that the brigantine was breaking up forward, she did not founder. Another hour, and both vessels were moored up tightly to a wharf in twelve feet of water with a soft mud bottom, and the *Osprey* was no longer in danger of sinking.

George sent Midshipman Dicken and the two expedition boats back to the *Vincennes* with a scribbled message requesting a survey, a carpenter, and a carpentering crew at first light. As he watched them disappear, and worked his sore shoulders to ease them, he abruptly became aware of how quiet it was, with just the rhythmic thud of the *Osprey* pumps to be heard, and the gush and ripple of water. The hulking shapes of shipyard gear rose up against the stars. He was sure he was alone, but when he turned round, he found that Captain Coffin was standing just behind him.

They looked at each other in the darkness, and then Captain Coffin said again, "Thank you."

George still couldn't decide if he was being sarcastic or not, and was too tired to think about it, so he snapped, "Midshipman Keith was right, you know. You were too slow to put down the helm."

"It was your lookouts who failed to see the *jangada,*" the other tartly pointed out. Then he sighed deeply and said, "But I thank you. Many others would have shoved free of me by force, and then left me to sink."

An abrupt light flared across the quay as someone lit a cresset on the *Swallow,* and in its flickering glow Rochester could see how exhausted and drawn the other man looked. It was very understandable, he thought—Coffin's ship had looked magnificent as she flew along with all her sails set, and now she was little more than a wreck. Not only was she totally unfit for sea, but, until she was fixed, no one could even live on board of her.

Regretting his loss of temper, he said, "What about your cargo?"

"Tortoiseshell. We'll unload it tomorrow, and once dried, it should be fine. In fact, I'll probably put it on the local market. There's no point in warehousing it for the time it will take to get the *Osprey* mended."

Thank heavens it hadn't been sugar, or rice, George thought. Then he wondered what price tortoiseshell fetched in Rio. To him, the cargo sounded very exotic. He supposed it had been loaded in some place like Manila, but thought that Coffin might have traded for it in some island in the Fijis, or that maybe his boys had gathered it themselves, picking it up on farflung beaches. They looked adventurous enough, he thought, and remarked, "Your crew seems very young."

"Those six lads are cadets," Captain Coffin said briefly, apparently unsurprised by the abrupt change of topic. "It's a Salem custom."

"Ah," said George. Undoubtedly, they were sons of prominent Salem shipmasters, shipowners, and merchants, and some would have brilliant careers in front of them. "Six is quite a number," he observed.

"They pull their weight, believe me—and I like them, anyway," Captain Coffin said. "Men bring problems on board that would have been better left on shore, but boys are uncomplicated."

George silenced, abruptly remembering that this man had sailed away from Salem when Wiki was sixteen years old. He thought how Wiki must have envied the cadets who had sailed with his father instead of himself.

Then Captain Coffin said with a hint of dry humor, "I couldn't help but notice that your first lieutenant is very young, too."

"Seventeen," said George ruefully. "And with an amazing capacity for doing the wrong thing—but he does the wrong thing so cheerfully that we have no trouble forgiving him, and so he survives to err yet another day."

To his surprise, the other man laughed, and before he knew it, George found himself inviting him to spend the rest of the night on board the *Swallow*—"And whichever of your hands are not on duty."

"I've sent the boys to the lodgings we use here, and the rest are tending the pumps. The mate is in charge of the lads; they'll be fine."

Rochester led the way up the gangplank that had been slung from the starboard side of the brig, and then through the small saloon to his tiny private cabin, which was crammed to bursting with just his berth, a sofa, and his chart desk and chair. As he took the chair, he observed, "You sound as if you come to Rio quite often."

"The market's good, and I have a good friend here." Captain Coffin sank back on the sofa with a deep sigh, and when George offered brandy, he accepted gratefully. For a long moment there was silence, as both men slowly relaxed. Then, with a sharply intelligent glance across the rim of his glass, Captain Coffin observed, "You make me very curious, Captain Rochester."

"I do?"

"Busy as we have been, I couldn't help but notice you studying me a lot of the time—and, right now, you're doing a great deal of that."

George smiled rather sheepishly, because he couldn't help casting constant glances at this man, and mentally comparing him with his son. Up until today he had thought that Wiki was the epitome of a New Zealand native—smoothly brown-skinned and muscular of physique, with long, snaky, black hair, and a nose that was Roman in profile, but flat in full-face view. Indeed, Rochester had suspected that when Captain William Coffin had claimed the quick-witted twelve-year-old Wiki as his son, he had been indulging in wishful thinking.

However, the resemblance was remarkable—especially when the color of the eyes was considered. Wiki's eyes, like this man's, were light brown in repose, but had the same ability to change to gray with anger. The eyebrows, too, were the same—fine, black, arched, and very expressive. There were differences that fascinated him, too—Captain Coffin's ears, for instance. They stuck out a little, while Wiki had neat, lobeless, Polynesian ears, set close to the sides of his head.

"In fact," Captain Coffin remarked, after waiting in vain for an answer, "you remind me much of a butcher sizing up a side of beef."

George was surprised into a hoot of laughter, suddenly liking this man.

"And, what's more, you knew my name—and yet I don't believe we've ever met."

"I am sure we have not," Rochester agreed, and leaned back in his chair with an amiable grin. "But I know your son, Wiki."

"Wiki?" Coffin echoed. His expression went blank.

"There's quite a resemblance," George assured him.

"Good God, is there?" Captain Coffin seemed absurdly pleased by the revelation. "Have you been shipmates?"

Rochester paused again, before he said gently, "We met eight years ago—at a college in New Hampshire."

Both he and Wiki had been sixteen, and had been sent to the missionary college as a punishment. On the first day, when George had galloped out of his grandparents' carriage into the dim college portal, he had fallen over Wiki, who was glaring at the massive door. After they had picked themselves up George had spotted Wiki's brown skin and black hair, jumped to the conclusion that he was one of the benighted Indians he was to be taught to save, and with a braying adolescent laugh had declared, "Should be converting you, old chap, not knocking you down!"

Luckily, there had been strength in George's gangling limbs, or Wiki would have finished him off in the first murderous rush. Instead, George had fended him away and talked very fast, and the boys had launched a friendship that despite their different seafaring careers—one in the U.S. Navy, the other traipsing from one New England whaleship to another—had lasted eight years.

Captain Coffin sighed, and said, "You must be George."

"Aye," George admitted.

"Wiki told me how you both absconded from the college."

George shook his head and grinned. "We didn't take long to get acquainted with the local Abnaki tribe, and after that, hunting the forest with the Indians was a damn sight more attractive than sitting in a dusty classroom. We got away with it for quite some months—because the college administration was laboring under the romantic delusion that we were converting the Indians, I think. Then they found that the Abnaki were converting *us,* and all hell broke loose, so we jumped out a window in the middle of the night, and paddled off down the Connecticut River in a birchbark canoe."

Captain Coffin's expression held more than a hint of envy. "Quite an adventure," he commented.

"Aye," said George. It had been the first of many adventures. "Neither of us was missionary material," he went on frankly. "My grandparents sent me there after I'd refused to carry on in the family law firm. Dusty books and deeds were most emphatically not my passion. It took just four months in the office for me to understand that, but my grandfather hoped the missionary teachers would put me straight."

"Rochester? The law firm of Boston?"

George nodded.

"And you're a scion of that house? I can see why your grandfather was disappointed. But you managed to persuade him that you prefer the navy?"

George smiled and said, "Wiki and I would have been happy to ship with the first skipper who would take us, but my grandfather refused to contemplate a *scion* of the family going to sea on anything less than a navy ship, and got me a commission as a midshipman. The

U.S. Navy was impossible for Wiki, but, as you know, your wife's brother was a Nantucket whaling captain, who shipped Wiki as a favor to her."

Captain Coffin winced. He said in a low tone, "When I left my son at home, I didn't expect . . ." Then he broke off, paused, and burst out, "I *couldn't* take him with me when I returned to the Bay of Islands—but I had not a single goddamned notion that my wife would send him to that college!"

"So what did you think would happen?" George queried dryly.

"I wanted to go back—to see Wiki's mother, *goddamnit,*" Captain Coffin exclaimed without answering, and then fell into a deep silence, staring into space while George watched him. Outside, it was very quiet, with just the faint thud of pumps and the occasional echoing voice to betray that others were awake in the depths of the night.

Then Captain Coffin said softly, as if he were talking to himself, "I taught her how to dress her hair in the French style, and she washed herself from head to foot with soap before coming to bed."

"You were fond of her?"

"I *loved* her."

George paused, carefully choosing his words, and then said, "You married her—after their fashion?"

Captain Coffin looked up, his expression curiously defensive. "You have to understand that at the time it was dangerous to trade in the country without the support of a *rangitira*—a local chieftain. Because of her father's influence, no one would try to steal from me, or cheat me—or eat me."

"So it was just a business arrangement?"

"You could call it that, I suppose," Captain Coffin said with an expression of self-disgust. "I'd come to the Bay of Islands to trade tobacco for sperm-whale teeth with the whaling skippers who congregated there at the time, because whale teeth were the best currency possible in Fiji, where I hoped to find a freight of pearl shell. But after Rangi's father gave her to me, I stayed the whole summer, trading in pork and potatoes, acting as a middleman for the tribe, learning their ways. Then, damn it, I sailed home, and married Huldah Gardiner. I returned next voyage, but Rangi was wed—in their fashion, as you say. She showed me our son—our boy, named after me—and we remained friends, but our love affair was ended. She was utterly loyal to her husband—just as she had been to me."

"And when Wiki was twelve?"

"I asked her to give him to me—to let me take him home. Huldah and I had not had children, and . . ." Captain Coffin broke off, and then exclaimed again, "I *couldn't* take Wiki back to the Bay of Islands."

"Not even for a visit?"

"If I did, he'd be a fully tattooed warrior and probably dead by now. Europeans who call the Maori treacherous couldn't be further from the mark—they are proud and revengeful, particularly of treacherous acts. Before the advent of the European, their wars were skirmishes—hand-to-hand combat, honor satisfied after just a few fatalities. But then they learned about our guns. We traders and whalers traded muskets to the northern tribes, and they set out on the warpath, taking white mercenaries as advisors. Can you imagine what it was like, with one side armed with muskets, and the other with traditional weapons? Thousands were killed, *thousands*. I saved Wiki from that, so how *could* I take him back?"

George was silent a moment, mulling it over. It sounded logical, he thought, but, while he didn't pride himself on having a deductive brain—not like Wiki—he thought that even he could see the flaw in the argument.

He said, "So why did you go back to New Zealand at all?"

William Coffin frowned. "What do you mean?"

"If you had gone to the Orient, or anywhere else but New Zealand, you could have taken Wiki with you."

There was a long silence, and then Captain Coffin burst out, "All right—I was angry with him!"

"On account of a woman?" guessed George shrewdly.

"Aye!" Captain Coffin exclaimed, and then looked surprised. "You know about Wiki and women? Oh, you're friends, so of course you do," he said impatiently before George could speak. "But, my God, I doubt you know the half of it! I was once forced to buy off the father of a Marblehead milkmaid after he'd found his daughter and my boy together in his byre—and Wiki was just fourteen!"

"My," said George, impressed.

"Two years after that, there was a friend of mine who married a girl who was just eighteen, less than half his age—an utterly unsuitable match, but he was quite besotted. Indeed, he was so delighted at landing such a young, beautiful bride that he entertained his friends at his estate for a whole week before the wedding, and during that week the girl and Wiki—"

"Had a passionate affair," said George.

He already knew about it, and had met the girl, too, and had found her strikingly beautiful, but also boldly seductive. Every time her huge, languorous eyes had slid sideways to smile secretly into his, George had helplessly pictured what it would be like to take her to bed. However, he could scarcely inform Wiki's father that his strong belief was that sixteen-year-old Wiki had been used by a pretty little tart who was determined to make the most of her last week of freedom, so he kept his mouth shut.

Captain Coffin grimly nodded. "And they didn't bother to be discreet about that passionate affair. Just an hour before the wedding ceremony, they waltzed together, and the familiar way they fitted into each other's arms . . . Well," he said, and sighed. "They made it obvious that they were lovers—even though she was wearing her wedding dress! Everyone saw it—it became the gossip of the village—and Wiki didn't seem to care that he had shamed me."

"And so you punished him by leaving him behind when you sailed?"

"Aye," said Captain Coffin grimly. "And it was one of the stupidest things I've ever done. At the time, I was too angry to think. I expected to be back from voyage within twelve months, and find him still in Salem, a year older, and a year wiser. I believed that we would pick up where we had left off, only on different terms. Instead, I got home to find he had gone to sea. Now, we only meet up in port, usually by accident, and that for a few days, at the most. Where, for a while, I had a son, I now just have a friend."

He was quiet, staring into space, and then looked back at George and asked quietly, "Where is Wiki now?"

"Great heavens!" exclaimed George. "Didn't you know? He's with the exploring expedition!"

Nine

First light dawned with no sign of a survey party from the *Vincennes,* or even a carpentering gang, let alone Wiki. The only visible activity in or near the shipyard was upon the survey ship *Peacock,* which was hove down fifty yards away—and even that wasn't much, just a few caulkers dangling on lines on the exposed side of her hull.

Captain Rochester and Captain Coffin stood on the jetty staring out to the flagship *Vincennes* as if they could glimpse Wiki on her deck. She lay anchored off the island called Enxados, where the old convent gleamed in the early sun, framed by the grass of a hilly meadow.

"Wiki should have heard about the accident by now," Captain Coffin said at last. He turned and studied his poor ship again, and the sad way she leaned to keep her wounded side clear of the mud.

"Aye," said George grimly. "And Wilkes should have read my message, too." Though both men, being shipmasters, were accustomed to nights with little sleep, their tempers were strained. After another half hour their patience evaporated, and they took one of the brig's boats out to the *Vincennes*.

Captain Wilkes, whom they found in conference with the second-in-command of the expedition, Captain William Hudson, was in an even fouler mood. His eyebrows snapped down as Captain Coffin was announced, and he didn't bother to introduce him to Captain Hudson, who had evidently come from the shipyard to report on the progress of repairs on the *Peacock*.

Instead, he resumed his cross-examination of Hudson, saying impatiently, "How long? Come on, give me a date! An estimate!"

"Impossible," Hudson exclaimed. "They're all foreigners—and there's no accounting for their style of work. My God, bring a gang of 'em to the Boston Navy Yard, and the crowds would line up in wonder. Where five of our men can put a seam on a ship, it takes five dozen of 'em, every single man waiting for a signal before they heave a mallet."

"And is she as badly off as we suspected?"

"Right now, she's utterly unfit to go to Cape Horn, let alone into high southern latitudes."

"The mizzenmast?"

"Has to be shortened by eighteen inches. It ain't as if those string-shanked bastards at the navy yard didn't know she was rotten—they patched up the worst hole with putty and ropeyarn, and then painted it over."

"My God! Evil and dishonor! Did they ever do anything to further the expedition? *No, they bloody well did not!*" Captain Wilkes closed his eyes tight, and George could see that he was shuddering with rage. Then he opened them, and exclaimed, "And, on top of that, I've had a bloody insulting letter from Commodore Nicholson, in reply to my *perfectly sensible* explanation for the lack of a gun salute! And where the hell is the storeship *Relief*, I ask?"

Captain Hudson shrugged grimly, and George Rochester wondered if the poor dog of a ship had sunk. Within days of leaving Norfolk the

Relief had demonstrated such awful sailing qualities that Captain Wilkes had sent her on ahead to Rio, so she wouldn't retard the rest of the fleet. She should have been waiting here, but instead, she was not, and there was no word from her captain, Andrew Long.

"So what the *hell* has happened to her?" Captain Wilkes was breathing heavily, and there was sweat on his brow. "And what the *hell* does Long think he is doing? Is he a seaman, or just another witless bastard?" he demanded in a shout. Then he swerved round at George, and shouted, "Well, Captain Rochester? When am I going to receive your written report of yesterday's disgraceful affair?"

Stung, George protested, "It was an unavoidable accident, sir."

"You think so? Then you're even less competent than I imagined! Your seamanship is an utter disgrace, lubberly beyond belief! And in full view of the whole port, by God! And where the hell is the bloody *report*?"

George winced, because he hadn't set pen to paper yet, and then to his surprise he heard Captain Coffin say firmly, "I have a detailed report right here."

Captain Wilkes's fine, large eyes blinked. "Report?" he echoed blankly.

"My accounting, Captain." And, as George watched, bemused, William Coffin produced several pages, all closely covered with arithmetic.

"What the devil is this?"

"My expense sheet, Captain Wilkes—and I would be obliged if you'd check it now, so that my account can be settled without undue delay."

Wilkes looked stunned. "Your account?"

"Exactly, Captain Wilkes. My ship has incurred a significant amount of damage as a result of her collision with a ship of the U.S. Navy, and it is my strong belief that the U.S. Navy should foot the expenses for her repairs."

Captain Hudson, George saw then, had beaten a hasty diplomatic retreat. Captain Wilkes reluctantly took the pages, winced as he got to the very impressive total at the end, and then looked up at William Coffin with scarlet patches of fury high on his cheeks. "You're a goddamned rogue, sir!"

"On the contrary, I'm an American shipmaster of good repute, who has always paid his taxes and duties," Captain Coffin informed him calmly. "I've heard a lot of soft soap in the past about how the U.S. Navy prides itself on being a bastion of support and succor to all its citizens everywhere, and those in evil straits at sea and in foreign ports, in particular. My ship was reduced to a wreck when run afoul of by a navy brig under your ultimate command; it lies now at the shipyard in dire need of heaving down and fixing by a carpenter's gang, and I claim that rightful support, sir."

George saw the fleet commander's mouth purse up tight, before he said curtly, "I'll send you a shipwright."

"*One* shipwright?" Coffin leveled a stare with his half-closed eye.

"All right, then, a gang of carpenters will come with him."

"For insurance purposes, I need a formal survey."

"I will instruct the shipwright to do the necessary paperwork."

"And the financial loss, being forced to sell my cargo locally—"

"Absolutely not!" Captain Wilkes snapped. "I have conceded enough!"

And, with that—or so George realized in his stupefaction—the horse-trading was over. Captain Wilkes scribbled a note, shoved it at Captain Coffin, and dismissed them.

"My God," said George Rochester with awe, and, though he was not, in fact, wearing a hat, went on, "I take off my hat to you, Captain Coffin."

"I was only asserting my legal rights," said the other. "And my name," he added, "is William."

They were back at the shipyard. In contrast to the plight of Captain

Hudson, who could be heard shouting with utter frustration over by the *Peacock*, William Coffin had accomplished a great deal. Not only had he managed to get the attention of a foreman, but he had introduced him to the navy carpenter, who had arrived accompanied by a gang; he had made arrangements for the pumping out and heaving down of the *Osprey*, and he had extracted a promise that the work would start that very afternoon.

Now, it was noon, and George, as he ushered him up the gangplank of the *Swallow*, said, "You are most welcome to stay on board while your ship is being fixed, William." The previous night, when they had finished talking, he had given Captain Coffin his bed, and had bunked very comfortably in Wiki's berth.

"That's very good of you, and I would very much like to accept," said William Coffin, casting an appreciative eye over the repast Stoker had set out. "But I have a friend here who would be offended."

George threw off his uniform coat, sat down in the captain's chair at the end of the table, and helped himself to ham and pickles, while Captain Coffin industriously buttered a thick slice of soft bread. "A Brazilian friend?"

"Well, he lives here, but he's an Englishman—though his wife is Brazilian, a member of a prominent local family. I met him three years ago when I rescued him from shipwreck," William Coffin added.

"Shipwreck?" George echoed.

"He'd been some years in Uruguay, collecting orchids, but was urgently summoned back to England to attend his father's deathbed, and had taken the first London-bound ship he could find. Three nights out, it foundered."

Disregarding the rest for the moment, Rochester exclaimed, utterly thunderstruck, *"Orchids?"*

"Orchids are big business, or so he told me."

"Good God," said George, greatly wondering. "And he was wrecked—and you saved him? How did it happen?"

"The ship struck something in the water, and sank within moments. He was the only passenger—and the only survivor, as it turned out. We found him floating in one of the ship's boats, with all his provisions and drinking water gone. He'd been exposed to the sun for nine days, and was so shockingly burned his face seemed scarcely human."

It was every seaman's nightmare, and the main reason most mariners refused to learn to swim, preferring drowning to such an awful prospect. George marveled, "It's a wonder the ordeal didn't kill him."

"I was so certain he would die before we got to port, that I ordered the carpenter to make a coffin. However, by the time we made Rio he was sitting up and telling me all about it. He credits me with his recovery, but I put it down to his constitution, myself."

"He must have been as strong as a horse to survive years in the jungle," Rochester agreed. "So, what happened after you got him here?"

"Put him in hospital—and then a Brazilian family took him into their house, just out of the kindness of their hearts. By the time he recovered, he had fallen in love with one of their daughters, so he sold his father's estate after he arrived home, came back to Brazil, married her, and settled."

Rochester, who always enjoyed a romantic story, shook his head very appreciatively, indeed. "The gods were surely on his side," he marveled.

"They were on the side of the girl, too," said William Coffin soberly. "After the marriage, his wife's parents took the chance to visit the old country, leaving the family businesses under his management, but caught smallpox in the first port their ship touched, and died soon after. Their two girls—his new bride and her sister—had no support in the world, save for the usual vast host of distant relatives, and would have been quite lost without him. As it was, he was there to take over the management of the family estates."

"Fortunate, indeed," said Rochester, and then both he and William fell silent. Footsteps echoed on the quay, and they waited for them to come up the gangplank, but instead they passed on by.

"Where the devil is he?" William Coffin demanded.

Rochester knew exactly whom he meant. Coming back through the afterhouse of the *Vincennes,* he had searched for any sign of Wiki. However, the only person he had recognized had been Robert Festin, who had been tending to someone who was obviously very ill. The squat little cook had been cradling the patient as gently as a baby, as he spoon-fed him something that smelled nourishing and good, but the sick man had been squirming feebly in the Acadian's hold.

So where was Wiki? He *must* have heard not only about the accident, but that his father was in Rio, too. "I haven't a single *damn* idea," said George.

Ten

"Here comes the storeship *Relief*," announced Commodore Nicholson. Lowering his spyglass, and cocking a bright eye at Wiki, he remarked, "They reckon she sails like a drover's nag."

"I've heard that, too," Wiki agreed amiably.

If he hadn't been so worried about Astronomer Grimes and Robert Festin, he would have quite enjoyed the past three days, because he liked his host so much. Commodore John Nicholson might be the august commander of the Brazil squadron, but to Wiki's hidden amusement the middle-aged, rolypoly fellow looked and behaved like the most affable of publicans.

It had been disconcerting to be kidnapped, though. When Nicholson had read the letter explaining the lack of a proper salute of guns, he had gone red in the face, and exclaimed, "I don't believe a word of it! Does Wilkes have no idea of the insult to my pennant? Within the past six months we've been saluted with proper ceremony by both the British and the Russians, and now a fellow national snubs us—and an upstart lieutenant, at that! Good God, man, it's insupportable!"

And with that, he'd wreaked what he called a "poetic" revenge—by stealing Wiki! As he kept on pointing out, *he* was the senior American officer in this port, and it was ridiculous that a mere lieutenant like Wilkes should have a Portuguese-speaking clerk when the commodore of the squadron did not, and so he had appropriated that clerk, forthwith—which meant that Wiki had found himself in the very strange position of penning a formal letter from one of his bosses to another, at the start of a campaign that over the next two days turned into a paper war.

The first of the barrage from the *Vincennes* was delivered by a junior midshipman by the name of Dicken. Wiki, recognizing his flushed face from a long-ago but well-remembered feast in the junior mids' wardroom, greeted him by name. Then he asked if Captain Wilkes was exceedingly furious that his linguister had been kidnapped.

"Of course, Mr. Coffin, sir!" said Midshipman Dicken brightly.

"Oh dear," said Wiki, though it was nothing less than expected. Then, with foreboding in his heart, he inquired about Grimes. Forsythe, who *had* been allowed to return to the *Vincennes*, had reported that Festin slept on his sofa as serenely as ever, but had no news of the sick instrumentmaker, save that he was still confined to his bed. Then, ominously, he had repeated that he had bloody well better not die, as he could not be responsible for what happened after that.

"Recovering well," Dicken assured him, to Wiki's huge relief, but then added on a doubtful note, "Well, Dr. Olliver says so. He found some new medicines in Rio, they tell me—though scuttlebutt still reckons the poor fellow was poisoned by that Festin's fancy cooking, and is utterly doomed."

That dire prediction delivered, he announced that the brig *Swallow* had run afoul of a merchantman. Wiki, greatly alarmed, said, "Is she badly damaged?"

"Nothing but a little rigging pulled astray and some railing smashed to splinters," said Dicken, and then puffed out his chest, saying, "*We*—that is, Captain Rochester, with the help of my men—sailed her to the shipyard, and she'll be as right as a cricket in a couple of days. She almost sank the poor barky, though," he added, still on a note of pride.

"What ship was it?" Wiki asked, but the young midshipman had gone, leaving Captain Wilkes's letter behind.

The contents did nothing to improve Commodore Nicholson's state of mind, being a peremptory request that he exchange volunteers from the *Independence* for the invalids in the expedition ships. "Goddamnit," expostulated Nicholson. "Don't he know we're shorthanded?"

However, as the letter also assured him that the invalids were fit enough to help work the ship, he sent back a reasonably obliging reply. Unfortunately, however, it was addressed to *Mister* Wilkes, over Wiki's most strenuous objections. Predictably, the answer that came back fairly sizzled, accusing the commodore of lack of respect for the great enterprise, and berating him in no uncertain terms for failing to address him as "captain."

"Good God," expostulated Nicholson, after reading it with his eyebrows bristling. "This ain't language that even the most senior officer would dare to use to me, without he was a child or an idiot." Forthwith, he dictated a sarcastic reply wishing him every success in his efforts to attain the rank he thought he deserved.

In the meantime, too, the invalids from the *Vincennes* arrived, and proved to be wholly unfit for duty, one being deranged, another epileptic, and the rest in the last stages of consumption. Nicholson promptly sent them all on shore to the hospital, and shot off another letter, informing *Lieutenant* Wilkes that he was responsible for the cost of shipping them back to the States, which Wilkes riposted with a long complaint about the surly nature of the volunteers the commodore had sent.

However, throughout the insults and acrimony, the lack of a proper gun salute was what rankled most. On the third day, Forsythe having lounged on board with yet another shrill epistle from Wilkes, this time hotly demanding that his clerk should be returned to the *Vincennes,* the commodore queried of the messenger, "How many confounded chronometers are you carrying, anyway?"

Forsythe shrugged. "Fifty?" he hazarded.

"Fifty? Good God." Then Nicholson read the letter, and said to Wiki, "I'd better let you go, I suppose—but make sure the letters you pen to me are a damn sight more moderate than those we've been getting of late, young man. This nonsense has gone on long enough, I say!"

Wiki, who thoroughly agreed, said, "Permission to leave now, sir?"

"Not just yet. There's fellows in the wardroom who say they're anxious for a word with Lieutenant Forsythe—probably on account of monies he owes 'em, but what the hell, it's time for supper."

The wardroom hospitality proved boundless, unfortunately, which meant that Wiki was detained for yet another night, because Forsythe got too drunk to get back into the cutter. The next morning, the southerner slumped at the tiller, his battered face cut in several places where a borrowed razor had slipped, while he contemplated the spectacular, mountain-rimmed scene with jaundiced eyes.

It was certainly busy enough. Fleets of fishing rafts were heading out to sea under their enormous gossamer lugsails, while *fallua* zigzagged everywhere, driven by the vigorous strokes of black crews who stood to work their huge oars. The *Swallow,* Wiki saw, was moored up to a quay at the shipyard, but the only activity on board of her was laundry, it seemed, because a host of shirts and drawers hung in the rigging. Beyond her, a ship was lying hove down with a gang of men at work on her exposed side. This, he deduced, was the "poor barky" that Dicken had described.

The *Vincennes* was now securely anchored off Enxados Island, where the turrets of the disused convent caught the early morning sun. On the summit of the grassy hill, men were setting up portable laboratories, and lighters loaded down with provisions, men, and implements were plying from the flagship to the beach. Captain Wilkes, having obtained permission to use the whole of the island for scientific purposes, had concluded to empty the *Vincennes* of everything possible, and then have her smoked to kill rats.

After clambering on board the ship, which felt much lighter already, Wiki hurried to the afterhouse. The saloon was empty, which seemed strange, as the table was set for breakfast. Jack Winter poked his head out of the pantry, and Wiki said, "Where's Dr. Olliver?"

"Gone off a-collecting," said the steward, looking very sulky about it.

"Where?"

"He and Couthouy requisitioned a boat and a crew, and are off about the harbor. They went off yesterday," he went on, more resentfully than ever.

"But what about Mr. Grimes?" Wiki glanced at the shut stateroom door. "Who's looking after him?"

"Me! That's the man—me!" the steward said furiously, and pointed a long, knobbled finger at his own chest. As he ranted on, Wiki gathered that Dr. Olliver, feeling perfectly sanguine about Grimes's recovery now that he had the new medications, had left bottles of medicine and a vial of pills in Jack Winter's care, along with instructions.

"But I don't like it, I swear I don't! What happens if he dies? I heard Dr. Olliver's wicked aspersions about me and his wine, you know, and it ain't nothing else but bloody lies—I've never touched his wine, I swear, and I didn't give none of his wine to Mr. Grimes, neither! In fact, I didn't give Mr. Grimes nothing to eat nor drink, except for the medicine, and if anyone is blamed for him being sick, it should be that Festin, with his poisonous foreign muck! And now

Mr. Grimes complains that the medicine is bitter and that it gives him pins and needles, but what am I s'posed to do about it, I ask?"

"I don't know," said Wiki, feeling very uneasy. They were interrupted by the echoes of a shrill of pipes from the starboard gangway, announcing the arrival of someone or other. A stamp of boots, and a challenge from the doorway of the afterhouse, and then not one, but two captains marched down the corridor—Andrew Long had come with Captain Hudson, for what would doubtlessly be an awful interview with Wilkes. Both looked grim-faced as they were ushered into the drafting room, and the corporal who had announced them rolled his eyes at Wiki as he retreated back to his post.

The big double doors slammed shut, and Wiki winced. After that, as he sat at the table eating breakfast alone, he couldn't help but overhear Captain Wilkes's rant, a tirade that was only occasionally interrupted by Captain Long's lower-voiced, apologetic replies. He'd been becalmed for days on end in the doldrums, and bedeviled with light, contrary airs, he explained. Even with all sail out, the *Relief* had never trundled faster than three knots.

Then, just as Wiki heard Captain Wilkes expostulate in a furious shout, "One hundred days—*one hundred days*, sir! Do you realize that this is a record, a goddamned *record*?" a dreadful, hacking, stifled groan echoed from the stateroom that had so briefly been his.

Grimes! Wiki threw down his knife, lurched out of his chair, ran around the corner of the credenza, threw open the stateroom door, and then stopped short, appalled. Grimes's thin frame was rigidly arched, his limbs thrown out from the blankets and convulsing rapidly. The skin about his nose and lips was pinched and blue. His eyes were half-open, but were rolled up in his head so only the whites could be seen.

"*Jesus Christ*," Wiki whispered, and then yelled, "Jack!"

"I'm here, I'm here," the steward exclaimed from just behind his shoulder. His voice held panic.

"What the hell is wrong with him? Has he been like this before?"

"He's been twitching for days, but nothin' like this, I swear!"

Even as the steward spoke, the convulsions stopped. Grimes flopped onto his back and then lay utterly still, save for the quivering in his stiffly held-out arm. His breathing was stertorous, and there was a waxy look about his brow, as if he were on the verge of death.

Wiki said urgently, "Get Dr. Gilchrist."

He heard Jack Winter scuttle off, but didn't know what to do next. There were bottles of medicine on the table by the head of the berth, but even if he had dared to administer anything, it was obvious it would be impossible to get it between Grimes's rigid lips. From the cabin he heard Captain Wilkes shouting with vicious sarcasm, "You've created a sensation, sir! It's the talk of the port! The longest passage recorded so far is ninety days—a record you've exceeded by ten!"

Wiki turned to the door with relief as he heard hurried footsteps, but it wasn't the surgeon—it was Festin, white-faced. Before the Acadian could gasp a single word, Dr. Gilchrist did arrive, coming up the corridor at a run.

Evidently, the surgeon had been at the dining table when Jack Winter found him, as he still had a large napkin tucked into his collar. However, his manner was brisk and professional as he examined the patient. Even he looked rattled, though, as Grimes spasmed into another fit, his lips pulled back from his clenched teeth, and his eyes rolling even farther up into his head.

He exclaimed, "This man has been poisoned!"

Robert Festin was on the verge of tears. "Not by me, sir, not by me!"

"What have you been feeding him, for God's sake?"

"Gruel—gruel, and good soup!"

"Then it must be the medicine. Make sure those bottles are kept safe," Dr. Gilchrist said to Wiki, and to the steward, "Get some saleratus and mix it with milk and water, quick. It's his only hope—sodium bicarbonate, and being walked about. You!" he said to Wiki again. "Help me get him onto his feet."

It was a lot easier said than done. Grimes had collapsed after the second convulsion, and despite his thinness was as heavy and unyielding as a sack of wheat. As Wiki grappled with the unresponsive form, he could hear Captain Wilkes still raving at the unfortunate commander of the storeship *Relief*. The words rang clear, snapped out with vicious irony: "An American resident has been kind enough to favor me with a table he has been compiling, showing the monthly average of passages from the United States to Rio de Janeiro—and do you know the record for the shortest passage? Twenty-nine days! And do you know the longest? Yours, sir—yours! One hundred days exactly! You are aptly named, Captain Long!"

"That figure of one hundred includes three days at the Cape de Verdes," Captain Long protested, aggrieved enough to allow his voice to rise. This only served to trigger yet another outburst, but Wiki had lost attention, struggling instead with the slack, bony body in the very confined space of the stateroom, while Robert Festin bobbed around, getting in the way in his panic.

"You have to admit, sir, that she is the dullest of sailers," Long was arguing while they heaved Grimes toward the corridor. It took an age, but at last they got out of the stateroom in a clumsy, struggling knot, with the sick man swaying in the middle. Together, Wiki and Dr. Gilchrist propelled Grimes into a walk toward the outside air, while Festin scuttled along behind.

"And a dull sailer demands smart seamanship," Captain Wilkes was shouting. "Which makes me wonder where you crossed the equator, sir! Show me your logbook!"

Rapid footsteps. Wiki looked up to see Jack Winter arrive in the corridor, his normally even gait quick and agitated. When a rat oozed out of a corner and ran across his boot he kicked out at it, and almost lost his balance. He was carrying a tumbler. "I mixed what you said," he gasped.

Wiki and Gilchrist lurched to a halt, gripping the slack body between them. They propped Grimes against the wall, and tipped the tumbler between his lips. His teeth were beginning to chatter, the skin about his lips had gone blue, and white liquid ran down his chin.

In the captain's cabin, Wilkes was shouting, "My God, you crossed at twenty-nine degrees west, where the equatorial current flows north! So what the hell did you expect? Can't you read a goddamned chart?"

Wiki looked at the open afterhouse door. At that moment, it seemed imperative to get the dying man out onto the deck, as if the fresh air would perform a miraculous cure. Dr. Gilchrist appeared to be gripped by the same impulse, because he put a hand under Grimes's left armpit again, and said urgently to Wiki, "Come on, man, help me."

Silently, Wiki grappled with the sick man's other side. As they reached the doorway, he heard a peculiar whistle echo from across the water. When he looked up, he glimpsed the smoke from a steamer chugging by—the Santos steamboat, he distractedly realized. When the wake washed against the flagship the half-empty *Vincennes* danced and bounced. He and Dr. Gilchrist, with their burden, staggered and crashed back into the corridor, slamming up against the larboard wall.

The marine corporal on sentry duty peered in to see what the noise was about, his face confused and alarmed. When Dr. Gilchrist snapped at him to hurry up and bear a hand, he set down his musket and contributed his shoulder to the struggle. Between the three of them they got Grimes out into the open air. Festin followed, wringing his hands.

The assistant astronomer stood a moment, swaying in their grip. Then his eyes opened, and he stared wildly all around at the decks, the busy waters of the harbor, the blue sky, Enxados Island, and the mountains beyond. "Oh, my God, they've done for me!" he cried, so unexpectedly that Wiki flinched.

Then he went into another paroxysm—but not a silent one, this time. Instead, while the instrumentmaker writhed and arched, a wordless scream issued from his rigid lips: *"Ah—ah—ah-ahhhh!"*

Despite their strenuous efforts to hold him, he buckled all the way to the deck. At the last instant, Wiki deliberately collapsed with him, to cushion his fall. They hit the planks together. For a terrible moment he was entangled with the man's convulsing limbs, but then he managed to extricate himself, while all the time Grimes's body threshed.

Jack Winter had arrived, clutching the tumbler, and shaking so much that the white saleratus mixture slopped onto the deck. "Get blankets," Dr. Gilchrist snapped. There was heavy sweat on the surgeon's brow, and he had lost his napkin. Jack Winter dropped the tumbler, turned, and ran, blundering past the three captains as they came out of the afterhouse, having at long last noticed the commotion.

"What the *hell* is going on?" Captain Wilkes demanded. His voice was high-pitched. No one answered.

With a last scream Grimes arched and then flopped back to the deck. His blank eyes stared up at the orb of the sun and his right arm was stiffly extended toward Festin, as if in silent accusation. When Wiki looked up to follow the dead gaze, he saw a whirl of seabirds directly overhead, rising on a pillar of air.

It was like an omen—a bad one. No sooner had Captain Wilkes heard the full details of the affair, than Robert Festin was charged with murder, and Wiki and Jack Winter were thrown into the brig with him, as accessories after the fact.

Eleven

The inquest was held in a room at the back of a small courthouse on the Praça da Constituição. Wiki, attired in his best broadcloth, was sitting in the front row next to Jack Winter, who was sweating heavily, while Festin, weeping and wearing handcuffs, was in the dock to one side.

Fortunately, none of them sported any further signs of battle, because they had had the shipboard prison to themselves. As regular as clockwork, at eight bells every evening watch, the crew of HMS *Thunderer* struck up "The *Chesapeake* and the *Shannon,*" just to taunt the patriotic Americans, who couldn't wait to get on shore and teach the saucy British a lesson. Accordingly, Captain Wilkes had issued orders that no leave was to be given, and so there had been no broken heads, and no aggressive drunks tossed into the brig, and Wiki had been spared from fights.

On the dark side, he did not have a notion of what was going to happen in this courtroom. At sea, there would have been an inquiry presided over by Wilkes and three other captains, and that would have been that, but, since they were in port, the Brazilian authorities had taken it over, and so the procedure was a mystery.

As it was, Captain Wilkes was not even present. Captain Andrew Long had asked for a survey of the stores the ship *Relief* was carrying, as he reckoned they were defective, and for a long time, Wilkes had refused to listen. Before he had taken command of the expedition, he had been assured that the provisions had been inspected and found in such good order that they were expected to last the expedition for at least a year. However, Long's officers backed him up, swearing that over the hundred-day passage they had had plenty of time to establish that even the flour was spoiled, and had probably been that way when loaded. The survey was held, and the decision the provisions must be replaced had been made. Accordingly, Captain Wilkes was too busy to turn up to a mere court procedure.

By contrast, it seemed that just about every citizen of Rio was intensely interested—that the poisoning had become a cause célèbre, in fact. Though the benches in the public part of the courtroom were packed, men were still shoving and fighting to find a place, ignoring the remonstrations of the two fat court officers who stood on either side of the door. Clouds of flies buzzed angrily in the high ceiling, and the atmosphere became heavy, hot, and humid, redolent with sweat, wine, and garlic.

To one side, there was a half-curtained alcove, like an opera box, where the grandees of the town were packed as tightly together as the men on the common benches. They were an animated lot of aristocrats, Wiki noted, talking to each other with great energy, pointing out people of interest. One of them was a lean, dark-haired gentleman with a strangely patchy complexion, and scars on his nose and cheeks. Wiki studied him, wondering what had caused the damage to his face. It looked as if he had run through a fire. While not particularly disfiguring, it made him stand out from the rest.

Then his attention was taken up by the arrival of the coroner, who proved to be a slight, elegant man with a narrow, aristocratic nose. According to the clerk's announcement, his name was Dr. Vieira de Castro. He studied the court through a pair of pince-nez, and then, with a bow, sat down behind the bench.

Once everyone had settled, Wiki stood up, and introduced himself in Portuguese as the expedition linguister. Then, as Captain Wilkes had instructed, he offered his services as translator. Dr. Vieira de Castro listened with interest, and congratulated him on his Portuguese—though with the added comment that he had obviously learned the language from Azorean shipmates, as his accent was so provincial. Then he remarked on his foreign appearance, and asked about his origins.

When Wiki admitted he was New Zealand Maori, he adjusted his pince-nez, studied him intently for a long moment, and declared himself overwhelmed with amazement that a man who had been raised as a savage could take on the trappings of civilization so completely. A few similarly grand compliments followed, and then this leisurely conversation came to an end. Senhor Coffin's services were unnecessary, he announced, as he, Dr. Vieira de Castro, would conduct the hearing in English.

This led to a lot of whispering in the crowd, some restlessness, and a few loud complaints. With a sniff and long, cold stare, Dr. Vieira de Castro informed the troublemakers that it was in the interest of saving time, as the members of the exploring expedition had many pressing matters for their attention. With that, he shifted to excellent English, which he spoke with an educated Boston accent. Wiki sat down, and Dr. Gilchrist was called.

A chair had been placed on a bare patch of floor in front of the coroner's bench. The surgeon's footsteps set up echoes as he approached. Then he sat down, arranged the tails of his coat to either side of his chair, and proceeded to describe Grimes's last moments, while the clerk industriously wrote down every word he said. Dr. Vieira de Castro listened very attentively, asking many questions and taking copious notes of his own.

When Dr. Gilchrist had finished the scratching of pens went on for quite a while. Then Dr. Vieira de Castro looked up and said, "So what, in your opinion, was the cause of death?"

"Strychnine," said Dr. Gilchrist.

"You sound very sure of that."

"I am. His jaw was stiff, his tongue was fixed, there were distinct convulsive movements of the body, his limbs were quivering violently, and there was great arching of the spine."

"Those are also the symptoms of tetanic convulsion."

"That's true. However . . ."

"And did you not also say that he was drowsy?"

"I agree that drowsiness could indicate a tetanic condition."

"But you still believe that the cause of death was poisoning with strychnine?"

"I am quite convinced of that, Dr. Vieira de Castro."

More scratching. "Dr. Gilchrist, how was the poison administered?"

"I have no idea. When I was called by Dr. Olliver, the day Mr. Grimes was reported sick, there were no symptoms of strychnine poisoning, so it must have been subsequent to that."

"Dr. Olliver called you?" Dr. Vieira de Castro looked surprised.

Dr. Gilchrist puffed out his chest a little, and said, "I am the official surgeon attached to the flagship of the expedition. Dr. Olliver was summoned when the deceased fell ill, and naturally consulted with me. After that, he remained the attending physician until called away by scientific duties."

"And you were happy about this?"

"Of course. I gave my permission quite freely. While Dr. Olliver is officially a naturalist with the expedition, he is also a practicing physician."

"I see," said Dr. Vieira de Castro, and with no further ado dismissed Dr. Gilchrist, and called for Dr. Olliver.

Dr. Olliver crossed the planks in almost total silence, his gait as neat and light as always, and sat down with ponderous dignity. He and Dr. Vieira de Castro conferred a few moments, exchanging qualifications and pleasantries, and then settled down to business.

"When did you first attend the deceased, Dr. Olliver?"

"At just after four in the morning on the seventeenth of this current month," Dr. Olliver replied instantly, without having to refer to notes.

"And the reason you were summoned?"

"Wiki Coffin called me, being alarmed about the state of the subject."

Again, the pince-nez were adjusted. The coroner looked at Wiki and said, "Senhor Coffin?"

Wiki stood up. "Sir?"

"What was the cause of your alarm?"

"Mr. Grimes had a nasty stomach upset."

"Do you have any idea what caused it?"

"He blamed the previous night's supper."

"What had he eaten?

"Fried fish and bread, and then a sweet potato pudding."

"And the same was eaten by all?"

"We all ate the fish." Wiki paused, and then added, "The pudding was an individual one that had been cooked for Mr. Grimes as a treat."

"And was anyone else ill?"

"No, sir."

"Ah. If the deceased was indeed poisoned by Senhor Festin's cooking, the individual pudding must be the culprit, is that not so?"

"Logically, yes," said Wiki. He, like Dr. Vieira de Castro and everyone else in the courtroom, looked at Robert Festin, who smiled uncertainly. The replaced tooth had turned black, and the effect was dismayingly villainous.

Wiki looked back at the coroner, waiting tensely for the next question, but instead he was told to sit down.

"Dr. Olliver? Did you suspect any kind of poisoning?"

"I gave the cause of the diarrhea very little thought," the naturalist admitted. "I was more worried about the subject's obvious state of bad health, which I had particularly noted the evening before. When I questioned the subject, he complained loudly of neuralgic pains in his head, and also of pains in his chest, yet it was still difficult to persuade him to let me examine him. When I did, it was to find that his temperature was high, and his pulse was rapid. Of greatest concern, however, was a severe congestion of the left lung, and a threatened pneumonia, the first symptoms of which had been brought on by the chills accompanying the intestinal cramps."

"And your prescription?"

"Carbonate of ammonia, and a pill which I made up from a compound of Peruvian bark, piperine, *ferri pulvis*, and gentian root, all of which I carried in my medical chest. These were administered four times a day. This regime worked reasonably well until the supply of bark ran out, when his condition deteriorated rapidly. There was none in the ship stores, and the ship had become becalmed off Cape Frio. Captain Wilkes was kind enough to send a cutter into port so that I could visit an apothecary."

"And this apothecary?"

"Dr. Elisha Tweedie."

"You knew Dr. Tweedie already?"

"No. The lieutenant who commanded the cutter recommended him, and escorted me to his place."

"Is he present in this court?"

There was movement on one of the benches near the back, and Wiki turned around, along with everyone else. Lieutenant Forsythe, wearing dress uniform and an extremely forbidding expression, stood up.

"You know Mr. Tweedie?"

"I've consulted with him in the past," Forsythe admitted, and sat down quickly, forestalling any questions about the nature of the illness.

Dr. Vieira de Castro looked at Dr. Olliver again, and said, "And Dr. Tweedie sold you the bark you needed?"

"And opium, too," Dr. Olliver said. "The patient was very irritable, and I attributed his slow recovery to his choleric temper. I also asked Dr. Tweedie to make up a bottle of a bismuth preparation—*mistura bismuthi cum soda et tragacanth*, to be exact—as his indigestion had persisted."

"And after you returned to your patient?"

"He improved so well that when Captain Wilkes issued instructions for a survey of the marine life in the harbor, I decided that it was safe to leave him." Dr. Olliver sighed deeply, and said, "I greatly regret that I was proved so wrong." He paused, and then added, "The subject had made some wild accusations, but I'd paid little attention. As I said before, he was a man of irritable temper."

"Accusations? What kind of accusations?"

"He raved about a conspiracy to kill him."

There was an instant hubbub, while those who could not understand English asked for translations from their more knowledgeable neighbors, and other men called out for an explanation. The clerk hammered on the desk, and slowly silence returned.

"And did the deceased name the members of this conspiracy?"

Dr. Olliver looked at Wiki, and said, "While he mostly pointed the finger at the cook, Robert Festin, he named Wiki Coffin, too."

Another commotion, silenced with more hammering. Wiki stood up again, and waited. The coroner surveyed him curiously, and then queried, "Why did the deceased think *you* wanted to kill him?"

Wiki shrugged. "He accused me of wanting to get rid of him so I could have our cabin all to myself—though, as it happened, *he* was the one who was unhappy that we were sharing a stateroom."

"But why should he feel that way?"

"He was frightened of New Zealand Maori."

"Meu Deus, a sério?" Dr. Vieira de Castro was quite astounded. Then he looked thoughtful, and remarked, "Well, your people do

have an ominous reputation for cannibalism, I suppose." Wiki kept an impassive silence, and when Dr. Castro inclined his head, he sat down.

Dr. Vieira de Castro looked at Dr. Olliver again, and the surgeon said, "Mr. Grimes also accused the steward, Jack Winter."

"Why, is he a New Zealand Maori, too?"

"No, but he *was* the man who carried the fish into the cabin."

"So you think the fish was poisoned, Dr. Olliver?"

"As Wiki Coffin said, the rest of us ate it with no ill effects—though there is the slight chance that the top two fish, which were the ones the deceased ate, might have been polluted with something. Personally, I had perfect trust in the steward—so much so that the subject, most unfortunately, was in his entire care at the time that he died."

Silence fell as everyone took in the implications of what the surgeon had said, so complete that Jack Winter's sharp intake of breath could be heard. When he was summoned, he moved with uncharacteristic awkwardness, dropping into the witness chair with a thud after being given permission to sit.

Dr. Vieira de Castro said, "Were you aware that the deceased considered you to be part of a murderous conspiracy?"

Jack said defensively, "No one paid no attention to his ravings. As you said yourself, sir, if anything poisoned Mr. Grimes, then it must've been the pudding what Robert Festin made specially for him."

"But you were the one in charge of his nursing?"

"If by *nursing* you mean getting medicine into him despite his wild complaints, then that's right, sir."

"Dr. Olliver gave you clear instructions?"

"There was two big bottles of medicine, and a vial of enough pills to last the time while he was away. One of the bottles held bismuth, and Dr. Olliver told me to give him a tablespoonful of that after food. The other ones he got four times a day. It worried me something horrible," the steward said plaintively. "He was asleep mostly, but his arm twitched all the time, and he complained of pins and needles and how the medicine tasted bitter—he complained a-constant, sir, but what was I to do?"

"Pins and needles?" Dr. Vieira de Castro looked at Wiki, and said, "What does he mean?"

Wiki did his best to explain the term in Portuguese, and after a while the coroner understood. Then he frowned at Dr. Olliver and said, "But is that not a symptom of strychnine poisoning?"

Dr. Olliver heaved himself to his feet and said angrily, "I assure you, sir, that the deceased never complained of anything like that to me!"

"But it certainly indicates that strychnine was administered while you were away—that he was, in fact, being poisoned." Dr. Vieira de Castro looked sternly at Jack Winter, and said, "What did you give the deceased to eat?"

"I didn't give him nothing but medicine, sir," the steward exclaimed. "Robert Festin was the one who cooked and fed him his invalid food!" His face had gone pasty, and he was beginning to sweat.

"Aha," said the coroner, and consulted his notes for what seemed a very long time, while everyone waited for the accused to be called. When Dr. Vieira de Castro finally looked up, however, he merely remarked, "I think it is time that we heard from the Colonial Analyst," and nodded to Jack Winter to stand down.

The steward, looking shaken and somewhat baffled, returned to his seat next to Wiki, and a blond, sturdily built man took his place. In a strong accent, he attested that his name was Johan Ohlsson, and then went on to state in matter-of-fact tones that he had received a jar of human organs from the postmortem.

Then, without needing any prompting from Dr. Vieira de Castro, he reported that he had also received the postmortem report, which had made particular remark of the congested and extremely inflamed left lung. Apart from the lung, the organs were anatomically normal, though the stomach was blackened in places by bismuth, and the liver contained a bitter substance that was probably strychnine, though the tests were inconclusive.

"And did you test the medicines?" Dr. Vieira de Castro asked.

"Of course," the Colonial Analyst replied. "First, I ground up the pills, of which there were fourteen in the bottle, and which had been competently made, in my professional opinion, and finished with powdered licorice root. The resultant powder proved to contain approximately fifteen grains of chinoidine, which is a common form of Peruvian bark, one grain of piperine, two and one half grains of *ferri pulvis*, one grain of gentian root, and four grains of opium."

Delivered in a thick accent, this was quite incomprehensible to most of the audience. Dr. Vieira de Castro, however, looked very thoughtful, indeed. He tapped the end of his pen against his lips, and then said, "Were any toxins present?"

"None that I could ascertain."

"So what about the bottles of medicine?"

There was a hushed pause as Dr. Ohlsson took out a notebook and waved away the flies that circled about his head. Then he said, "The first bottle contained carbonate of ammonia, and the second, a bismuth carbonate compound."

"And?"

"I found the first free of poison."

Total hush, while everyone waited. Then Dr. Castro prompted, "The second?"

"By distillation I obtained a precipitate which, when evaporated to dryness, answered all the tests distinctive of strychnine hydrochloride."

Blank silence, and then absolute commotion. People shouted at each other, and the clerk banged on his desk with his fist. It took a long time for the man who had risen to his feet at the back of the room to make himself noticed. Then he was heard to say, "Dr. Vieira de Castro, I think I can provide an explanation."

"I certainly hope so, Dr. Tweedie," said Dr. Vieira de Castro, and motioned to him to come forward.

Apothecary Tweedie was a short man with stiff red hair which stood out all around his head. In a broad Scotch accent, he said, "As I found out only this morning, when I made up the bismuth mixture I used a contaminated mortar. A most regrettable lapse, but completely inadvertent."

"You—*what*!"

"It was a combination of circumstances, Dr. Vieira de Castro," said the apothecary. "Earlier the same afternoon that I made up this medicine, I was working in the factory at the back of my property. My son called to tell me that a customer wanted some strychnine for destroying mice, and when I told him to look in the bottle where we normally kept the strychnine, he said he had already looked there, but it was empty. So I went to the shop, and ground some in a mortar kept specially for such purposes, and give the customer a portion of it, putting the rest in the bottle. No sooner had I done it, than I was called back to the factory on an urgent but unrelated matter, so I left the mortar at the back of the counter, for my son to clean and put away. After that, I did not think about it anymore. About an hour later, when my son called me again, this time to tell me that Lieutenant Forsythe had brought in a customer who wished me to make up some medicine, the mortar was gone, so I assumed he had taken it away for cleaning."

"And what was this medicine?"

"The lieutenant's friend, Dr. Olliver, had two orders he wanted urgently filled. The first was for Peruvian bark, which he needed, he said, for making up *pilula cinchona composita*. He had the other ingredients on board, he said, but had run out of bark. Accordingly, I supplied him with chinoidine. He also consulted me about the addition of opium to the pills, and, after advising him, I sold him that, too. The second order was for a gastric sedative of compounded carbonate of bismuth. After collecting together the various ingredients—bismuth oxycarbonate, sodium bicarbonate, tragacanth flakes, and so forth—I went to the shelf where we keep the mortar for pounding medicines, took it down and used it, assuming it was the right one. Unfortunately, as we found today, it was the same mortar that had been used to grind up the strychnine."

"Meu Deus!" Dr. Vieira de Castro shook his head in horror, and said, "How did this unfortunate blunder come about?"

"I have no idea. My son says that though he hadn't had a chance to clean the mortar I used to grind the strychnine, he had put it back in its proper place. When we checked this morning, however, we found it on the wrong shelf. Regrettably, the traces of strychnine left in the mortar must have polluted the medicine."

"Traces," said Dr. Vieira de Castro thoughtfully. There was dead silence in court. Everyone watched him as he studied his folded hands. Then he looked up again, and said to the analyst, "Dr. Ohlsson, how much strychnine did you find in the mixture?"

"Perhaps one fifth of a grain per dose, Dr. Vieira de Castro."

"Enough to be fatal?"

"It is very rare for even one half of a grain to prove mortal."

"Were there any other contributing factors?"

"The deceased's precarious state of health was the major feature, I believe. The left lung was adherent to the chest wall, and was congested and extensively inflamed. Though the small amount of strychnine I detected might have exacerbated the problem, the state of the left lung was sufficient to bring about a terminal crisis, to which the strychnine, though it caused unfavorable symptoms, did not contribute."

"So what, in your professional opinion, was the cause of death?"

"In my professional opinion, Dr. Vieira de Castro," Dr. Ohlsson pronounced with grave certainty, "the death was due to natural causes."

Twelve

To Wiki's surprise, when the verdict was given a cheer started up in the body of the court, swiftly quelled by the portly court officers. Then, as he followed the Acadian cook, now freed of handcuffs, through the packed room to the door, men reached out and clapped Festin on the shoulder, uttering congratulations, and calling him by affectionate names.

More strangely still, when they came out on the plaza a dozen women of various ages swooped in on Robert Festin with cries of delight. Two of the women seemed particularly ecstatic, smothering his face with kisses. They were obviously mother and daughter, both full breasted, and with clouds of black hair and flashing black eyes. Though the daughter would undoubtedly be as fat as her mother in another few years, Wiki thought she was extremely beautiful. However, as they carried Robert off, the look the Acadian cast back at Wiki was unmistakably desperate.

Wiki stood watching Festin and his ardent aficionadas disappear, feeling most mystified. While he'd known that the cook had shipped on board the sealing vessel in Rio de Janeiro, he had not given much thought to what kind of life he had passed here—or even whether he'd been here any significant time, as it had seemed so likely that he was just another transient sailor.

"So, who the devil is he?" he asked the men around him, and, as everyone vied to talk the loudest, he learned that Festin was a celebrated chef—the genius behind the far-famed table of a restaurant called the House of the Ewer! When he had arrived back in town in handcuffs—accused of poisoning!—it had been the sensation of the year. It was inconceivable that Maestro Festin's food would give even the most delicate stomach the slightest difficulty! Grandees paid magnificent sums to the House of the Ewer to borrow him for their banquets—so would he poison a man? Unthinkable!

Not only that, the gossip ran on, but Robert Festin was destined to become a substantial man. The daughter of the House of Ewer was determined that she would marry him, and him alone. It was a romantic affair! Tragically, though, he had been kidnapped, and put on board some departing ship. Some said that the poor fellow was suffering from the effects of a knock on the head, and undoubtedly, if so, he had sustained this blow during the abduction, did not Senhor Coffin agree?

"Perhaps," said Wiki, frowning. While the mystery of why the courtroom had been packed with spectators was solved, the discovery that Robert Festin was locally famous raised interesting questions about the inquiry itself. He craned to look over the heads of the crowd, but Dr. Gilchrist was nowhere to be seen. He was anxious to talk to Lieutenant Forsythe, too, but the southerner had also vanished.

Finally, one whiskery fellow produced a gap-toothed, meaningful grin, pointed over one shoulder, and indicated that the big lieutenant had left early in the proceedings, muttering that he needed a drink. *Damn*, thought Wiki, remembering the hundreds of *tabernas* in the maze of stone-paved alleys between the Praça da Constituição and the waterfront, but nonetheless he set off.

Within moments, he was hemmed in by squat, solid buildings, their frames built of great wooden beams, which were filled in with roughly squared stones. These had been cemented into place with clay, and then plastered over and washed with a variety of pastel colors. Their roofs jutted out, hiding most of the sky overhead, and were heavily tiled with terra-cotta. All the shops were open-fronted, strung with ropes of garlic and onion, and packed with tables loaded down with goods that included sweets and fruit and pastries. The wrought-iron balconies of the living quarters above the stores were hung with bright fabrics. Showy Brazilian soldiers and drunken foreign sailors jostled on the narrow sidewalks, growling at each other like dogs, while barefooted slaves undulated through the throng with tall water jars on their heads, on their way to or from the nearest public fountain.

Wiki paused to buy a bunch of ripe bananas from a passing fruit seller. It was growing late, and he was hungry, but still he kept up the search. He had just about run out of likely places when he finally tracked down his quarry in an alley off the big market at Rua Ouvidor. The dark, smoky interior of the tavern, ancient enough to be decorated with frescoes on the plastered walls, was packed with carousing sailors, mostly Englishmen from the British man-of-war. When Wiki asked for Forsythe by name, several pointed to the courtyard outside, where Wiki found the southerner drinking in a corner behind the privy.

The lieutenant was alone, slumped on a bench with his elbows on the table, his tattooed arms curved around a pitcher of fiery local *aguardiente*. His coat and hat were tossed onto the bench beside him, and a branch of purple bougainvillea dangled bizarrely over his head. There were just a few other men in the yard. One of them was lying in the tiny fountain in the middle, in imminent danger of drowning, so Wiki lifted him out with a fist in his collar, and deposited him dripping on the cracked flagstones. Then he walked over to Forsythe's table.

The southerner betrayed no amazement at all when he looked up and saw him, instead waving a beefy hand at the bench opposite, and pushing the pitcher toward him. He didn't look surprised, either, when Wiki shook his head and called for hot coffee. Instead, he turned his mouth down when the serving maid brought it at the run, commenting sourly that he never got that kind of attention.

"That's because I'm better looking than you are," Wiki complacently informed him, and offered him a banana, which was rudely refused. Peeling one for himself, he said, "Did you know that Robert Festin is famous around here?"

"Famous?"

Wiki told Forsythe the story. "So when he absconded onto the sealing schooner he was running away from a woman, huh?" the southerner said at the end, and enjoyed a hearty guffaw. "So what else happened after I left?"

"When *did* you leave?"

"Right after that cold-blooded little Swede started on about human organs. Bloody repulsive, I thought, enough to turn a normal man's stomach." Forsythe picked up the pitcher and took a swig. Rather a lot dripped down his shirtfront, and Wiki realized that he was drunker than he looked.

"You didn't think you might be called up for more testimony?"

"Nope." Then Forsythe asked rather aggressively, "Why would they want to question me some more, anyways?"

"Your apothecary friend, Dr. Tweedie, gave some rather startling evidence after you had gone, and the coroner might have wanted to cross-examine you about it."

Forsythe said uneasily, "Why, what did Tweedie say?"

Nothing about the disease you once consulted him for, e hoa, Wiki thought with amusement. He said aloud, "The analyst testified that the bottle of bismuth mixture was adulterated with strychnine—which raises a lot of questions, including some I want to ask you myself."

"It was the *medicine* what poisoned Grimes?"

"That's what he said."

"I thought all along that that po-faced steward was to blame," said Forsythe with satisfaction, and toasted himself with a draft from the jug. "I'd reckoned it was those top two fish he put somethin' nasty on, though, and nothin' worse than a heavy dose of salts. He put strychnine into the medicine, huh?"

"That's not what the court heard. Instead, Dr. Tweedie calmly stood up and confessed it was his fault the strychnine got into the medicine."

"What!"

"Apparently he has one mortar for grinding poisons, and another for medicines, and the two mortars got mixed up. He used the poisoned one to grind up something that went into the bismuth preparation."

"Christ! That's the last bloody time I'll buy anything from him!"

"I should imagine a lot of people feel the same way, which makes his candor impressive as well as surprising," Wiki said dryly.

"So how did they get mixed up?"

"An hour or so before you came in with Dr. Olliver, someone had called for strychnine to kill mice, he said. The jar was empty, so he had to grind some up, and then he left his son to clean the mortar and put it away after the customer had gone. Apparently, instead of cleaning it, the boy put it on the wrong shelf."

" Wa'al, there's one bloody lie, for a start. When we arrived the woman who was after the strychnine for mice was still in the store."

Staring at him very thoughtfully, indeed, Wiki ate a second banana, and then finished off his coffee. When he set down the mug he said, "Why do you think Tweedie got it wrong?"

"Maybe she had been there an hour, on account of she was the gossipy sort. She was natterin' away to Tweedie's boy when we arrived, and then latched on to old Olliver like he was a long-lost friend; told him all about her problems with her mice and her poor bastard of a husband."

"In English, or Portuguese?"

"English. Her name's Dixon. Tweedie's place is in the *quinta* at Botafogo, and it's a proper little outpost of old Europe, there."

"Is that so?" said Wiki meditatively. So there had been a lot to distract Dr. Tweedie while he was getting his ingredients and pestle and mortar together, he thought, and asked, "Did you see Tweedie's son pick up a mortar and shift it somewhere else?"

"Nope."

"How about Tweedie himself?"

"He hurried into the shop, and talked to Dr. Olliver about what he wanted. Then he turned around to work at his bench. After he'd finished, he turned round again, handed the bottle and other stuff over, and took the money for it. Then we left. We was in a rush, remember."

So the apothecary had had his back to them while he made up the medicine, Wiki mused. "Was Tweedie's son in the courtroom?"

"Not that I saw. His father had to leave someone in charge, as he'd be too tight to shut it up and lose custom while he was attending the inquest—which is bloody pointless, anyway, because the shop is bound to be closed down."

"Why do you say that?"

"Tweedie's confessed to goddamned manslaughter, hasn't he?"

"Not according to the coroner."

"What! You mean he ain't been charged, not even with goddamned carelessness? After all, he caused a man's death!"

"Dr. Vieira de Castro was so impressed with Dr. Tweedie's candor and honesty that he broke into Portuguese to tell the whole court about it," Wiki informed him, going on in an ironic tone, "He trembled to think what would have happened if Dr. Tweedie had not come forward. He admitted that some authorities might think that the gross negligence he had committed merited a charge of manslaughter, but in his own opinion Dr. Tweedie's frankness deserved both acknowledgment and credit, he said, and completely absolved him of blame."

"But that's a crock-up!"

"There's certainly something very wrong," said Wiki soberly. The words Dr. Gilchrist had exclaimed when he had first seen Grimes convulsing—*"This man has been poisoned!"*—kept on echoing in his head, and he wished for the hundredth time that he had been able to see the surgeon's face when the verdict was pronounced.

"So how did the case end?"

"The coroner banged his gavel, and issued a verdict of death by natural causes exacerbated by misadventure. The case is now closed, and *no one* is suspected of murder."

"So Jack Winter got away with it," the lieutenant said in disgust. He picked up the jug to wash the nasty thought out of his mouth, only to find it empty. He shook it disbelievingly, peered inside, came up for air, and opened his mouth to yell for another.

Wiki said, "You've had enough."

"What the hell—"

"It's time we left."

"The devil it is. Order some more to drink, and forget those bloody bananas. When you eat them in your hands like that it makes you look more like a goddamned savage than ever."

Wiki cast him an impatient glance, and said, "I want you to take me to Tweedie's shop."

"Why, for God's sake?"

"To talk to Tweedie's son."

"Oh, Jesus Christ," said Forsythe in utter disgust. "What can you prove by talking to him? Look at the bright side—Robert Festin is a free man!—or until that woman drags him to the altar, anyway. I don't like the idea of Jack Winter getting away with it, but what's the point in stirring up trouble?"

"Because I was there when Grimes died—and whoever did that to him should *not* get away with it," said Wiki, and pushed himself to his feet.

However, after he finally persuaded the big Virginian to stand up, getting out of the *taberna* was not nearly as easy as envisaged, Forsythe being even more inebriated than he had thought. He staggered in drunken circles until Wiki grabbed his elbow to hold him still, and then, though he consented to put on his hat, setting it rakishly over one eye, it was impossible to get him into his coat.

Finally, Wiki steered them both toward the gate with Forsythe's arm draped over his shoulders, Forsythe's coat over his free arm, and the remaining bananas in his free hand. By the time they arrived at the entrance to the alley, Forsythe had picked up the rhythm of walking, and everything seemed set. However, just as they were moving through the gate and into the street, a couple of harlots stepped up.

"Wiki," said Forsythe, lurching to a stop. He was loosely grinning.

"No," said Wiki firmly.

"One of 'em's quite pretty. What are they saying?"

"That they can show us a good time. What else did you expect?"

"Wa'al, why don't we let 'em?" said Forsythe, and wrapped his free arm around the prettier one's neck.

"Because," said Wiki. Then he saw that he had lost Forsythe's attention. Instead of listening, the southerner was staring up the street.

"Wa'al, lookee who's here," said he. "And who's that with him?"

Wiki looked. The tall figure of George Rochester was threading through the crowd toward them, and the man with him was Captain William Coffin.

Thirteen

Wiki's face creased up with delight and astonishment. Then, as he recognized the stiff, fast way Captain Coffin was striding, his smile faded.

As the older man got close, Wiki could see that his normally hazel eyes were an icy blue-gray, and his mouth was tightly compressed. His father walked right up to him, stopped, and said, "So there you are."

"Aye," said Wiki uneasily. George Rochester didn't look very pleased to see him, either, he noticed. He searched his conscience, but couldn't think of a reason. To make matters still worse, the prettier of the two girls detached herself from Forsythe's drunken embrace, went up to Rochester, and tucked her hand into his arm, smiling up at him invitingly while he looked down at her like a loftily inquiring heron.

Wiki returned his gaze to his father, who still did not deign to smile. The pause had gone on for far too long, and had become awkward, so he said lamely, "It's good to see you." At other times when they met up in some foreign port, they shook each other's hands warmly, but right now Wiki didn't have a free hand.

William Coffin nodded. "It's good to see you, too. Why don't you pay off those girls and come along?"

"But we weren't—" Wiki blurted in embarrassment, but then gave up, realizing that whatever he said was going to make matters worse. Instead, he introduced Forsythe, whose expression turned to blatant curiosity when it seeped into his foggy head that this stranger was none other than Wiki's natural father. Abruptly realizing what a bad impression he was making, he tried to improve the situation by stepping away from Wiki and straightening up. Unfortunately, his equilibrium was not up to the challenge. Rochester had to grab hold of him to stop him from toppling into the gutter.

Wiki, searching his father's face for any hint of what had made him so angry, saw Captain Coffin look the southerner up and down with a deep frown of disapproval. Nothing was said to acknowledge the introduction. Instead, as soon as the girls had been sent off, he said to Wiki, "Let's go someplace where we can talk."

Without waiting for an answer, William Coffin turned on his heel, and headed for the market. After a moment of hesitation, Wiki followed, listening to Forsythe and Rochester trailing behind. George had taken over the job of keeping the lieutenant upright, it seemed, because he could hear a lot of muttered swearing and stumbling, but he did not look behind to check, all his puzzled attention being fixed on his father's rigid rear view.

First, Captain Coffin led the way through the market, and then he crossed Rua Direita, heading for Praça Quinze. As they passed the ancient jail, Wiki realized that his goal was the Hotel Pharoux—a logical destination, because that was where all the European travelers and American sea captains stopped, even though the food was reputed to be bad, and the smell when the wind blew in from the harbor was notoriously foul.

The famous hotel was quite plain in appearance, its thick white-washed walls three stories high. The windows on the bottom floor were barred, while the windows on the second and third floors were more elegantly arched, each one provided with a square wrought-iron balcony. The street entrance was halfway along the frontage, with an embellished stone tympanum above it, but instead of heading there, Captain Coffin led the way to an iron gate at the side of the long building, and opened it to let them all through into a bricked, open-air passage. It was overhung with trees, the low branches half hiding the hotel privies that were sited along the left-hand side of the walk like a row of smelly huts.

Still, not a word was said. Wiki became conscious that Forsythe was staring from his face to his father's, and that he had lost his ingratiating grin. However, the lieutenant tagged along behind as Captain Coffin strode along the walk to the curving stone stairway at the end, and climbed it to a doorway. This led into the hotel, opening onto a balcony on the second level which ran round the four sides of a big inner courtyard.

Plants climbed and hung everywhere; it was like being in a tropical forest. Two more stairways led off this balcony, one going up to the topmost floor, and the other curving down to a marbled hallway on the ground level. Captain Coffin passed these by, walking along the balcony to a curtained arch at the far end, which opened into a dining room.

Though the windows were wide open, they were also hung with curtains, so the light was dim. However, it was possible to see that the walls were covered with great oil paintings, some well done, others very bad. Four big round tables were laid for meals, but the room was empty. Then, in a hurried rattle of footsteps, the manager arrived. He greeted Captain Coffin and George Rochester effusively, with many nods and bows, evidently because they were expected. There was an awkward pause when he turned round and realized that one of Captain Coffin's guests looked like an Indian, and that the other was drunk, but he covered up his discomfiture by talking a lot while showing them to a table.

With his own hands, the restauranteur placed decanters of wine on the table, before hurrying away to the kitchens. Without waiting for an invitation, Forsythe reached out, grabbed one of the carafes, and poured. As Wiki watched him lift his filled wineglass in a sardonic salute to Captain Coffin, he realized with a sinking heart that Forsythe had decided to be insulted by his father's rudeness, and that trouble was definitely in the offing.

He didn't have to wait long. "So you're Wiki's father," the Virginian observed, and jerked his chin in Wiki's direction. "Fine lad," he went on, much to Wiki's surprise, and added with meaningful emphasis, "You *should* be bloody proud of him."

Wiki winced. Captain Coffin contemplated Forsythe quizzically, his fine black eyebrows arched, and his half-closed eye piercing.

"He won't never make an officer, of course—except on blubber-hunters, where the skippers don't care if their mates are black, brown, or brindle—and certainly never a captain. How could he, bein' what he is? But he's done bloody well, considering. Did you know he's the agent of U.S. law and order on the expedition? That he has the same powers in the fleet as a sheriff does on land?"

William Coffin turned his half-closed eye on Wiki. "Good God," he said without expression. Wiki smiled uncertainly. Then his father looked back at Forsythe, and said, "No, I didn't."

"Wa'al, he's got a fancy document to prove it—and I bet you've got it in your pocket, Wiki," guessed Forsythe in one of his disconcerting flashes of shrewdness. "I bet Wilkes ordered you to carry it, in case you needed to establish your credentials at the inquiry."

"Inquiry?" Rochester echoed. He had been looking from Wiki to his father and back again, his expression worried, and now his face held consternation. *Inquiry* was an ominous word for a navy man.

"Assistant Astronomer Grimes is dead," Wiki told him. "He was poisoned. The coroner held the hearing today."

"Who?" said George, and then, thunderstruck, *"Poisoned?"*

"However, the coroner came to the conclusion that it was a mere misadventure, and that Grimes actually died of something else," Wiki went on more sardonically than ever. "So absolutely no one is under suspicion of murder."

"It's a crock-up," Forsythe idly observed, and then said to Wiki, "Show your father that letter."

He behaved as if he were showing off a clever child, which embarrassed Wiki considerably. However, Forsythe's guess was right, as Captain Wilkes had indeed instructed him to carry the letter of authority. For the sake of peace, he produced it from the inside pocket of his coat.

It was a grand parchment affair, embellished with a lead seal and a scarlet ribbon, which commanded the reader to provide whatever assistance the bearer, William Coffin, Jr., required, as he was the accredited agent of the sheriff's department of the Town of Portsmouth, Virginia. Captain Coffin received it with an air of caution, opened it very slowly, and then studied it for what seemed a very long time, while everyone watched.

"How on earth did this happen?" he said at last.

Wiki grinned sheepishly. "It was an accident, really. When the expedition left Norfolk, the sheriff strongly suspected that a man who had committed a murder was with the fleet, and so he gave me the job of tracking down the killer, and this certificate to back me up."

"Did you catch him?"

"Aye," said Wiki, without mentioning that there had been more killers since. Then a pretty mulatto maid with a great deal of bouncing black hair came in, providing welcome distraction. She was carrying a tray piled with small bowls of assorted tidbits, and Wiki automatically swayed to one side so the food would not pass over his head. She placed dishes in the center of the table until the tray was empty, and then cast Wiki a flirtatious smile over her shoulder as she left.

His responsive grin was absentminded. The moment she had

gone, he turned to George and said, "I heard that the *Swallow* run afoul of a merchantman."

George's fair brows shot up. "Weren't you on deck when the fleet came into the harbor, old chap?"

"Aye, but the last I saw of you was when you were a long way astern, racing a brigantine through the heads—well, that's what it looked like, the way you were both flying along. Then Captain Wilkes sent me off to the *Independence* to deliver a letter, and I guess you run afoul after that. Was it with the brigantine?"

"It was indeed the brigantine," George agreed thoughtfully.

"Well, I didn't know that anything amiss had occurred until Midshipman Dicken told me about it." Wiki paused, very aware of both his father and George staring at him, and added rather awkwardly, "He also said that the *Swallow* got off very lightly."

"He's right," agreed George, looking even more pensive.

"He went on to say that you almost sunk the poor barky."

"He did," said William Coffin grimly.

Light dawned. Wiki exclaimed, "She was *your* ship?"

"She was."

"Oh dear! And she's badly damaged?"

"As your informant told you, the *Swallow* almost sunk me."

"It was not *like* that," Rochester exclaimed. "Tell him the truth, old chap—that it was you who run into me, and *not* the other way around."

Instead of answering, William Coffin watched Wiki broodingly. "You didn't recognize the *Osprey*?"

"No, I did not," said Wiki, and shook his head. So this was the reason his father was so cross with him, he thought. He reached out, picked up a pastry triangle in his fingers, and ate it. It was warm and tasted of cheese. He liked it, so took another as he said, "The last time I saw her, she was a full-rigged brig, and I remember her as a topsail schooner. What do you expect, if you keep on changing the rig?"

"You sailed on her often enough!"

"The last time I sailed on her," Wiki said deliberately, looking his father right in the eye, "I was fifteen years old."

There was a short, dead silence. Then Wiki became conscious that Forsythe was looking very alertly from Captain Coffin to himself, with an ominous air of being on the verge of some shrewd conclusion. Before he could say anything disastrous, however, George Rochester forestalled him by complaining, "The accident happened *days* ago. Where the devil have you been?"

So this was why George was annoyed with him, too, Wiki thought. "It was quite out of my control," he assured him. "I was kidnapped by the commander of USS *Independence*, and after that I was in prison."

His father thundered, *"What?"*

Wiki reached out for another snack. This one was a cube of fried meat. He put it in his mouth and immediately wished that he hadn't. Not only was it tough, but it had been cooked in a very hot pepper sauce. Sweat broke out on his brow, and his ears felt as if they were on fire.

"Prison?" George exclaimed.

Wiki swallowed the fiery morsel, wondering at the same time what damage it would do to his vitals. *"E hoa,"* he told him, "you do not have the slightest notion what a fascinating few days I've spent. No sooner was I on board the *Independence* than Jovial Jack Nicholson jumped to the conclusion that it was outrageously unfair that Captain Wilkes should have a man to write his letters when he did not, and so he purloined me."

His father exclaimed, "What did you do to get into *prison*, for God's sake? What the hell have you been up to *now*?"

"Nothing," said Wiki, rather haughtily.

"They must have charged you with something!"

"As a matter of fact, they did not. They threw me into the brig as an accessory to murder, that's all. Robert Festin was the one they charged."

"Festin?" George exclaimed. "The *cook*?"

"He's no mere cook," Wiki reproved him.

"And he got off," Forsythe reassured Rochester.

"What the hell is this about letter-writing?" demanded William Coffin.

"It's all George's fault," accused Wiki.

"Me?" Rochester exclaimed.

"Aye. Because of you, I shipped as the expedition linguister, and I went on board the *Vin* as the expedition linguister, too," Wiki said. "After that, I somehow ended up as Captain Wilkes's amanuensis."

"Amanuensis?" said William Coffin, rather faintly. It was obvious that he had never heard the word before, and George looked equally baffled.

"Captain Wilkes and Commodore Nicholson have engaged in a paper war, and I'm the chief wielder of the pen."

"Paper war?" asked Rochester with lively interest. When Wiki reached out for another of the pastry triangles, he pulled the plate out of range, sampled one with appreciation, and then proceeded to eat the rest.

Wiki told him all about it, feeling a lot better now that George was back to his normal placid self. Indeed, he felt quite relaxed, and was beginning to wonder if the *real* food would ever arrive, when he abruptly realized that his father's expression was more thunderous than ever.

"It sounds as if you're nothing better than a bloody clerk," he exclaimed.

"You're right," agreed Wiki.

"But I didn't bring you up for that!"

"No?" said Wiki, lifting an ironic eyebrow. "And what *did* you bring me up for, pray?"

Captain Coffin's own eyebrows snapped down, but before he could reply Forsythe interrupted, stabbing an unsteady finger at him.

"I bet I know your problem," he said triumphantly.

They all stared at the Virginian, while Wiki struggled to think of some way to forestall whatever disastrous conclusion he was on the brink of revealing. However, with terrible lack of judgment, his father jumped in.

"What the devil do you mean?" he demanded.

"As I told you afore, you should be bloody proud of your boy, but you seem to be constant upset, instead, and I reckon it's because he don't behave like the respectable, scandal-fearin' Yankee that would be a credit to you and your wife. You're expectin' far too much, you know," Forsythe said wisely. "Even though he might be half American, it's the Maori half that counts."

William Coffin had gone red in the face, but now the scarlet ebbed, leaving his cheeks very white. Leveling a gray-eyed stare at the southerner, he said very evenly, "You don't know what you're talking about."

"On the contrary, *sir*, I know a goddamned lot," Forsythe replied, taking drunken umbrage at this perceived affront. "Back in the year 1828 I hired myself out to a Ngapuhi chief, and it was a bloody interesting experience. I learned a *lot*. They might be goddamned cannibal savages, and *savage* savages, at that, but you have to admire their—"

He broke off and hunted for the word he wanted, while Wiki stared at him in speechless horror. "Their *appetite*, I guess you can call it," he said at last, and smiled and nodded with satisfaction at his choice. "That's it, their *appetite* for life. They might be scoundrels what will steal anythin' what ain't nailed down, but they're bloody brave warriors and seamen, too, and are as fond of the girls as any proper sailor—only earlier. And I bet that was a real big problem for you, Captain Coffin, sir. They mature goddamned early—their balls drop at the age of ten, or so I was informed—and you took him to Salem when he was twelve, right? Or was it thirteen? Whatever, I bet it wasn't long at all before Wiki was *waltzing* with pretty Yankee women what rightfully belonged to others, and creating scandals that set you at odds with your neighbors and friends, not to mention your wife."

Captain Coffin swerved round to George. "What the *hell* have you been telling him?"

"Nothing," said Rochester quickly. "I haven't even had the chance—" Then he stopped and grimaced, evidently on the verge of a horrible blunder.

Wiki put down his napkin, and stood up. He was hot with embarrassment that that long-ago headstrong affair should come back to haunt him yet again, and his mouth was dry with disappointment that the unexpected reunion with his father should turn out like this. When they all looked at him he said quietly, "I think it would be a good idea for me to go."

"You stay right where you are!" Captain Coffin thundered—and the restauranteur came back into the room, accompanied by the lean, elegant gentleman with the patchy complexion Wiki had noticed in the courtroom.

When Captain Coffin and Rochester stood up, Forsythe stumbled to his feet, too. Wiki watched his father walk up to the newcomer and vigorously shake hands. Though Captain Coffin was still very pale, his manner was as everyday as if nothing out of the usual had happened. Then the two men turned, and walked toward the table.

William Coffin indicated George. "Captain Rochester—my good friend, Sir Patrick Palgrave," he said. Then, after George and the newcomer had shaken hands, he said, "Lieutenant—Forsythe, isn't it?"

Palgrave shook hands with Forsythe, too, urbanely ignoring his tipsy condition. Then, when he turned to Wiki, an expression of surprise crossed his face. "Haven't I seen you before?" he inquired. He reached into a pocket for a pair of spectacles so he could study Wiki closely, while Wiki, growing angry, stared right back.

Close up, it was obvious that Sir Patrick Palgrave had lost a lot of the natural pigmentation in his skin, because only parts of his face were tanned, while the rest had been reddened by the sun instead of going brown. The scars on his cheeks and nose were shiny. Otherwise, he looked rather a lot like a squirrel, with the same broad nose and bright, rather protuberant eyes.

"William, who is this?" he asked Captain Coffin.

"My son," Captain Coffin said gruffly.

"Your . . . *what?*"

"My son, Wiki."

"You old dog! Tell me, which voyage was it?"

Silence—dead silence. Instead of answering, Captain Coffin numbly gestured at them all to sit down. Wiki was angry enough to stay, so took his seat, as well. In the awful quiet, the scrape of chairs seemed deafening.

George Rochester, obviously desperate to fill the embarrassing hush, blurted out, "Captain Coffin told me how he saved you from shipwreck."

Sir Patrick's eyebrows lifted higher than ever, and George went red in the face, obviously appalled at the possibility that he had broken a confidence. However, Palgrave smiled affably at him and agreed, "I owe my life to my friend."

Wiki was puzzled, because his father had never mentioned this. He said, "When did this happen, Sir Patrick?"

Palgrave glanced at him as if surprised that a man who looked like Wiki should interrupt with such natural confidence, but answered readily enough, "Three years ago."

"In a storm?"

"No, the weather was calm."

"So how, then?"

Captain Coffin said, "Wiki, I don't think—"

However, Sir Patrick Palgrave had already begun to reply. "We were just three days out from Montevideo," he said. "Or nights, I should say," he amended, "as we sailed in the evening. On the third night we struck something—a whale, perhaps. The thud woke me, and then I realized that the ship was rapidly filling. By the time I got out of my berth and grabbed some clothes, the water was knee-deep in the stateroom. I was the only passenger, and how I managed to get onto the deck, I have not a notion. A moment later, the ship rolled over, and I found myself swimming. I was fortunate enough to strike up against a boat, and struggle into it. I heard a few cries, but saw no one, and when morning dawned I was all alone in an empty sea."

Wiki frowned. "No other survivors at all?"

Sir Patrick Palgrave shook his head, and Captain Coffin said, "I asked the master of every vessel I spoke to to keep a sharp lookout for other boats, and posted the news at the seamen's Bethel in Rio, when we got here. Later, the Bethel informed me that official tidings had come from Montevideo—that the entire crew of the *Pagoda* had been lost."

Wiki turned back to Sir Patrick. "How long were you in the boat?"

"Later, I learned that I had been drifting for nine days when the lookout on the *Osprey* raised me. I must have been unconscious for at least three. My drinking water had run out, and the few provisions long before that. Another day, and I would have been dead. It's a miracle that I survived at all."

It certainly was, Wiki thought—and it accounted for Sir Patrick's odd appearance, too, because he must have been terribly burned by the sun. "And the *Osprey* brought you to Rio?"

"Aye." Sir Patrick paused, and then said sentimentally, "That was when I fell in love with the woman who is now my wife, and made up my mind to settle."

"You're English, judging by your accent."

Palgrave frowned; it was as if he prided himself on having become so cosmopolitan that he had lost his accent, and was chagrined to find that his origins were still identifiable. There was a pause as everyone waited, and when he remained silent, Wiki said, "I saw you at the inquest today."

"The coroner's inquest into the death of the poor man who was poisoned?" inquired the other, suddenly relaxing. "Of course—I remember now, you're the interpreter from the expedition!"

"Aye," said Wiki. He remembered that he had had his back to the courtroom during the greater part of the proceedings, and supposed that was the reason Palgrave had taken so long to recognize him. Then he remembered the spectacles, and thought that Sir Patrick's sight might be poor.

"Terrible affair, terrible," the Englishman said. "The entire town was appalled when Robert Festin was charged with the poisoning, and when the verdict of not guilty was heard, the relief was felt by all."

"So I noticed," Wiki murmured. He saw Forsythe open his mouth, and tensed, but luckily they were interrupted as the maid came in to clear away the dishes and used wineglasses.

It was the same pretty girl. As she left she cast Wiki another bold smile. As he winked in return, he heard Rochester clear his throat and observe, "This is a very fine hotel."

When Wiki looked at him, George was politely pretending to admire the array of huge paintings. "They say it is the equal of Astor House in New York City," said Palgrave. "But, as I haven't been there myself, I cannot comment. There is even talk of fitting the place out with pipes and drains!" he went on. "A huge mistake, in my opinion!"

"But ain't it a great luxury to have running water on tap?" George objected. "And drains save an awful lot of labor, surely."

"A luxury indeed—but pipes and drains *leak*, Captain Rochester, they burst, and disgorge their contents! And who wants water running loose inside a building, eh? If too many buildings had pipes and drains, we'd need a complete workforce trained to mend those pipes and drains and put the water back in its proper place—a truly ridiculous situation! No, no, it will never work."

Wiki stopped listening. A marvelous smell was wafting to his nostrils, and he saw that the maid was on her way back into the room with a huge tureen of some kind of bean and sausage stew. Then he heard a meaningful cough.

When he looked at Sir Patrick Palgrave, the Englishman was smiling slightly. He said, "My guests will be arriving very soon. You and your friend are most welcome to join us, but . . ."

Wiki shoved back his chair, mortified and flustered. He had thought his father was the host, but now, with a lurch, he realized his mistake. "Duty calls—the *Vincennes,*" he blurted, and looked at Forsythe and jerked his head. For a horrid moment he thought the southerner wasn't going to take the hint, but then Forsythe stumbled to his feet, and bowed elaborately and vertiginously to all the company before wavering unsteadily toward the arched doorway.

Wiki hurried after him, just in time to straighten him up. A clumsy pirouette later they were out of the room, *thank God,* though for a moment it looked as if the southerner were in great danger of tumbling over the balustrade. Then Wiki realized that George Rochester had joined them.

George said determinedly, "I'm coming with you."

"*E hoa,* don't be a fool." Then Wiki moderated his tone, saying with a wry smile, "I'm sorry about all the misunderstandings, and I'll call on board the *Swallow* the first chance I get."

"Fine—but right now I think you need help."

Wiki wanted to refuse, but Forsythe was teetering so precipitously on the top stair that he was glad to accept. Together, he and Rochester worked him down the stairway to the ground floor, and across the marbled hall. Then at last they were standing in the main entrance, and the plaza lay before them, lamplight gleaming off the paving stones.

It was fully dark, and the sounds the carriage made as it rattled up to the main entrance were very loud in the night. On either side of the driver's bench there were flambeaux in holders, which flickered as the carriage jolted to a stop, and then burned steadily, so that the woman who emerged from the vehicle was framed in gold. Her form was hidden in a shapeless black cloak, above which her face was an alabaster oval, crowned by a wealth of coppery hair which tumbled out from the gold-embroidered blue silk mantilla draped over her head.

Wiki forgot his chagrin and embarrassment, instead lost in profound appreciation. The young woman was nibbling her full lower lip in concentration as she put out a dainty slippered foot to step down from the coach, lifting her skirts to display a pair of elegant ankles. Then, halfway through the movement, she looked up and saw Wiki.

He was standing in a patch of light himself, so that her eyes focused at once on his admiring expression. Instead of glancing modestly away, as expected, she surveyed him right back, taking her time while she studied his stalwart frame. When her gaze returned to his face her expression became mischievously teasing, and she lifted her ruffled petticoats, just a little, not quite as far as a rounded knee.

Then the skirts were hastily dropped. From behind, Wiki heard a servant cough, then say in Portuguese, "Madame de Roquefeuille, you will find Sir Patrick Palgrave's party dining in the ordinary on the second floor."

Wiki heard the servant's footsteps retreat, but hadn't taken his gaze off Madame de Roquefeuille's wickedly enchanting face. As soon as they silenced he executed a gallant bow, and said in Portuguese, "Madame, may I introduce Captain Rochester? He's another of Sir Patrick's guests, and would be glad to escort you to the dining room."

"How kind," she murmured. Her eyes sparkled.

"Enchanted," said George, once he understood. He looked extremely taken aback, but had the natural good manners to gracefully extend his arm.

"Obrigado," she said demurely. As Wiki watched George lead her toward the stairway, she glanced back, and when Wiki winked, she giggled. Then she and George headed upward. As they receded from sight, Wiki could hear her talking to George, first in rudimentary English, and then in fluent French, asking questions.

When he looked back at Forsythe, the lieutenant was shaking his head reprovingly, as owlish as a drunken Dutch uncle. "My God, you really do ask for bloody trouble," he said, but Wiki, feeling very much more cheerful, merely laughed.

Fourteen

By noon next day, the *Vincennes* had been completely discharged, and rang like an empty barrel. Wiki's sea chest and bedding, which had been the last dunnage to be removed, were down in the cutter. Apart from him, Lieutenant Forsythe, a caulking gang, and a squad of marines, the entire crew, including the thirty surly volunteers from the USS *Independence*, had been lightered ashore. Now, they were living in a city of tents that had been pitched on the grassy ramparts of Enxados Island.

Now, those still on board the *Vincennes* had the job of making a chemical smoke in the bilges, and battening down the hatches so that the smoke would kill off the plague of rats. Lieutenant Forsythe had been put in charge of the operation, with the squad of marines to patrol the ship for stragglers, the gang of caulkers ready to stop gaps in the deck seams, and Wiki to write an official report.

After the squad formed up in the bright sunlight, the marines listened to the lieutenant attentively, because Forsythe was taking pains to impress on them the importance of making absolutely certain that there was no one left below decks. In pungent phrases he told them about past experiences where dead men had been found in among the dead rats when ships had been opened up after smoking, and described in gross detail how nasty the discovery had been. Then he sent them below.

In order to rouse these hypothetical men, some of the soldiers were carrying side drums. After Wiki arrived in the holds, he could hear the rat-tat, rat-tat noises progressing here and there around and above him, near at times, and faraway at others. As he went forward, bulkheads, oozing dampness, reared up on all sides. It was very dark, and the lantern he was holding flickered every now and then in the stale, foul air. Every time it flared up, he could see hundreds of rats' eyes gleaming red in the corners, and could hear their squeaking as they skittered away from the light.

When a corporal spoke from just a couple of yards away, Wiki jumped a foot. "There's thousands of the brutes," the man said. His voice echoed against the wet iron walls of huge water tanks. There was a squeal as he kicked out, and a whole wave of skittering as a dozen rats fled.

"Releasing a coupla dozen snakes would work a treat," said Forsythe in his Virginian accent. He emerged from the dark with his rifle propped over his shoulder, giving every appearance of enjoying the job.

The very idea of serpents let loose in the bowels of the ship sent shudders up and down Wiki's spine. Even though he knew the southerner was joking, he couldn't help saying, "You'd have trouble getting the men back on board."

Forsythe, who knew very well how Wiki hated snakes, let out a loud, echoing guffaw, while all the time the drums went rat-tat, rat-tat, and boots stamped to and fro. There was a sudden shout of, *"Goddamnit, what the hell are you doing there?"* from one of the marines on the deck above. They all broke into a startled run in that direction, convinced that he had found a stowaway. However, it turned out that he had blundered into another marine who had taken a wrong turning, and so they returned to the search.

Gradually, the reports came back that the field was clear. The squad, led by Forsythe, and Wiki bringing up the rear, trailed down to the bowels of the ship where a row of barrels, filled with a mixture of sawdust, brimstone, birchbark, charcoal, and other devilish ingredients, had been firmly wedged in the ballast. The corporal struck a spark, and set the first, and then the others, to slowly burning. Acrid smoke billowed out, carrying a throat-clenching smell of bad eggs. As they waited to make sure the fires would not go out, the marines shifted nervously from boot to boot, and there was general relief when Forsythe gave the word to retreat.

It was a good feeling to get into the bright light again, and batten down the hatches. Then they all waited to see which deck seams needed stopping up to keep the ship smoke-tight. Meantime, the marines sat in the sun and practiced on their instruments. First, "Hail Columbia" racketed out over the water, and then the marines sang, "The Parliaments of England," while the drummers beat out the rhythm, and derisive cheers echoed from the British ship, a couple of hundred fathoms away. Smoky threads were beginning to curl out from gaps in the seams. The caulking gang set to stopping them up, while Wiki and the marines searched inside the various deckhouses for other leaks.

He and the corporal, along with a couple of others, went into the afterhouse, where Wiki checked the big drafting room. The afterquarters seemed eerily silent, but then the corporal's Yankee voice spoke up.

"Hello," he exclaimed. "We got one of the bastards already."

Wiki stepped through the double doors into the corridor, to see the corporal holding up a dead rat by the tail. He was standing by the credenza. As Wiki arrived beside him, he put the corpse down, and dropped to hands and knees to look underneath the big dresser.

"Look," he said. "There's a hole." Smoke was threading up and wafting out.

So that was where the rats had gone, Wiki thought—and how they had come, no doubt. He hunkered down by the corporal to have a look for himself, but then his attention was caught by the dropped rat. It was lying on its side in a rigid, hooked attitude, as if it had been grotesquely deformed by whatever had killed it. When he pushed the cold, limp body with one finger, to turn it onto its back, the spine was so strongly arched that it flopped over onto its other side instead. Its abdomen was purple, and distended. Under the stiff whiskers its nose was tinged blue, and the gaping lips exposed tightly clenched teeth.

The sight brought Grimes's final convulsion so vividly to mind that Wiki's stomach clenched. Without a word, he stood up, and searched through the cabins until he found a suitable box. Then he dropped the dead rat inside this, put on the lid, and put it in his pocket before he and Forsythe climbed down the side of the ship to the cutter.

When they got to the boat, the lieutenant propped his rifle against Wiki's sea chest, and said, "Orders are to carry your duds to the *Swallow*."

Wiki blinked. "Captain Wilkes is sending me back to the brig?" It was great news, but the first he had heard of it. "Why the change of mind?" he asked.

"Dunno," said the southerner, and the cutter headed for the shipyard.

The brig was dancing at her mooring lines as they braced up to the dock, and as pretty a sight as ever. George and Captain Coffin were nowhere to be seen, and the old boatswain was in charge of the ship. After shoving his chest under the double berth in the cabin he shared with Midshipman Keith, Wiki came out on deck again, looked down at Forsythe, and said, "I need to go to Botafogo."

"What? Why?"

Wiki jumped down into the boat. "To see Dr. Tweedie."

To his surprise and relief, Forsythe didn't argue. Instead, the lieutenant directed the men into setting the sail, as the breeze was in their favor. They headed south, coasting past a fortified island and then around Flamingo Point to arrive at the secluded bay of Botafogo. There, it was breathtakingly beautiful. The deeply curving foreshore lay before them, fringed with riotous tropical growth. Low white walls surrounding pastel-colored buildings stood out against the dark green. Beyond the shorefront settlement, more villas were dotted among coffee plantations and orange groves, as far as the forested foothills that swooped up to the abrupt heights of Corcovado Mountain.

The cutter touched sand. Wiki and Forsythe jumped out, leaving the men to paddle off a short distance, and amuse themselves fishing. As they walked up the beach, Wiki studied the beachfront village. Though small, it looked prosperous, made up of a number of substantial, flat-fronted structures, some several stories high. The houses had French doors, and windows with wooden shutters, and were set in luxuriant gardens of ferns, tamarinds, and trees with enormous yellow blossoms. Rippling creeks wound between the trees, noisy with frogs, and crossed with little footbridges. The air was perfumed with myrtles and mimosas, along with the honeyed scent of ripening bananas. Unseen insects chirped, and every now and then flocks of tropical birds burst out of the growth. In the hot brightness of the afternoon the colors were intense.

It was all quite a contrast to the alleys of the port and the polluted waters of the anchorage, and it was hard to believe that the city was just a walk away. "Is Tweedie rich?" asked Wiki.

"Made a fortune selling spectacles and thermometers to the English population when he first arrived, but whether he managed to keep a grasp on it is open to question," said Forsythe. He led the way along a paved road that followed the curve of the beach and was densely edged with palms and filmy-leaved trees. There was no movement in the heat of the afternoon, save for a line of black slaves undulating along gracefully with burdens on their heads.

Elisha Tweedie's place turned out to be a complex of three single-floored buildings, set in an extremely botanical garden, and surrounded by a low wall. The one at the front, Forsythe told Wiki, was the dispensary, and that at the back was the place he had called his "factory," while the third, which was set on the other side of a brook, was the house where he and his family lived.

When they came around the end of the wall, it was to see a boy, aged about seventeen and with bristling red hair, standing knee-deep in the stream. He was scrubbing pieces of equipment, including a pestle and mortar. They walked onto the bridge that crossed the stream, stopped, and looked down.

Forsythe said with disgust, "What was in them basins and stuff? Ain't you worried about gettin' poison in that creek?"

The boy looked up, his expression resentful but unsurprised. He said, "That mix-up weren't my fault, Lieutenant. I never touched the mortar."

"So how d'you reckon it happened, huh?"

The boy shrugged. "Dunno."

"Was Mrs. Dixon there when it happened?"

Mrs. Dixon, Wiki remembered, was the gossipy woman who had bought the strychnine for mice. The boy said, "Yup."

"Wa'al, if you didn't do it, she might've spoke up in your defense."

"Doubt it," the boy said in his offhand way.

"D'you know where she is?"

"At home, if she ain't in town shopping. Can't think of nowhere else."

"What about your father?"

"In the dispensary, of course. What else did you think?"

Forsythe looked as if he would have liked to deliver the boy a clip about the ear, but instead he growled, "Wa'al, then," and headed for the building closest to the road, with Wiki close behind.

The sign outside the porch read *Elisha Tweedie, Druggist &*

Apothecary, and was hung from the traditional red and white striped barber's pole. It looked extremely odd in the tropical setting, and once they had crossed the veranda and gone inside, it was like entering a different world.

The place was dim, and smelled of aromatic spirits. Posters and shallow glass-fronted cases displaying spectacles and small items of household medical equipment hung from the walls on either side of the customers' area of the shop. At the far end, Dr. Tweedie was standing behind a wide counter that extended from one side of the room to the other, blocking him off from his clients. He was wearing a leather blacksmith's apron, and had evidently been making up medicine at a marble-topped bench set against the back wall, because his hands were stained. The marble was very scarred and discolored, evidence of years of use. On the wall above it, racks held glass jars, many of them wondrously shaped. Some of the exotic contents were strangely colored, while others were a crystalline white.

Wiki, who found *pakeha* glass almost as fascinating as *pakeha* guns, studied the jars with great interest. On their labels words like **ACONITI RADICUS**, **STRYCHNINA**, and **ZINGIBER** were printed in elaborate script. The bottle of white strychnine powder, he noted, was full. On the side walls, wide shelves stacked with items of equipment were neatly labeled on their forward edges. There were gaps in the ranks, and undoubtedly the utensils the boy was washing in the creek would be placed there, once cleaned.

Like his son, Dr. Tweedie looked neither pleased nor surprised to see them. He said, "How can I help you, Lieutenant?"

"I'm fine," said Forsythe, his tone rather aggressive. He indicated Wiki, and said, " 'Tis Wiki Coffin, here, what wants to consult."

"He does?" Dr. Tweedie tipped his head a little on one side, studying Wiki with an air of grave curiosity.

"Aye," said Wiki, and put the box on the counter. Taking off the lid, he said, "Could you tell me what killed this rat?"

The apothecary picked up the rat by the tail. He peered at the body as it slowly revolved before his face, and then dropped it back in the box.

"It was poisoned," he said in his Scotch accent.

"With strychnine?"

"Probably, though it's hard to tell. It's a ship rat," he added.

Wiki wondered how he knew that, but instead of asking said, "In court, yesterday, I heard you say that the bismuth medicine was contaminated with strychnine because you inadvertently used the wrong mortar."

"Aye, that's so," said the apothecary, looking perfectly calm about it.

"But the analyst testified that there was too little poison in the mixture to kill a person. Would there have been enough to kill a rat—if, for instance, some of the medicine was spilled, and the rat lapped it up?"

Dr. Tweedie frowned. He looked at the rat again, and then back at Wiki. "It's possible," he admitted.

Forsythe, who was shifting from foot to foot and scowling down at the rat, said, "How long would it take this rat to die from strychnine poisoning?"

"About a week—or even longer, if the dose was small."

"That long?" exclaimed Wiki, appalled.

"It's not a fast-acting poison—not like others I could name."

"Ah," said Forsythe, and nodded as if this confirmed something. Then he lost interest, going over to the pharmaceutical posters and reading their ominous messages with his eyebrows going up and down.

Wiki asked, "Would the rat have had to drink a lot of the bismuth to get a fatal dose?"

"Definitely," said Tweedie, and nodded.

Somehow, thought Wiki, it was hard to see it happening, because Jack Winter, for all his faults, was too clean and tidy to leave a puddle of spilled medicine around for long. Trying to think of an alternative, he queried, "What about the pills? Could eating one of those kill a rat?" Dr. Olliver, he remembered, had suggested that a rat might have eaten the pill that was lost under the credenza.

"What pills?" Tweedie stared. "The pills Dr. Olliver made up? Good God, my lad, those pills would do no harm to man nor beast!"

"Even though they contained opium?"

"I assure you they were safe."

"The analyst—Dr. Ohlsson—mentioned something about the pills being *finished*. What did he mean?"

"Once the pills are made, it's usual to coat them with something to keep them from sticking together in the bottle, and to make them easier to swallow. Common flour makes a nice cheap coating, though carriage varnish is popular. Men who can afford it ask to have their pills finished in gold leaf."

"Gold?"

"The vanity of man prevails even in the extremity of illness," Tweedie informed him dryly.

"Good heavens," said Wiki, wondering greatly. Then he went on, "The analyst said something about licorice root."

"You have an excellent memory, my boy. Dr. Olliver's pills were finished with licorice root powder, which is an excellent coating for anything containing Peruvian bark, as it goes very sticky in the heat."

"What about the carbonate of ammonia? Would that kill a rat?"

Tweedie laughed, and shook his head.

"So, if the rat was poisoned by any of Astronomer Grimes's medicine, it would have to be the bismuth?"

"Definitely."

"Even though it was so dilute?"

"The rat might have eaten the bismuth several times. Strychnine is a cumulative poison—with repeated applications the amount of strychnine in the body builds up until there is enough in the system to finish the job."

"It's hard to believe that this rat was given more than one chance to get at the bismuth," Wiki objected.

"It's much more likely that someone laid poison for rats," Dr. Tweedie agreed. "Do you have many rats on your ship?"

Thousands, thought Wiki, and said, "The ship is being smoked for rats right now. While we were on passage the steward threatened to lay poison, but if he did do it, it certainly didn't work."

"There may be more dead rats in the bilges than you think."

"That's possible." Wiki remembered what it had been like down in the black bowels of the ship. "But that means the steward had the wherewithal to add poison to the medicine," he pointed out.

Dr. Tweedie exclaimed, "That's ridiculous! You know perfectly well it was my fault that the medicine was contaminated—and that it was Robert Festin who was charged with the crime, not the steward!"

Wiki watched him, feeling surprised. With the mix-up of the mortars on his conscience, Dr. Tweedie should have been uneasy, awkward, and anxious, but instead, he had been remarkably calm. Now, for some reason, he looked rattled.

He said casually, "Of course you're right—it was Festin who was charged, and not Jack Winter. However, the fact remains that if you hadn't confessed to the mix-up of mortars, the court could have concluded that *someone* added strychnine to the mixture, but didn't know enough to do it properly. The intention of murder would have been assumed."

Tweedie hesitated, and then said reluctantly, "I suppose it's possible that the coroner could have come to that conclusion."

"Other men would have kept quiet instead of confessing to something that was so likely to have a bad effect on business."

The apothecary went red. "I would have been boneheaded not to come forward! The juicy story that a patient had died after taking my medicine would have gone around the port in no time at all, and got a bit more embellished every time it was told. As it is, I might lose some business—but if I had kept silent and my blunder had been discovered later, it would have looked a great deal worse!"

And Mrs. Dixon, the woman who had bought the poison, was a

gossip. As a frequent customer, she might have unconsciously noticed that Tweedie's lad had put the mortar in the wrong place, and then remembered it later.

Wiki looked at the rat. It lay there in the box, arched in its last agony.

"And strychnine *is* a poison," he said slowly.

"A very active poison, as everyone knows," Dr. Tweedie grimly agreed.

Fifteen

It wasn't until some moments after they had walked out of the apothecary shop that Wiki realized that his memory wasn't so wonderful, after all, because he had forgotten the dead rat. However, he did not turn back. He and Forsythe strode on in silence along the hot, dusty road, and then the southerner said, "That rat got poisoned before we got to Rio, and the bismuth ain't nothin' to do with it."

Wiki frowned. "What gives you that idea?"

"It took a week to die, and it's been dead for at least four days—any goddamned fool could see that. So it was poisoned eleven days ago, and we've only been here for six."

"So you, too, think that Jack Winter must have laid poison for rats?"

"Nope," said Forsythe with an air of utter certainty. "Jack Winter put strychnine on those top two fish, and the rat got at the remains. Then it staggered around for the next few days, until it finally dropped dead."

"So what was his motive?" Wiki inquired dryly.

"I told you, he wanted to get at Wilkes and Smith."

"As you said yourself, he would have used a dose of salts."

"Mebbe so, but I still reckon Jack Winter was *bloody* lucky that Tweedie 'fessed up about the mix-up with the mortars."

"Oddly enough," Wiki said thoughtfully, "Tweedie was very insistent that it was Robert Festin—*not* Jack Winter—whose skin he saved."

"Wa'al, you told me that Festin is famous round here."

"And the strychnine got into the medicine *somehow,* so Tweedie must have been telling the truth—but why did the coroner come so easily to the conclusion that he wasn't guilty of misadventure? After all, he had confessed to it! He should have been tried for manslaughter, even if it was obvious that the verdict was going to be a not guilty one, just to satisfy the letter of the law."

They had walked out onto the beach, and Wiki came to a stop, studying the scene with his hands propped on his hips and his eyes narrowed against the glare. The cutter was about fifty feet off. He saw one of the oarsmen wave, and the boat started on the way to shore. Then he said, "And what puzzles me, too, is that Dr. Tweedie was so surprisingly calm and collected."

Forsythe said dismissively, "He's always like that."

"But he made no attempt to explain how the mix-up happened."

"He didn't need to—the boy put the mortar in the wrong place, that's all. You saw how the shelves are labeled. Tweedie looked at the label, and assumed that the mortar he picked up was the right one."

Dr. Gilchrist's words—*"This man has been poisoned!"*—rang through Wiki's mind. Had Dr. Tweedie confessed in order to spare his son from a charge of misadventure leading to manslaughter—to save him from prison, perhaps? Maybe there had been more than his reputation as an apothecary at stake.

The boy had denied putting the mortar away, Wiki remembered. He said, "Did you see Dr. Tweedie look at the label before he picked up the mortar?"

"I didn't pay all that much attention," Forsythe said, rather defensively. "That bloody woman was blathering on, and Dr. Olliver aidin' and abettin' by urging her on with questions."

"So, what *did* you see?"

"I saw Tweedie doing exactly what he usually does," Forsythe snapped. "He took down the jars and set them up in a row on the workbench, picked up the mortar from the shelf, and ground up the ingredients. Then he poured the powder into a beaker of liquid, stirred it around, poured it into a bottle, shook the bottle a few times, and handed it over."

"You told me that he had his back to you. There could have been something you missed."

"If you're thinkin' that someone leaned over and switched the mortars, then you should shove that little idea right out of your head. You saw the setup yourself—to get to the other side of that counter a man would have to go out of the store and round the outside to the other door, at the back. It's too wide to reach across and touch any goddamned thing."

Wiki stared out to sea, narrowing his eyes against the bright sun bouncing off the water. Logic said that the southerner had to be right, because the counter was indeed too wide for anyone to lean across and exchange the mortars, certainly without the rest of them noticing. The only people who had known that the strychnine had been ground up earlier were the woman, the boy, and Tweedie himself—and why would anyone switch the mortars in the farfetched hope that the contaminated medicine would poison Grimes? Back in the Bay of Islands, Wiki's people had a saying: *Ko nga take whawhai, he whenua, he wahine*—for the source of trouble, look for property and women, but Grimes had had neither of those. While the thin, gray-faced man had been unpleasant, he had been harmless enough. No one who knew him had a motive to kill him, particularly in such a complicated, hit-and-miss fashion, and Tweedie, his son, and Mrs. Dixon had never even met the man!

Then the boat arrived, and both men waded into the sea. As Wiki steered the craft just offshore of the Praia de Santa Luzia, past the gardens, the lakes, the great peaks, and the craggy hills, he didn't take in any of the magnificent view, however. Instead, he was going over the interview with Dr. Tweedie, and battling with the niggling thought that there had been something else he should have asked. Try as he might, he couldn't put a finger on it.

Then, as they rounded Calabuça Point, and the city came into view, he felt Forsythe nudge his shoulder. "There's that French filly what snared your fancy," the lieutenant said.

Wiki looked around, and saw one of the felucca-rigged craft close by. This specimen was a pleasure boat, a large, smart affair that was undoubtedly the toy of someone very rich. She was dashing along on the breast of the breeze under her long, triangular sails, with a dozen husky black men standing at the massive oars. Under a striped canvas awning four or five gentlemen were relaxed in padded seats, chatting with a couple of women. Wiki recognized Sir Patrick Palgrave, but the Englishman's face was turned away as he talked to a man who sat deep in the shadows of the awning, and so he didn't see the cutter.

One of the women, as Forsythe had said, was Madame de Roquefeuille. She was seated on the side nearest to the cutter, and this time, because she was not swathed in a cloak, Wiki could see that she was very slender. Her silk taffeta gown was a haunting shade of gray-blue, like dawn light on the sea, and the sun glittered on the many jewels she wore. Bracelets extended all the way up her white forearms, and the hand lying languidly on the gunwale was heavy with rings. The bodice of her dress was low-cut and very tight, pushing out the upper swell of her breasts. Her head was uncovered, and her rich copper hair was drawn up from a center parting, and braided into a thick chignon high on her long slender neck. There were flowers pinned into her hair.

Despite the awning she was holding a parasol, so was sitting in a double shadow, but still Wiki could distinctly see her eyes as her contemplative gaze passed over his face, focused briefly, and passed on without expression. Then the other boat had gone. For the first time, Wiki realized that it had come from the direction of Enxados Island, where the expedition fleet was based. Now, he wondered where the *fallua* was going.

Forsythe said, "One of 'em must've been her husband."

"Aye," said Wiki, feeling depressed. Then he put his attention to steering the cutter to the shipyard.

As they arrived alongside the *Swallow*, Midshipman Keith came out onto the bow, cupped his hands about his mouth, and hollered that Captain Wilkes wanted to see Lieutenant Forsythe and Mr. Coffin *instantum*.

"Why?" shouted Wiki.

The young man lifted skinny shoulders in a shrug.

"Where, then?"

"In the observation chamber at the convent."

Five minutes later, the cutter touched the boat stairs of Enxados Island. As he and Forsythe clambered out, Wiki contemplated the convent. It was an odd edifice, he thought, being such a strange mixture of building styles. Its flat, two-storied face was interrupted with two rows of rectangular windows in the local fashion, but it was also embellished with a round turret in the medieval style, with a pointed roof. The large portico boasted an arched Gothic doorway, four arrow-slit windows on two levels, a stone balcony, and Dutch gables. To its left-hand side was a large barnlike building with equally oddly assorted corner bastions.

Wiki had not a notion what the barn had been employed for in the past, but right now it was used as a barracks for the marines. The sailors who had come off the *Vincennes* were housed in rows of tents which were smartly set out in military squares on the flat top of the hilly meadow above and behind the convent. Lines of trees and thickets of scrub served as windbreaks, along with cairns of rocks.

The effect was surprisingly rustic, considering that the bustling port of Rio de Janeiro was so close by. However, there was plenty of activity in progress, with many carpentering gangs marching to and fro with their tools and timber. Portable huts that had been carried in the holds of the *Vincennes* were being set up, and instruments—barometers, diurnal variation machines, and thermometers—were being fixed in their stands, both in the shelter of the huts and out in the steaming sun.

The marine on sentry duty at the boat stairs directed them along the shoreside path to the portico, where they paused in the deep shadow for their sight to adjust after the bright light outside. Forsythe had shouldered his rifle, and his meaty left hand fidgeted with the stock as he stared through the inner gateway to the sunbaked expanse of the courtyard beyond. "Where the hell is the observation chamber?" he demanded.

"Who knows," said Wiki. The courtyard was bounded by a bewilderment of columns, walls, corridors, stone rooms, and steep, winding flights of stairs. Then, he heard the echoes of voices, and led the way across the cracked flagstones and through the cloisters on the far side, toward the noise.

They arrived in a large stone chamber, which was so crowded that it immediately became apparent that all the officers of the *Porpoise* and *Vincennes* had been summoned there for a lecture. Most were huddled in a large knot, with just a few more independent souls standing somewhat apart. They were all gazing with various degrees of bafflement at a very long pendulum, which was suspended from a high tripod that had been set up at the far end of the long room. It wasn't moving, but was frozen instead at the fullest extent of its swing, which looked odd, as if time itself had abruptly stopped. Then Wiki spied the thin string that had been tied just above the bob, which led to a hook in a side wall, and kept the pendulum at its highest point.

Directly behind the tripod, a tall case clock had been lashed up against the back wall, its door clipped open to expose its much smaller movement. While this wall had no windows to interrupt its white-plastered stonework, long casements in the walls to either side let in plenty of light, so both the pendulum and clock could be seen clearly. A telescope had been set up at the nearest end of the long room, close to the archway where Wiki and Forsythe stood, positioned at the right height for a man to peer into the eyepiece. Its nose pointed at the case clock. The sun reflected obliquely off brass.

Captain Wilkes was standing alongside the tripod, a lit candle in his hand, and his large, intelligent eyes glowing with enthusiasm. "As you all know," he was saying as Wiki and Forsythe arrived, "Isaac Newton's theory of gravitation explains the motion of terrestrial objects and celestial bodies by assuming that there is a mutual attraction between all pairs of massive objects proportional to the product of the two masses, and inversely proportional to the square of the distance between them. This, according to his Law of Gravitation, can be summed up in an equation—one which I am certain you are all fully familiar with already."

"$F = Gm_1m_2/r^2$, sir," piped up a junior midshipman, while his peers turned and surveyed him with open astonishment and veiled disgust.

"Well done, Mr. Fisher! However, the element G of that equation is the least well-measured constant in nature," Captain Wilkes declared. "Isaac Newton himself concluded that it is impossible to obtain it with any accuracy, because the gravitational attraction between any pair of objects that we can sensibly measure is so weak. *We*, gentlemen, are here to prove him wrong. Before we leave, *we* are going to quantify the constant G. *We*, gentlemen," he dramatically pronounced, "are going to weigh the earth."

Dead silence. The senior officers cast uneasy glances at each other, while all the midshipmen, save the young genius, Fisher, looked completely bewildered. Wiki, on the other hand, was extremely impressed. Standing in the archway with his arms folded, he had trouble to stop himself from shaking his head in admiration. While scientifics like Dr. Olliver and Captain Couthouy might despise Captain Wilkes for his carping approach to the collection and storage of specimens, and while the midshipmen, who had unstintingly worshipped him at the start of the voyage, might be expressing dismay at his increasing attacks of hysteria, Wiki himself held great respect for the man.

Because of his background in whaleships, Wiki was acutely aware of the stresses that afflicted the commander of the expedition. Being responsible for just one vessel was a great strain on any conscientious captain, yet Wilkes was in charge of *seven* of them, all with different sailing characteristics, and in varying states of repair. Most of the time, he did not even have them all in sight! Too, his job was far beyond the usual one of getting a ship from one port to another as quickly and safely as possible. Not only did he have to get this sevenfold fleet along a highly ambitious track about the world, but he had to satisfy the demands of a scientific corps who, apart from Captain Couthouy, had no idea what the job of a shipmaster involved. And yet, Captain Wilkes had time for a complicated experiment that sounded as if it could be a revolutionary forward step. Weigh the world with a pendulum, a clock, and a telescope? Incredible—amazing!

Then Wiki was distracted. A chink, right at the bottom of the wall behind the clock, suddenly opened up, letting in light. He wondered what had happened, and then saw a big rat run along the skirting. The hole led outside, he realized, and the rat had finally come through it after sitting there and blocking the light for a while. Some of the ship's rats must have come ashore with the provisions—dozens of them, he mused, as the light was momentarily obscured again and two more rats wriggled through the hole into the room. When Wiki glanced at Forsythe he saw that he was watching the rats, too, and that his hands had shifted their grip on his gun. *Don't shoot,* he prayed.

His prayer was answered. Just as the glint of light was blocked again—and stayed blocked, the animal in the hole choosing to stay there instead of coming into the chamber—Lawrence J. Smith stepped forward, and Forsythe's stare shifted to his despised fellow officer.

"Perhaps it would clarify the issue if we all repeated Cavendish's classical experiment," Lieutenant Smith suggested, while the expressions of all those about him turned from open perplexity to muted loathing.

"Excellent idea!" returned Captain Wilkes. "The Cavendish gravitational torsion balance that I use for experiments is stored in one of the tents, I think. If you'd be kind enough to locate it and take charge of the project, Lieutenant Smith? You could start with the most senior officers, and then *graduate* to the junior midshipmen."

Both Captain Wilkes and Lieutenant Smith laughed merrily at the little joke, and then Smith said, "Of course, Captain Wilkes!"

"This invariable pendulum," said Wilkes, sobering as he returned to his subject, "was provided to me by the astronomer Francis Baily, who has encouraged enterprising commanders to set up the experiment in as many latitudes of the world as possible. Because our mission is so wide-ranging, he nurses the most lively hopes that we will collate enough data to ascertain the gravitational constant G, by determining the median density of the earth."

No one said a word. Wiki, like everyone else, watched raptly as Captain Wilkes lifted the candle, and carefully set fire to the part of the string that was closest to the bob. As they gazed, the string burned through, and the pendulum, smoothly released, began its great swing. Back and forth it went, powerfully but gently, with such obstinate force that it looked as if it would swing like this forever. It was a grand and solemn moment.

"This pendulum, which is exactly sixty-eight inches long," said Captain Wilkes, "is naturally swinging at a different rate from the much shorter pendulum in the clock behind it, because the period of a pendulum's swing depends on that pendulum's length."

Again, he paused. His face was tilted upward and he stroked his chin as he searched for words, gazing unseeingly into space—which was lucky, thought Wiki, because it meant that he didn't notice that he had lost his audience. The midshipmen, who had glimpsed the rats, were jogging their shipmates in the ribs as they surreptitiously pointed them out. One by one, the senior officers saw them, too. Their eyes moved from side to side as they watched the animals scurry along the walls.

"Every now and then, however," said Captain Wilkes, returning his contemplative stare to the men, but still unaware of what was happening, "the arcs will coincide—the big pendulum will be in line with the smaller pendulum in the clock. *Your* job, gentlemen, is to record the exact time when this happens," he informed them, and all the stares jerked back to his face, the rats forgotten as everyone abruptly grasped the implications of what he'd just said—that there was a long, exacting task ahead of them, one that was guaranteed to be stupefyingly boring.

"The constant watch will be kept by officers in turns," Wilkes went on, "so that precise observation continues for twenty-four hours a day. By conscientious notation of each and every coincidence, we will eventually obtain sufficient data to ascertain the *exact* period of time taken by the big pendulum to execute a single swing from one extremity to the other in this place. And, once we have that *exact* period, gentlemen, we can calculate the force of gravity here."

"Weigh the world, sir?" said Midshipman Fisher brightly.

Captain Wilkes smiled. "As Henry Cavendish prophesied as far back as the year 1783, once G is known, the mass of the earth can be calculated from the rate of gravitational acceleration on the earth's surface. In other words, we can indeed weigh the world," he benignly agreed—and a deafening shot rang out.

Everyone jumped a foot, and the officers who'd had battle experience threw themselves flat on the floor. Wiki jerked round to look at Forsythe, and found, as expected, that his rifle was smoking. Then he turned his stare to Captain Wilkes, who was definitely shocked but not at all scared, shaking with pure rage instead.

"What the bloody *hell* do you think you are doing?" he screamed at the Virginian. "Don't you realize that gravitational experiments demand a low-noise, low-vibration environment—or are you just a completely *ignorant* goddamned bastard?"

Low noise, low vibration—and Captain Wilkes carried out private gravitational experiments? Wiki suddenly put two and two together, and realized that there might be a very good reason for the infamous tirades that happened each time some unfortunate soul in the room next door dropped something heavy or made a commotion.

At the same time, however, he was staring raptly at Forsythe, just like everyone else, as Captain Wilkes screamed, "Give me a reason, sir—why the *hell* did you do it?"

Instead of answering, the Virginian pointed his rifle at the six-foot, rust-red-colored snake that was writhing out the last of its life against the back wall. Evidently it had wriggled into the hole in pursuit of the rats, blocking the light as it waited there until it sighted its prey—and then it had hurtled out, ready to strike, but instead to meet an abrupt end.

A marine sergeant shoved past Wiki, closely pursued by a half-dozen marines. "Is all well, sir?" he hollered, and then lurched to a stop as he sighted the serpent, which had worked itself into a final knot. "Aha," he said, "is that what it is, sir? 'Fer-de-lance,' they call 'em here, sir, and vicious reptiles they are, too. There's a nest of 'em somewhere about this place, and they've come out after the rats. I'm glad you got him first, sir, afore he could get at you. We've surprised two already, sir, and lucky not to lose a man, we were, on account of they strike on sight, without warning. Nasty creatures, very nasty."

Captain Wilkes had his eyes tight shut, and was obviously battling with his emotions. When he opened them, he turned to Lieutenant Smith, and demanded, "Was there a ricochet? Was the equipment damaged?"

A hurried inspection, and then Lawrence J. Smith reported that all was well. The great pendulum swung on in oblivious grandeur.

However, when Captain Wilkes turned to face Forsythe, his pallor was marked, and the lips that had been so happily upturned during his lecture were now pressed tightly together.

"I have decided to deny you the privilege of taking part in this historic experiment, Lieutenant Forsythe," he said frostily. "Instead, you can practice your marksmanship elsewhere. The brig *Swallow* will be making a week-long survey of the coast as far as Macae, while a party of scientifics will trek through the jungles and marshes on a parallel path, charting the natural phenomena of the region—and you will accompany those naturalists, and take charge of them, and—and protect them from these—these fer-de-lance."

"Aye, sir," said Forsythe very humbly.

Wiki had never seen him so polite and submissive. Then he realized that the big southerner was undergoing a Herculean internal struggle—to hide his utter disbelief and boundless delight at this highly unexpected reprieve.

Sixteen

Having vented his wrath, Captain Wilkes embarked on the much more pleasant task of assigning men to the job of rostering the pendulum observations—which, as threatened, were to be kept up day and night until it was time for the fleet to leave Rio. During the process, Wiki suddenly recognized one of the officers—Passed Midshipman Ernest Erskine, who had been George Rochester's second-in-command when Wiki had first joined the brig *Swallow*, in Norfolk, Virginia, back in August. Erskine, who looked older than the rest of the senior midshipmen because of a certain primness in his demeanor, was a courtly fellow with old-fashioned good manners. After Captain Wilkes, in one of his tempers, had shifted him onto the *Porpoise*, everyone on the *Swallow* had been sad to see him go.

When Wiki accosted him, Erskine immediately said, "How goes it with the brig?" After being reassured that she had survived the collision, he remarked, "I heard that she got off very lightly—much more lightly than the other ship."

"That's true," said Wiki. "The *Osprey* is hove down at the shipyard now."

"And lucky to be there. Other men would have left her to sink." It was obvious by Erskine's tone that he admired George Rochester greatly.

"What do you mean?" asked Wiki, puzzled, and for the first time learned about George's gallantry in saving the *Osprey*, when he could so much more easily have taken her captain and crew on board, and then left her to founder. He had wondered about the warm friendship that his father and his best shipmate had evidently struck up, and now could guess the reason.

Then he said, "Did you have much to do with Astronomer Grimes when he lived on the *Porpoise*?"

"He kept to himself. I had the impression he was reclusive by nature."

"What about mealtimes?"

"He took a tray to his room. I think he worked while he ate."

"Was he ever sick?"

"He coughed at lot, I noticed, but I never heard him complain of being ill."

"Did he ever seek the attentions of the surgeon?"

"Dr. Guillou? Not that I noticed. You will have to ask him."

Wiki had to be satisfied with that, because a bell was struck in the convent portico, and Erskine bid a hasty goodbye. Belatedly, he realized that Captain Wilkes, looking very impatient, was beckoning imperiously in his direction.

Captain Wilkes turned and stalked out into the cloisters, and Wiki hurried after him, up a winding flight of narrow stone stairs that led to a small chamber. This, it was immediately evident, had been taken over by the captain as his private quarters. A narrow bed had been set up in a corner, but otherwise the room was packed with desks, chairs, and tables.

In his characteristic fashion, Captain Wilkes walked to the other side of a desk before turning to face Wiki; it was always as if he wanted to put some official barrier between himself and his listener. Then he said, "I've assigned you to the brig *Swallow*, to assist with the survey that I mentioned earlier."

So this was why he'd been so unexpectedly posted back on board the *Swallow*, Wiki mused. As careful as Forsythe not to betray his pleasure, he said, "May I ask which scientifics will be going?"

"The scientific party will be made up of the naturalists Dr. Winston Olliver, Joseph Couthouy, and Charles Pickering, assistant taxidermist John Dyes, and draftsmen Joseph Drayton and Alfred Agate. They will be land-based, exploring the jungle and the general terrain, while the brig will follow them up the coast. Lieutenant Forsythe will be in charge of the land party, while Captain Rochester will be in command of the ship."

Wiki paused, thinking that this was one of the most sensible plans Captain Wilkes had ever devised. Not only was he getting six of the irritating scientifics out of his way while he carried on with his pet pendulum experiments, but he was doing it in a useful and orderly fashion.

Then he said, "And my part in the operation?"

"You will live on the *Swallow*, and act as the liaison between the scientific party and the Brazilians. Every afternoon, after the brig has dropped anchor, you will go ashore, and meet up with the scientifics, who should be at the assigned meeting place by nightfall. There, you will take orders from Lieutenant Forsythe, who will requisition any necessary provisions and gear, and put anyone who might be sick or hurt on board the brig. You will also inspect whatever specimens the scientifics collected that day, and choose which are fit to be taken on board. I strongly urge you to be both strict and judicious! If the specimen is large, instruct the collector to replace it with a smaller one; if a sketch will do instead, then insist that he throws it away."

Wiki winced at the thought of the many loud arguments that

would be the certain outcome of this, and Captain Wilkes snapped, "If you meet any objections, simply repeat that you have strict instructions from me. Be firm! Take no heed of even the strongest protestations! As well as that," he went on, "you must make sure that they do nothing—I stress, *nothing!*—to offend the patron of the survey."

Wiki, completely baffled, said blankly, *"Patron?"*

"Sir Patrick Palgrave!"

"Who?"

"Though an Englishman, he feels a lively interest in our great enterprise; he came here this very day to express that enthusiasm in person, along with extremely courteous and attentive friends and family." Wilkes's smile had widened wonderfully. "He has not only volunteered to provide horses, mules, servants, and ostlers, but when he left me he was setting off to contact other friends who have plantations along the proposed route, to ask them to host the land party each night. His own estate is at the remotest part of the survey, on the Macae River, and he informed me that the party could stay there in comfort to write up their reports, before everyone boards the *Swallow* for the return trip to Rio—a most significant contribution to our mission!"

"It certainly is," said Wiki, feeling puzzled about Palgrave's motives.

"And he was most specific that *you* should go along."

Wiki blinked. A stray draft must have come into the stone-walled room, because gooseflesh rose on his arms. He said involuntarily, "Why me?"

Captain Wilkes frowned. "Isn't Sir Patrick your father's close friend? I certainly got that impression when Captain Coffin brought him here today."

So his father had been the unseen man in the *fallua,* Wiki realized. Not seeming to notice either his silence, or his sudden lack of enthusiasm, Captain Wilkes chatted on. "It should be a capital excursion, and I do wish I could have come along, too. However, not only do I want to closely supervise the gravitational observations, but I have too many pressing engagements on shore. Did you know that the quality here speak French?"

Wiki shook his head.

"A great convenience for me," Captain Wilkes confided, and then went on in that language. "You're not the only linguist with the fleet, you know! Had you heard that my French is considered excellent?"

"*Assurément*," lied Wiki, who hadn't known at all. He thought he should have guessed that Captain Wilkes could speak French, though, because he had toured Europe extensively in his search for scientific instruments. In fact, Wiki mused, Captain Wilkes's French was probably a lot better than his own.

Captain Wilkes laughed as he said jokingly, "We mustn't be wasteful—we must be prudent with our resources—so why use a translator when I can deal with the local gentry perfectly well myself?" Then he said, "Which reminds me," picked up a folded card from the table, and handed it over.

Wiki took the card, unfolded it, and read it twice, with growing disbelief. It was from Sir Patrick Palgrave, inviting him, with Lieutenant Forsythe, to a dinner party at his house on Praia Grande, on the opposite side of the bay to Rio de Janeiro, at seven in the evening in three days' time.

He looked at Captain Wilkes again, and said quietly, "I don't think I can accept this."

Captain Wilkes flushed. "You certainly *will* accept it."

"But surely I will have sailed with the survey by then?"

"Certainly not. December second is the emperor's birthday, and it would be most undiplomatic for the *Swallow* to leave before that."

"But why *me*?" demanded Wiki. Even more pertinently, he meditated, why *Forsythe*? Inviting him to a formal affair was a recipe for disaster.

Captain Wilkes's lips pressed together. "I trust you will both behave with the good reputation of the expedition in mind."

"Of course, sir," said Wiki, hiding a wince, and was dismissed.

When Wiki arrived at the boat stairs, it was to find that the cutter crew had disappeared, so he asked the sentinel to hoist a signal for a boat from the *Swallow*. Then, instead of waiting, he went along the gravel walkway to the far end of the convent. Here, another path wound up to the plateau where the sailors and marines were camped. He followed this to the top, and found that a deep ditch, maybe once a moat, lay between the hilltop and the back wall of the building.

The convent reared above him. The stonework was unplastered, and the visual effect was solid and dramatic in the afternoon sun. Very few windows interrupted the rugged expanse, and so it took a while to work out where the pendulum chamber lay. Then Wiki spied a small pile of rubble, which looked as if it marked the place where the rats and the snake had wriggled into the room, and skidded down the steep side of the ditch to that spot.

At the bottom, he found that the hole was much bigger than it had looked from the inside of the chamber. He wondered about the thickness of the wall. About two feet from the outer side to the inner, he decided, judging by the size of the stones. Then he speculated about the size of the cavity. That snake had been six feet long and sturdy in build, and it had been coiled up in the hole for quite some time before it had lunged out after the rats. More crevices might fan out from it, winding through the gaps in the stones and crumbling mortar—indeed, there could be a complicated network of holes inside the wall. *A nest of snakes*, the sergeant had said. When he hunkered down and tossed in a pebble, he heard rustling sounds from the darkness.

Wiki had contemplated putting his ear to the hole to see if he could hear the swish of the pendulum and the tick of the clock from this side of the wall. Instead, however, he stood up in a hurry, and, abandoning dignity, he scrambled hastily up the steep slope, and headed briskly for the waterfront.

Back at the boat stairs, he found the boat from the *Swallow* waiting, with Tana at the tiller, and Sua at one of the oars. Because of the other four boat's crew, they couldn't talk in Samoan, but their broad grins testified to their pleasure that he was part of the brig's complement again—because of Sir Patrick Palgrave, Wiki remembered. Instead of going straight on board the brig, he walked along the quay to where the *Osprey* was hove down, just in case the *fallua* had brought Captain Coffin back.

However, he was nowhere to be seen, though it was noteworthy that even in his absence the carpenters were working hard. Wiki could hear Captain Hudson, in the distance, shouting with obvious frustration as he tried to harry along the workers who were supposed to be mending his poor, hard-used, ill-maintained ship, while on the *Osprey* the air was loud with the busy clangor of hammers and thump of caulking mallets. It was a testament to the force of his father's personality.

Lying over the way she was, the *Osprey* appeared clumsy and vulnerable. There was certainly nothing about her to remind him of the times he had sailed with his father as a lad—but then, it was hard to know what a ship looked like when you were constantly on board of her. Wiki remembered an incident on one of his whaling voyages when his captain had called him to the rail to look at another whaler passing by. She looked kinda familiar, the old salt had said, but he was damned if he could put a name to her. It wasn't until after the old man had hailed her and got an answer, that he realized that he had once commanded her—on a three-year Pacific voyage! Both the captain and Wiki had considered it a huge joke, but now he wondered if his father would laugh.

In truth, he hardly knew his father at all. Captain Coffin had sailed away when he was barely sixteen, after he had been in New England for just three years. Before that, Captain Coffin had taken him on the *Osprey* for short West Indies voyages, but now it was hard to remember what that had been like, except for the balmy evenings when his father had regaled him with yarns—which were probably far-fetched, Wiki realized now, but which he had absorbed greedily at the time. While he had helped out with the work of the ship to the best of his ability, he'd had no role on board except that of the captain's son.

Since then, Wiki had sailed with a dozen or more masters, because he had quickly adopted the habit of jumping ship whenever it suited him—when he was keen to visit home in the Bay of Islands and the ship was not steering for New Zealand, for instance, or when he had become so disgusted with whaling that he needed a break. At other times, he had deserted to get away from a captain he disliked, though he had been lucky enough to never have served under one of the sadists who were the subject of ghoulish whispers all about the whaling fleet.

Whaling captains were an assorted lot, he'd found. There were some who were gentlemen, and others who were hogs in human form; there were poets, and musicians, and men who were so morose they did not seem sane. He'd been second mate for a master who'd carried a complete set of Hume's *History of England* to sea, and had willingly loaned the books to Wiki. They had walked the deck in the quiet spells, discussing wars and kings and politics, and though they had been steering for the northwest coast, where Wiki did not want to go at all, he had delayed jumping ship until he had finished the last volume. Would sailing with his father have been like this? It was impossible to tell.

Hearing a step behind him, Wiki turned hopefully, but instead of Captain Coffin, it was George Rochester. The afternoon sun glinted on his fair hair and fluffy side whiskers, and lighted up his broad smile. "I see you've shifted your duds into your cabin," he observed. "It's good to have you back."

Wiki grinned, and then said, "I wondered where my father was berthed."

"Living with Sir Patrick Palgrave until the *Osprey* is back on her keel. I offered him a bed on the *Swallow*, but he didn't want to offend an old friend."

Wiki looked at the *Osprey* again. "Tell me about running afoul of her."

"*He* ran afoul of *me*, remember," Rochester reminded him, and then described the incident with drama and flourish. "I doubt it would have happened with you at the helm," he admitted at the end.

Or if he'd had a more experienced first officer, Wiki thought silently, but merely said, "It sounds as if it happened too fast to do much. What amazes me," he added, "is that you recognized my father."

"There's quite a resemblance, you know."

"Good God!"

"*He* was flattered."

"And *I* am, too."

"You are?" George looked surprised.

"Of course," Wiki said complacently. "My father is a handsome man."

George laughed, and then said more soberly, "He's very fond of you."

"And I of him," said Wiki lightly.

"I wondered—well, knowing that he left you behind in Salem, and how you felt about it, old chap . . . And I couldn't help but notice how many young lads he ships along . . ."

"Carrying cadets is a Salem custom," Wiki told him. "And an efficient one, too, if you belong to a port where every substantial man has his sights on foreign trade. If they don't turn into good seamen, with careers as shipmasters ahead, then they can be employed as supercargoes until a trading post becomes available in the Pacific or Indian Ocean. Some even turn into reasonably respectable United States consuls! And those who are not fit to take charge of either a ship or some farflung station can always find jobs as clerks in Salem."

"Clerking being the last resort?" George said shrewdly.

"Aye," said Wiki, remembering his father's disgust at the news that he'd become Captain Wilkes's clerk.

"Ouch," said George with sympathy.

Carpenters were filing off the *Osprey*, and Wiki and George moved out of the way. Then they walked back toward the *Swallow*. As Wiki stepped onto the gangplank he said, "Tell me about what happened at the Pharoux Hotel last night."

"After you left?" said Rochester. They crossed the deck, and he led the way down the companionway stairs to the saloon. "Room crowded, many people chattering," he related as he sat down at his end of the table. "Came away deafened, but the grub was good. That sausage casserole was first rate—*feijoada*, they call it; apparently it's a national dish. But God, they were a bunch to talk."

Wiki swung a leg over the small bench at the forward end of the table, which was his usual seat, sat down, and said, "In Portuguese—or French?"

"A lot of it was indeed in French."

"For the benefit of Madame de Roquefeuille?"

"She's Brazilian. As a matter of fact, she's Sir Patrick's sister-in-law."

"Good God, really?" exclaimed Wiki. So the other woman in the *fallua* was probably Madame de Roquefeuille's sister, he deduced, but he had not a notion what she looked like, because he hadn't noticed her at all. It had been quite a family party—one that included his father.

He inquired, "And what language did my father speak after I'd gone?"

Instead of answering, George studied him with a troubled frown. For a moment he was silent, obviously choosing words, but then merely said, "Wiki, your father—"

Wiki said flatly, "Girls."

"You don't want to take any notice of Forsythe, old chap," George protested. "He was fearfully drunk."

"Nevertheless, he was right. Come on, 'fess up—you've apparently got to know my father quite well, and I'm sure he's shared a few confidences."

George grinned. "You never told me about the milkmaid."

"Who?" For a moment Wiki's mind went quite blank, and then he suddenly remembered her hands. He saw them as clearly as if the girl were in the cabin—large, competent, experienced hands, the curled palms smoothly callused. "Oh," he said, disconcerted, and George laughed.

At that moment, rather to Wiki's relief, Stoker came in, bearing a good repast of bread, butter, ham, cheese, and pickles. Looking down as he buttered bread, he said, "Did you know that Sir Patrick Palgrave is the guiding hand behind this survey of the coastal jungle?"

"Wilkes told you about it?"

"Aye. And I wonder why Palgrave should be so interested in the exploring expedition—which is an American enterprise, after all."

Rochester scratched one fluffy sideburn meditatively while he chewed. "It must be on account of orchids," he decided at last.

"Orchids?"

"Aye. He has a passion for them—well, he must have, considering he spent years at it. Before he inherited his father's estate and married into Brazilian high society, he was an orchid collector. Have you ever heard of such a thing?"

"I've actually met a few orchid collectors, *e hoa,*" Wiki told him.

"Good God, dear fellow, you never fail to surprise me. Where?"

"Brazil and Uruguay, particularly in the smaller ports. They'd come in from the jungle, driving mule carts loaded to the gun'ls with orchid plants in wet sacking bundles, looking for a vessel to freight them to New York, or London, or Boston. I don't think there was much money in it for them, as they were such a miserable lot, poor fellows. Their complexions were bright yellow, and they were invariably shaking with fever. I never saw the same man twice, because they died so easily."

George frowned. "Sir Patrick doesn't fit that description, old chap."

"That's right," said Wiki slowly, as the same thought occurred to him. "Perhaps he employed collectors, instead of going after them himself?"

"You'll have to ask the man himself. All I know is that Palgrave sent the plants off to his father's estate in Cambridge, England, where the gardeners cultivated them in heated glasshouses until they were ready to be sold."

Glasshouses. Palgrave. Cambridge. Wiki put down his knife, and stared at his friend in startled speculation.

Seventeen

The sun was barely up next morning when Lieutenant Forsythe marched on board to take charge, and within an hour the brig *Swallow* was a hive of activity, taking on fresh water and provisions, as well as scientific and drafting equipment. Hollering around in his usual hectoring fashion, the southerner looked as if he couldn't wait to get into the jungle and start decimating the wild life. When Wiki asked him if he knew about the dinner party at Sir Patrick Palgrave's mansion on Praia Grande, he was most matter-of-fact about it, simply nodding before turning to roar at some innocent seamen who were delivering a raft of freshwater casks.

To keep Midshipman Keith out of range of Forsythe's unpredictable temper, Rochester gave his young first officer the day's liberty, along with one of the brig's boats.

"You spoil the lad," said Wiki, looking Keith severely up and down.

"He deserves it."

"For running your ship afoul?"

Pausing only to cast Wiki a deeply reproachful glance, Constant Keith set off. Wiki saw him take the boat to Enxados Island and sprint up the boat stairs, and about a half hour later saw it sail off into the harbor. He imagined the boy spending the day exploring the riotous, exotic markets, but instead, when young Keith arrived back, well after dark, he reported with pride that he and Midshipman Dicken had climbed Sugar Loaf Mountain.

It had been quite a struggle, he declared; he and Dicken had taken turns to haul each other over numerous precipices and many rocky crags. They had been somewhat dashed to get all the way to the summit, only to find a message in a bottle, telling the world that some British officers had beaten them to it. "But never mind," he ebulliently went on. "We wrote our names on the bottom of the paper, announcing that we were the first *Americans* to do it, and put it back in the bottle." Then he and Jack Dicken had toasted the great United States Exploring Expedition in a flask of wine, and had scrambled and slid all the way back down to the bottom.

Even more dampening was the official reprimand that was borne to the brig early next morning by Midshipman Dicken, who was redder in the face than ever, and still flinching from a verbal battering. Captain Wilkes had been *surprised* and *disappointed* to learn that two of his officers had climbed Sugar Loaf—just to have something to boast about later!—that they had climbed all that way without taking a single measurement! And, forthwith, he had ordered them to repeat the feat this very day, this time with a team of volunteers, and carrying the proper equipment. And, he had snapped at the conclusion of the tirade, the two midshipmen were not to dare to even *think* of returning until they had a set of reliable figures!

"*Volunteers?*" Midshipman Keith exclaimed. "Where the devil am I going to find *volunteers*?" he demanded of Wiki.

He, like his friend Jack Dicken, was hefting a number of enigmatic contraptions, including a two-foot-long mahogany case which held a mysterious assemblage of glass tubes filled with various oils. "A sympiesometer," said Constant Keith grumpily, when Wiki asked about it, and then unbent to explain, "It's a kind of barometer that tells variations in the weather."

"You're using a barometer to measure a *mountain*?"

"Why not?" said Keith.

Wiki had no answer to that. Shaking his head in bemusement, he walked along the wharf to watch the work on the *Osprey*, which was a lot more comprehensible. As he perched on his favorite bollard, he could hear Keith and Dicken trying to talk Sua and Tana into volunteering, and the two Samoans having a lot of fun at the lads' expense. Then he was distracted by the sight of his father stalking down the quay with six young mariners in tow.

Wiki straightened, and Captain Coffin, looking rather harried, introduced his cadets. Wiki shook hands solemnly with them all. They had solid Salem names like Derby, Cheever, and Follansbee, and, while they immediately set out to impress Wiki with grand tales of Canton and the Pearl River, Macao and Manila, they all looked very young and somewhat overawed.

For a while, he thought they were intimidated by meeting a strongly built brown man with long black hair, as so many *pakeha* were, but then he saw that they cast many flickering looks from Captain Coffin and back to him again, secretly comparing their faces, and Wiki realized that they knew their captain was his father. Because of that, no doubt, they treated him with vast respect, asking him many questions about how and why he had joined the exploring expedition, and what adventures he had experienced before and since, while Captain Coffin listened with an air of relief that time was being wasted like this.

"You're wondering how to fill in your day," Wiki shrewdly guessed when the questions ran to a stop.

They looked at each other, then back at Wiki, and nodded. Usually, the mate found them jobs to do, but today he was in town on business. Captain Coffin had brought them to the *Osprey* in the hope of finding work on the hove-down hull, but the carpenters didn't want them, and so they were at a loose end.

"Ah," said Wiki, with perfect understanding. To his hidden amusement, his father had a hopeful glint in his half-closed eye. "Would you like me to find them something to do?" he asked him.

His father cleared his throat, fought unsuccessfully to hide his mighty relief, and said, "Well, now that you mention it—"

"How would you like to measure a mountain with a barometer?" Wiki inquired of the boys. The cadets looked baffled, but gamely nodded.

"Well," he said. "I have just the thing for you. Not only is there a mountain for you to measure, but I know just the men to lead you to it."

"You young devil," said his father, five minutes later. They were standing together on the quay watching the string of boys carried off by a hugely thankful pair of midshipmen.

"They'll enjoy it," Wiki confidently assured him.

"With two wet-behind-the-ears junior officers in charge, God alone knows what they'll get up to," Captain Coffin grumbled. "I thought you were offering to take care of them yourself."

"I'm far too busy," said Wiki loftily.

"You don't look very busy to me. What does linguisting involve, anyway?"

"It's too complicated to go into now. And I want to ask you some questions."

"In your capacity as sheriff?"

Wiki ignored this. "Have you ever heard of Grimes before?"

"Isn't he the man who was poisoned?"

"I'm glad to see you still have all your faculties, including your memory," Wiki dryly observed, and then said, "I wondered if you've heard Sir Patrick Palgrave mention him."

"Why the devil should he mention that man? He's never met him, has he?"

"Grimes told us that in Cambridge, England, he worked as a gardener and glasshouse designer for a man named Sir Roger Palgrave."

"Good God," said his father, looking extremely startled. "It certainly sounds as if he worked for Sir Patrick's father—but what a coincidence!"

"Not really," said Wiki. "Sir Roger Palgrave paid to have him trained in the science of optical glass, with such impressive results that he was hired by an American astronomer as his assistant—and when the astronomer joined the expedition, it was only natural that he brought Grimes with him."

"It proved fatal for Grimes."

"Perhaps—and perhaps not."

"What do you mean? He died from poisoning, didn't he? It's a fate he would have escaped if he hadn't sailed with the expedition, surely."

"According to the colonial analyst—who, presumably, knows what he is talking about—the strychnine that accidentally got into his medicine wasn't the primary cause of death. Grimes had weak lungs, and so forth—and so I wondered if his health had always been bad."

"I wouldn't have a notion," his father said. "Sir Patrick has certainly never mentioned the man to me. If you're desperate to know, you can ask him tomorrow night."

Wiki said, surprised, "You know I've been invited?"

"Of course. Lieutenant Forsythe and the six scientifics have been invited, too, as well as all the men who have offered to host the survey party."

"So it's going to be a conference? I thought it was a social occasion."

"Is that wrong?" his father demanded, taking exception to something in Wiki's tone of voice that Wiki hadn't intended. "It's obvious that you dislike Sir Patrick Palgrave, but once you get to know him, you'll find that he is a very clever man, extremely artistic. Wait until you see his gardens, and then you will understand what I mean—they're really quite spectacular. A feast is an enjoyable way for the surveying party and their prospective hosts to get acquainted."

"Do you have any idea why he stipulated that I should go on the survey?"

"Consider it an honor," his father said grumpily, without answering. "Just concentrate on making an effort to be pleasant—and don't eat with your fingers, either. I know it's the way you were brought up to eat, but in Brazil it's not considered polite."

Wiki looked away. It was moments like these that he almost wished he used tobacco. Back home in the Bay of Islands, smoking had become all the rage. Everyone had a pipe almost constantly in his or her mouth, down from the most ancient *kuia* to children who could barely walk. Wiki found the smell and taste of tobacco foul, but if he had a pipe right now, he would be able to light it with great concentration, and pretend he hadn't heard.

Lacking one, he tilted his head and studied the clouds swimming in the sky above the two tall masts of the *Swallow*. Then he heard his father add, "And when you talk to Sir Patrick, don't start cross-examining him, either. He won't like the implications at all."

It almost sounded as if his father had told Sir Patrick Palgrave about his letter of authority from the sheriff's department of the Town of Portsmouth, Virginia. Surely not, Wiki thought with a frown.

Then his father distracted him by saying even more irritably, "You should take a damn sight more care when choosing your friends."

Wiki said frostily, "I beg your pardon?"

"He's a crass, ignorant, foulmouthed boor."

It was obvious who he was talking about. Much of the time, Wiki had the same opinion of Forsythe, but nonetheless his silence was chilly. Without even noticing, his father ran on, "And I'm not at all happy about him being in charge of the survey. I don't want Sir Patrick and his friends to be offended or insulted, so I made up my mind to join the group."

Dear God, thought Wiki, this was looking for trouble with a vengeance. The prospect of Forsythe and Captain Coffin trekking through the jungle together was quite horrible.

He couldn't say that, however, so asked, "You will be at Sir Patrick's house tomorrow night?"

"Of course," said his father loftily. "I look forward to seeing you there."

A whole fleet of small boats converged on Praia Grande the night of the feast, because the officers and captains of the discovery expedition had been invited to a grand ball that was staged in rooms just a couple of hundred yards from the Palgrave mansion. George Rochester had declined, taking the chance of a quiet evening without Forsythe charging around, and had sent Constant Keith in his place. Accordingly, the young man was in the boat, dressed up to the nines in his best uniform.

The row across the bay was beautiful. The water was like a sheet of satin, undisturbed by even the slightest breeze. Men's voices echoed back and forth in the cool, soft air, and the drops falling from the blades of the oars glowed with phosphorescence. The landing was rather hard to find, and they milled around uncertainly until an orchestra struck up in the distance, creating a musical beacon. Wiki, stepping out onto the beach, watched Midshipman Keith and the other expedition officers head off toward the ballroom, following the strains through the trees.

Then Forsythe materialized out of the darkness, and together they turned in the other direction, following a gravel driveway into the shadows of an avenue. Their footsteps crunched and then silenced as they left the path and started walking across a soft lawn. The smell of grass rose up to merge with the perfume of night-scented flowers. In the moonlight Wiki could glimpse formal gardens stretching out into the dark distance like the spokes of a wheel, with a fountain in the center. Even in the dimness, it was impressive.

Sir Patrick Palgrave's mansion lay right ahead, a dainty affair surrounded by a colonnaded patio, and with shafts of lights streaming out of many windows. As they neared, Wiki could smell tobacco, wine, and brandy, and hear masculine voices, mostly speaking Portuguese. Through open French doors women could be seen clustered on chairs in a long salon, listening to the strains of a mandolin. To Wiki's surprise, the musician was Madame de Roquefeuille. She was wearing white, and her copper hair was coiled into a bright, unadorned knot in the nape of her bent neck. The varnish of the pear-shaped instrument gleamed, and the long neck of the mandolin was decorated with colorful ribbons.

There seemed to be some sort of separation of the sexes. While the women were gathered in the brightly lit salon, sipping wine, eating tidbits, and gossiping as they listened to the music, the men were on the loggia, clustered in the rectangles of light that fell from inside. A couple of maids progressed from dimness to brightness, passing around trays of drinks and *aperitivo* plates.

In one of the shafts of light, Wiki could see Sir Patrick Palgrave deep in conversation with Dr. Olliver. He stopped to watch them, amused by the contrast they made, one scar-faced and as lean as a greyhound, the other heavily bearded and positively balloonlike in form. Yet, somehow, it was possible to tell that they were both English—because of their erect backs, he supposed, and the way they tucked in their chins. In another illuminated patch, farther along the loggia, Captain Coffin was talking animatedly with Captain Couthouy. As far as he knew, the two Massachusetts shipmasters had never met before, but they had obviously struck up an instant friendship, having so much in common. No doubt, he thought, his father was in full imaginative flight, and telling tall yarns. Then, with a frown, he noticed that Forsythe was heading with intent toward the two men.

Quickly, he set after him, intent on preventing trouble, but as he stepped onto the veranda, a strong hand came out from behind a pillar and grasped his arm.

It was Sir Patrick Palgrave. His smile exposed square, strong teeth, while his protruberant brown eyes gleamed, and Wiki was reminded again of a squirrel, except that he smelled of wine and soap. The Englishman's grip on his elbow was tight, and Wiki had to control himself not to pull his arm away.

Palgrave said, "I hope you didn't mind being drafted for the survey."

"Of course not," replied Wiki, but wondered if his father had told his friend about their conversation. One of the maids progressed toward them, a tray held high, and Wiki stepped to one side so the food would not pass over his head, managing to detach himself from Sir Patrick at the same time. Then the tray was lowered, while the maid smiled prettily at him, and Wiki contemplated an array of little plates. Some were loaded with enticing tidbits, while others were invitingly empty, each fitted out with a little fork.

Very conscious that Sir Patrick was watching, Wiki took over an empty plate, and then helped himself to a small fried rice ball, carefully wriggling it onto his plate with a serving fork. Then, with equal care, he snared it with his own fork, and popped it into his mouth. It was filled with ground meat, and quite delicious. He looked for another, but the maid had moved on.

He finally glanced back at his host, and said, "It will be an adventure."

"That's how I hoped you would feel. Your fluent Portuguese will be a great help."

"But Captain Couthouy speaks good Portuguese—didn't you know?" Wiki watched the bright eyes blink, and said, "He was a shipmaster before he joined the expedition, and a brilliant scholar before that. He went to the Latin school in Boston, he told me."

Palgrave seemed confounded. Then he waved the hand that was not holding a wineglass, and said, "Do you like my garden?"

"It seems quite magnificent."

"You must see it in the daytime. I designed the layout myself."

Wiki hesitated, took a mental gamble, and said, "I suppose you learned a lot from Grimes when he was your father's gardener?"

"Probably—though I disliked him intensely," said Sir Patrick Palgrave, without even a blink of surprise. He paused to drink wine, watching Wiki over the rim of his glass, and then said, just as candidly, "I was only seventeen when I ran off to Montevideo, and old Grimes was one of the prime reasons I went."

"You had that much to do with him?"

"I was always keen on horticulture—what a pity he was such a nasty creature! He could have been like a father to me, considering that we had so much in common. Instead, I remember him chasing after me with a spiky hawthorn stick because I had accidentally knocked the first blossom of the season from a two-year-old magnolia sapling—as if it were a major calamity!"

"I thought he was more of an orchid fancier."

"Why do you say that?"

Sir Patrick's query was sharp. The maid with the tray of food arrived again, and Wiki, deliberately taking his time, concentrated on selecting a little pastry package, fiddling from fork to fork as he got it from one plate to another and then at last into his mouth. It was stuffed with shreds of chicken in a mouthwatering savory sauce.

Swallowing crumbs, he said, "I heard you were an orchid collector."

Sir Patrick laughed, and exchanged his empty glass for a full one as another maid went by. "That's not quite the truth. My first sight of tropical jungle convinced me that all I wanted to do in this life was find new species, and have plants named after me. Accordingly, I wrote home to announce that I was stopping on in Uruguay to become a famous naturalist. My father was a businessman to the bone, so instead of ordering me to come back home he made up his mind to wrest a profit from my rebellion, and decided on orchids."

"Why orchids?"

"There was a craze for orchids in London at the time. My father—Sir Roger—set about the business in a very well organized manner, too, which was quite typical of him. He sent me the wherewithal to pay expenses while I searched the jungle for choice plants, but, unbeknownst to him, I declined to do any of the collecting myself. I simply set up a little trading post in a town on the upper reaches of the Rio de la Plata, posted a notice saying that cash would be paid for orchid plants in good condition, hired an agent to look after the shop, and used the rest of the money to ride south and roam the pampas. I'm a passionate horseman, and once I learned to get along in Spanish the pampas proved irresistible."

"I've ridden the pampas myself," said Wiki reminiscently. A year ago, he and George, having met up in Montevideo, had taken off for a month to ride with the gauchos, an amazing and memorable experience.

"Wonderful, ain't it," Sir Patrick said with enthusiasm, and continued. "When I got back to the post it was to find that enough for a shipment had been collected, and so I carried the plants to England, thus resuming my relationship with the dreadful Grimes, who had been ordered to adapt a barn for their reception. Despite his awful nature, he was a clever fellow, you know—he even invented steam machinery to keep the barn warm and moist inside. Later on, he designed propagation houses entirely made of glass."

The maid with the tray of little edibles came by again, and this time Wiki selected something crunchy and golden. It was quite an art to get it from one plate to another, but when he finally sampled it, he found it to be a deep-fried pork crackling, dusted with salt and spices. It was so good he would have liked another, but the maid had gone, so he said, "The plants thrived?"

"Not only did they thrive, but they made a lot of money. Grimes was still the same miserable, complaining, bullying creature, though. That cough preceded him when I was working, echoing down the aisles of plants like an oncoming ghost. I hear that ghastly hacking cough in my nightmares!"

Wiki had nightmares about Grimes, too. "Was he born with that cough, do you think?"

"I'm sure of it!"

"What were his circumstances? Was he married?"

"Can you imagine any woman marrying that man?" Palgrave demanded, and laughed. "The next time I went home, he wasn't there, thank God. He'd gone to America with a famous astronomer—exactly what my father deserved, having had him taught to grind optical glass! And if my father hadn't been dead by the time I arrived, I would have told him that, too."

"And now Grimes himself is dead," murmured Wiki.

"It was certain that cough would kill him."

"I was there when he died," Wiki said soberly. Again, he remembered Dr. Gilchrist's exclamation: *"This man has been poisoned!"*

"How terrible! Was it awful?"

"I wouldn't wish a death like that on my worst enemy."

There was a pause, during which Wiki became conscious that his host had moved into the shadows, so that it was hard to see his face. Then he said, "Are you enjoying the food?"

"It's delicious."

"I was fortunate enough to be able to borrow Robert Festin from the House of the Ewer."

Wiki was amazed. "Festin! You mean that he's here?"

"In the kitchen, of course—in a supervisory capacity. The whole town was aghast when he was arrested for the so-called murder, so you can imagine the general relief when he was acquitted. Don't you agree that it was lucky for him that Dr. Tweedie confessed?"

"Dr. Tweedie's honesty was quite remarkable."

Palgrave's stare flickered. Then he stepped into the light, and said, "The ladies have been trying to get your attention for quite some time, you know. Come, let me introduce you before we all go in for dinner."

He said it so smoothly that Wiki wondered if he had imagined the expression of cold hatred that had so briefly crossed the shadowed face.

Eighteen

The dining room was as beautiful as everything else about the house. Italian frescoes decorated the walls, and the floors were made of inlaid wood. Apart from the long table and the chairs around it, there was very little furniture, so that the voices of the animated diners echoed up to the ornately plastered ceiling. The French doors to the colonnaded patio and garden were wide open, letting in a balmy breeze, the scent of many blooms, and distant strains of music.

Wiki, toward the head of the table, was seated among strangers who gossiped together, and ate his meal in virtual solitude, so unnoticed that he felt relaxed enough to pluck up the occasional tidbit with his fingers. Then he saw that Madame de Roquefeuille, halfway down the table, was watching him with a secret smile. Her white gown did not suit her pale skin, but she still managed to look bewitching. He wondered which of the men was her husband. When their eyes met, she twinkled mischievously instead of looking away. A creased-up grin got an answering smile. When he winked, she put up a slender hand to hide her giggle—and so the silent conversation went on.

It was little wonder that Madame de Roquefeuille was bored enough to flirt with her eyes, he thought. Like himself, she was being neglected. Lieutenant Forsythe, on her right, wasn't bothering with southern gallantry, having other things on his mind. Dr. Olliver was seated on the Virginian's other side, while Captain Coffin, with Couthouy, Pickering, Dyes, Drayton, and Agate, sat opposite, and it was obvious that Forsythe had grabbed the opportunity to instruct them about the responsibilities of the land-based survey party.

Captain Couthouy, though, was not paying proper attention, as he and Captain Coffin had their heads together as they continued to gossip. Wiki could hear their roars of laughter. This, he also discerned, was beginning to annoy Forsythe, because the southerner snapped something, and both shipmasters glanced at him dismissively before turning away. A quarrel was developing, Wiki thought with great misgiving, but then was distracted by the woman on his left, who was trying to pose a question in rudimentary English.

He turned. She was a pleasant, plump, middle-aged person who looked at him fully in the face, in the frank Brazilian way. Her name—or as much of it as he remembered from the introductions—was Senhora Mercedes. When he greeted her in Portuguese she laughed with relief, and immediately embarked on a lively conversation.

While Wiki appreciatively sampled as much as he could of the gigantic meal that arrived in numerous courses, he heard how desolated the whole port had been when the genius behind this repast—"Maestro Festin himself!"—had mysteriously disappeared—"Stolen by a ship!"—and then returned to the fold in shackles—"An astonishing error of justice!" His acquittal had been achieved by the angels of heaven, truly. What a triumph of Sir Patrick's, to obtain the maestro's services for this banquet! A true compliment to his guests.

Then she said, "I hear you are the son of Captain Coffin."

Wiki admitted it.

"Aha," she said. They all knew Captain Coffin well. "What a rascal, to keep his interesting son such a secret!" Was Wiki really a New Zealand native, as well as American? When he confessed to that, too, she produced many questions about his exotic background that became more personal as she grew bolder, and which Wiki fended off with the expertise of long experience.

At the same time, he ate, selecting judiciously. Side dishes had arrived with various relishes to garnish the meats—sliced fresh oranges, shredded kale sautéed with onion, dressed rice, manioc, eggs that had been fried in garlic—and he sampled them all with great interest.

"That is very hot and spicy," she said, breaking off the interrogation to point at a bowl of harmless-looking sauce that smelled of lemons.

"Obrigada," said Wiki, and took care to avoid it. The next hour passed very pleasantly indeed, except for ominous signs that Lieutenant Forsythe was becoming more irritable by the moment. When he glanced in that direction, he saw Madame de Roquefeuille roll her eyes.

For her, no doubt, the arrival of the little cups of warm chocolate that signaled the end of the banquet came as a relief. Forsythe, too, looked as if he were glad it was over. He was assembling a pile of scrap notes from various places about his person, undoubtedly getting set to lead the discussion when the women left the table, and the men got down to work. Then, just as Lady Palgrave was glancing meaningfully from one of the female guests to another, and was picking up her skirts ready to stand and lead the way out of the room, Senhora Mercedes found another personal question.

In the silence as everyone looked at their hostess, her voice rang out in the echoing room. "Tell me, Senhor Coffin," she said prettily, "why do you wear your hair so long? Is it a custom with your people?"

Wiki, who was halfway out of his chair, sat down again with a sense of entrapment. His thick black hair had been braided for the occasion, knotted at the bottom of the plait and tied with a black bow into the nape of his neck, but he realized now that over the months of voyage it had grown very long.

He saw Forsythe turn to his companions to ask what Senhora Mercedes had said. Then, to his horror, he heard him say, very clearly indeed, "Because there ain't anyone of high enough rank to cut it for him."

Dead silence, as all those who understood English absorbed this, and the rest wondered what he had said. Then the southerner turned to Captain Coffin and said smugly, "You didn't think I knew that, did you."

Senhora Mercedes said, "What did he say?"

Someone translated it for her. She turned back to Wiki, looking very impressed. "You are of very high rank in your society back home?"

The whole room listened for the answer. When Wiki looked helplessly at his father, Captain Coffin was no help at all, merely lifting his glass in an ironic salute, so he prevaricated by saying, "My mother was of high rank—the daughter of a chief, and the granddaughter of one, too."

"And Captain Coffin is a famous Salem shipmaster, so your ranking is high, indeed!" exclaimed Senhora Mercedes with a naïve and sunny smile.

"Well," said Wiki uneasily, glancing at his father again.

"But why do men of high rank have to wear long hair?"

"Most New Zealand men have long hair, whatever their rank," Wiki told her. "The head is *tapu,* the most sacred part of the body, and great attention must be paid to everything to do with it."

He had lost the lady, he saw, because she was looking quite baffled. She frowned, and then ventured, "Sacred—like in church?"

"Not really." Wiki paused, working out how to try to explain. Then he said, "We believe in two states of being—commonplace and special. *Tapu,* being important and dangerous, is the opposite to *noa,* which is commonplace and safe. *Tapu* is a force that governs the whole of Maori life; it affects places and objects, as well as people. For example, cooked food, being *noa,* must never be taken into the *wharehui,* the meetinghouse, which is *tapu.* No one would drink rainwater from the *wharehui* roof, even if he were dying of thirst."

Naturally, apart from the Maori words, he had spoken in Portuguese. Forsythe's voice lifted again, demanding, "What was all that about?" Couthouy answered, but the words were lost, and, thankfully, Forsythe did not produce any intriguing item of information. Then, to Wiki's vast relief, the women took their leave, happily discussing the strange customs of the Pacific as they went.

There was a bustle as the white tablecloth was removed and fresh decanters and wineglasses set out on the bare mahogany, along with bowls of nuts. Then, after Palgrave suggested that they all move to join Lieutenant Forsythe and the scientifics at the middle of the table, Wiki became aware that the southerner, with a consciously dramatic gesture, had set an object on the table in front of his father.

The six scientifics swooped in to inspect it, and the Brazilian men were flocking about, too. Then Wiki was close enough to recognize the object, and stopped dead.

Forsythe demanded of Captain Coffin, "Now do you believe that I lived and fought with Wiki's people?"

"I never disbelieved you," Wiki's father said tiredly.

"Then you know what this is, huh?"

"Of course," Captain Coffin said. "It's a *mere*—a greenstone club."

The greenstone weapon was just eight inches long and three inches at its widest part; its edges, once ground with sand to razor-sharpness, were stained dark, and the spiral carving on the knoblike handle was blurred. It had a presence much greater than its size—that of a *mere pounamu,* the supreme hand weapon and mark of a chief. Wrought with dogged patience from the hardest jade, clubs like this one were given proud names; some, by changing color, were reputed to have the power to foretell the future; some had such great *mana*—prestige—that prisoners of war of high rank requested the honor of being killed by them.

Forsythe said proudly, "I killed the chief what brandished it."

"By shooting him, I suppose," Captain Coffin said, even more wearily.

"Aye—from one hundred ninety yards. Killed him first shot."

"And he was armed with this *mere*, and did not have a gun?"

"Aye." A note of uncertainty had entered Forsythe's voice.

"It hardly seems sportsmanlike."

Forsythe's attitude became aggressively self-defensive. "I was only doing the job I was hired to do, and the warriors with me were firing guns, too! If the tables had been turned, he would have shot me!"

"I believe you, more's the pity," said Captain Coffin. "Damn it," he said softly, and to Wiki's surprise, his eyes glistened with tears.

"Put it away," he said then, more loudly. "You're insulting my son."

"*Me?* Me insult *him*? *How*, for God's sake?"

"Didn't you listen to what he was saying? This club is *tapu*, and you've set it down in a *noa* place, on a table that is used to serve cooked food."

Forsythe looked puzzled. Then he straightened and looked around. It was as if he were suddenly aware of his audience. Dr. Olliver was plucking at his plump lower lip, his eyes bright and alert; as Wiki watched, his hand dropped to stroke his bushy beard. The other scientifics were staring down at the *mere*, blatant greed in their faces. Forsythe noticed that, too, because he pulled it back before anyone could touch.

He looked at Wiki, shoved the club at his chest, and said, "Take it."

Wiki said blankly, "What?"

"Take it. I hadn't realized you set such store by it."

For a long moment, Wiki couldn't move. He clenched his right hand to stop its trembling, but when he slowly held it out the shake was still there.

"It's that important, is it?" Forsythe said, looking embarrassed.

Important? It was *taonga*—treasure. Wiki took it. The stone was warm. When he blinked, tears fell out of his eyes and ran down his cheeks. Incapable of saying a single word, he turned and walked out of the room. Captain Couthouy could do the translating, he thought.

As he descended the shallow veranda steps into the scented garden, Wiki softly sang a *karakia* to restore *tapu* to the *mere*. As always, he didn't know if he had the right words. There were *karakia* for laymen, for children, for priests, and chiefs, and he didn't know one from the other. However, it didn't matter. When the rapid chant was finished, he tucked the *mere* into his belt at the back, where the weapon fitted into the small of his spine as if it had been made for it.

Then, letting his jacket drop, he looked around. Pergolas radiated out from the fountain, their trellised archways leading into moonlit gardens, and the air was soft and cool. He could hear the women chattering in the salon, and the music of a waltz wafted from the ballroom beyond the trees.

The moon was so bright that the shadow of the nearest trellis was black. It wasn't until Madame de Roquefeuille called out his name that he realized that she was perched on a nearby bench. Her gown was as white as the moonlight.

He went over, sat down, and said, "What are you doing here?"

"Ah, they talk about babies," she said, and made a kind of *pshaw* noise. "I'm not interested in that. So I came out for the air."

Her voice was light and breathy, as if she were eternally on the verge of a giggle, and she shifted closer, in the cozy way of Brazilians, so that he could smell her scent and feel her warmth. Her skin was very white, the upper swell of her breasts gleaming faintly.

Wiki was finding it hard to concentrate. He said, "Were Lieutenant Forsythe and my father quarreling at the table? Or was Forsythe just bragging?"

Her white shoulders rose and fell in a shrug. "It was hard to tell. Men are such strange, rough creatures. Too, they spoke English. I suspect the lieutenant considers himself your friend, and your father does not approve at all."

"Good God," said Wiki. She was probably right, he thought, remembering Forsythe's strange loyalty to the men who had crewed the cutter.

"Fathers are like that," she said, and snapped her fingers in an emphatic dismissal of the vagaries of paternal parents. "You waltz, they tell me."

"That I do," Wiki admitted uneasily, wondering how she had heard.

"Listen," she urged.

Wiki listened. He could hear men's voices, and realized that the men had settled down to their conference, because Forsythe's Virginian accent predominated. The orchestra in the distant ballroom had struck up yet another a waltz. Then, close to hand, there was a sudden startling swish of fabric, as Madame de Roquefeuille impatiently stood.

When he looked up into her face she crinkled her eyes at him in her provocative way. Then she held out her hand, and said, "Let's go."

"To the ball?" He laughed. "You're joking, surely."

"I'm serious."

"But what would your husband say?"

"I don't have one," she said, and grabbed his hand and hauled.

Her hand was small, warm, and imperious, but he held back, protesting, "We can't just walk into the ballroom."

"Why not?"

"For a start, we haven't been invited."

"Talk for yourself," she said pertly. "I was most surely invited—why do you think I wear white, and have no jewelry? Because that is the stipulated costume, you see. But my sister insisted that I stay and help entertain my brother-in-law's guests instead of going, which was tedious. Come *on*," she said, and let go his hand, picked up her skirts, and ran off across the lawn.

Obviously, she kept herself in wonderful physical trim, because she was as fleet as a nymph. She was wearing little satin slippers, Wiki noticed as he pursued her. He thought she was giggling, but it was hard to tell, because she was moving so fast. He followed her across the lawn; and under the trees, and then onto the gravel path that wound up to the blazing windows of the ballroom.

Like Sir Patrick Palgrave's place, the building was colonnaded, and the portico was elaborate. When they were within yards of the entrance Madame de Roquefeuille stopped and dropped her skirts, allowing him to catch up with her, and then tucked her hand demurely into the crook of his elbow. They walked sedately up the short flight of steps and into the anteroom, to find several dignified gentlemen chatting over their claret and cigars.

"Madame de Roquefeuille," exclaimed one in a tone of surprise. "An unexpected pleasure! You decided to join us, after all?"

"Just for one waltz," she said, without bothering to introduce Wiki, and with no further ado tugged him into the brightly lit ballroom.

The temperature immediately rocketed, fueled by the heat of what looked like a million candles. The room was huge enough for a thousand to dance. Men gossiped in groups about the fringes, while older women fanned themselves from the clustered chairs where they perched, but most of those present were galloping about the floor in the throes of a hectic Boston waltz.

Everyone, Wiki immediately saw, was wearing white, just as Madame had predicted. He, by contrast, was wearing black. However, he was not the only one to stand out, because Captain Wilkes and the other officers from the expedition were wearing uniform. Wiki glimpsed Midshipman Keith's stunned expression just as Madame de Roquefeuille stepped into his arms.

She was definitely laughing, Wiki decided as he took charge of their revolutions, because he could feel her quivering. Her face, pressed against his upper arm, had gone quite pink. Across the floor and round and round they charged, while Wiki's braid flopped up and down between his shoulders, and Madame's copper hair started to tumble out of her chignon. Her merriment was so infectious he had trouble not to laugh out loud while he swung them both round and round.

"The gossip was true—you really can waltz," she gasped when the music slowed, and she was able to loosen her convulsive grip on his hand. "And very well, too," she added.

"*Gossip* is putting it mildly," he said, intent on keeping on the far side of the crowd from Captain Wilkes. "Are you sure you don't have a husband?"

"I'm a widow."

"Oh," he said, thinking he should have guessed, and added, "I'm sorry."

"I am sorry, too. He was rich and generous. I liked him."

"A lot?"

"Definitely too much to let any other man take his place," she said.

Wiki thought about her widowhood as they revolved in intimate circles, meditating, too, on how young and lithe and alive she felt—far too young to be a widow, though it was patently obvious that she managed to enjoy herself. She was the perfect height to fit against his shoulder as they slowly circled, their bodies close together. He could feel her every breath, and smell her warm scent.

Forcing himself to think about her dead husband, Wiki asked, "He was French?"

"His father was French, but he—Pierre—was as Brazilian as the rest of us. Unfortunately, he was a very keen horseman."

"He died while riding?"

"With Sir Patrick, yes. They were playing a Persian game that Pierre's father learned in India—it is called polo. The players ride round and round on fast horses, chasing a wooden ball with clubs called mallets, which they toss from hand to hand with astounding skill. When Pierre fell he was accidentally hit with a mallet on the head. It was very sudden and sad, but he died doing what he liked most."

She let go his hand to make a casual, flyaway gesture, and as if at a signal, the orchestra stopped. "Let's go," she said abruptly. "Come, quick, before the captain who is staring this way arrives with difficult questions."

Wiki was more than willing. There was a door open nearby, and he briskly followed her through it. The night was cool, and the stars twinkled in their multitudes. He pursued the sound of her giggles down the path, then onto the lawn, and at last the bright windows of the ballroom were hidden behind the trees. Sir Patrick's perfumed gardens enfolded them. Voices still drifted out from the long, lit windows of his house. It was as if they had never been away.

Instead of going back to the bench where she had been seated when Wiki had found her, Madame de Roquefeuille dropped to the grass on a slope that overlooked a bed of roses. Though the flowers were lost in the dark, Wiki could smell their heady scent as he took off his jacket and spread it on the ground. "Sit on this," he said. "You'll get grass stains on your dress."

"And ruin my reputation?"

"I was thinking about *my* reputation."

She laughed again, and shifted to sit on the coat. Then she saw the *mere* tucked into the back of his belt, and said, "What's that?"

He showed it to her, and sat down on the grass with the *mere* in his hands, and told her about it.

She listened carefully. "And the lieutenant gave it to you—just like that?"

"He—at long last, he understood its importance. He doesn't know as much about my people as he thinks he does," Wiki added.

"So what are you going to do with it?"

"I must return it to its rightful owners."

"But won't that be very dangerous?"

"I'll have to talk very fast," he agreed.

She was silent a long moment, and then looked sideways at him with her characteristic twinkle, and said, "You won't let me hold it, I suppose."

"Why do you say that?"

"Because I am certain that women are commonplace—*noa*."

He was startled by her astuteness. "How did you guess?"

"Because I am very sure that men are *tapu*."

He laughed, and shook his head, but confessed, "You're right."

"And you have priests to make sure that men and women not only know their rightful places, but keep them, too. What do you call them, the priests?"

"Tohunga."

"And these men, the *tohunga*, what would they say about a man who laid his *tapu* head in a woman's *noa* lap?"

He was surprised into another laugh. "I don't like to even think about it."

"Well, I dare you to do it." Her expression was full of mischief. "There are no *tohunga* here, you know."

It was a completely irresistible challenge. Without another word, Wiki swung around, and then lay down with his head in her lap. Then he wriggled and eased himself into a comfortable position. She was too slender to make a good pillow, but it was very pleasant to recline there on the cool grass, his long legs crossed at the ankle, and the *mere* a smooth weight on his chest, held with both loose hands. He turned his face into the cradle of her abdomen and closed his eyes and breathed in, enfolded in her scent.

She said, sounding insulted, "Are you going to sleep?"

"M'm," he said.

Then he felt her hands in his hair, playing with the loose strands, tugging at the ribbon and the braid. He opened his eyes, and ordered, "Stop that."

"Because it is forbidden?"

"Because it takes a devil of a time to get it tidy again."

"Tell the truth," she said. "You didn't braid it yourself."

"How did you guess?"

"Because a woman can always tell. So who was it who fixed your hair?"

"Sua. He's Samoan. One of my shipmates."

"Is he of high rank?"

"At home, he is of very high rank, indeed. At sea, he is just a seaman."

"Would you let me braid your hair?"

Of course he would; at that moment Wiki would have gladly allowed her any liberty with his body that she wanted. Instead of answering, though, he joked, "But I don't even know your name."

"Manuela Josefa Ramalho Vieira de Castro de Roquefeuille." Then she added demurely, "You may call me Josefa."

He sat up with a jerk, and swung round to stare at her, only dimly hearing the noise of the party breaking up as people started to take their leave.

He said, "Vieira de Castro was your father's name?"

"It's a very common name," she said, rather defensively.

"So the coroner is related to you?"

"A distant cousin."

"My God," said Wiki, and stared at her very speculatively, indeed.

Nineteen

By first light next day, on board the *Swallow* all preparations were being made to sail. Having been warped out from the dock the afternoon before, she was moored in the stream, ready for the anchor to be raised. The two artists, Drayton and Agate, were on board, as were Pickering, and Dyes, Captain Coffin and Lieutenant Forsythe. However, Dr. Olliver and Captain Couthouy were conspicuous by their absence, not having come off from Enxados Island.

Finally, a boat was lowered, and Wiki was sent in it with instructions to hurry them up. It was a perfectly calm morning, the surface of the water glossed with low shafts of early sun. As the boat drew up to the stairs, the first ripples disturbed the serenity—the offshore breeze was arriving, Wiki saw, and knew that George would be chafing at the bit. To his relief, three men were waiting on the strand. However, while Couthouy was one of them, and the other two were surgeons, neither of the surgeons was Dr. Olliver. Instead, Wiki recognized Dr. Gilchrist, and quickly found that the other was Dr. Guillou, assistant surgeon on the *Porpoise*. Interest stirred immediately, and all at once he hoped the wind would be slow to rise.

Captain Couthouy, by contrast, had the fire of sharp impatience in his eye. "Goddamn the man," he growled when Wiki inquired about Olliver. "He keeps on remembering another bit of dunnage he reckons he can't manage without—and you know how silently he moves. He's gone before I can grab him. Believe it or not, the last time I tracked him down, he was indulging in idle conversation with a marine about home remedies back in Maine, for God's sake! And the marine was advising him that a sore throat could be cured by wrapping a dirty sock about the neck! Does the man have no sense of time at all?"

"He always turned up in good time for dinner," said Wiki with a grin.

He sent Captain Couthouy off in the boat with instructions to the boat's crew to return as soon as he had been loaded onto the brig. As it rowed off, the two doctors turned to walk away, but Wiki quickly stepped in front of them.

"I'd be obliged if you'd answer a couple of questions," he said.

Dr. Gilchrist hesitated, and then said, "In your capacity as sheriff?"

"Aye," said Wiki, and hoped that he wouldn't be asked to produce his letter of authority, because it was back in his chest on the *Swallow*.

"Questions about Grimes?"

Wiki nodded.

"But the case is over," Gilchrist reminded him. "You were one of those under suspicion—you should be relieved, so why are you pursuing the matter?"

Ignoring this, Wiki said, "The coroner—Dr. Vieira de Castro—said something about tetanic convulsions. Did he mean lockjaw?"

"He did—but the similarities between tetanus and the convulsive attack that carried off Grimes are only superficial. If Dr. Vieira de Castro had been there at the time, he would not have entertained the theory for very long at all."

"I wondered if Grimes could have been infected with lockjaw while he was still on board the *Porpoise*—I've heard that it can remain dormant for a number of weeks," Wiki suggested, and both surgeons interrupted at once, Dr. Guillou declaring righteously, "He didn't come to me with any open wounds," and Dr. Gilchrist snapping, "I would have picked it up during my first examination of the patient, I assure you!"

Wiki looked at Dr. Guillou. "His state of health on board the *Porpoise* didn't give you any concern?"

"He had a very severe cough, certainly, but he had an equally violent dislike of doctors," Guillou said dryly. "I couldn't persuade him to let me offer a word of advice, let alone give permission to examine him."

"But you were surprised when you heard that he'd died?"

"You're putting words into my mouth, young man. Doctors can only do their best; Providence is the ultimate decider."

"Exactly," said Dr. Gilchrist, and nodded pontifically.

"But weren't you surprised when he expired so suddenly and violently?" said Wiki, remembering this man's exclamation when he had first seen Grimes convulsing: *"This man has been poisoned!"*

"How was I to know that the bromide—a perfectly apt and sensible prescription—was polluted with strychnine?"

"But not enough strychnine to kill him," Wiki reminded him.

Dr. Gilchrist cleared his throat instead of answering, and then said gruffly, "The case has been heard, and the case has been dismissed, Mr. Coffin. Face it, young man, there's no case for you to investigate."

Wiki said doggedly, "I was reliably informed that strychnine is a cumulative poison, so, logically, if he had taken that medicine long enough on a daily basis, even that small amount would have killed him."

"Who told you that?" Dr. Guillou demanded.

Wiki said reluctantly, "Dr. Tweedie." And, with that, the question he had forgotten to ask the apothecary jumped back into his mind. "How long does it take for a man to die from strychnine poisoning?" he asked, and thought how stupid he had been not to think of this question back then, because it was the obvious follow-up to the revelation that it took a rat a week to succumb.

There was a long pause, and Wiki noticed that the two surgeons carefully refrained from looking at each other. Instead, they contemplated the path, rocking back and forth on their heels, and he began to form the indelible impression that they did not have a notion of the answer.

"It depends on the size of the dose," Dr. Guillou said at last.

"And the state of the patient's health," added Dr. Gilchrist.

"Strychnine poisoning is very rare," pronounced a third voice. They all looked up, startled, to find that Dr. Olliver had joined the group in his usual silent fashion. When he encountered Wiki's inquiring gaze, the fat surgeon smiled blandly, and Wiki wondered how long he had been there.

"Mr. Grimes did not display symptoms of any kind of poisoning at all when Dr. Olliver first consulted me," said Dr. Gilchrist very firmly. "Except for the diarrhea, of course," he added. "Which could have been caused by anything that he had consumed in the previous ten hours—anything whatsoever."

And with that, the two ships' surgeons nodded with an air of finality, and walked away, leaving Wiki alone with Dr. Olliver.

The boat arrived, and after Dr. Olliver and his dunnage had been loaded, it was rowed briskly back to the brig. Wiki shoved Dr. Olliver up the side, then clambered up himself, onto a bustling deck where six seamen were already at their places at the windlass.

"Heave away!" cried Captain Rochester with an air of relief, and the windlass clacked around as the seaman heaved down on the handles. Inch by inch, the brig worked up to the anchor chain, which rattled up through the water until the last links were straight up and down. "Anchor a-peak—anchor a-trip," called a man from the foredeck, and: "Avast the heaving!" shouted Captain Rochester. "Lay aloft and loose sail!"

Men swiftly sidled along the yards, whipping off gaskets, working on earrings and buntlines as the men on deck tailed onto sheets and halyards. "Heave!" cried the boatswain, and yards creaked and squealed as they rose.

Wiki, at the helm, watched the *Swallow* put on her wings. When all light sails save jibs were set, and the brig was held back only by the taut, short anchor chain, he heard the loud command, "Man the windlass!" Clack went the handles, and slowly, but surely, the *Swallow* began to gather way, plucking up her anchor as she went.

On the top of the hill of Enxados Island a few men cheered, and signals lifted on the flagstaff at the boat stairs, wishing the brig a profitable voyage and a safe return. Wiki kicked off his boots so that he could feel the sway of the deck beneath his bare feet. Then he tested the helm, watching the spread sails progress across the scud of the sky, and listening to the silky rush of the current against the coppered hull. They were off, he thought—at last they had sailed, complete with their cargo of scientifics and their equipment.

They were soon to get rid of them, too—at the Praia Grande beach, where Sir Patrick Palgrave was waiting impatiently on horseback, along with a string of horses and mules and a dozen retainers. He was a fine figure, straight-backed and elegant, his blunt-featured face so haughty with annoyance that he looked loftily patrician. There were some pointed remarks passed about unwarranted tardiness, during which everyone looked at Dr. Olliver, and the plump naturalist looked surprised that anyone should care about the passing of time when so much of the day still lay ahead. After that, the mules were meticulously loaded by sweating sailors and servants, while the scientifics shrilly supervised, and the sun became increasingly hot.

When it was finally all organized, another problem arose, because

Dr. Olliver proved to be so inept on a horse. First, he had to be bodily hoisted into the saddle, and then he sat like an unyielding sack of wheat. His steed immediately realized that this was no master, and disliked the massive weight of its rider as well, so it impudently cavorted in frisky circles while the surgeon wobbled dangerously from side to side. He was hastily taken down, and put on board a huge, meaty mule, which looked annoyed but did consent to walk after a lot of persuasion and prodding.

At long last Wiki watched the procession trail off across the sloping meadows toward the woods. When the party had disappeared into the forest he and the sailors, hugely relieved, rowed back to the brig. Again the sails were set, and again the anchor was raised, and, with Wiki at the helm, the *Swallow* coasted out of the harbor on the breath of the balmy wind.

They passed between the two sentinel ports with a dip of the flag, and then steered due east, coasting along under short sail, and hugging the shore. The colors were intense, the bright sun striking gold off the cerulean of the sea, while beyond the beaches the forested hills rose rhythmically against a lapis lazuli sky in shades of dark green, interspersed with the glossy emerald of the occasional banana plantation. Once, Wiki saw the sublime white of an ancient convent on the top of a hill. Every now and then the scientific party could be glimpsed by anyone who wielded a spyglass. Inevitably, however, the brig drew ahead.

The assigned meeting place was Ithocaia, just twelve miles from Praia Grande, and though the brig had much farther to sail, having to negotiate the harbor mouth, it did not take long to get there. After a short search for good holding ground, George dropped anchor in a secluded bay at five bells in the afternoon watch, when the sun was still very high.

It was siesta, and far too early to go on shore, so Wiki lingered on the quarterdeck, leaning on the rail under the shade of an awning. The sand was blinding white, and he could hear the rhythmic thud of surf. A road ran parallel to the beach, branching off into a path that led through trees to an ancient-looking building on a hillock, painted white, with a row of blue-shuttered windows, and a solid stone bastion at one end. This, Wiki knew, was the fazenda where the scientifics were scheduled to stay the night, but there was no movement on the road, not even when the shadows grew long.

Wiki gave up waiting, and asked for a boat to be lowered to take him to shore. The sand was still burning hot when he waded onto the beach, so he hopped about, putting on his boots, and by the time he looked up again, the boat was well on the way back to the brig. Turning, he found a well-kept walkway leading up the slope through filmy trees. Immediately below the building, it became a wide granite stairway with shallow steps, and at the top of this he passed through a gateway in one of the walls, and found himself in a courtyard.

With wonderful timing, the owner of this establishment rode into the courtyard at the same moment that Wiki walked up to the house, and his wife appeared at the door. They made Wiki very welcome, and expressed great pleasure at the prospect of entertaining the scientifics and their escorts for the night. Then, they sat at a big refectory table and nibbled at snacks, made polite conversation, and waited. The sun set without the appearance of the party. At midnight, when the huge meal was finally served, Wiki was the only guest, and when he was ushered to the capacious guest quarters, he had them all to himself.

At ten the next morning dust puffed at the far end of the road, and gradually specks resolved into men, mules, and horses. Dr. Olliver smiled benignly from the shade of his large straw hat as he swayed from side to side on his huge mule, which was being hassled along by Lieutenant Forsythe, who was very obviously in a foul temper. The other five scientifics looked tired and frustrated, and Sir Patrick Palgrave was very tight-lipped. As Captain Coffin communicated to Wiki in an infuriated undertone, Dr. Olliver had vanished into the jungle not once, but three times, retarding the party so greatly that they had been forced to spend the night at a miserable little *venda*. Then, despite instructions from both Sir Patrick and Forsythe to turn out bright and early this morning, Dr. Olliver had not only risen late, but had delayed them still further by engaging in a long argument with the proprietor of the *venda*—quite ignoring the fact that the innkeeper did not understand a word of English.

Dr. Olliver couldn't see what all the fuss was about. Instead of deigning to notice that everyone else was maddened by his complete lack of consideration for others, he rhapsodized to Wiki about the forests—and the insects!—and the frogs, lizards, snakes, and monkeys!—quite unaware that Couthouy, Drayton, Agate, Pickering, and Dyes had been equally entranced with the abundance of plant and animal life, but had been forced to stand around waiting for him, instead of investigating these wonders. Dr. Olliver's unfortunate fellow scientifics had done hardly any collecting—but, as Wiki saw with alarm when the mules were unloaded, Dr. Olliver had not just fallen in love with the riotous plants, but had gathered twigs, seeds, and blossoms from them all.

Captain Wilkes's reaction if even a fraction of this were transported back to the flagship was quite predictable—and Wiki felt sure that George Rochester would refuse to take it all on board the brig, anyway. Going out of earshot of Dr. Olliver, he asked Drayton and Agate, who were good, obliging fellows, to draw the specimens as soon as they had finished breakfast, and suggested to Forsythe that they should be discarded as soon as they were sketched.

Then, belatedly, he saw that Sir Patrick was trying to get his attention. The scarred Englishman was standing by his horse, with the reins in his hand. "The party will stop here tonight," he said curtly. "I'm going on ahead to tell the rest that from now on they'll be twenty-four hours later than scheduled." Without waiting for an answer, he sprang into the saddle and rode off, his horse's hooves clattering as he cantered down the flight of shallow steps.

Wiki walked to the beach, put up a signal for a boat, boarded the brig, and told Rochester about the twenty-four-hour delay. "Well, at least it means we have a day at leisure, old chap," said George placidly.

Consequently, when Captain Coffin walked down the strand and hailed the *Swallow*, he had to wait a while for anyone to notice, because Wiki and George were loafing in the captain's cabin. Rochester was slouched in the wooden armchair at his chart desk, his bare feet waving in the breeze that wafted in the open sternlights, while Wiki lay stretched out on the sofa, with a mug of coffee propped between his hands on his chest. Midshipman Keith, who was the only officer on deck, was the one who eventually sent a boat for the visitor.

As Captain Coffin came into the cabin, the folio of completed drawings under his arm, both Wiki and George straightened up guiltily. Wiki moved along to make space on the settee, and, while his father told them about Dr. Olliver's screams and protestations as Forsythe had obdurately discarded the specimens, he sorted through the sketches. He was entranced, and wished he had watched the draftsmen creating these miraculous things. Orchids and insects, exquisitely detailed, seemed to leap off the pages.

As he admired them, he listened to his father and George exchange yarns. George reminisced about his dog days as a junior midshipman, and his father told tall tales about his adventures as a privateersman in the war for free trade and sailors' rights, when the *Osprey* was very new. The atmosphere was very companionable, he thought, and marveled yet again at the warm friendship his friend and his father had struck up so quickly. In fact, he felt quite neglected. However, when shadows became long, and Sua and Tana sent a message down into the cabin inquiring if Wiki wanted to lower a boat and go fishing, Captain Coffin asked if he could come, too.

The fish were biting well, and after returning the first one caught as a tribute to the ancestor guardian of the sea, they made a great haul. For the first half hour, Wiki thought his father was enjoying himself, but then he noticed his withdrawn expression as he listened to the two islanders chatting in their own language. Wiki had been translating for his father's benefit, but got so little response that he stopped trying, giving himself over to the fishing and good companionship instead.

Dusk loomed, and after leaving enough fish for a good mess for all hands, Wiki and the two Samoans accompanied his father to the fazenda, carrying the rest of the haul as a contribution toward the party's supper. They found the six scientifics sitting around the big table. Dr. Olliver, by some magic, had his decanter with him, and lifted his wineglass, saying with a jocular air, "What a pity Robert Festin isn't one of our number, so we know who to blame if that fish gives us all the squits!"

Wiki winced, and Olliver himself was the only one who laughed. "What was that about?" his father demanded, as he kept Wiki company on the walk back to the beach.

Wiki told him about Festin, the fish, and Grimes.

"Grimes got the gripes, and blamed it on Festin's fried fish?"

"He also blamed me for bringing the fish on board, and the steward for carrying the fried fish to the cabin—even though it made no one else sick."

"So, what *did* give him the diarrhea?"

Wiki frowned. He hadn't given this enough thought, he realized. "Forsythe reckons the steward sprinkled a dose of salts on the top two fish—the ones Grimes took, as he was the first to be served."

"But the steward had no idea who would take the top two fish—so why would he do it?"

Wiki didn't want to go into the strange processes of Forsythe's logic, so he merely said, "Just to make trouble, I suppose."

"Forsythe's a fool," said Captain Coffin. Though not, Wiki noticed, with quite the same contempt that had been in his voice when he had talked about Forsythe before. Evidently, the day of shared trials had made a difference.

"But *something* upset Grimes's stomach," he went on. "So what else could it be?"

Wiki said slowly, "Dr. Guillou said that Grimes was in his usual state of health when he left the *Porpoise*, and Dr. Gilchrist said that whatever gave him the diarrhea had to be eaten within the past ten hours, which means it was something he ate on the *Vincennes*—so it must have been the pudding."

"Pudding?"

"Festin made a special pudding for him, one that no one else was given."

However, Wiki thought, that wasn't logical, either, because Festin's obvious—and very naïve—motive had been bribery, pure and simple. It was impossible to believe that he would deliberately make the instrumentmaker sick. If it was something in the pudding, it must have been there by accident.

His father was scratching one ear, deep in thought as he watched the two Samoans stride with stalwart dignity ahead of them.

"Festin's cookery is thought of very highly around here," he observed.

"So I gathered," said Wiki dryly.

"Maybe it wasn't the food. What did Grimes have to drink?"

Wiki paused, abruptly remembering that just before Grimes had died, Jack Winter had been most insistent that not only had he not touched the wine that belonged to Dr. Olliver, but that he'd given none to Grimes. Now Wiki wondered if Jack Winter had been hinting that there was something wrong with the wine. Dr. Olliver—just like today—had never shared the wine with anyone, but on that particular evening, Wiki remembered, Forsythe had helped himself liberally, and had suffered no ill effects. But had Grimes drunk something else? He resolved to ask the steward about it, after getting back to Rio.

"Well," said Captain Coffin, getting tired of the long silence. "I'll see you tomorrow afternoon." The next rendezvous was at Lagoa Maricá, which should be no more than a five-hour trek away—if all went well. Which depended very much on Dr. Olliver, Wiki thought with great misgivings.

Twenty

To the great satisfaction of all on board the brig, the sun was only barely above the horizon when they watched the scientific party trail out onto the road and gradually disappear. As soon as the morning breeze rose, the *Swallow* put on her sails, and followed them, wafting gently along a coast that was becoming a great deal more barren, and rimmed with loud surf. Though they were taking observations and sounding the bottom at regular intervals while George marked up his charts, it didn't take long at all to reach their goal.

Another safe cove was found, the anchor dropped, and Wiki contemplated a new scene from under the re-rigged awning. In the middle distance, within thin groves of filmy trees and clumps of palms, he could see a broad patch of shimmering light—a marsh that exploded with spectacular birdlife. Cranes and egrets swarmed and swooped, while, in the distance, granite hills marched across the sky. Nearer, the house where the scientifics would stay for the night hunched close to the arid, cactus-studded ground under its heavy terra-cotta roof. Cattle grazed in the scanty shade of stubby trees, but if they lowed it was impossible to hear them. Wiki's ears were filled with the rush and thunder of surf.

It was only just past noon when he glimpsed the scientifics in the distance, and hastily asked for a boat. Getting through the surf was exciting, but then the bottom bumped on grit, and Wiki jumped out and waded through the waves. After putting on his boots, he headed up the beach, finding to his surprise that the miserable-looking trees smelled very sweet. On investigation, he found that most of what he had thought of as their foliage was a kind of parasitic orchid which was richly perfumed, and he wondered if they were the kind that Sir Patrick collected.

He walked on, while the cattle looked at him curiously and he wondered what they ate. The fazenda proved to be a sprawling complex focused on one main house, a big place built of thick upright posts with plaster in between, the wood of the pillars cracked and pale. The front of the building was open, and the massive tiled roof extended over it for some distance, creating an outdoor place for eating. In a corner of the courtyard a spit with a whole dressed sheep was turning over a low fire. As if drawn by the good aroma, the scientific party arrived, just as their host, a good-looking older man by the name of de Silviera, appeared at the door.

Forsythe was looking grimly pleased with himself, while the six scientifics were very subdued. Then Captain Coffin revealed to Wiki that a man on a horse had been glimpsed lying in wait in a thicket beside the trail—a bandit, obviously, because he had shot at them. Luckily, he had been too impatient to hold his fire until they had come within range. Forsythe and Couthouy had galloped toward him, firing their own guns, and the horseman had fled through the trees.

Senhor de Silviera was very concerned when he heard about it, as it sounded very much as if the armed man had been a lookout for a gang. "They're cimarrons," he said. "Runaway slaves."

After they had first escaped, these cimarrons established a settlement of thatched huts high in the hills, and scratched a quiet living from the soil. Then, however, the village had been stormed by a contingent of Brazilian soldiers. The troopers had recaptured everyone they had found, save for one woman who had thrown herself off a cliff rather than be enslaved again. Those of the young men who had been out hunting had escaped, and were now living in the wilderness, and preying on passing travelers.

"They're desperate men," their host gravely concluded. "Thank God you had the lieutenant to protect you."

So this, Wiki mused, was why Dr. Olliver had obeyed orders, for once, and kept with the party. Then, however, he learned another reason—that the trail had led through marshes and lagoons, with no dense jungle to conceal him. There had been plenty of specimens to gather, however. The insect life had been abundant, there had been frogs and exotic birds aplenty, and there had been many foreign flowers in the reeds, as well as the scented orchids in the trees.

While he was willing to carry the boxes of insects to the brig, Wiki again directed the two draftsmen to apply themselves to their sketchpads, and asked Assistant Taxidermist Dyes to skin the animals, so that Forsythe could discard their bulky innards. This time, however, he stayed, first to watch, and then to assist. As he discovered the fascinating logic behind the recording of plants—that the pattern of leaves was repeated forever, that the number of petals was always a multiple of the sepals, to the tune of one, or five, or three—he became absorbed in helping, by cutting sections of buds, and tearing calyxes neatly apart. There was a regularity and symmetry within flowers that was remarkably satisfying, he found.

When he looked up once, he found his father studying him with an odd little smile, the lizard eye more than usually half-closed. After

Wiki left Forsythe to deal with the hysterically angry scientifics, Captain Coffin kept him company on the walk to the beach.

After a meditative silence, he said, "You remind me of yourself as a child—so eager to learn, and so quick about it."

Wiki laughed. "You Americans are endlessly amazing—you weigh the world with clocks and telescopes, measure mountains with barometers, and make patterns out of plants. How could I not be intrigued?"

His father didn't smile back. "*You* Americans?" he echoed. Then he was silent for a long time, his expression grim as they walked down the grass slope to the sand. Finally, he said flatly, "So, even after all these years, you still don't think of yourself as American."

Wiki shrugged. "It doesn't help that I don't *look* American," he pointed out. "People take one glance and assume I'm a South Seas savage, and then marvel because I've assumed the trappings of civilization."

Captain Coffin flushed. "But you *are* American—an extremely well educated and cultured American! And you're no darker than most Brazilians! You talk about *trappings* of civilization? Dear God, Wiki, you're more civilized than most Americans I know—you speak several European languages with ease; you talk philosophy and politics! Don't get me wrong," he went on in a more moderate tone, "I think your mother's people are wonderful—they are gallant, brave, intelligent, and good-looking, but their culture is outdated and dying, and if they are to become part of the future, they will have to change. That is what *you* have done—*you* have adapted quite magnificently. I'm proud of what you have accomplished, Wiki—very proud—so why can't you accept that when I carried you home from the Bay of Islands you left your Maori past behind?"

Wiki was quiet, thinking this over. "Come on board the *Swallow* so I can show you something," he finally said.

The boat from the brig arrived, and after stowing the boxes of insects, they clambered into it. As soon as they were on board, Wiki led the way aft. Opening the companionway door, he stepped down to the top stair, and then turned around. The wall above the door was broad enough to store a few weapons, out of sight and yet easily reached from both the saloon or the deck. There, George hung his sword, a few cutlasses, and his pistol, and below them, immediately above the lintel, a spearlike weapon lay on a couple of hooks.

Wiki lifted it down, and carried it outside. After motioning to his father to get out of the way, he whirled it around his shoulders, swinging it from hand to hand, and closing and unclosing his fists as its balance shifted. *"Ko te rakau na Hapai,"* he sang, while the weapon hummed through the air;

Ko te rakau na Toa
Ko te rakau na Tu, Tu-ka-riti, Tu-ka-nguha.
This is the weapon of the Ancestors,
This is the weapon of the Warriors,
This is the weapon of Tu, furious Tu, raging Tu.

Then, with a flourish, he handed it to his father.

"Good God," Captain Coffin said. "It's a—a—"

"A *taiaha,*" said Wiki, tired of waiting for him to find the long-forgotten word. The shaft of the four-foot-long *taiaha* was highly polished by constant contact with his hands. One end, teardrop in shape, was elaborately carved into a stylized head with a protruding tongue, while the other—the *rau,* the business part of the weapon—was shaped like a paddle, and hardened by smoking and heating to the smoothness of a hatchet.

"I made it myself," Wiki said.

"It's—quite magnificent," his father said, sounding awed. He turned it in his hands, and then spun it about his head a couple of times before examining it again. The teardrop-shaped head, the *arero,* had been intricately engraved with curves and whorls. A sennit collar had been twisted about its neck, and into this Wiki had braided feathers, along with long tufts of his own black hair, to distract the enemy by being flicked across his eyes. This spearlike end was for jabbing and feinting, while the other end, the *rau,* was used as a club.

"But I have indeed adapted, and I'll tell you something to prove it," said Wiki, taking the *taiaha* back. "While I was making this, I kept it in the galley, on hooks over the stove."

Captain Coffin's lizard eye closed even further. As usual, his quick intelligence caught on fast. He said, "Where food was being cooked? But wasn't that defying the law of *tapu?*"

"My reasons were practical—the smoke from the fire did a capital job of hardening the wood. Even if I had remembered that I was breaking the code, seasoning the wood seemed more important."

At the time, too, Wiki had believed that making the *taiaha* was just an interesting and challenging project, a harking back to his roots. Then, he had been forced to use it in self-defense, and in the heat of the battle the force of Tumatauenga, the ancestor guardian of war, had flooded into the weapon. He had *felt* it—he had felt the wood *sing* as it absorbed the savage power. Because of *Tu, Tu-ka-riti, Tu-ka-nguha,* his life had been saved, and abruptly his *taiaha* had become *tapu.*

Wiki was reluctant to tell his father about that, fearing he would be derisive, so he said, "Now, I store it over the stairs that lead to the saloon—so that it is under the roof of the place where we eat. However, I have very little choice. George would let me put it in his cabin, but he entertains guests there, which involves eating, too. When I live on board, I share a stateroom with Constant Keith, who eats day and night, I swear—he keeps biscuits beneath his pillow! The *tohunga,*" he said wryly, "don't have to grapple with the limitations of life at sea. In fact, I wonder how the people coped during the long migrations across the Pacific."

His father asked curiously, "What have you done with the *mere* that Forsythe gave you?"

Wiki shrugged. "I braided a string for it, and it hangs on a hook by the *taiaha.*"

"I would have thought you'd keep it in your sea chest."

His father was thinking like a seaman, Wiki knew, because a sailor's chest was his special private storage place, and therefore considered inviolate by his shipmates. He shook his head, and said, "It's much safer where we can see it from the table. *Pakeha* don't think of *mere* and *taiaha* as weapons, you know, as they're so obviously outclassed by knives and guns. Instead, they call them 'curiosities,' and consider them valuable in terms of money, not *mana*. I've seen shipmasters bear them in triumph back to the States, where they sell them at an immense profit—and scientifics are even worse, because they so greatly benefit their careers by donating them to museums. No, there are too many opportunistic thieves who know the value of such things."

Captain Coffin was quiet a moment, and Wiki wondered if he had traded in curiosities himself. Then he looked out at the darkening land, and said with a sigh, "I must go. Someone is bound to be doing or saying something to offend our hosts."

"Forsythe is giving you trouble?"

"I had Olliver in mind. He'll be screaming for his dinner—which, as he knows perfectly well, won't be served until ten. Then, when it does come, he'll complain about the barbaric hours that Brazilians keep, right in front of our hosts, who understand more English than he thinks."

"Well, thank the Lord that he seems to have seen sense about getting up early and keeping with the party—and long may it continue," said Wiki.

Twenty-one

For the next forty-eight hours it looked as if Wiki's wish would be granted. While the brig ghosted gently north, charting shoals and rocks on the way, the party trekked through a maze of lagoons and marshes to Mandetiba, where the fazenda was a twin of the one they had left behind at Maricá, and then fifteen miles through dunes to the next stopping place, near Ingetado. After that, however, the trail led inland. Not only did lush forests beckon, but from now on the brig would have to sail up uncharted rivers to keep in contact with the scientifics.

George Rochester ordered the anchor weighed before dawn on the day they left the cove by Ingetado, because the challenge of doubling Cape Frio lay ahead. Link by clattering link, the anchor chain writhed up the hawse pipe, and then, "Brace the yards, there!" Midshipman Keith cried. Luminous canvas slapped hollowly as it dropped, and then was swiftly sheeted home. The *Swallow* heeled slowly as she took the damp, dark breeze, and nosed gently out to the open sea.

Soon she began to pitch uncomfortably, but George held her on to the easterly course, because he wanted to get a safe offing. As the sun rose, the great bulge of Cape Frio loomed. This was where the *Vincennes* had been becalmed, back when Grimes had still been alive, but now, there was a wind, and a fair one, too. The brig sailed sweetly on, leaving the cape astern, and then George ordered a change of course, to bring her closer to the coast. A half hour later, they started to search for their next anchoring place, the San João River.

Clouds had descended. The landscape was flat, and heavy with mist-shrouded trees, and the hot, damp atmosphere clung to the skin. Thick vapor drifted up from the surface of the water, and an amazingly evocative smell surged out from the land, of leaves and flowers, rampant growth and equally speedy decay, and incredibly fecund earth. Water ran on every visible surface, so that the lookouts didn't recognize the river until the brig was actually crossing its mouth.

Sua, setting the foremast to creaking and swaying, waved and hollered, and Tana was sent out into the chains with a lead line. George hesitated, going aloft to study the prospect minutely through his spyglass, and then, when the tide turned, he came down and gave orders to sail cautiously upriver, sounding the bottom all the way.

It was a nerve-racking business. The dense trees on either side stole their wind, so that the big lower sails slatted, and finally George ordered the foresail brought in. The *Swallow* crept against the river current; the only reason she was getting upriver at all was because of the tide and the landward breeze in the topsails.

"How deep?" asked George.

Tana had the lead line loosely wound about his hand. He spun it out, the lead line revolved in great circles with the ten-pound lead weight at the end whistling, and then the lead dropped. A silent moment as the brig glided up to the rope, and up came the line again.

"By the mark, three!"

Three fathoms was barely enough to float the little brig. Great green clots of camalote weed bumped along her sides, and the banks were lined with palms which rose higher in the air than her masts. Alligators floated like fallen logs, watching with cold bubble eyes. At last, the forest was interrupted with sugarcane fields, and after that, fences, and dirt roads could be glimpsed between the fields, and, in the hilly distance, a track that was evidently the way the scientific party would come. The sugarcane grew tall, its seasonal growth already twice as high as a man, and the jungle loomed and threatened. From aloft, however, Wiki could glimpse a sprawling building, which had a sugar factory with a couple of tall chimneys behind it—their destination, thank God.

A primitive wharf jutted out into the river, but George chose not to try it. Not only did he suspect that the water there would be too shallow at low tide, but the middle of the stream was out of the range of mosquitoes. Accordingly, they dropped anchor in the deepest part of the river, and Wiki was sent on shore in a boat. There were a few shacks among the palms, with their owners sleeping in the shade beneath. As the boat arrived, they didn't even waken.

The road that led from the jetty to the house ran through the fringe of the primeval forest. It was wide and well used, but there was a constant feeling that the jungle was waiting to take over. Bright birds flickered through branches bearing huge, vibrant flowers. Wiki heard the cry of a monkey, and once a muffled growl from somewhere beyond the factory. Then he emerged onto the lawn in front of the house, which was studded with a row of old brass cannon set in stone. While he was contemplating these, his host came out onto the veranda.

This man, Senhor da Silva, was bright yellow from past bouts with fever, but remarkably cheerful and energetic. Being a lonely old bachelor, he was delighted to have company. Wiki was taken on an extensive tour of the sugar house, which was full of idle, apparently derelict machinery, the harvest being over. Then he was taken to a mysterious pond, where, it was rumored, a giant alligator lived, but the beast remained invisible.

Having run out of things to look at, they returned to Senhor da

Silva's shadowy tropical mansion. Wiki's host wished much to regale his guest with pale rum, and seemed quite put out when Wiki asked for coffee instead. Perhaps because of this, Senhor da Silva did double justice to the bottle, and became garrulously drunk. It was rather like an evening with Forsythe, Wiki mused. Otherwise, there was an awful similarity to the fazenda at Ithocaia, because as the hours went by the scientific party still failed to appear.

Instead, just as the sun dropped behind the trees, Sir Patrick Palgrave arrived, having come upriver in a felucca. His friend, da Silva, was too inebriated to care about the nonarrival of his guests, but the Englishman made a great fuss about bad manners and goddamned arrogance. In the middle of the tirade, Senhor da Silva passed out, and Wiki seized the chance to escape down the road to the jetty, and get back on board the brig.

When the next day dawned, and the party had still not put in an appearance, the felucca set sail, Sir Patrick calling out as he passed that he was headed for the next rendezvous to warn the expectant host that his guests would be late by at least a day. As it happened, however, it was thirty-six more hours before the scientifics hove into sight at the end of the trail, and the shadows of the third day were very long by the time they arrived at the house.

The news his father communicated was just as Wiki had feared. Dr. Olliver had reverted to his early grossly inconsiderate habits—though his mule was also partly at fault. Not long after leaving Ingetado it had mutinied, and they had not been able to persuade any other beast to take its place. Accordingly, the surgeon had been forced to travel on foot, with the inevitable result that the rest of the party, moving faster, had overtaken him on several occasions—and each time he had been left behind, Dr. Olliver had seized the chance to disappear into the trees. By the time they realized he was out of sight, they'd not only had to retrace their steps, but had been forced to wait around for hours, until Lieutenant Forsythe or Captain Coffin found him, or the surgeon returned of his own accord to the trail.

Dr. Olliver seemed absolutely unaware of the maddened expressions on the faces of his companions, instead reveling in the prize he'd brought with him—a twenty-foot anaconda! Wound up into a massive coil, it had been loaded on a wild-eyed mule by the gang of men who had captured it. Never had Wiki imagined anything so awful. When he violently objected to taking it on board the brig, Dr. Olliver refused to listen. "How could a savage New Zealander possibly understand the priorities of science?" he loftily demanded.

"Want me to handle him?" queried Forsythe with a grin.

"You really think you can make him see sense?" Wiki said dubiously.

"Wa'al, I surely haven't had any luck so far," Forsythe drawled, then grinned evilly. "But this is going to be fun."

Accordingly, Wiki followed the snake-loaded mule to the wharf. Then, the load of snake plus fat scientific being as much as the boat could bear, he stood with Forsythe at the fringe of the forest, waiting for the boat to come back.

Dark was falling fast. As always, Forsythe had his rifle slung over his shoulder, and Wiki could see his big left hand moving on the weapon as his eyes shifted about, checking out the river and the trees. The whine of insects had intensified. The air, which had been so hot and humid it was scarcely breathable, became cool, and Wiki felt the nape of his neck ruffle up with the breeze. Birds began to call eerily from the sugarcane fields, *Whip, whip, whip, poor Willy, weep, Willy, weep,* and Wiki remembered that someone had once told him that whippoorwills were the ghosts of dead slaves. He thought of the runaway cimarrons, and when he heard a rustling in the trees, he felt another chill.

It was a relief when the boat reappeared from the darkness, and he and Forsythe jumped into it. As they clambered onto the brig's deck, the companionway door opened, throwing a shaft of lantern light into the area covered by the awning. It silhouetted the massive shape of Dr. Olliver, and the great snake heaped in a circle around him.

George emerged from the doorway. Over the past two days he had put the time to profit by surveying the river, and he now had a pen in his hand, and looked preoccupied and busy. He took one look at the anaconda, stepped back a smart pace, and said, "I am *not* taking that on board the brig."

"But a pristine example of *Eunectes murinus* is a rare and wonderful find!" Dr. Olliver exclaimed.

"I don't give a damn about that," said George, who seldom resorted to strong language. "It's too bloody big, for a start."

"But this is a very small specimen," the naturalist informed him. "I have read travelers' accounts that have spoken reliably of one-hundred-forty-foot anacondas!—of anacondas which have crushed and engulfed grown men with their extensible jaws! So huge are they, the Indians believe they metamorphose into ships!"

"Well, I most certainly don't want it on board *this* ship."

"You'd like it overboard instead?" inquired Forsythe.

"Most certainly," replied George, and with marvelous communion of spirit he and Forsythe bent, gripped, heaved the anaconda up, and returned it to its natural element by dropping it over the rail. Dr. Olliver gobbled incoherently. Wiki, fascinated, watched the snake disappear beneath the black ripples like a bit of old hawser—and a shot blasted out from the night.

Cimarrons! It happened so fast—first the flash, and then the roar, and then an abrupt crash and clatter as the awning collapsed. Wiki, fighting to fend off the descending weght, glimpsed Forsythe swinging up his rifle. He heard the sound of his shot, and another from the shore, and then he was engulfed in canvas.

There was a great deal of muffled shouting as everyone fought to get free, and then Wiki got his head out just in time to hear the sound of distant galloping. A confused moment later the last man struggled out of the stiff, heavy folds. A babble of questions followed, and then, as the canvas was shoved about, everyone realized that the cimarron's first shot had snapped one of the ropes that held the awning up. It had been a shock when it came down, but it could well have saved their lives.

"I'm almost sure I winged one of the bastards," said Forsythe, and jumped down into the boat, yelling for some oarsmen and a lantern.

Wiki went with him. On shore, the birds had been shocked into silence, but the insects still whined. He and Forsythe clambered onto the jetty, and kept low as they ran into the trees, though it was obvious the cimarrons had fled.

Forsythe headed unerringly for a small clearing. "They waited here," he said, and pointed. The lantern light fell on hoofprints in the mud, which swelled and filled with water. Then his tone became puzzled as he said, "It looks like there was only one."

"But why would one man attack so many?"

"I'd reckoned they planned to pick us off, one by one, and then take the brig," Forsythe said. "But that would need a whole gang." He paused, and Wiki could imagine him pursing his thick lips in and out. Then, he said slowly, "So what the hell did he think he was doing?"

Wiki had no answer. The whippoorwill birds started up again, and gooseflesh rose on his arms.

Twenty-two

Two days later, the brig worked her way up the Rio Macae, which—thank God, thought Wiki—was their last rendezvous. This was where the scientific party would meet up at Sir Patrick Palgrave's fazenda, and then, after they had organized their notes and drawings, everyone would board the brig for the swift passage back to Rio.

The cautious upriver passage was very like the exploration of the San João river, except that the landscape about the banks was flatter and the forest was lower. Being more open to the long afternoon sunlight, the water was not so brown, being a pewter color. It was also a lot deeper. Beyond the margins of the river, dense jungle beckoned, rising over foothills to the mountains.

"Let's have a haul on the starboard mainbrace," said George to Constant Keith. The river was executing a wide bend. Then, as they made the turn, a small village came into sight, an assemblage of flimsy houses on stilts, painted bright colors, and with flat-sterned, high-prowed boats and log canoes drawn up on the mud beneath them. As the brig neared they could see another street beyond the waterfront, lined with more substantial buildings, including one flying the Brazilian flag. Another paved street led down to the river, with a wharf at the end. It was the most civilization the crew had seen in a week.

Sir Patrick Palgrave's estate was high in the hills, some miles away, and, according to Wiki's instructions, someone from the fazenda would come with a horse to take him there. Sure enough, only an hour after the brig had moored up to the jetty and furled her sails, a couple of horses arrived, one with a rider, and the other led by the rein. However, though both George and Wiki waited on deck expectantly, no one came on board. Instead, the horseman waited. In the end, with a shrug and an eyebrow lifted quizzically in George's direction, Wiki vaulted down to the soggy planks of the wharf. Then he strode up to the pair of horses, looked up at the rider, and exclaimed, *"Meu Deus!"*

Manuela Josefa Ramalho Vieira de Castro de Roquefeuille twinkled down at him. "Aren't you pleased to see me?"

She was riding astride, Wiki noticed, which was the reason he had assumed the rider was a man. He said, "How did you get here?"

"I've been at the fazenda for *days*—all alone save for servants. It has been very restful, but also very boring. Now I am your guide to our country estate, which used to be my father's. Why aren't you pleased to see me?"

"But I am," Wiki assured her. "You are very much more beautiful than Lieutenant Forsythe, and more fun than the scientifics. But where are they? I thought they would be at the fazenda by now."

"You'll see them soon enough," she promised.

Wiki went on board again, collected his kit bag, waved a hand to George in farewell, and jumped back to the wharf, while Madame patiently waited and all the villagers watched. As soon as he was aboard the second horse, she clicked her tongue, rattled the bridle, and led the way along the waterfront street to a narrow path, which wound past small fields, climbed a steep slope, and then plunged into the primeval jungle.

The air became thick with humidity. Great trees blotted out the sun. Spanish moss and woody lianas dripped and swayed, spectacular orchids clung to the branches that sprang from massive white tree trunks, great spiderwebs stretched from twig to twig, and the filtered light was green. The sweetish smell of leaf mold was overwhelming. The trail of hoofprints left by Josefa's horse pooled with moisture and then swelled back to the original mud. Every now and then there was a bloodcurdling cry as an unseen monkey swung from branch to branch high above, and for some magical moments an enormous blue butterfly fluttered about the flicking ears of Wiki's horse.

He called out, "I thought we were going to Sir Patrick's estate."

"Oh, he likes to pretend that it's his," she called back casually, and waved a dismissive hand.

"It's yours?"

"It belongs to my family, yes, but he does the business."

He wondered if she resented that, but couldn't ask, so shouted instead, "What do you grow there?"

"Coffee, of course," she shouted back. "What else?"

What else, indeed, Wiki mused; after all, he was in Brazil, the land of his favorite beverage. Then conversation lapsed, because Josefa, being a much lighter burden, was drawing farther ahead. The air had become filled with the thunder of an unseen waterfall, and was even wetter, and the potholes were full of water, which splashed up. The trees on either side were overhung with great ferns.

Then, just as Josefa disappeared about a bend, the path turned into a ribbon of pure mud, and Wiki's horse, growing tired of his weight, staged a mutiny. It stopped dead, and refused to take another step. When Wiki kicked at its sides, it turned its head and delivered him a grin of baleful derision. Finally, he gave up and jumped to the ground, right in a hole where the mud was higher than the tops of his boots.

While he was struggling to get out of the morass, the horse grabbed its chance to lash out with its hooves. Wiki dodged the kicks, but was liberally sprayed with mud from head to toe.

By the time he got to the turn in the path, Josefa was beyond the next bend, and well out of sight. Wiki trudged after her, knee-deep at times, hauling the horse along by the reins. The world was filled with the rush and crash of unseen water, and bright birds flickered in and out of the trees. It was as if he were alone in this lavishly primeval world—a daunting prospect, as dusk was fast descending.

Then the path widened until it was almost the width of a road, looking much more traveled, and a couple of bends later Wiki abruptly broke out of the trees. A mountainside that he hadn't even suspected existed suddenly reared up before him, its aspect black because of the red sun setting behind it.

The last light glittered on a magnificent waterfall that hurtled down its side, rushing through lush vegetation and tumbling over rocks. Close to where Wiki stood, it widened into an artificial pool, walled with rocks and ferns, before disappearing into the forest. A surprisingly formal garden stretched beyond it, reminding him of Sir Patrick's place at Praia Grande. The road he was following blazed through the first part of the garden to where a complex of low, well-maintained buildings surrounded a quadrangular courtyard. Their terra-cotta roofs were a warm color in the last light, surmounting white-plastered walls.

One big house dominated the scene, and was obviously where the Vieira de Castro family lived, when in residence. The stables were on the opposite side of the square from this, while the sides were taken up with servants' quarters, kitchens, and storerooms. Beyond the compound, plantations swooped up to the highest foothills of the mountain—growing the coffee that Josefa had talked about, Wiki supposed.

A bell began to toll, the noise a rhythmic accompaniment to the clatter of hooves as he led the horse into the courtyard. Servants appeared from all directions, and formed a ragged line behind Josefa, who was giggling immoderately at his bedraggled appearance. The reason she had been able to ride astride, Wiki saw, was that her shortened skirt was divided into two. Beneath it, she was wearing shiny black boots that were scarcely muddy at all.

"Why are they ringing the bell?" he asked.

"Oh, in the old days they used to fire a cannon when someone arrived, but now they use a bell," she replied. Waving a hand at the assembled servants, she went on, "Just as in the old days, they have come out to welcome you."

Feeling hot, sweaty, and dirty, Wiki bowed to the assemblage, who smiled vaguely and then disappeared, save for a man who took away his horse. He noticed that the beast cast a triumphant look over its shoulder as it went.

Josefa said in a thoughtful kind of tone, "You won't see the servants again for quite a while, as we don't eat until ten."

"I thought you said the scientifics would be here?"

"I didn't say that—what I said is that you will see them soon enough. I thought perhaps they might be here, but they are not. Perhaps they will join us for supper, but I don't think they like to travel in the dark."

So Dr. Olliver had delayed them yet again, Wiki mused—which meant that he and Sir Patrick's sister-in-law were alone for the night. When he looked at Josefa, she was watching him with a definitely wicked twinkle in her eyes.

She murmured, "So how would you like to fill in the time?"

"Swim," Wiki said, and jerked his chin at the darkening pool.

"But it's freezing, and the insects will eat you to pieces. The servants use it for laundry. Come inside, and see the bathing pool that my brother-in-law designed. There is glass in the roof, so the sun warms the water by day, and it is very pleasant and pretty. You will enjoy a swim there."

Before following her inside, Wiki kicked off his boots and washed his muddy feet in the pool the servants used for laundry. As predicted, the mountain water was icy. Then he went barefoot into the building, stepping from the great entrance door straight into a reception room with white-plastered walls and black beams in the roof. Bizarrely, it was furnished with gilt chairs, tables, and settees in the current French mode.

There was a row of French doors, too, leading to an inner courtyard, which was floored with flagstones and tiles, and had baskets of plants hanging from the beams. As Josefa had said, a decorative pond rippled quietly in the middle of this. Panes of glass had been let into the roof, so that the sunset light reflected on the water, which was edged in places with ferns and tropical flowers. Fallen blossoms floated.

"It's romantic, don't you agree?" she said.

Wiki said sincerely, "Your brother-in-law is a very talented designer."

On the three far sides of the courtyard, the doors that were open revealed bedrooms, a dining room, and an office. "Take what bedroom you like," she said with a casual flip of her hand. "Help yourself to whatever you need." Then she walked around the pool and disappeared through one of the doors, closing it behind her.

Wiki went inside the nearest bedroom, dropped his kit bag on the floor, stripped to the skin, and made a great splash as he executed a shallow dive into the pool. The water was like silk, just warm enough not to shock the breath out of his chest, but cool enough to be refreshing. It was deep enough to swim, and he stroked lazily to and fro a few times. Feeling clean at last, he floated with his eyes shut.

The soft step could have been a servant—or one of the survey party arriving—but Wiki thought he knew better. He heard the rustle of silk as the intruder perched on the edge of the pool, and then Josefa said in her challenging way, "I think perhaps you won't let me wash your hair."

Wiki smiled, still with his eyes shut. "Your rank is higher than mine."

She laughed, and her hands gripped his shoulders and floated him closer. His hair was lashed into a ponytail, now very wet. He felt the tug as the yarn was pulled free, and then she dunked his head. He relaxed, and didn't resist her. She pulled him up again, and poured a cold liquid onto his scalp. There was a smell of rosewater, and foaming noises as her fingers slid through his hair. She pushed him under again, and then repeated the process, massaging while he luxuriated.

A second rinse, and then she said, "Am I allowed to comb it, too?"

"There are no *tohunga* here." He felt the comb teeth set in, pull, yank, and tug, and opened his eyes a fraction as he winced. Then the tangles and knots were sorted out, and he felt the comb run smoothly to the ends of his long, black hair. Then, out of the corner of his eye, he saw the flash of metal.

A knife! Wiki whipped around, grabbed, and jerked her into the water. Through the great splash, he heard the rattle and plink as something fell into the pool. Then, as the water stilled, he saw it through the ripples—not a knife, but scissors. "Damn it," he exclaimed in English, and accused in Portuguese, "You were going to cut my hair!"

Josefa's only reply was a giggle. She was wearing a blue gown which clung wetly, making it obvious that she had stripped completely when taking off her riding clothes, and was naked beneath the thin silk. She laughed up at him through the dripping strands of her drenched hair, which hung down to her waist. When he kissed her in the European fashion, she wound her arms around his neck, and pressed her taut, wet breasts against his chest.

"Mischievous little witch," said Wiki, and she chuckled in his ear. Then, with a movement that was so abrupt it took him by surprise, she jerked out of his arms, leapt out of the pool with marvelous litheness, and ran like a gazelle into the bedroom he had chosen. By the time he caught up with her, the gown was lying in a puddle on the floor.

When Wiki woke for the second time, it was almost dawn. The graying light was what he noticed first. Then he thought about how quiet it was, with no servants moving about. While their mistress was otherwise occupied, they were taking things easy, he thought—and it also meant, thank God, that the survey party hadn't arrived. There had been times in the night when he had listened for the warning clatter of hooves, and other times when he wouldn't have cared—or even noticed—if the whole complement, including his father, had been crowded about the bed.

After that, he thought about the mistress of this establishment—the sister-in-law of his father's good friend Sir Patrick Palgrave. He was sprawled over and around and beside Josefa, with his head nestled in the hollow of her shoulder. Slender white legs were entwined with his muscular brown ones. When he shifted, he realized she was awake—and, when he tried to sit up, he realized that Josefa had been busy.

"What the devil?" Wiki said, and felt and heard her giggle. He opened his eyes and tucked in his chin to look down at his chest, and saw she had braided their hair together. Her copper tresses merged with his snaky black hair, woven into a variegated plait that gleamed exotically in the light that slanted across the bed.

"You were drooling on my breast," she accused, and he laughed. Then he realized he had a problem, but when he tried to unreeve the braid, her fingers stopped him.

"I have to get up," he said.

"Why?"

"Don't ask," he said. "It's indelicate." He was hungry, too. A feast of beef, beans, and vegetables had been served at ten, but he and Josefa had been seated at either end of a long refectory table, forced to communicate in shouts, and they had both found it so funny that they hadn't eaten much.

"Kiss me first," she teased—and he heard a queer thud at the outside door.

Though the sound wasn't loud, it echoed from beyond the front room. Another thump, and a low, hoarse, muffled cry. "What's that?" whispered Josefa.

"Someone—something at the door," he said. This time, she allowed him to unravel the braid, but his fingers were thick and clumsy, and she had to take over, while all the time the desperate thump-thump echoed. Then, when he was halfway out of the room, Wiki realized he was naked. It seemed to take an age to get his legs into his trousers and get the trousers buttoned, while he heard rustles as Josefa found her gown and hurried into it.

Wiki didn't wait to put on anything else. The flagstones felt gritty under his feet as he ran around the pool. He slipped on wet tiles, but managed to keep his balance. Then he was hurrying across the dark reception room. The gilt furniture glittered in glimpses of light. He found the latch of the front door, but when he jerked at the handle, the door wouldn't budge. It took him two heartbeats to realize what was wrong. Then the bolts at both top and bottom screeched as he hauled at them. The thudding on the other side had ceased, but there was still a strong sense of a presence.

Finally, he got the heavy wooden door opened—but the rectangle that should have let in the early light was blocked by a great form that seemed to be wedged there. The fat surgeon. Dr. Olliver. His eyes were staring unseeingly, and blood ran from his nose and ears and matted his beard. Paralyzed, Wiki watched the small, plump-lipped mouth open wide.

Dr. Olliver shrieked in a tone of utter disbelief and horror, *"William!"*

He began to fall, very slowly, his massive shape inclining forward. For a horrible moment Wiki thought the great mass was going to collapse on top of him, and smother him with its weight. Instead, however, the scientist buckled at the knees, and the great body slowly folded. The sightless eyes turned upward, and suddenly focused. It was as if Dr. Olliver recognized him in the throes of his last extremity. A painfully intense expression crossed his bloodied face and his mouth opened again.

"I *killed* for him," he husked, so low that Wiki had to strain to hear him. Then, with a heartbreakingly soft sigh, Dr. Olliver fell the rest of the way to the floor, landing facedown so that Wiki could see the gash in the back of his head. It was a terrible wound; it was a miracle that he had stayed alive long enough to get to the door and deliver his enigmatic message.

An awful silence had descended. Then Wiki heard clattering in the outer courtyard, and looked up to see that the survey party had arrived. The closest man to the door was his father.

He was holding a bloodied cudgel, and looked dazed. Someone cried, "What's happened?" No one answered. Instead, someone called to William Coffin, "I heard him shout out your name." The tone was puzzled, but definitely accusing.

Captain Coffin didn't answer. Instead, he looked confused. Then, like everyone else, he turned as the thump of hooves came fast down the track from the forest. A horse burst out of the tangled trees, with Sir Patrick Palgrave in the saddle. Instead of heading for the courtyard gateway, he drove the steed right at the pool where the mountain water gathered. Then, right in the middle of the thigh-deep water, he hauled the horse to a stop, and stood in the stirrups, a magnificent silhouette in the light of the rising sun.

"In God's name, what happened?" he cried.

No one answered. Instead, everyone looked at Captain Coffin, who stared back numbly with the murder weapon in his hand, while Forsythe, closely pursued by two officers of the law, came galloping down the track.

Twenty-three

Wiki did not have a chance to talk with his father until they were back at Rio, and then it was in his father's cell in the jail on Praça Quinze. The warder, rattling keys, let him in, and Wiki looked about curiously. The cool little room was irregular in shape and walled with stone, but was reasonably comfortable, with a narrow bunk at the back, and a small table with two kitchen chairs in the middle. Wiki supposed that was because Captain Coffin was quite well known about town as a respectable and affluent shipmaster—and, indeed, he still had the bearing of a man of dignity and substance, even if he had been charged with the murder of Dr. Winston Olliver.

Now, he indicated one of the chairs as if he were the master of this domain, and Wiki sat down. Then, when they were both seated, they contemplated each other in silence. To Wiki, it felt as if they had never studied each other properly before, and that they were both worried that the other would disappear forever if they stopped looking. He had dressed for the occasion in his best black broadcloth, because visiting someone in prison had seemed oddly like going to church, and his hair was neatly clubbed into the back of his neck. His father was similarly attired, except that one of his favorite brocade vests glinted secretly in gold and silk beneath the open front of the jacket. The heavy-lidded left eye was lowered even more than usual, so that he looked older, and very wise.

Then he said abruptly, "Son, I swear I didn't kill Olliver."

"Of course you didn't," Wiki replied readily. He hadn't believed it for an instant, even when the two guardsmen had hauled his father off in shackles.

The soldiers had come to the estate with Forsythe, after he had reported to the justice of the peace in the village on Rio Macae that the scientific party was being shadowed by cimarrons, who had shot at them twice. There had been a lot of trouble with the desperadoes locally, and so the justice had immediately assigned two soldiers to the job of providing an armed escort until the time that the scientific party was safely on board the brig. Instead, they had arrived at the fazenda to find that they were faced with a case of murder.

They had taken no time at all to jump to the obvious conclusion. The victim had cried out the name of his killer, "*William,*" and a man with that name had been discovered holding the murder weapon. Accordingly, they had carried off Captain William Coffin to the village of Rio Macae, and there, in the building that flew the Brazilian flag, the justice had issued a formal arrest, and sent him on board the brig, with four soldiers to guard him until he was locked up in prison.

The inquest would take place at the coroner's bidding, probably within a couple of days. If Captain Coffin was indicted, he would be tried before a *juiz de decrito* and a jury of forty, all men who were prosperous enough to pay taxes. Looking at his confident bearing now, Wiki felt dreadfully afraid that the coroner would consider him cocky, and rule for an indictment.

He said, "How did you come to be holding that cudgel?"

"You sound as if you don't believe me."

For God's sake, Wiki thought. He said patiently, "I do believe you."

"So why are you questioning me like this? Like an officer of the law?"

"Because that's exactly what I am."

His father arched his brows, and then shrugged, and said, "I saw it lying in the mud about a hundred yards before the end of the track, and got off my horse to see what it was. Then, when I ran the rest of the way, I kept it in my hand."

"Why?"

"Because it had blood on it—and hair."

"You were alone?"

"Aye."

"But you were so angry when Dr. Olliver strayed from the group."

"That's why I was alone! I was hurrying after him to make him see sense and rejoin the party. For God's sake, Forsythe and I had done that often enough over the past few days. The rest weren't far behind."

"You arrived on foot. Where was your horse?"

"I didn't think it was worth remounting, being so close—and I wasn't thinking straight, because of what was on the club. I suppose the horse followed me, but I'm not sure. What I do recollect is hearing my name shouted, and then I saw the open door—and you standing in the doorway."

Wiki found himself the object of a penetrating stare, and then his father demanded, "Did you spend the night at the estate?"

Wiki nodded.

"Did you *sleep* with that woman?"

Wiki thought about it. He had definitely slept with Josefa, because he could remember waking up with her. However, he said nothing.

Captain Coffin snapped, "There will be hell to pay if Sir Patrick ever finds out that you seduced his sister-in-law!"

Wiki didn't doubt that for an instant. Instead of commenting, he said, "When I woke up, I heard hammering at the door—a queer kind of thudding—and managed to get it open just before Dr. Olliver died. He said something."

"I know," said his father harshly. "He said my name."

"That was what he shouted. What he whispered to me was even more shocking—he husked out the words *I killed for him!*"

Dead silence. Captain Coffin's brows shot up, and then frowned. Finally, he said, "Killed who? And for whom?"

"Exactly," said Wiki. "And why did he call out the name William?"

There was another long pause, and then his father said, "That's three questions," and added in reminiscent tones, "I learned something during the war for free trade and sailors' rights—the importance of single-ship actions."

Wiki blinked. "I beg your pardon?"

"One needed a cool head. I once raised three vessels in convoy—a sixteen-gun ship, a fourteen-gun brig, and a twelve-gun ship, and took 'em all with great ease, simply by going alongside of each of them one at a time. If I'd tried them all at once, I would've been dead and done."

"Ah," said Wiki, understanding. "So we tackle these three questions one at a time?"

"Exactly," said his father with great satisfaction. He beamed at Wiki as if he had always known that he was bright.

"So let's look at the name William, first. Why do you think he shouted it?"

"Because the man who attacked him was named William, of course," said his father with great confidence.

"That's what the coroner is going to assume," Wiki dryly agreed.

"It's a common name, so it didn't have to be me! What about the scientifics?"

"You don't know their first names?"

"Of course not," his father said loftily.

So, despite all the fuss and contention, the scientifics had addressed each other formally, by surnames. Wiki had trouble not shaking his head in wonder. He said, "They were Charles Pickering, John Dyes, Joseph Couthouy, Alfred Agate, and Joseph Drayton. Not a William among them, unfortunately."

"What about Lieutenant Forsythe?"

"His name is Christian."

"What?"

"It's peculiarly inappropriate, I agree, but nonetheless it's his name."

There was a long silence, and then his father said softly, "Oh, damn."

Wiki, feeling sorry for him, said gently, "The next question is easier."

"You're thinking of Olliver's confession?"

"Aye—his confession that he killed someone. It must have been Grimes."

"But why would he kill Grimes, of all people?"

"I don't even know *how*," said Wiki in frustration. Dr. Olliver hadn't even *been* there when Grimes had died. Instead, he'd had an alibi, because he had been surveying part of the harbor with Couthouy, and it had been Dr. Gilchrist who was summoned to attend the dying man.

Wiki remembered the way the flagship surgeon had hurried into the stateroom with his napkin still under his chin, and how he had cried out with shock, *"This man has been poisoned!"* Then, Dr. Gilchrist had ordered him to make sure that the medicine bottles were kept safe—a wise precaution, because the bismuth had proved to be contaminated with strychnine. But, Wiki's thoughts flew on, the analyst had testified that there had not been enough strychnine in the bromide—

Suddenly Dr. Tweedie's voice was as clear in his head as if the apothecary were in the room: *"Strychnine is a cumulative poison."* Inspiration hit, and he stood up so abruptly that his chair tumbled with a clatter.

His father demanded, "Where are you going?"

"To the *Vincennes*, to ask the steward some questions."

"Why?"

"Because Forsythe's theory that Grimes was given a dose of salts might not be as crazy as we thought."

"You surely don't think the steward put salts on the top two fish!"

"The salts could have been added to anything. What is important is that they made him sick enough to be put under Dr. Olliver's care."

His father's half-closed eye was shrewder than ever. "So he could kill him?"

"At leisure," agreed Wiki grimly.

The *Vincennes* still smelled of brimstone and sulfur, and goods were being lightered back on board. Wiki found the plump steward in the saloon, peevishly muttering as he wielded a mop. The marines who had cleared the ship of rats had also made free with his pantry, he grumbled; they had used up his store of coffee and molasses, and had even broached a cask of spirits. "And how the hell am I going to account to the purser for the shortfall?"

Then his eyes glistened at the chance of learning gossip. "I hear that Dr. Olliver is dead," he said promptingly.

"Aye," said Wiki unhelpfully.

"Murdered, huh?"

"Aye."

"And by none other than the captain of that brigantine what Captain Rochester nearly sunk?"

"The case has not been tried yet," said Wiki.

Then Jack Winter gave him the opening he needed, by uttering in portentous tones, "The Lord giveth, and the Lord taketh away, and

He surely taketh away our scientifics—two in Rio alone! Mr. Grimes, and now Dr. Olliver. Ain't it an ever-living wonder?"

Wiki said, "What I wonder is how Mr. Grimes got the gripes in the first place."

"I've reckoned all along that it was that foreign pudding of Festin's," Jack Winter said at once.

"On the other hand," Wiki suggested, "Mr. Grimes might have drunk something that upset him."

"It wasn't my coffee!"

"I remember you mentioning wine."

"Not wine *I* gave him, I assure you! The only wine he drank was what Dr. Olliver gave him hisself."

"What!" Wiki's heart bumped, and he said quickly, "When did this happen?"

"Right after supper, after everyone had left the table. Dr. Olliver came into the pantry, poured a glass of wine, stirred in a powder, and then went into Mr. Grimes's stateroom and gave it to him—for medicinal use, he told me privately, on account of he was concerned at his appearance. Then he said I was to keep quiet about it, because Mr. Grimes would object if he knew there was something else but wine in the glass."

Wiki exclaimed, "Why didn't you tell me at the time?"

"How could I?" Jack Winter aggressively demanded. "Dr. Olliver was right there listening when you was talking about it! He was the bloody *doctor*, and I'm just the afterhouse steward, if you'll excuse the biblical language, and he'd already ordered me to keep quiet! I wasn't even allowed to make a fuss when I was told to take over the nursing, even though I had severe prognostications of an untimely demise, and I had nothing to do with his death, neither! All I did was follow instructions, I bloody swear it. Dr. Olliver made up the new pills, and showed me the medicine, and I repeated the instructions until I could recite them off to his satisfaction."

"He didn't write them down?" Wiki asked curiously.

Instead of answering, the steward produced a rag and started polishing the credenza. His expression, Wiki saw, was defensive. Light dawned. "You can't read?"

"I can write my name," Jack Winter muttered. "And that's enough for me. It ain't no trouble to learn instructions off by heart."

Wiki studied him very thoughtfully. "Where is Dr. Olliver's medical chest?"

"Back in what was his stateroom, of course."

"Let's fetch it out, shall we?" Wiki suggested, and when Jack Winter seemed inclined to argue, he got it out of the stateroom himself. Returning to the saloon, he sat down, set the box on the table, and took the bottles out, setting them up in a long row. The names on the labels were in Old English script, a miniature version of the big labels he had seen on the much bigger bottles in Dr. Tweedie's apothecary shop.

"Did you watch him make up the new pills?" he asked.

"Aye. I saw him make the pills both times."

"I don't expect you can remember which bottles he used."

Jack Winter cast him a surly look, and said, "Of course I can."

It was no idle boast. Without hesitation, he picked four bottles out of the row, and set them in front of Wiki. Their labels read CINCHONAE RUBRAE CORTEX, PIPER NIGRUM, FERRI PULVIS, and GENTIANAE RADIX. His memory was impeccable—they were exactly the same bottles Wiki had seen the naturalist use when he had made up the first lot of pills.

"That one reads *'Peruvian Bark,'*" Jack Winter said proudly, pointing to the one that read CINCHONAE RUBRAE CORTEX.

Wiki nodded, because the steward's unknowing translation of the Latin was perfectly correct. That bottle, of course, was empty, but the others—those holding piperine, powdered iron, and gentian root—were one quarter full.

"Which bottles did he use for the second batch?" he asked on a hunch, partly because he had not been around to watch Dr. Olliver make up the second lot of pills, and partly to check what had been said at the inquest.

"These three," said Jack, and sorted out the ones that held the piperine, *ferri pulvis,* and gentian root. "Plus these," he went on, and picked out two more, one reading CHINOIDINE, and the other, OPIUM.

Chinoidine and opium, thought Wiki. It was exactly as Dr. Tweedie had testified at the inquest. He was silent, staring at the labels, thinking about Dr. Olliver's last words—*I killed for him!*—and Grimes's final ghastly convulsion. He remembered the dead, contorted rat that had been found under the credenza, where one of Dr. Olliver's first lot of pills was lost—the rat that, according to Dr. Tweedie, had taken at least a week to die, and which Forsythe reckoned had been dead four days when they found it. Had it been poisoned by the pill, even though Dr. Tweedie had said that the pills were harmless?

But Dr. Tweedie had only known about the *second* lot of pills, the ones that Dr. Ohlsson had analyzed. The apothecary's Scotch voice echoed again in his head: *"Strychnine is a cumulative poison—with repeated applications the amount of strychnine in the body builds up until there is enough in the system to finish—"*

Wiki exclaimed, "Those pills had to be *finished*!"

"I don't know what you mean, Mr. Coffin," the steward replied in his prissy way. "The pills never ran out, not before Mr. Grimes died. I could show you, except that they were taken away for that analyst to work on. Far as I know," Jack Winter went on moodily, as if he resented it, "he's still holding on to that bloody bottle, and the ones with the liquid medicine, too, specially the one what turned out to be poisoned."

"I didn't mean that," said Wiki. "Dr. Olliver had to coat the pills with some kind of powder to stop them from sticking together in the bottle. That, apparently, is called 'finishing.' "

"I didn't see him do anything like that. All what I saw him do is add some powder after he'd put the dried pills inside the bottle, and shake them around."

That was an easy way of finishing them, Wiki supposed. If enough powder was left in the bottles, the pills would remain separate, instead of sticking together. He asked, "Do you remember which powder he used?"

"Of course," said Jack Winter loftily. He pulled out a bottle with the label GLYCYRRHIZAE RADIX.

Licorice root, Wiki thought; it was as both the analyst and Dr. Tweedie had said. He had a depressing feeling of getting nowhere.

Then Jack Winter added, "That powder was for the second lot of pills."

Wiki sat up straight. "He used a different powder to finish the first lot of pills?"

"Aye. After Dr. Olliver made up a *first* lot of pills, after Mr. Grimes *first* got sick, he added *this* powder to the bottle."

And the bottle that Jack Winter picked out was labeled STRYCHNINA.

Twenty-four

The inquiry into the death of Dr. Winston Olliver was held in the same small courthouse on the Praça da Constituição, and Captain Coffin's Brazilian friends were crowded into the same alcove, with Sir Patrick Palgrave in the front. Wiki recognized several, who inclined their heads when they saw him. Even Senhor da Silva was there: he waggled his yellowed fingers in comradely fashion, obviously remembering their encounter with affection.

Then Captain Coffin was escorted into the court, flanked by two guards even though he was wearing shackles. Wiki contemplated him with misgiving, because he looked as calm and confident as ever, not at all intimidated by the circumstances and setting. They hadn't had another chance to talk privately, even though Wiki had called at the prison several times, as his father had always had other visitors—the U.S. consul, once, and at other times, Brazilian friends. Sir Patrick Palgrave had been there at least twice, to Wiki's certain knowledge, as he had found the two men engaged in deep discussion, which had stopped the moment he had entered the cell. Now, he wondered what they had been talking about—surely not Dr. Olliver's gasped confession, he hoped. While he now knew how Dr. Olliver had murdered Grimes, he still had not a notion why. *"I killed for him!"* Him? Who? After forty-eight hours of puzzling, he had come no closer to the answer.

A door opened, and the clerk of the court rang a bell and announced the arrival of the coroner, setting the flies to buzzing in the ceiling. To Wiki's surprise, it was Dr. Vieira de Castro. Just as before, the lean, elegant figure studied the court through a pair of pince-nez, and then, with a bow, sat down behind the bench. A long moment passed as he sorted papers, dipped his pen in a pot of ink, and finally nodded to the clerk, who summoned Lieutenant Christian Forsythe to the bench.

Forsythe's testimony was necessary because Dr. Olliver's corpse had been buried back at Rio Macae, on account of the tropical heat, and so there had been no postmortem. Being an officer of the U.S. Navy, he was considered the man most competent to testify to the cause of death. "He was struck over the back of the head, and bl—very hard, too," he informed the court. "From behind. Someone approached from the back and hit his head hard with a cudgel—a lump of wood."

The southerner was repeating himself, and speaking very loudly and slowly, as if the coroner not only had a poor grasp of English, but was deaf and mentally deficient, as well.

"Just once, or several times?" Dr. Vieira de Castro queried patiently.

"Just once," Forsythe confirmed. "But very accurately, and very hard. It's bl—incredibly amazing that the victim got himself any farther up the trail. Most men would have curled up on the spot."

"You ascertained the place on the trail where he was attacked?"

"Aye, sir, that I did, not that it was difficult. There was blood on the bushes where it had sprayed from his head, and big splotches in the mud."

"Showing the path of his struggle to the ranch?"

"Aye, sir, though the struggle was bl—entirely pointless, in my candid opinion, on account of what he was going to die, whatever," Forsythe said flatly. "There was nothin' in this mortal world what was going to fix that great hole in his head."

"And was he still alive when you and the soldiers arrived in the courtyard?"

"No, sir, he was as dead as a duck."

"So how did you determine the identity of his attacker?"

"Wa'al, when you find a man holding the cudgel what did the dirty work, and hear everyone who was present declare that the victim called out that man's name in his last accusing breath, jumping to a conclusion is not so very hard."

"But you were relying on the testimony of others?"

"Wa'al," said Forsythe, and his lips pursed with a judicious air. "I guess that testimony is reliable when a whole bunch of people say the same thing?"

"They all informed you that they heard the deceased call out 'Captain Coffin'?"

"Nope. They all told me he called out the name William."

"Captain Coffin's first name is William? I believe," Dr. Vieira de Castro said with an air of great sophistication, "that the English often shorten the name William to Bill."

Everyone, including Wiki, looked at his father. Someone in the alcove actually laughed, because the thought of calling Captain William Coffin something as common as Bill was so outrageous.

"No, sir, no one called him Bill," Forsythe expressionlessly assured him.

"They called him William?"

"No, sir. Everyone called him Captain Coffin."

"But they knew his name was William?"

"Aye. That's what they told me, anyways."

"So when they heard the deceased call out the name William, they assumed that he was referring to Captain Coffin?"

"Aye, sir."

Dr. Vieira de Castro shook his head, his expression surprised. "But didn't the rest of the party address each other by first names?"

"Nope, they did not; it was Mister this, and Doctor that, and Captain whoever."

"But I've always considered Americans remarkably informal people, who get on a first-name basis in an astonishingly short time, usually without waiting for an invitation. This survey doesn't sound like a very amicable affair."

"If you mean unfriendly, sir, then you've hit the nail right on the head."

"Why? What was the problem?"

"Partly on account of they're scientifics—who are mighty dignified fellows, and get insulted if that dignity ain't noticed. And then," Forsythe added, "there was the nature of the victim, Dr. Olliver."

"What about him?"

"He caused a lot of muttering in the ranks, partly on account of his lateness, and also because he wandered off when he'd been ordered to stay on the trail. One of us would have to go and look for him in the jungle while the others waited around, and the scientifics got all riled up on account of missing out on collecting time."

"And this habit of wandering away irritated you, as well?"

"For me, it was a bl—a confounded nuisance, because we were forced to stop an extra night in some places, which put the schedule out of whack. Captain Coffin was even angrier about it than I was, on account of his friend Sir Patrick Palgrave, who was the patron of the survey. He had organized his friends to lodge and feed us nighttimes, and it really upset Captain Coffin when we didn't turn up on schedule."

"It sounds a *most* contentious journey," Dr. Vieira de Castro commented. Then, after a pause in which he scribbled a great deal on his notepaper, Forsythe was dismissed and Captain Couthouy called.

"You are a shipmaster, Captain Couthouy?"

"Aye, sir, out of Boston."

"Yet you are a scientific with the exploring expedition?"

"I most certainly am, Dr. Vieira de Castro."

"And you heard Dr. Olliver cry out a name in his moment of crisis?"

"I arrived in the courtyard in time to hear him cry out the name William."

"Were you aware that Dr. Olliver and Captain Coffin were on bad terms?"

"We were *all* on bad terms with Dr. Olliver, and I want to make it plain right here and now, Dr. Vieira de Castro, that whatever terms they might or might not have been on, Captain Coffin did *not* kill Dr. Olliver."

Patrician eyebrows lifted. "And what makes you so certain of that?"

"Knowledge of human nature, Dr. Vieira de Castro."

"Which is very extensive, I'm certain, being in the company of sailors so often," said Dr. Vieira de Castro dryly. "So whom do you blame?"

"Cimarrons," said Couthouy.

"I beg your pardon?"

"Runaway slaves who live in the forest."

"I know that cimarrons are runaway slaves, Captain Couthouy. What intrigues me is why you have jumped to this conclusion."

"We were shot at on the way to Ingetado, once, and another shot was fired at the brig at San João. Dr. Olliver told me about it—he was most agitated, as he reckoned that the party on the quarterdeck was only saved from slaughter by the fact that the first shot cut a rope, and the awning fell down on them all. It is easy to imagine one of these desperate creatures lashing out when Dr. Olliver blundered across him, and then throwing down the cudgel as he made his escape."

"It does not require a vivid imagination," Dr. Vieira de Castro agreed, his expression ironic. Then he dismissed Couthouy, and called up Captain Coffin.

Wiki's father stood up with an impressive dignity that was not diminished in the slightest by the rattle of handcuffs, while Wiki watched in suspense, wondering what damage he would do to himself with his testimony.

"Your name is Captain William Coffin?"

"Aye, sir."

"And you were a member of this surveying party?"

"I helped oversee the operation, Dr. Vieira de Castro."

"Captain Wilkes requested you to go along as a guide, perhaps?"

"I was there at my own request."

"Because Dr. Olliver was one of the party?"

"Not at all," said Captain Coffin. "I simply wanted to make sure that everything went smoothly."

"And you did not think this . . . smoothness would come about if you didn't accompany them?"

"Exactly, Dr. Vieira de Castro."

"But it did not go smoothly, alas."

Captain Coffin heaved a sigh, and said, "Unfortunately, sir, you are right."

"And this is why you quarreled with Dr. Olliver?"

"I didn't quarrel with him at all, sir. He was an eccentric who liked to dominate the conversation with crazy statements, but that didn't bother me. What *was* irritating was his constant confounded lateness, and the fact that he went missing all the time, which kept the rest of us waiting about. It was all exactly as Lieutenant Forsythe said." Then Captain Coffin added broodingly, "He was also far too fat."

"Fat?" Dr. Vieiro de Castro glanced complacently down at his trim stomach, then looked back at Captain Coffin—who was equally lean—and suggested, "And this fatness, it annoyed you?"

"The plain fact of the matter is that he was too heavy for any decent mount to carry. We managed to get him aboard a giant of a mule at the start, but a few days later the mule gave out, and we couldn't persuade any of the others to take its place. They all took one look at him, and buckled at the knees."

"So Dr. Olliver walked, while the rest of you rode along the trail?"

"Aye—which gave him every opportunity to disappear into the forest. We'd all pleaded and argued with him, and did our best to ride at his pace, but he defied us by lagging behind and then taking off into the trees the instant no one was looking. It was an aggravation, a nuisance, and a confounded waste of time."

"And you are a shipmaster—a man to whom time is of the essence."

"Exactly, Dr. Vieira de Castro."

"So, did you devise a remedy for this exasperation?"

"I asked Lieutenant Forsythe to order him to get his lazy carcass out of bed earlier, so that we would have more time on the trail, and it wouldn't be quite the same vexation when he went missing."

Dr. Vieira de Castro looked at his notes, rustling papers back and forth, and then looked up and said, "And this earlier rising is what happened on the day of his death?"

"As far as I know, that is what happened."

The coroner adjusted his pince-nez, and studied him with an air of interest. "You weren't there?"

"No, sir, I was on board the brig *Swallow*."

"How could this be?"

"According to the schedule, we should have arrived at Sir Patrick Palgrave's estate the night before, but Dr. Olliver held us up so much that when night fell we had only got as far as the village on the Rio Macae. The brig was moored there, and I accepted Captain Rochester's invitation to stop the night. The others stayed at a *venda* in the village. When I went on shore after breakfast, I was told that Dr. Olliver had gone up the trail and vanished into the forest."

"So what did you do?"

"I went after him."

"Alone?"

"Aye, sir. I'd done it before, believe me. This time, I left the scientifics packing their collections, and consulting with Captain Rochester about loading them onto the brig. Lieutenant Forsythe was nowhere to be seen. As I found out later, he'd gone to the office of the local justice of the peace to report that we'd been shadowed by bandits."

Silence, while Dr. Vieira de Castro scribbled. Finally, the coroner looked up and said, "And you met up with Dr. Olliver, Captain Coffin?"

"I did not. I never saw him alive again."

"What *did* you see?"

For the first time, Captain Coffin's tone became ragged. "About a hundred yards before the plantation—where the path gets wide—I saw a cudgel lying on the ground, in the mud. The sun was starting to rise, and—and something about the cudgel's appearance puzzled and alarmed me. I dismounted to look closer, and when I picked it up I saw that the end was smeared with blood and hair—and worse—so I ran to the ranch."

"On foot?"

"It wasn't far away. My horse followed me—I think, or maybe the others brought him along—I didn't really pay attention. When I got to the courtyard I saw my son open the door, and—and Dr. Olliver fell inside."

"Did Dr. Olliver say anything?"

Wiki held his breath, but his father simply replied, "He called out my name."

"William?"

"Aye—but he didn't look around, and I don't believe he knew I was there."

"So why do you think he called your name?"

Captain Coffin paused. Then he looked down at the floor, and said in a very low voice, "Dr. Vieira de Castro, I have absolutely no idea."

Wiki was the next to be called. He stood up, walked to the chair, and bowed before he sat down.

Dr. Vieira de Castro pushed his pince-nez farther up his long, narrow nose, and said amiably, "So, Mr. Wiki Coffin, we meet again."

Wiki smiled back. "So we do, Dr. Vieira de Castro."

"Your expedition is experiencing a great deal of bad fortune."

"We certainly are, sir."

"Do you think that by the time the journey is over you will have any scientifics left?"

"I'm beginning to wonder about that myself, Dr. Vieira de Castro."

"I am not surprised!" said the coroner. Then, with a little cough, he returned to business, saying, "You were inside the house when Dr. Olliver collapsed at the door?"

"I had arrived the previous evening, expecting to find the surveyors there."

"Were you surprised to find they had not come?"

"Not in the slightest," Wiki said frankly.

"Because Dr. Olliver had retarded their progress so often in the past?"

"Exactly, Dr. Vieira de Castro."

"Did this annoy you?"

"Sometimes it was inconvenient. I was stationed on board the brig *Swallow*, which was following the land party along the coast, and my orders were to drop ashore at regular intervals, hear Lieutenant Forsythe's report, and lend any assistance necessary. Instead, I spent most of the time waiting for them to arrive, and trying to soothe hosts who had everything ready to welcome them. Every time the surveying party had been forced to stop somewhere else, it was because Dr. Olliver had held them up so much."

"So what did you do, when they failed to arrive?"

"Once, I stayed at the fazenda, because the hosts had waited so long to serve the meal that it was the small hours of the morning before we finished. Otherwise, I went back on board the brig *Swallow* for the night, and then went ashore again next morning."

"And this is what happened this time?"

"No," said Wiki, careful not to look at the alcove where the grandees were intently listening. "Sir Patrick Palgrave's estate is several miles away from the village on the Rio Macae where the brig was moored."

"So you stayed at the fazenda instead of returning to the brig?"

"Aye, sir."

Dr. Vieira de Castro scribbled, and then adjusted his pince-nez as he looked at Wiki again. "Tell me about the morning of Dr. Olliver's death."

"It was dawn, and I had only just woken up. Then I heard a thudding at the door. I got there as fast as I could, and when I opened it, he fell inside."

"And what did you hear him say?"

"He looked up at me, and cried out the name William."

"And why do you think he said that?"

Wiki said very deliberately, without even glancing at his father, "Because William is my name."

Dead silence in the court, and then a sudden outburst of comment. The clerk called for quiet, and the hubbub gradually silenced, while Dr. Vieira de Castro rustled his way through his notes.

After some moments he looked up and said, "According to my records, your name is Wiki."

"That's my other name," said Wiki blandly.

"It's a shortening? Like Bill is a nickname for William?"

"Wiki is my Maori name."

Dr. Vieira de Castro stared at him, frowning. "Yes?"

Wiki explained, "It's common for Polynesian seafarers to have two names—a Polynesian name and what we call a 'sailor name,' which is usually the one given to the sailor by his first captain, because *pakeha* people find our names so difficult to write down and pronounce. As I am only half Polynesian, I am *te kakano whakauru,* a man of two tribes, which is even more complicated. As a result, I have two birth names. One is Wiki, and the other is William."

"But which one is your name in the eyes of the law?"

"Under United States law, William Coffin is my legal name."

"Do you have anything to prove this?"

"Aye, sir. Permission to approach?"

Dr. Vieira de Castro nodded, and Wiki walked up to the bench and handed over his letter of authority. He watched the coroner's expression as he read it. Amazement came first, and then, to his surprise, respect.

"You're the legal representative of the sheriff's department of the Town of Portsmouth, Virginia?"

"Aye, sir. But only with the fleet, of course," Wiki added.

"But I would hope that the administrators in any of the ports you touch would realize its significance!" the coroner declared with vigor. Then, dropping his tone to an informal level, he said, "May I ask how you came to be appointed to this office?"

Wiki didn't want to go into it, so prevaricated, "It was a convenience for the department, as they wished to have a representative sailing with the fleet."

"And a great honor, I am sure." Dr. Vieira de Castro paused, deep in thought, and then looked up and said, "So, Dr. Olliver recognized you when you opened the door—and that is why he called out your name?"

Wiki paused a moment, remembering the dying scientific's unseeing eyes. Then, with all the conviction in his voice that he could summon, he declared, "That is exactly what happened, Dr. Vieira de Castro."

Twenty-five

Wiki still did not have a chance for a private chat with his father. Instead, they were both commandeered by Sir Patrick Palgrave, who insisted that the grandees who had attended the hearing should celebrate the reprieve, with Captain Coffin and his son as guests of honor. He had already arranged to meet Lady Palgrave and her sister, who were in town on a shopping excursion, at the Hotel Pharoux, and so he hired the private dining room on the second floor of the hotel for a festive afternoon feast.

Lieutenant Forsythe was not invited. He didn't seem to mind, tipping Wiki an ironic salute as they left the courthouse, and agreeing to meet him at the boat stairs, where the cutter and crew were waiting. Wiki thought that it was unlikely he would honor the promise, as without a doubt he would head off to some taberna, but there were plenty of expedition boats going back and forth between the city and the fleet.

Wine and *tira-gosto* were served by the flurried-looking restaurateur, and everyone partook freely, though it was noteworthy that the quality of the food was not even close to the standard of the fare Festin had conjured up for Sir Patrick's banquet. Captain Coffin was the center of much congratulatory attention, while Wiki was cajoled into producing his letter of authority. As he watched, it was handed around the table in a babble of flattering comment, while the readers glanced up at him with obvious respect. Even if they couldn't comprehend the flowing English script, the seal, ribbon, and flourishing signatures were evidence enough of its importance.

Then, just as Sir Patrick returned it, commenting that though his father had told him about Wiki's being deputized, he'd had no idea it was such a formal appointment, Manuela Josefa Ramalho Vieira de Castro de Roquefeuille arrived with her sister. "Is Captain Coffin still in jail?" she cried, and then, when she glimpsed Wiki's father, clapped her hands and cried, *"Maravilhoso!"*

Then, as she and her sister were cermoniously placed at the round table, she demanded to know the details, and the grandees competed to tell her, while Wiki watched expressions chase each other across her pretty face. She was wearing blue, a color with vivid connotations for him.

"To the escape!" she cried at the end, lifting her glass and smiling at him across the rim. She was seated on the opposite side of the round table, while Wiki sat at Sir Patrick's right hand. His father was seated at Lady Palgrave's right hand, so was on the far side of the table, too, with Josefa at his other elbow.

Then Josefa mused aloud, "The coincidence of names was very lucky, was it not?"—and Wiki held his breath. When Dr. Olliver had cried out the name William, Josefa had been at the back of the reception room, but still she must have seen Dr. Olliver's unseeing look, and the blank, suffering eyes. To Wiki's relief, however, she silenced, simply looking very thoughtful.

"The coincidence might have tipped the issue," Senhor de Silveira argued in knowledgeable tones. "But it still must be recognized that there was not much of a case to start with. Finding Captain Coffin holding the murder weapon was not at all conclusive, and the name William is a common one. Surely the man who brought about his arrest was a fool."

"As Captain Couthouy said, it must have been a cimarron," said Senhor da Silva wisely. "They are desperate men, those runaways. The rebels recruit them, you know."

"An unplanned crime, obviously," agreed Senhor de Silveira. "He blundered across Dr. Olliver, lashed out in a panic, threw the cudgel down, and ran away."

Wiki remembered how Sir Patrick Palgrave had galloped headlong out of the jungle, and full-tilt into the outdoor pool before he had dragged his steed to a halt. He turned to him and said, "Did you see anyone running away when you came down the track?"

His host lifted his shoulders in a rueful shrug. "I was in too much of a hurry to see much at all. To tell the truth, I had completely forgotten that I was supposed to be at the plantation to greet the party—I had lost all track of time. I sailed to Rio Macae, but was told the survey party had just left. So I took a horse, hoping to overtake them before they arrived at the fazenda."

"It was a dramatic entrance," Wiki commented.

"Aye, but definitely overdue," said Sir Patrick, with chagrin in his squirrellike face. "I should have been there the day before—then I could have greeted you, too." He paused, and though he smiled, the protruberant brown eyes were cold with dislike. "My sister-in-law looked after you well?"

When Wiki glanced at Josefa, she was watching him, her expression grave, for once. "As always in Brazil, the hospitality was impeccable," he said lightly.

The grandees who had hosted the scientific party clapped with pleasure at the compliment. Then a man who lived locally said, "Tell us about the latest antics of this exploring expedition."

"I beg your pardon?" said Wiki, puzzled.

"The big ship *Peacock* and the little schooners *Flying Fish* and *Sea Gull* have been behaving incomprehensibly."

"Why, what have they been doing?"

Several men competed to tell him, but he gradually gathered that all three were anchored in the outer harbor, and were engaged in firing guns at each other.

"An exercise?" he hazarded.

"Perhaps," someone agreed judiciously. However, each ship was firing four guns in turn, and so perhaps exercising the guns was not a good reason.

"It must be a survey," Wiki decided. "The bangs and flashes would give them the means to measure something, perhaps."

"But measure what?" Sr. de Silveira queried.

"Something astronomical, I suppose."

"But is this not the same expedition that refused to fire a salute to our national flag, on the grounds of the *fragilidade* of the chronometers?"

Wiki winced, and spread his hands to indicate that the strange lack of diplomacy was incomprehensible to him, too.

"This is a *most* strange expedition," Senhor de Silveira said.

"It is indeed," Wiki fervently agreed, watching a casserole of the famous *feijoada* arrive. Silence fell as plates were filled, and he said on a note of whimsy, in an effort to lighten the mood, "But what can one expect when it is founded on a crackpot theory?"

"Crackpot?" Josefa echoed.

"That the earth is hollow, and that habitable land, with jungles and meadows—and coffee plantations, undoubtedly—can be discovered in the center of the globe."

This had the desired effect of amusing the company greatly, so that a patter of lively questions followed. At the end, Josefa said, "It sounds as if one could find a most desirable country retreat in such a place—but how does one get there?"

"By sailing to the poles," Wiki told her. "Where, according to the theory, there are holes that lead to the interior."

"And that is what your expedition hopes to find—a hole in the South Pole, which will lead perhaps to this paradise?" asked Senhor da Silva.

Wiki laughed, and said, "Not at all. No one believes in that crackpot theory now, but it gave birth to the idea of a discovery expedition."

Josefa confided, "Sir Patrick's grandfather was a crackpot, too. He believed the sun was habitable."

Everyone looked at her attentively. The grandees were smiling, but the hairs on the nape of Wiki's neck were rising in an icy chill.

Sir Patrick drank wine, and said, "Josefa, we don't want to hear that."

"But it was so amusing—and it is so like this story of the inside of the earth being warm and friendly and a good place to live. You told me your crackpot grandfather declared that the sun is a temperate planet, and that if only we could get there we would live quite comfortably! That's what Sir Patrick told us—isn't that right, Ramona?" she said, and looked at her sister, who nodded.

"Meu Deus," said someone. "Truly, Sir Patrick?"

Sir Patrick smiled, and said he hoped it wasn't the kind of craziness that was handed down from father to son, and they all laughed and agreed, while all the time Wiki sat utterly frozen, terribly afraid that he had betrayed himself in the first moment of shocked realization, and desperately trying to hide the fact that he now knew who had bludgeoned Dr. Olliver to death, and why Dr. Olliver had poisoned Astronomer Grimes. *"I killed for him,"* he'd whispered with his dying breath, and at long last Wiki understood.

No wonder Sir Patrick had invited him to the banquet at Praia Grande! He had learned from his friend, Captain Coffin, that his son was an agent of the law. That was why he'd spun that long, convincing story about his childhood memories of Grimes—based on what

Dr. Olliver had told him. When Wiki had first met this man who called himself Sir Patrick Palgrave—in this very room, and at this same table!—he had simply referred to Grimes as "the poor man who was poisoned." *Dear God, how did I miss the contradiction?*

And how did I miss that Dr. Olliver and the so-called Sir Patrick Palgrave were brothers? Wiki's thought was bleak with chagrin. He, of all people, should have picked up on their relationship—he'd come so close, that night at Praia Grande when he had been amused by a certain sameness of stance and attitude, and yet it had taken Josefa's little story, and the realization that the two men had the same grandfather, to trigger it.

It took a physical effort to stay in his seat and pretend to hold a normal conversation, but at long, long last the closing toast was given, Captain Coffin was congratulated for the final time, and the guests began to take their leave. Wiki shook hands with everyone, smiling mechanically as he received still more encomiums, and then made his way down the curving stone stairway to the marbled hall, forcing himself not to hurry.

There was a carriage drawn up outside the portico—the same carriage that had brought Josefa here the first time, only this time it was standing in the afternoon sun, and Wiki could see that it was drawn not by horses, but by smart little mules. A patter of feet sounded from behind him. Josefa, her expression anxious. He wondered how much she had guessed.

"You are fine?" she queried in her soft, breathless voice.

Instead of answering, he said, "Can I kiss you good-bye?"

"Fie, you cannot. You would ruin my reputation." She smiled, but a warning was there in her eyes. After looking around to make sure no one was watching, she said, "I have a gift for you to remember me by," and pressed something hard and small into his hand. Then she said, "It's your important color—green. It will bring you luck, and keep you safe."

Before he could say anything more she was inside the carriage, with a swish of blue silk and a last glimpse of slender ankles. The coachman flicked the reins, and then Manuela Josefa Ramalho Vieira de Castro de Roquefeuille was gone.

The others had not come down the stairway. Wiki grabbed the chance to get away unnoticed, hurrying across the square and breaking into a run once he was around the corner. He had not a notion of where the office of the local Seamen's Bethel might be, but had seen the distinctive blue and white Bethel flag flying from a beached hulk near the boat stairs, with a gangplank that led from the shore to the deck. The wreck probably just housed a reading room for sailors who preferred books to carousing, but the librarian would know the address of the office on shore. And there, Wiki knew he had a good chance of locating the information he so desperately needed, because part of the mission of the Seamen's Bethel was to look after shipwrecked or marooned seamen, and keep records of their deaths. His father had said that he had gone to the office here to report the loss of the *Pagoda* and the rescue of one man, the passenger, and so their files should have the details—including a crew list.

Forsythe's cutter was moored at the steps, but there was no sign of the lieutenant. The boat's crew grinned resignedly when they saw Wiki, and then went on with smoking their pipes and contemplating the passing view. Wiki carried on up the gangplank of the hulk that flew the Bethel flag, ducking to avoid a beam as he clattered down the companionway. A smell of bilge and old books rose to meet him. At the bottom he found the reading room, and a clerk who told him where to find the office on shore—off Rua Mata Cavalo, a frustratingly long distance away.

It was still siesta, but Wiki's timing was good, because an ancient sacristan opened the door just as he arrived. The old clerk was yawning, but became politely attentive once he saw Wiki's certificate from the sheriff's department in Virginia. As Dr. Vieira de Castro had promised, it carried more authority in this foreign port than Wiki had ever dared hope or expect.

Files labeled *P* were hauled out, and after a short discussion about the date of the wreck, a box with the label *PAGODA* was produced. Inside were copies of the letters that had been sent to the families of the men who had died, plus a few sad little acknowledgments. Right at the bottom was the crew list the Bethel had received from Montevideo.

Wiki grabbed it eagerly. The name of the dead captain of the *Pagoda* was unfamiliar, but the next name on the list jumped out of the page.

William Olliver, first officer.

Twenty-six

"We've had two callers, both asking for you," Midshipman Keith informed Wiki after he finally arrived on board the brig *Swallow*.

Wiki looked at him distractedly. Forsythe had still not been with the cutter when he had got back to the boat stairs from the Bethel office, and so he'd had to wait until he found a ride with another of the expedition boats, making him so late that the abrupt equatorial night had fallen while he was still out on the harbor.

He asked, "Where is Captain Rochester?"

"With Captain Hudson, on the *Peacock*. They've been making a triangulation survey at the mouth of the harbor, with the lighthouse as a central point, and tomorrow they are to commence making another survey off Enxados Island, with the observatory as the focus. They've decided to release the crew of the *Flying Fish* for the day, and so we'll be taking over."

It was terribly scientific and quite meaningless. No doubt it was the mysterious exercise the grandees had discussed. Wiki looked about the dark deck, and said, "Callers?"

"One was Midshipman Fisher, with a message for you from Captain Wilkes. He wants to see you, the instant you're back."

That suited Wiki, because he was very anxious to talk to Captain Wilkes himself. He said, "On the *Vincennes*?"

"No—on Enxados Island. He's staying there to keep an eye on the gravitational observations, until the end of the first watch."

The watch didn't end until midnight, so Captain Wilkes would certainly still be there. Wiki looked around again, and said, "And the other caller?"

Midshipman Keith said importantly, "Sir Patrick Palgrave."

"*What!*"

"He came in a *fallua*."

Wiki's heart was thudding with alarm. "What did he want?"

"He didn't say. I told him that you would have to head off to Enxados Island as soon as you got back from the city, so wouldn't be available until the morning. However, he said it was very urgent and wouldn't take long, so I invited him to wait in the saloon. He went down, but after just a few moments he came back on deck, and said he had changed his mind, and would come and see you tomorrow. Then he went off in the *fallua*."

Wiki, beset by a terrible sense of emergency, felt more anxious than ever to report to Captain Wilkes. When he asked for a boat to take him to Enxados Island, though, Constant Keith mumbled a bit, and then came out with it—the boat would have to come right back, as George had taken the other boat to the *Peacock*, and it was against orders to leave the brig with no boat at all.

Wiki understood. "I'll find my own way back," he said. It wouldn't be a problem. If necessary, he could stay the night on the island or on the *Vincennes*, and signal for a boat in the morning.

Once, on the way across the stretch of water to the island, he thought he heard the splash of an oar, but when he looked over his shoulder he saw nothing unusual, just the lights of the city reflected in the quiet water. There were several boats moored by the stairs at the foot of the convent, but the only man there was a sentry, who challenged him in a jumpy sort of way. The encampment on the flat hillock was abandoned, as the men had all returned to the *Vincennes*, and there were very few lights in the convent windows. Next day, the *Porpoise* would be discharged to be smoked for rats, and her men would come to this camp, the marine told him. Meanwhile, however, the only activity was the round-the-clock monitoring of the scientific instruments.

Wiki headed to the convent, his steps crunching on gravel. To his surprise, there was no sentry in the portico. His footsteps echoed under the gateway roof, and then quietened as he walked into the central courtyard. Once he paused, because he heard a step on the gravel outside. Then he decided it must have been the sentry, returning from wherever he had been. The columns of the cloisters gleamed ghostlike in the light of the moon, their thrown shadows very black.

He headed for the gravitational chamber first, anticipating that Captain Wilkes would be there. Even before he arrived at the archway, Wiki could hear the ticking of the tall case clock, and the heavy, almost palpable swish of the big pendulum. There was no sound of voices, but he could see the glow of reflected light from the lanterns set in the walls.

He entered the chamber without calling out, as he didn't want to take the risk of disturbing Captain Wilkes's concentration. However, the precaution wasn't necessary, because the chamber seemed to be empty. Then, just as Wiki was about to turn back, to go up the winding stairs to Captain Wilkes's room, he glimpsed a black heap at the foot of the telescope stand.

He arrived beside it in a couple of quick strides, and hunkered down—to find a body. It was the young genius, Midshipman Fisher. Wiki saw blood leaking from the smashed head, and felt terrible sadness at the loss of that bright young mind. Then, with another sick lurch, he saw the *mere pounamu* lying on the stone flags beside the dead boy. So it had been stolen from the brig, he realized—by Sir Patrick. Had his father told him where it was stowed—or had the Englishman glimpsed it as he waited in the saloon?

Then he heard the man who had impersonated Sir Patrick Palgrave speak out from the flickering shadows at the far end of the room. He ordered, "Pick up the club, Wiki Coffin."

Instead, Wiki stood up. His eyesight had adjusted. The scar-faced Englishman stood in front of the case clock, and behind the swinging pendulum. Wiki could also see the gun that he held aimed.

He took a breath to steady his voice, and then said calmly, "William Olliver, I understand—first mate of the ship *Pagoda*."

"What a clever young savage you are!" the other mocked, but after a pause he confessed, "I'm curious to know how you deduced it."

"As soon as I understood that you and Dr. Olliver were brothers—that you had the same grandfather—it was easy to guess that you were one of the crew of the wrecked ship. The crew list," Wiki added, "was at the bethel."

"Ah." William Olliver was quiet a moment, and then burst out, "I should never have told those women about our crazy grandfather and his crackpot theory about the sun—but I tend to be loose-mouthed in the company of pretty females, my wife in particular. Winston told you the same yarn?" he asked.

"He did—but the moment I first saw you together, I should have realized that you and he were brothers."

William Olliver let out a grunt of sour laughter. "Most people refused to believe that Winston and I were brothers even when they knew it for a fact! He was grotesquely fat; I was thin; he affected that great beard; I preferred to be clean shaven. Winston fancied he was the cleverer man, because he was a surgeon and I was a common seaman. The truth of the matter was that he was fat, lazy, selfish, and gluttonous, a slobbering lump. That's what killed him, you know—his greed."

"I thought it was your cudgel that killed him."

"Don't try to be clever—not when I'm holding the gun." William Olliver wagged the pistol, and snapped again, "Pick up the club."

"So you can shoot me dead by the corpse of poor young Fisher, and then claim I'd shamed one of the most honorable weapons of my people by using it to slaughter a defenseless boy?" Wiki took four angry steps from the telescope to the side wall, to distance himself from the treachery.

William Olliver exclaimed, "Get back where you were!" Then, more calmly, he pointed out, "It's easy enough to shoot you first, and then put the club in your hand."

"It would, indeed, be easy—for the man that you've become. You know something?" Wiki asked, without moving.

The other paused, and then said unwillingly, "What?"

"I think that before you met Patrick Palgrave—before he came on board the *Pagoda* for the passage back to England—you had the makings of a fine man. You certainly have imagination—the stories you spun about Grimes had me completely fooled. You have the talent of a fine artist, too—the beautiful gardens you created are evidence of that."

"Condescending compliments—from a half-breed cannibal! Who would ever have guessed the day when such a thing could happen?" William Olliver spat with vicious sarcasm.

"I'm quite serious—and I did not intend to be condescending," Wiki told him quietly, then asked, "Is that how you struck up a friendship with the passenger on the *Pagoda*? By talking about plants and gardens—and learning a lot about his background at the same time? When did it occur to you to impersonate him?" he demanded. "When you found you were the only survivor of the wreck? Or when you realized that your face was so badly burned that you were no longer recognizable as William Olliver, first officer?"

"Does it matter?" Olliver's tone was distant.

"Not really," said Wiki, and took a surreptitious pace. "What *did* matter was your brother Winston, who had to be kept quiet. You paid him?"

"I paid him well," the other spat. "But the bastard was greedy."

"And to teach him a lesson, you stopped the payments?"

Wiki glimpsed William Olliver's involuntary nod. "So that's why he was so anxious to join the expedition," he meditated aloud. "Having a paid berth to Rio must have seemed like a dream come true." And whatever money remained would have allowed him the luxury of carrying that butt of Madeira, he thought as he moved a few more stealthy inches along the wall. His right hand was in his pocket, gripping the ring that Josefa had given him.

"And you have to admit that your brother did you a significant favor," he pointed out. "It was as big a shock for him to learn that Grimes had worked for Palgrave's father as it would have been for you, if you'd been there—and he did what he thought you would have done. That was the last thing Dr. Olliver said before he died, you know—after he had cried out your name, he whispered to me, 'I killed for him!' "

William Olliver recoiled. "Winston thought he was so clever, but he couldn't have made a bigger mess if he'd tried! He was quite content for Festin to take the blame, but the maestro's revered around here!"

"So you persuaded Dr. Tweedie to confuse the issue by pretending the mortars had been mixed up?"

"His son had been in trouble and I'd fixed it with the judge, so he owed me a favor. He didn't know the details, of course, but I promised it wouldn't rebound on him."

So Forsythe had been right, Wiki thought. When he had watched Dr. Tweedie make up the bismuth medicine, the apothecary had done everything just as usual. Just as the lieutenant had stated, he hadn't missed a thing. And Dr. Vieira de Castro? Obviously, he had been persuaded to let Tweedie off lightly, but Wiki didn't want to think about that, because he'd liked the coroner—who was a cousin of Josefa's family. Instead, he asked, "What about the Swedish analyst? Did you have a hold over him, as well?"

"Johan Ohlsson?" Olliver let out a laugh that sounded genuinely amused. "Utterly incorruptible! But, as it turned out, he really did believe that Grimes died of natural causes. That lung must have been in a shocking state."

"You took quite a risk," Wiki commented.

"As you should have understood by now, taking calculated risks is my specialty."

That was indeed very true, Wiki mused. He said, "But when you covered up the murder, it meant that your brother had an even bigger hold over you. Were you trying to kill him, when you fired at the brig?"

"If you want the truth, you clever young savage, I was aiming at *you*!"

There was such cold venom in Olliver's voice that Wiki flinched. Then the imposter admitted, "But my brother would have been the next target—and I would have got you both, if that bloody awning hadn't fallen down."

Would he? As he moved another stealthy pace, Wiki remembered how Palgrave had put on spectacles to see more clearly. "*He* was the one you killed on the trail," he commented, and asked, "Did you take him by surprise—or did you go along the trail together?"

"What's the difference?" the other demanded. However, he answered the question, saying abruptly, "We kept company on the road—and it was his idea."

"How stupid of your brother—when you're so good at playing polo."

"Who the *hell* told you that I'm good at playing polo?"

"It's well known," said Wiki quickly, to protect Josefa. "I imagine you kept pace with him until the path widened, and then swerved round, cantered away, and then came back and galloped past him, swinging the cudgel as if his head were a wooden ball—or did you make him run first, to make it more fun?"

"Do you really think I'm that cold-blooded?"

"I do think that's the kind of man you've become," said Wiki very soberly. "After you had clubbed him you galloped off, and it was not until the rest of the party had gone past that you realized that he had struggled to his feet and blundered to the fazenda. So you joined us in a panic-stricken hurry—just in time to see my father arrested for the crime you'd committed. It could have been a disaster when your brother lasted long enough to cry out your name, so it was an enormous piece of luck for you that my father is another William. What was your original plan?" he queried, after moving another surreptitious pace. "To pretend to spy a runaway slave, go galloping off after him, and come back later to report that he'd eluded you? After all, you had taken great pains to establish those mythical cimarrons!"

"You think you know it all, don't you," William Olliver spat.

"I think perhaps I do," Wiki quietly agreed. "When you galloped out of the jungle and into the mountain pool, you were a magnificent sight—but I suppose you did it simply to clean both yourself and your horse. The blood must have splashed over the horse's withers and flanks as well as your boots and legs."

He was almost within reach of the pendulum spike, but just as he was bracing himself he was distracted by a flurry of movement. Two rats squirted out of the hole in the wall beside the case clock, and scuttled along the skirting.

William Olliver saw the flicker of movement, too. He said, with sick disgust in his voice, "The place is alive with rats."

Searching for food, because the provisions had been restowed on the *Vincennes*, Wiki thought. Revolted, he saw that the rats had been distracted by the smell of blood, and were heading for the midshipman's corpse.

William Olliver was watching, too—and, glancing back at Wiki, he realized at the same time how far he had moved. "Get back!" he exclaimed, and hissed, "And pick up that club."

Instead, Wiki pitched Josefa's ring straight at the gleaming eyes. Next, in a fast burst of movement, he snatched the pendulum, spun it at Olliver's face, dived for the floor, and frantically rolled. A shot roared out from Olliver's gun, struck the pendulum bob, glanced off it, and crashed back and forth around the room. Then he heard William Olliver's terrified scream.

When Wiki struggled to his feet he saw the man who had impersonated Patrick Palgrave kneeling on the floor, staring in horror at the snake that reared over him. It was just a glimpse. The fer-de-lance struck—once, twice, and raised its head to strike again.

Another shot rang out, this time from the doorway. Wiki was watching the snake, mesmerized, and saw the snake's head disappear.

It was impossible to believe that even Forsythe could shoot so accurately in this deceptive light. Wiki was trembling so much it took a violent effort to turn and check. The lieutenant was standing in the archway, holding his gun in the crook of his arm, and grinning loosely. Even from this distance Wiki could smell the fumes of *aguardiente*.

"Reckon that snake got him," the southerner observed with detached interest, and jerked his chin at William Olliver, whose convulsions were growing weaker. "They say that the fer-de-lance got the quickest-acting poison of 'em all."

Wiki heard shouts—Captain Wilkes, and the officers who had been with him. He looked at the pendulum, still oscillating wildly, and thought with a remote part of his mind that there was going to be hell to pay. "I thought I heard you following me," he said to Forsythe.

"I was advised by a certain lady to do just that, and damn lucky for you that I did," the lieutenant said smugly. "You'd be dead and done, if I didn't."

Wiki wondered about that, since William Olliver had actually been killed by the snake, but wasn't disposed to argue. He listened to the steps come closer as Captain Wilkes hurried down the winding stairs, and braced himself.

"How much did you overhear?" he hopefully asked.

"Not a bloody thing," said Forsythe, and grinned.

Epilogue

The shipyard foreman called out, "Easy now, easy!" Four carpenters turned a capstan on the wharf, and the cable running from the heaving post to the head of the *Osprey*'s mainmast gradually slacked away, releasing the brigantine from the hold that had kept her hove down on her side. Slowly, she groaned and shuddered. Then, all at once, she shook herself like a dog, and came upright, floating in the water as triumphantly as if she hadn't been lying down in ignominy just a handful of minutes ago.

"One—two—three," recited Captain Coffin, holding his conductor's baton at the ready, and his ship's band, composed of six cadets with assorted instruments and a boatswain with a pipe, struck up "Yankee Doodle." The strains rose boldly in the warm summer air. When the music finished all the carpenters cheered, and Wiki, perched on his favorite bollard, clapped.

"Reminds me of the first time I dropped anchor in Whampoa,

when the *Osprey* was on her maiden voyage," his father said with great satisfaction, as his band trailed on board the brigantine, and then disappeared below to get reacquainted with their seagoing home. "The Chinese *hoppo* was accustomed to big American ships by then, and jumped to the conclusion I was the tender to something more magnificent. 'Where is the big ship?' he inquired, so I informed him that *this* was the big ship, and my band played 'Yankee Doodle' to prove it."

"Wonderful," commented Wiki, who didn't believe the story for an instant, and followed his father on board. Down in the cabin, which served as the saloon as well as his father's sleeping quarters, the brigantine looked much more familiar than she had from the outside, especially when hove down. However, he had almost forgotten his father's eccentric choice of red cushions on the port side of the horseshoe-shaped settee in the stern, and green cushions at the starboard end.

Wiki perched on the green end, and looked about as his father yelled for coffee. In the middle of the racket, a man walked into the saloon, and said, "Give the chap a chance to get his pantry shipshape, for God's sake, Captain. We ain't even taken on provisions yet, let alone settled the ballast! Can't you feel the poor ship bobbing about like a drunkard's empty bottle?"

This, Wiki gathered, was the mate, the paragon who kept the cadets safely occupied both at sea and on shore, and, apparently, kept his father organized, as well. He was lean, but very athletic, wearing a loose shirt with rolled-up sleeves that displayed his trimly muscled arms. "This is Alf," said Captain Coffin, and then the two of them had a conference where the mate informed Captain Coffin exactly how the ship was going to be reloaded, and which ended with Alf stamping off up the stairs to take charge of the arrangements.

"Sour as a crabapple, but the lads revere him," Captain Coffin said in an apologetic sort of way.

"And you couldn't manage without him," Wiki guessed with a grin.

"Unfortunately, no." Captain Coffin sat down on the red end of the settee. Then, with an abrupt change of subject, he said, "So Patrick Palgrave's name was really William."

"William Olliver," Wiki agreed.

"And when Dr. Olliver shouted out the name William, it was actually Patrick he was calling—the brother who had bludgeoned him?"

"Exactly," said Wiki.

"But you testified in a court of law that it was *your* name the dying man was saying."

"Well . . ." said Wiki.

"Did you know at that particular moment that Sir Patrick's name was William?" his father demanded.

"No, of course I didn't."

"You *lied* for me, son."

"Aye," said Wiki placidly.

The lizard eye studied him for a long time, its warmth almost lost beneath the half-lowered lid. Then his father remarked in a musing kind of way, "Not long after I carried him into port, someone came into the room and called out my name—and Palgrave automatically turned to see who it was, just the same as I did, but of course I didn't pay any attention at the time." His tone became cynical as he added, "It was very handy for him that it was my name, too."

"It's only natural that he made errors," Wiki said. "It's amazing that he carried it off so well—but then, he was opportunistic by nature."

His father nodded. "After I rescued him, he might have regained consciousness much sooner than I realized, because when he finally came out of his coma the first thing he asked for was a looking glass. I didn't want to hand it to him, because his face was scarcely human, but instead of recoiling, he studied his reflection for what seemed a very long time. When I think back, it's as if he had considered the idea of impersonating Palgrave already."

Wiki lifted his brows. "I wonder what the real Palgrave looked like?"

"It probably didn't matter, just as long as they were about the same shape and size. He rose from his sickbed to go to Cambridge and claim the inheritance, as you know, and when I saw him off, his face was bandaged."

"The scars would have helped, even without the bandage," Wiki opined. "But if Grimes had met Patrick Palgrave in Rio, he would have known at once that he was an imposter—and it was very likely that he would seek him out, having worked for his father."

"So Dr. Olliver poisoned Grimes to prevent it?"

"Aye," said Wiki soberly, yet again hearing Dr. Olliver's gasped confession in his mind: *"I killed for him!"* "He gave Grimes a dose of salts in wine, so he would get the gripes, and then, by exaggerating his symptoms, he made sure that Grimes was put under his medical care, so that he could poison him at leisure—first with the strychnine-coated pills, and then with the bismuth, to which he'd added just enough poison to finish him off. In agony," Wiki added with a grimace, remembering the instrumentmaker's terrible end.

Captain Coffin shuddered. "We all found Dr. Olliver inconsiderate and arrogant, but I didn't think he was capable of such callousness. He deserved his awful death, really."

"They were *both* cold-blooded," Wiki said harshly, remembering penning the official notification of his death to Midshipman Fisher's parents. As Captain Wilkes had dictated the words, tears had run down the long face. "The waste," he had exclaimed, and had thumped the desk with his fist—"the goddamned waste!"

The desecrated *mere pounamu* had been returned to its hook, because Wiki was still berthed on the *Swallow*, even though he was back to serving as Captain Wilkes's amanuensis. He wondered again if his father had told his friend where the *mere* was stored, but didn't want to ask, so said instead, "What are your plans, now that the *Osprey* is back on her keel?"

The *Swallow,* like all the other expedition ships in port, was preparing for departure. Longitude, latitude, tides, and the radiation of the sun had all been calculated, and, as far as Wiki could tell, this part of the world had been weighed. The *Peacock* had been fixed and repainted, and was fit to double Cape Horn, and maybe even venture into the Antarctic, too. The *Relief* had been restowed and reprovisioned, and had been sent ahead, hopefully to get to Orange Harbor, at the tip of South America, before the rest of the fleet arrived. The *Vincennes* and the *Porpoise* had both been successfully smoked free of rats (though the cockroaches, by some insect-miracle, had survived), Enxados Island had been cleared of vermin and venomous snakes, and now it was time to go.

Captain Coffin said, "I've sold my freight of tortoiseshell, and bought a cargo of coffee for the New York market." Judging by his smug expression, both deals had been good ones. Then, however, his face lengthened, and he asked, "Did you make a call on your stepmother before you joined the expedition?"

"I wouldn't have dared not," said Wiki dryly. He always paid her a duty visit, carrying a gift from some exotic landfall. After all, she had found him his first berth, on her brother's Nantucket whaleship, and had even provided a sea chest. As usual, they had drunk tea, and eaten cake, and made stilted conversation—always about herself and domestic Salem affairs, as she wasn't at all interested in his travels.

"She's well?"

"Exactly the same as ever."

Captain Coffin grimaced. "Well, I guess I'll see her myself before long."

As Wiki stood up to leave, he stood up, too. With an abrupt movement he reached out and gripped Wiki's hand, very hard. Then he cleared his throat with an embarrassed sound, and said, "I never raised you to tell lies, son, but I thank you for your belief in me, and I cherish you for it."

"It was an honor," said Wiki gently.

It was January 6, 1839, and the great U.S. Exploring Expedition was about to depart. The weather was bright and clear, with a light breeze from the land, and the atmosphere about the harbor was festive. Boats sailed and tacked over the glittering water, one of them a familiar-looking *fallua*, which was steering straight for the brig *Swallow*. As Wiki watched, it hauled about and then aback, seething to a halt under the sheer of the stern.

He leaned inquiringly over the taffrail, to find himself gazing down into Manuela Josefa Ramalho Vieira de Castro de Roquefeuille's pretty face. She was wearing black, as befitted a woman mourning the loss of a brother-in-law, and the color reminded him of the night he had seen her getting out of the carriage at the Hotel Pharoux—the first time they had made love with their eyes.

"I'll just be a minute," he said to Captain Rochester, who was firmly in charge of the quarterdeck for the departure from the harbor. Then, without waiting for permission, Wiki vaulted down into the *fallua*.

"Hulloa," she laughed. "Jumping ship?"

"Not this time," he said with a creased-up grin. "But I am very glad to see you, because I owe you a great big thanks."

"Thanks for me?"

"When Forsythe finally arrived at the cutter, you were waiting for him."

"Ah," she said, and nodded, not needing to ask what he meant. "It is very entertaining to stop by the stairs and watch the drunken sailors while waiting for the *fallua* to go back to the Praia Grande."

"And—for some reason—you advised him to follow me." Which Forsythe had done—first to the brig, where Midshipman Keith had told the southerner where he was going, and then to the convent.

Josefa looked meditative, and said, "You know, I have always thought that perhaps Pierre did not die accidentally in that polo match. I noticed afterward that it gave my brother-in-law great pleasure to be the one in charge of our estates. He enjoyed the money that allowed him to build pretty things—it was as if it were a great novelty for him to be rich."

Unanticipated sadness washed over Wiki. He remembered the beautiful gardens at Praia Grande and at the fazenda; he thought of the romantic pool that William Olliver had designed. At that moment it seemed a tragic failing of society that William Olliver had been forced to descend to deception and murder before he could realize such potential.

He shook his head to clear off the thought, and said, "How is your sister?"

"Desolate, naturally. She will get over it, but one of us will have to remarry. It is difficult for two sisters, you know, particularly rich ones, when there is no man of power and influence in the family." With an elaborate sigh, Madame Manuela Josefa Ramalho Vieira de Castro de Roquefeuille looked musingly around the harbor, and decided aloud, "I suppose it will have to be me. There are plenty of suitable men," she mused. "The problem is which one to choose."

Wiki felt a stab of jealousy, combined with some sympathy for whoever the man might be. Josefa would not be nearly as easy to manage as the family estates, he thought, and he wondered, too, if the new caretaker of the fortune would do as good a job as William Olliver had done.

Then he was distracted—by the sight of a short, square man sliding out from under a tarpaulin canvas in the stern of the *fallua*, and climbing stealthily up the side of the brig.

Involuntarily, he exclaimed, "That's Robert Festin!"

"Robert Festin?" Josefa echoed, without turning round to look. "It can't possibly be Robert Festin," she assured him with wide-eyed innocence. "Didn't you know he's getting married on Saturday?"

"No, I didn't," confessed Wiki.

"His bride's family treat him very badly, I hear. They charge a great deal for his services, but he never sees any of the money. And his mother-in-law slaps him about to make him understand better, because he isn't very bright."

"I wonder what happened to my invitation?" Wiki wondered aloud, and she laughed. When he looked again, Festin was safely out of sight, so he turned back to Josefa and said, "Here is the present you gave me."

He gave her the ring he had thrown at William Olliver's gleaming eyes—a huge emerald, probably worth more money than he would ever make in his lifetime, impossible to wear, impossible to sell, and impossible to give away.

"It saved my life, and I don't need it anymore," he said. "Instead, I want to give you something to remember me by."

Josefa didn't argue. Instead, she put out her hand. Then her mouth fell open in vast surprise—he had given her a length of his own black hair, neatly braided and tied. He wondered if she would ever understand what a declaration of trust this gift involved.

Instead of thanking him, she ordered, "Turn around!"

He turned his head, grinning at her over his shoulder.

"You cut your hair!"

"Aye." Though it was actually Sua who had done the cutting.

A voice called down from the deck, politely informing him that they were about to sail, and that Captain Rochester would be vastly obliged if Mr. Coffin would take the helm.

"So we say good-bye?"

"Aye," said Wiki. "May I kiss you?"

"Certainly not," she said, sounding scandalized, and he laughed, bowed, and lifted her fingers gallantly to his lips, before scrambling back up to deck. As he climbed over the rail, he heard her distinctive giggle, along with a few derisive cheers from the crew.

The *fallua* bore away with a last wave of a ring-laden hand.

Aloft, the men were unfurling the sails, which fluttered delicately before being tamed and clewed down. The other ships of the fleet were doing likewise—and the brigantine *Osprey*, too, was putting on her canvas for her journey home. Where, Wiki wondered, would he see his father next?

The vessels at anchor in the bay were flying flags in salute. Whistles sounded, and the crew of the USS *Independence* gave six hearty hurrahs as the *Vincennes* sailed grandly by—which, considering the circumstances, Wiki thought, was very gallant of Jovial Jack. Out of the harbor sailed the *Vincennes*, with Captain Wilkes in charge of the quarterdeck, while the other expedition ships followed in grand formation. Captain Coffin's *Osprey* was picking up pace on the larboard tack, and putting on more sail as Wiki watched.

Then all at once yells of utter outrage disturbed the happy scene, along with the sounds of a nasty collision. Sails fluttered on the *Vincennes* as she hurriedly reduced canvas. Wiki shaded his eyes to see what had happened, and then exclaimed, "My God, I don't believe it!"

The *Vincennes* had blundered off her course, and run afoul of the *Osprey*.

Suggested Reading

Darwin, Charles. Beagle *Diary*. Edited by Richard Darwin Keynes. Cambridge, UK: Cambridge University Press, 1988.

Erskine, Charles. *Twenty Years Before the Mast: with the more thrilling scenes and incidents while circumnavigating the globe under the command of the late Admiral Charles Wilkes 1838–1842*. Washington, D.C.: Smithsonian Institution, 1985.

Philbrick, Nathaniel. *Sea of Glory: America's Voyage of Discovery, the U.S. Exploring Expedition 1838–1842*. New York: Viking, 2003.

Reynolds, William. *The Private Journal of William Reynolds: United States Exploring Expedition, 1838–1842*. Edited by Nathaniel Philbrick and Thomas Philbrick. New York: Penguin, 2004.

Reynolds, William. *Voyage to the Southern Ocean: The Letters of Lieutenant William Reynolds from the U.S. Exploring Expedition, 1838–1842*. Edited by Anne Hoffman Cleaver and E. Jeffrey Stann (and with an excellent introduction and epilogue by Herman J. Viola). Annapolis, Md.: Naval Institute Press, 1988.

Stanton, William. *The Great United States Exploring Expedition of 1838–1842*. Berkeley, Calif.: University of California Press, 1975.
Viola, Herman J., and Carolyn Margolis, eds. *Magnificent Voyagers: The U.S. Exploring Expedition, 1838–1842*. Washington, D.C.: Smithsonian Institution, 1985.
Wilkes, Charles. *Narrative of the United States Exploring Expedition*. 5 vols. 1844. Reprint, Upper Saddle River, N.J.: Gregg Press, 1970.